The Treasury
—of—
Children's Classics

The Treasury
—of—
Children's Classics

WEATHERVANE BOOKS
New York

Compiled and edited by Samuel Carr and Carolyn Jones
Designed by Yvonne Dedman
Jacket illustration by John Blackman

First published in 1987 by Octopus Books Ltd

Arrangement and Design © 1987 Octopus Books Ltd
Text of 'King Arthur' and 'Thor, Loki and the Enchanter' by Jane Ives
© 1982 Octopus Books Ltd
Text of 'Cinderella', 'The Tinder Box', 'The Ugly Duckling' and 'Puss in Boots',
retold by Carolyn Jones, © 1987 Octopus Books Ltd
Illustrations on pages 334, 426, 461, 466, 613, 619, 625, 640, 661, and 666
© Octopus Books Ltd

This 1987 edition published by Weathervane Books,
distributed by Crown Publishers, Inc.,
225 Park Avenue South,
New York, New York 10003

Filmset in Linotron Bembo by J&L Composition Ltd, Filey, North Yorkshire
Printed in Czechoslovakia

ISBN 0–517–63343–4

h g f e d c b a

Contents

Nursery Rhymes

Comic Verse and Nonsense

Animal Verse

Stories in Verse

Fables (Traditional)

Fairy Tales

Myths and Legends

Comic Stories

Animal Stories

Contents

School Stories

Voyages and Shipwrecks

Favourite Stories

Acknowledgements

'Matilda, who told Lies, and was Burned to Death' by Hilaire Belloc from *The Bad Child's Book Of Beasts*, reprinted by kind permission of Gerald Duckworth & Co.

'The Shark' by Lord Alfred Douglas and accompanying illustration by Brian Robb, from *Tales With a Twist*, reprinted by kind permission of B. T. Batsford Ltd

'Skimbleshanks' by T. S. Eliot from *Old Possum's Book of Practical Cats*, reprinted by permission of Faber and Faber Ltd and Harcourt Brace Jovanovich, Inc. U.S. Copyright 1939 by T. S. Eliot; renewed 1967 by Esme Valerie Eliot.

Chapter 15 from *Anne of Green Gables* by L. M. Montgomery reprinted by permission of Harrap Limited and Farrar, Straus and Giroux, Inc and the Estate of L. M. Montgomery. U.S. Copyright 1908 by L. C. Page & Company. Copyright renewed 1935 by L. C. Page and Company, now a division of Farrar, Straus and Giroux, Inc.

Illustrations by Charles Robinson from *The Big Book of Fables* reproduced by kind permission of Blackie and Son Ltd.

Illustrations by H. J. Ford from *The Story of Robin Hood* and *Tales of Troy and Greece* by Andrew Lang reproduced by kind permission of the Longman Group Limited.

Nursery Rhymes

Jack and Jill

Jack and Jill went up the hill,
  To fetch a pail of water;
Jack fell down, and broke his crown,
  And Jill came tumbling after.

Rain, Rain, Go Away

Rain, rain, go away;
Come again another day;
Little Harry wants to play.

There Was an Old Woman

There was an old woman tossed up in a basket
   Seventy times as high as the moon;
Where she was going I couldn't but ask it,
   For in her hand she carried a broom.

Doctor Foster

Doctor Foster went to Gloucester,
 In a shower of rain;
He stepped into a puddle up to his middle,
 And never went there again.

Ring-a-Ring-a-Roses

Ring-a-ring-a-roses,
A pocketful of posies,
A-tish-oo, a-tish-oo,
We'll all fall down.

London Bridge is Broken Down

London Bridge is broken down,
 Dance o'er my lady Lee;
London Bridge is broken down,
 With a gay lady.

How shall we build it up again?
 Dance o'er my lady Lee;
How shall we build it up again?
 With a gay lady.

Silver and gold will be stole away,
 Dance o'er my lady Lee;
Silver and gold will be stole away,
 With a gay lady.

Build it up again with iron and steel,
   Dance o'er my lady Lee;
Build it up with iron and steel,
   With a gay lady.

Iron and steel will bend and bow,
   Dance o'er my lady Lee;
Iron and steel will bend and bow,
   With a gay lady.

Build it up with wood and clay,
   Dance o'er my lady Lee;
Build it up with wood and clay,
   With a gay lady.

Wood and clay will wash away,
   Dance o'er my lady Lee;
Wood and clay will wash away,
   With a gay lady.

Build it up with stone so strong,
   Dance o'er my lady Lee;
Huzza! 'twill last for ages long,
   With a gay lady.

The Man in the Wilderness

The man in the wilderness asked me,
How many strawberries grew in the sea.
I answered him, as I thought good,
As many red herrings as grew in the wood.

There Was an Old Woman

There was an old woman who lived in a shoe,
She had so many children she didn't know what to do;
She gave them some broth without any bread;
She whipped them all soundly, and put them to bed.

Little Bo-Peep

Little Bo-peep has lost her sheep,
   And can't tell where to find them;
Leave them alone, and they'll come home,
   And bring their tails behind them.

Little Bo-peep fell fast asleep,
   And dreamed she heard them bleating;
But when she awoke, she found it a joke,
   For they were still a-fleeting.

Then up she took her little crook,
   Determined for to find them;
She found them indeed, but it made her heart bleed,
   For they'd left all their tails behind 'em.

Ding Dong Bell

Ding dong bell,
Pussy's in the well!
Who put her in?
Little Johnny Green.
Who pulled her out?
Big Johnny Stout.
What a naughty boy was that
To drown poor pussy cat,
Who never did him any harm,
But killed the mice in his father's barn!

Old King Cole

Old King Cole
Was a merry old soul,
And a merry old soul was he;

He called for his pipe,
And he called for his bowl,
And he called for his fiddlers three.

Every fiddler, he had a fiddle,
And a very fine fiddle had he;
Twee tweedle dee, tweedle dee, went the fiddlers.

Oh, there's none so rare,
As can compare
With King Cole and his fiddlers three!

Old Mother Hubbard

Old Mother Hubbard
Went to the cupboard,
　To get her poor dog a bone;
But when she came there,
The cupboard was bare,
　And so the poor dog had none.

She went to the baker's
　To buy him some bread;
But when she came back,
The poor dog was dead.

She went to the joiner's
　To buy him a coffin;
But when she came back,
　The poor dog was laughing.

She went to the fruiterer's
　To buy him some fruit;
But when she came back,
　He was playing the flute.

She went to the tailor's
　To buy him a coat;
But when she came back,
　He was riding a goat.

She went to the cobbler's
　To buy him some shoes;
But when she came back,
　He was reading the news.

She went to the seamstress
  To buy him some linen;
But when she came back,
  The dog was spinning.

She went to the hosier's
  To buy him some hose;
But when she came back,
  He was dressed in his clothes.

The dame made a curtsey,
  The dog made a bow;
The dame said, 'Your servant,'
  The dog said, 'Bow, wow.'

Little Polly Flinders

Little Polly Flinders
Sat among the cinders,
   Warming her pretty little toes!
Her mother came and caught her,
And whipped her little daughter
   For spoiling her nice new clothes!

Simple Simon Met a Pieman

Simple Simon met a pieman
   Going to the fair;
Says Simple Simon to the pieman,
   'Let me taste your ware.'

Says the pieman to Simple Simon,
   'Show me first your penny;'
Says Simple Simon to the pieman,
   'Indeed I have not any.'

Simple Simon went a-fishing
For to catch a whale;
All the water he had got
Was in his mother's pail.

Simple Simon went to look
If plums grew on a thistle;
He pricked his fingers very much,
Which made poor Simon whistle.

Hey! Diddle Diddle

Hey! Diddle diddle
The cat and the fiddle
The cow jumped over the moon.
The little dog laughed
To see such fun
And the dish ran away with the spoon.

Please to Remember the Fifth of November

Please to remember
The Fifth of November,
Gunpowder, treason, and plot;
I know no reason
Why gunpowder treason
Should ever be forgot.

Please to Remember the Fifth of November!

One, Two, Three, Four, Five

One, two, three, four, five,
Once I caught a fish alive.
Why did you let it go? –
Because it bit my finger so.

The Queen of Hearts

The Queen of Hearts
She made some tarts
All on a summer's day.

The Knave of Hearts
He stole the tarts
And took them clean away.

Sing a Song of Sixpence

Sing a song of sixpence,
    A pocket full of rye;
Four and twenty blackbirds
    Baked in a pie;

When the pie was opened,
    The birds began to sing;
Was not that a dainty dish
    To set before the king?

The king was in the parlour,
    Counting out his money;
The queen was in the kitchen,
    Eating bread and honey;

The maid was in the garden,
    Hanging out the clothes;
There came a little blackbird,
    And snipped off her nose.

Mary Had a Little Lamb

Mary had a little lamb,
  Its fleece was white as snow;
And everywhere that Mary went,
  The lamb was sure to go.

He followed her to school one day;
  That was against the rule;
It made the children laugh and play
  To see a lamb at school.

And so the teacher turned him out,
  But still he lingered near,
And waited patiently about
  Till Mary did appear.

Then he ran to her, and laid
    His head upon her arm,
As if he said, 'I'm not afraid –
    You'll keep me from all harm.'

'What makes the lamb love Mary so?'
    The eager children cry.
'Oh, Mary loves the lamb, you know,'
    The teacher did reply.

Humpty Dumpty

Humpty Dumpty sat on a wall
Humpty Dumpty had a great fall.
All the King's horses and all the King's men
Could not put Humpty together again.

Monday's Child

Monday's child is fair of face,
Tuesday's child is full of grace,
   Wednesday's child is full of woe,
   Thursday's child has far to go,
Friday's child is loving and giving,
Saturday's child works hard for its living;
   And a child that is born on the Sabbath Day
   Is fair, and wise, and good, and gay.

See-saw, Margery Daw

See-saw, Margery Daw,
   Jenny shall have a new master:
She shall have but a penny a day,
   Because she can't work any faster.

23

A Frog He Would a-Wooing Go

A Frog he would a-wooing go,
   Sing heigho, says Rowley,
Whether his mother would let him or no;
With a rowley, powley, gammon, and spinach,
   Heigho, says Anthony Rowley.

So off he marched with his opera hat,
   Heigho, says Rowley,
And on the way he met with a rat,
With a rowley, powley, gammon, and spinach,
   Heigho, says Anthony Rowley.

And when they came to Mouse's Hall,
   Heigho, says Rowley,
They gave a loud knock, and they gave a loud call,
With a rowley, powley, gammon, and spinach,
   Heigho, says Anthony Rowley.

'Pray, Mrs. Mouse, are you within?'
   Heigho, says Rowley;
'Yes, kind sir, I am sitting to spin,'
With a rowley, powley, gammon, and spinach,
   Heigho, says Anthony Rowley.

'Pray, Mrs. Mouse, will you give us some beer?'
   Heigho, says Rowley.
'For Froggy and I are fond of good cheer,'
With a rowley, powley, gammon, and spinach,
   Heigho, says Anthony Rowley.

Now while they all were a merry-making,
   Heigho, says Rowley,
The cat and her kittens came tumbling in,
With a rowley, powley, gammon, and spinach,
   Heigho, says Anthony Rowley.

The cat she seized the rat by the crown,
  Heigho, says Rowley;
The kittens they pulled the little mouse down,
With a rowley, powley, gammon, and spinach,
  Heigho, says Anthony Rowley.

This put poor Frog in a terrible fright,
  Heigho, says Rowley.
So he took up his hat and wished them good-night,
With a rowley, powley, gammon, and spinach,
  Heigho, says Anthony Rowley.

But as Froggy was crossing over a brook,
  Heigho, says Rowley,
A lily-white duck came and gobbled him up,
With a rowley, powley, gammon, and spinach,
  Heigho, says Anthony Rowley.

So there was an end of one, two, and three,
　Heigho, says Rowley,
The rat, the mouse, and the little Frog-ee!
With a rowley, powley, gammon, and spinach,
　Heigho, says Anthony Rowley.

Hickory, Dickory, Dock

Hickory, dickory, dock,
The mouse ran up the clock,
　The clock struck one,
　The mouse ran down;
Hickory, dickory, dock.

I Had a Little Nut-tree

I had a little nut-tree; nothing would it bear
But a silver nutmeg and a golden pear;
The King of Spain's daughter came to visit me
And all was because of my little nut-tree.
I skipped over water, I danced over sea,
And all the birds in the air couldn't catch me.

Little Miss Muffet

Little Miss Muffet
Sat on a tuffet,
Eating her curds and whey;
There came a spider,
And sat down beside her,
And frightened Miss Muffet away.

Little Jack Horner

Little Jack Horner
Sat in the corner,
Eating a Christmas pie;
He put in his thumb,
And he took out a plum,
And said, 'What a good boy am I!'

Higglepy, Piggleby

Higglepy, Piggleby,
   My black hen,
She lays eggs
   For gentlemen;
Sometimes nine,
   And sometimes ten,
Higglepy, Piggleby,
   My black hen!

There Was a Crooked Man

There was a crooked man, and he went a crooked mile,
He found a crooked sixpence against a crooked stile:
He bought a crooked cat, which caught a crooked mouse,
And they all lived together in a little crooked house.

Little Boy Blue

Little Boy Blue, come blow your horn,
The sheep's in the meadow, the cow's in the corn;

Where's the little boy that tends the sheep?
He's under the haycock, fast asleep.

Go wake him, go wake him. Oh! no, not I;
For if I awake him, he'll certainly cry.

The North Wind

The north wind doth blow,
And we shall have snow,
And what will the robin do then,
    Poor thing?

He'll sit in the barn
And keep himself warm,
And hide his head under his wing,
    Poor thing.

The north wind doth blow,
And we shall have snow,
And what shall the honey-bee do,
   Poor thing?

In his hive he will stay
Till the cold's passed away,
And then he'll come out in the spring,
   Poor thing.

The north wind doth blow,
And we shall have snow,
And what will the dormouse do then,
   Poor thing?

Rolled up like a ball
In his nest snug and small,
He'll sleep till warm weather comes back,
   Poor thing.

The north wind doth blow,
And we shall have snow,
And what will the children do then,
   Poor things?

When lessons are done,
They'll jump, skip, and run,
And that's how they'll keep themselves warm,
   Poor things.

For Want of a Nail

For want of a nail, the shoe was lost,
For want of the shoe, the horse was lost,
For want of the horse, the rider was lost,
For want of the rider, the battle was lost,
For want of the battle, the kingdom was lost,
And all from the want of a horse-shoe nail.

How Many Miles to Babylon?

How many miles to Babylon?
 Threescore miles and ten.
Can I get there by candlelight?
 Yes, and back again.
If your heels are nimble and light,
You may get there by candlelight.

Comic Verse
and Nonsense

Matilda, Who told Lies,
and was Burned to Death

Matilda told such Dreadful Lies,
It made one Gasp and Stretch one's Eyes;
Her Aunt, who, from her Earliest Youth,
Had kept a Strict Regard for Truth,
Attempted to Believe Matilda:
The effort very nearly killed her,
And would have done so, had not She
Discovered this Infirmity.
For once, towards the Close of Day,
Matilda, growing tired of play,
And finding she was left alone,
Went tiptoe to the Telephone
And summoned the Immediate Aid
Of London's Noble Fire-Brigade.
Within an hour the Gallant Band
Were pouring in on every hand,
From Putney, Hackney Downs and Bow,
With Courage high and Hearts a–glow
They galloped, roaring through the Town,
'Matilda's House is Burning Down!'

Inspired by British Cheers and Loud
Proceeding from the Frenzied Crowd,
They ran their ladders through a score
Of windows on the Ball Room Floor;
And took Peculiar Pains to Souse
The Pictures up and down the House,
Until Matilda's Aunt succeeded
In showing them they were not needed
And even then she had to pay
To get the Men to go away!

    ★   ★   ★   ★

It happened that a few Weeks later
Her Aunt was off to the Theatre
To see that Interesting Play
'*The Second Mrs. Tanqueray.*'
She had refused to take her Niece
To hear this Entertaining Piece:

A Deprivation Just and Wise
To Punish her for Telling Lies.
That Night a Fire *did* break out –
You should have heard Matilda shout!
You should have heard her Scream and Bawl,
And throw the window up and call
To People passing in the Street –
(The rapidly increasing Heat
Encouraging her to obtain
Their confidence) – but all in vain!
For every time She shouted 'Fire!'
They only answered 'Little Liar!'
And therefore when her Aunt returned,
Matilda, and the House, were burned.

HILAIRE BELLOC

Illustrated by B.T.B.

Little Billee

There were three sailors of Bristol city
Who took a boat and went to sea.
But first with beef and captain's biscuits
And pickled pork they loaded she.

There was gorging Jack and guzzling Jimmy,
And the youngest he was little Billee.
Now when they got as far as the Equator
They'd nothing left but one split pea.

Says gorging Jack to guzzling Jimmy,
'I am extremely hungaree.'
To gorging Jack says guzzling Jimmy,
'We've nothing left, us must eat we.'

Says gorging Jack to guzzling Jimmy,
'With one another we shouldn't agree!
There's little Bill, he's young and tender,
We're old and tough, so let's eat he.

'Oh! Billy, we're going to kill and eat you,
So undo the button of your chemie.'
When Bill received this information
He used his pocket-handkerchie.

'First let me say my catechism,
Which my poor mammy taught to me.'
'Make haste, make haste,' says guzzling Jimmy,
While Jack pulled out his snickersnee.

So Billy went up to the main-top gallant mast,
And down he fell on his bended knee.

He scarce had come to the twelfth commandment
When up he jumps. 'There's land I see:

'Jerusalem and Madagascar,
And North and South Amerikee:
There's the British flag a-riding at anchor,
With Admiral Napier, K.C.B.'

So when they got aboard of the Admiral's
He hanged fat Jack and flogged Jimmee;
But as for little Bill he made him
The Captain of a Seventy-three.

W. M. THACKERAY

Nightmare

When you're lying awake with a dismal headache, and repose is
    taboo'd by anxiety,
I conceive you may use any language you choose to indulge in,
    without impropriety;
For your brain is on fire – the bedclothes conspire of usual
    slumber to plunder you:
First your counterpane goes, and uncovers your toes, and your
    sheet slips demurely from under you;
Then the blanketing tickles – you feel like mixed pickles – so
    terribly sharp is the pricking,
And you're hot, and you're cross, and you tumble and toss till
    there's nothing 'twixt you and the ticking.

Then the bedclothes all creep to the ground in a heap, and you
  pick 'em all up in a tangle;
Next your pillow resigns and politely declines to remain at its
  usual angle!
Well, you get some repose in the form of a doze, with hot eye-
  balls and head ever aching,
But your slumbering teems with such horrible dreams that you'd
  very much better be waking;
For you dream you are crossing the Channel, and tossing about in
  a steamer from Harwich –
Which is something between a large bathing machine and a very
  small second-class carriage –
And you're giving a treat (penny ice and cold meat) to a party of
  friends and relations –
They're a ravenous horde – and they all come on board at Sloane
  Square and South Kensington Stations.
And bound on that journey you find your attorney (who started
  that morning from Devon);
He's a bit undersized, and you don't feel surprised when he tells
  you he's only eleven.
Well, you're driving like mad with this singular lad (by-the-bye
  the ship's now a four-wheeler),
And you're playing round games, and he calls you bad names
  when you tell him that 'ties pay the dealer';
But this you can't stand, as you throw up your hand, and you find
  you're as cold as an icicle,
In your shirt and your socks (the black silk with gold clocks),
  crossing Salisbury Plain on a bicycle:
And he and the crew are on bicycles too – which they've
  somehow or other invested in –
And he's telling the tars, all the particulars of a company he's
  interested in –
It's a scheme of devices, to get at low prices all goods from cough
  mixtures to cables

(Which tickled the sailors) by treating retailers, as though they
were all vege*t*ables –
You get a good spadesman to plant a small tradesman (first take
off his boots with a boot-tree),
And his legs will take root, and his fingers will shoot, and they'll
blossom and bud like a fruit-tree –
From the greengrocer tree you get grapes and green-pea,
cauliflower, pineapple, and cranberries,
While the pastrycook plant, cherry brandy will grant, apple puffs,
and three-corners, and Banburys –
The shares are a penny, and ever so many are taken by Rothschild
and Baring,
And just as a few are allotted to you, you awake with a shudder
despairing –
You're a regular wreck, with a crick in your neck, and no wonder
you snore, for your head's on the floor, and you've needles and
pins from your soles to your shins, and your flesh is a-creep, for
your left leg's asleep, and you've cramp in your toes, and a fly
on your nose, and some fluff in your lung, and a feverish
tongue, and a thirst that's intense, and a general sense that you
haven't been sleeping in clover;
But the darkness has passed, and it's daylight at last, and the night
has been long – ditto ditto my song – and thank goodness
they're both of them over!

W. S. GILBERT

A Child's Primer of Natural History

I. A WHALE

The con-sci-en-tious art-ist tries
On-ly to draw what meets his eyes.
This is the Whale; he seems to be
A spout of wa-ter in the sea.
Now, Hux-ley from one bone could make
An un-known beast; so if I take
This spout of wa-ter, and from thence
Con-struct a Whale by in-fer-ence,
A Whale, I ven-ture to as-sert,
Must be an an-i-mat-ed squirt!
Thus, chil-dren, we the truth may sift
By use of Log-ic's Price-less Gift.

2. THE ELEPHANT

This is the El-e-phant, who lives
With but one aim – to please.
His i-vo-ry tusk he free-ly gives
To make pi-a-no keys.
One grief he has – how-e'er he tries,
He nev-er can for-get
That one of his e-nor-mous size
Can't be a house-hold pet.
Then does he to his grief give way,
Or sink 'neath sor-row's ban?
Oh, no; in-stead he spends each day
Con-tri-ving some un-sel-fish way
To be of use to Man.

3. THE PLATYPUS

My child, the Duck-billed Plat-y-pus
A sad ex-am-ple sets for us:
From him we learn how In-de-ci-sion
Of char-ac-ter pro-vokes De-ri-sion.
This vac-il-lat-ing Thing, you see,
Could not de-cide which he would be,
Fish, Flesh, or Fowl, and chose all three.
The sci-en-tists were sore-ly vexed
To clas-si-fy him; so per-plexed
Their brains that they, with Rage at bay,
Called him a hor-rid name one day, –
A name that baf-fles, frights, and shocks us, –
Or-ni-tho-rhyn-chus Par-a-dox-us.

4. AN ARCTIC HARE

An Arc-tic Hare we now be-hold.
   The hair, you will ob-serve, is white;
But if you think the Hare is old,
   You will be ver-y far from right.
The Hare is young, and yet the hair
   Grew white in but a sin-gle night.
Why, then it must have been a scare
   That turned this Hare. No; 'twas not fright
(Al-though such cases are well known);
   I fear that once a-gain you're wrong.
Know then, that in the Arc-tic Zone
   A sin-gle night is six months long.

Illustrated by the author   OLIVER HERFORD

The Walrus and the Carpenter

The sun was shining on the sea,
  Shining with all his might:
He did his very best to make
  The billows smooth and bright –
And this was odd, because it was
  The middle of the night.

The moon was shining sulkily,
  Because she thought the sun
Had got no business to be there
  After the day was done –
'It's very rude of him,' she said,
  'To come and spoil the fun!'

The sea was wet as wet could be,
The sands were dry as dry,
You could not see a cloud, because
No cloud was in the sky:
No birds were flying overhead –
There were no birds to fly.

The Walrus and the Carpenter
Were walking close at hand:
They wept like anything to see
Such quantities of sand:
'If this were only cleared away,'
They said, 'it would be grand.'

'If seven maids with seven mops
Swept it for half a year,
Do you suppose,' the Walrus said,
'That they could get it clear?'
'I doubt it,' said the Carpenter,
And shed a bitter tear.

'O Oysters, come and walk with us!'
The Walrus did beseech.
'A pleasant walk, a pleasant talk,
Along the briny beach:
We cannot do with more than four,
To give a hand to each.'

The eldest Oyster looked at him,
But never a word he said:
The eldest Oyster winked his eye,
And shook his heavy head –
Meaning to say he did not choose
To leave the oyster-bed.

But four young Oysters hurried up,
  All eager for the treat:
Their coats were brushed, their faces washed,
Their shoes were clean and neat –
And this was odd, because, you know,
  They hadn't any feet.

Four other Oysters followed them,
  And yet another four;
And thick and fast they came at last,
  And more, and more, and more –
All hopping through the frothy waves,
  And scrambling to the shore.

The Walrus and the Carpenter
  Walked on a mile or so,
And then they rested on a rock
  Conveniently low:
And all the little Oysters stood
  And waited in a row.

'The time has come,' the Walrus said,
  'To talk of many things:
Of shoes – and ships – and sealing wax –
  Of cabbages – and kings –
And why the sea is boiling hot –
  And whether pigs have wings.'

'But wait a bit,' the Oysters cried,
  'Before we have our chat;
For some of us are out of breath,
  And all of us are fat!'
'No hurry!' said the Carpenter.
  They thanked him much for that.

'A loaf of bread,' the Walrus said,
  'Is what we chiefly need:
Pepper and vinegar besides
  Are very good indeed –
Now, if you're ready, Oysters dear,
  We can begin to feed.'

'But not on us!' the Oysters cried,
  Turning a little blue.
'After such kindness, that would be
  A dismal thing to do!'
'The night is fine,' the Walrus said.
  'Do you admire the view?'

'It was so kind of you to come!
    And you are very nice!'
The Carpenter said nothing but
    'Cut us another slice.
I wish you were not quite so deaf –
    I've had to ask you twice!'

'It seems a shame,' the Walrus said,
    'To play them such a trick.
After we've brought them out so far,
    And made them trot so quick!'
The Carpenter said nothing but
    'The butter's spread too thick!'

'I weep for you,' the Walrus said:
　'I deeply sympathize.'
With sobs and tears he sorted out
　Those of the largest size,
Holding his pocket-handkerchief
　Before his streaming eyes.

'O Oysters,' said the Carpenter,
　'You've had a pleasant run!
Shall we be trotting home again?'
　But answer came there none –
And this was scarcely odd, because
　They'd eaten every one.

LEWIS CARROLL

Illustrated by John Tenniel

Skimbleshanks: the Railway Cat

There's a whisper down the line at 11.39
When the Night Mail's ready to depart,
Saying 'Skimble where is Skimble has he gone to hunt the thimble?
We must find him or the train can't start.'
All the guards and all the porters and the stationmaster's daughters
They are searching high and low,
Saying 'Skimble where is Skimble for unless he's very nimble
Then the Night Mail just can't go.'
At 11.42 then the signal's nearly due
And the passengers are frantic to a man –

Then Skimble will appear and he'll saunter to the rear:
He's been busy in the luggage van!
   He gives one flash of his glass-green eyes
     And the signal goes 'All Clear!'
   And we're off at last for the northern part
     Of the Northern Hemisphere!

You may say that by and large it is Skimble who's in charge
Of the Sleeping Car Express.
From the driver and the guards to the bagmen playing cards
He will supervise them all, more or less.
Down the corridor he paces and examines all the faces
Of the travellers in the First and in the Third;
He establishes control by a regular patrol
And he'd know at once if anything occurred.
He will watch you without winking and he sees what you are thinking
And it's certain that he doesn't approve
Of hilarity and riot, so the folk are very quiet
When Skimble is about and on the move.
   You can play no pranks with Skimbleshanks!
    He's a Cat that cannot be ignored;
  So nothing goes wrong on the Northern Mail
    When Skimbleshanks is aboard.

Oh it's very pleasant when you have found your little den
With your name written up on the door.
And the berth is very neat with a newly folded sheet
And there's not a speck of dust on the floor.
There is every sort of light – you can make it dark or bright;
There's a handle that you turn to make a breeze.
There's a funny little basin you're supposed to wash your face in
And a crank to shut the window if you sneeze.
Then the guard looks in politely and will ask you very brightly
'Do you like your morning tea weak or strong?'

But Skimble's just behind him and was ready to remind him,
For Skimble won't let anything go wrong.
   And when you creep into your cosy berth
     And pull up the counterpane,
  You ought to reflect that it's very nice
  To know that you won't be bothered by mice –
  You can leave all that to the Railway Cat,
     The Cat of the Railway Train!

In the watches of the night he is always fresh and bright;
Every now and then he has a cup of tea
With perhaps a drop of Scotch while he's keeping on the watch,
Only stopping here and there to catch a flea.
You were fast asleep at Crewe and so you never knew
That he was walking up and down the station;
You were sleeping all the while he was busy at Carlisle,
Where he greets the stationmaster with elation.
But you saw him at Dumfries, where he speaks to the police
If there's anything they ought to know about:
When you get to Gallowgate there you do not have to wait –
For Skimbleshanks will help you to get out!
  He gives you a wave of his long brown tail
    Which says: 'I'll see you again!
  You'll meet without fail on the Midnight Mail
    The Cat of the Railway Train.'

T. S. ELIOT

The Owl and the Pussy-Cat

I

The Owl and the Pussy-Cat went to sea
In a beautiful pea-green boat,
They took some honey, and plenty of money,
Wrapped up in a five-pound note.
The Owl looked up to the stars above,
And sang to a small guitar,
'O lovely Pussy! O Pussy, my love,
What a beautiful Pussy you are,
You are,
You are!
What a beautiful Pussy you are!'

II

Pussy said to the Owl, 'You elegant fowl!
How charmingly sweet you sing!
O let us be married! too long we have tarried:
But what shall we do for a ring?'
They sailed away for a year and a day,

To the land where the Bong-tree grows,
And there in a wood a Piggy-wig stood,
With a ring at the end of his nose,
His nose,
His nose,
With a ring at the end of his nose.

III

'Dear Pig, are you willing to sell for one shilling
Your ring?' Said the Piggy, 'I will.'
So they took it away, and were married next day
By the Turkey who lives on the hill.
They dined on mince, and slices of quince,
Which they ate with a runcible spoon;
And hand in hand, on the edge of the sand,
They danced by the light of the moon,
The moon,
The moon,
They danced by the light of the moon.

EDWARD LEAR

Illustrated by the author

The Shark

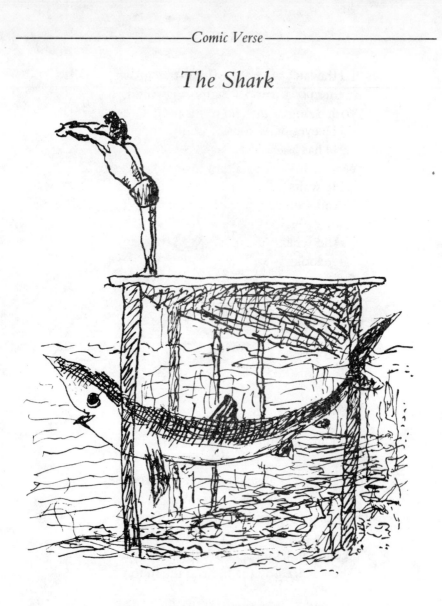

A treacherous monster is the Shark,
He never makes the least remark.

And when he sees you on the sand,
He doesn't seem to want to land.

He watches you take off your clothes,
And not the least excitement shows.

His eyes do not grow bright or roll,
He has astounding self-control.

He waits till you are quite undrest,
And seems to take no interest.

And when towards the sea you leap,
He looks as if he were asleep.

But when you once get in his range,
His whole demeanour seems to change.

He throws his body right about,
And his true character comes out.

It's no use crying or appealing,
He seems to lose all decent feeling.

After this warning you will wish
To keep clear of this treacherous fish.

His back is black, his stomach white,
He has a very dangerous bite.

LORD ALFRED DOUGLAS

Illustrated by Brian Robb

The Jumblies

I

They went to sea in a Sieve, they did,
    In a Sieve they went to sea:
In spite of all their friends could say,
On a winter's morn, on a stormy day,
    In a Sieve they went to sea!
And when the Sieve turned round and round,
And every one cried, 'You'll all be drowned!'
They called aloud, 'Our Sieve ain't big,
But we don't care a button! we don't care a fig!
    In a Sieve we'll go to sea!'
        Far and few, far and few,
            Are the lands where the Jumblies live;
            Their heads are green, and their hands are blue,
            And they went to sea in a Sieve.

II

They sailed away in a Sieve, they did,
　In a Sieve they sailed so fast,
With only a beautiful pea-green veil
Tied with a riband by way of a sail,
　To a small tobacco-pipe mast;
And every one said, who saw them go,
'O won't they be soon upset, you know!
For the sky is dark, and the voyage is long,
And happen what may, it's extremely wrong
　In a Sieve to sail so fast!'
　　Far and few, far and few,
　　　Are the lands where the Jumblies live;
　　Their heads are green, and their hands are blue,
　　　And they went to sea in a Sieve.

III

The water it soon came in, it did,
　The water it soon came in;
So to keep them dry, they wrapped their feet
In a pinky paper all folded neat,
　And they fastened it down with a pin.
And they passed the night in a crockery-jar,
And each of them said, 'How wise we are!
Though the sky be dark, and the voyage be long,
Yet we never can think we were rash or wrong,
　While round in our Sieve we spin!'
　　Far and few, far and few,
　　　Are the lands where the Jumblies live;
　　Their heads are green, and their hands are blue,
　　　And they went to sea in a Sieve.

IV

And all night long they sailed away;
  And when the sun went down,
They whistled and warbled a moony song
To the echoing sound of a coppery gong,
  In the shade of the mountains brown.
'O Timballo! How happy we are,
When we live in a sieve and a crockery-jar,
And all night long in the moonlight pale,
We sail away with a pea-green sail,
  In the shade of the mountains brown!'
    Far and few, far and few,
      Are the lands where the Jumblies live;
      Their heads are green, and their hands are blue,
      And they went to sea in a Sieve.

V

They sailed to the Western Sea, they did,
  To a land all covered with trees,
And they bought an Owl, and useful Cart,
And a pound of Rice, and a Cranberry Tart,
  And a hive of silvery Bees.
And they bought a Pig, and some green Jack-daws,
And a lovely Monkey with lollipop paws,
And forty bottles of Ring-Bo-Ree,
  And no end of Stilton Cheese.
    Far and few, far and few,
      Are the lands where the Jumblies live;
      Their heads are green, and their hands are blue,
      And they went to sea in a Sieve.

VI

And in twenty years they all came back,
   In twenty years or more,
And every one said, 'How tall they've grown!
For they've been to the Lakes, and the Terrible Zone,
   And the hills of the Chankly Bore;'
And they drank their health, and gave them a feast
Of dumplings made of beautiful yeast;
And every one said, 'If we only live,
We too will go to sea in a Sieve, –
   To the hills of the Chankly Bore!'
     Far and few, far and few,
       Are the lands where the Jumblies live;
     Their heads are green, and their hands are blue,
      And they went to sea in a Sieve.

EDWARD LEAR

Illustrated by the author

Jabberwocky

In Through the Looking Glass, *Alice climbs through her drawing-room mirror into a strange land, where she finds a book containing these odd verses*:

'Twas brillig, and the slithy toves
   Did gyre and gimble in the wabe:
All mimsy were the borogoves,
   And the mome raths outgrabe.

'Beware the Jabberwock, my son!
    The jaws that bite, the claws that catch!
Beware the Jubjub bird, and shun
    The frumious Bandersnatch!'

He took his vorpal sword in hand:
    Long time the manxome foe he sought –
So rested he by the Tumtum tree,
    And stood awhile in thought.

And, as in uffish thought he stood,
    The Jabberwock, with eyes of flame,
Came whiffling through the tulgey wood,
    And burbled as it came!

One, two! One, two! And through and through
    The vorpal blade went snicker-snack!
He left it dead, and with its head
    He went galumphing back.

'And hast thou slain the Jabberwock?
    Come to my arms, my beamish boy!
O frabjous day! Callooh! Callay!'
    He chortled in his joy.

'Twas brillig, and the slithy toves
    Did gyre and gimble in the wabe:
All mimsy were the borogoves,
    And the mome raths outgrabe.

'It seems very pretty,' she said when she had finished it, 'but it's *rather* hard to understand!'

Illustrated by John Tenniel   LEWIS CARROLL

Nonsense Limericks

There was a Young Lady of Norway,
Who casually sat in a doorway;
When the door squeezed her flat,
She exclaimed, 'What of that!'
This courageous Young Lady of Norway.

There was an Old Man of Corfu,
Who never knew what he should do;
So he rushed up and down
Till the sun made him brown,
That bewildered Old Man of Corfu.

There was an Old Person of Cromer,
Who stood on one leg to read Homer;
When he found he grew stiff,
He jumped over the cliff,
Which concluded that Person of Cromer.

There was an Old Man of the Dee,
Who was sadly annoyed by a flea;
When he said, 'I will scratch it,'
They gave him a hatchet,
Which grieved that Old Man of the Dee.

There was an Old Man of Calcutta,
Who perpetually ate bread and butter,
Till a great bit of muffin,
On which he was stuffing,
Choked that horrid Old Man of Calcutta.

There was an old Man of the Hague,
Whose ideas were excessively vague;
He built a balloon
To examine the moon,
That deluded Old Man of the Hague.

There was an Old Person of Dutton,
Whose head was as small as a button;
So, to make it look big,
He purchased a wig,
And rapidly rushed about Dutton.

There was an Old Man who said, 'Hush!
I perceive a young bird in this bush!'
When they said, 'Is it small?'
He replied, 'Not at all!
It is four times as big as the bush!'

Illustrated by the author   EDWARD LEAR

Animal Verse

The Robin

When up aloft
I fly and fly,
I see in pools
The shining sky,
And a happy bird
Am I, am I!

When I descend
Towards their brink
I stand, and look,
And stoop, and drink,
And bathe my wings,
And chink and prink.

When winter frost
Makes earth as steel,
I search and search
But find no meal,
And most unhappy
Then I feel.

But when it lasts,
And snows still fall,
I get to feel
No grief at all,
For I turn to a cold stiff
Feathery ball!

THOMAS HARDY

To a Butterfly

I've watched you now a full half-hour,
Self-poised upon that yellow flower;
And, little Butterfly! indeed
I know not if you sleep or feed.
How motionless! – not frozen seas
More motionless! And then
What joy awaits you, when the breeze
Hath found you out among the trees,
And calls you forth again!

This plot of orchard-ground is ours;
My trees they are, my Sister's flowers.
Here rest your wings when they are weary;
Here lodge as in a sanctuary!
Come often to us, fear no wrong;
Sit near us on the bough!
We'll talk of sunshine and of song,
And summer days, when we were young;
Sweet childish days, that were as long
As twenty days are now.

WILLIAM WORDSWORTH

The Tyger

Tyger! Tyger! burning bright!
In the forests of the night,
What immortal hand or eye
Could frame thy fearful symmetry?

In what distant deeps or skies
Burnt the fire of thine eyes?
On what wings dare he aspire?
What the hand dare seize the fire?

And what shoulder, and what art,
Could twist the sinews of thy heart?
And when thy heart began to beat,
What dread hand? and what dread feet?

What the hammer? what the chain?
In what furnace was thy brain?
What the anvil? what dread grasp
Dare its deadly terrors clasp?

When the stars threw down their spears,
And water'd heaven with their tears,
Did he smile his work to see?
Did he who made the Lamb make thee?

Tyger! Tyger! burning bright
In the forests of the night,
What immortal hand or eye,
Dare frame thy fearful symmetry?

WILLIAM BLAKE

The Vixen

Among the taller wood with ivy hung,
The old fox plays and dances round her young.
She snuffs and barks if any passes by
And swings her tail and turns prepared to fly.
The horseman hurries by, she bolts to see,
And turns again, from danger never free.
If any stands she runs among the poles
And barks and snaps and drives them in the holes.
The shepherd sees them and the boy goes by
And gets a stick and progs the hole to try.
They get all still and lie in safety sure,
And out again when everything's secure,
And start and snap at blackbirds bouncing by
To fight and catch the great white butterfly.

JOHN CLARE

The Snake

A narrow fellow in the grass
Occasionally rides;
You may have met him – did you not,
His notice sudden is.

The grass divides as with a comb,
A spotted shaft is seen;
And then it closes at your feet
And opens further on.

He likes a boggy acre,
A floor too cool for corn.
Yet when a child, and barefoot,
I more than once, at morn,

Have passed, I thought, a whip-lash
Unbraiding in the sun, –
When, stooping to secure it,
It wrinkled, and was gone.

Several of nature's people
I know, and they know me;
I feel for them a transport
Of cordiality;

But never met this fellow,
Attended or alone,
Without a tighter breathing,
And zero at the bone.

EMILY DICKINSON

The Frog

The Frog by Nature is both damp and cold,
Her Mouth is large, her Belly much will hold:
She sits somewhat ascending, loves to be
Croaking in Gardens, though unpleasantly. . . .

JOHN BUNYAN

A popular personage at home

'I live here: "Wessex" is my name:
I am a dog known rather well:
I guard the house; but how that came
To be my whim I cannot tell.

'With a leap and a heart elate I go
At the end of an hour's expectancy
To take a walk of a mile or so
With the folk I let live here with me.

'Along the path, amid the grass
I sniff, and find out rarest smells
For rolling over as I pass
The open fields towards the dells.

'No doubt I shall always cross this sill,
And turn the corner, and stand steady,
Gazing back for my mistress till
She reaches where I have run already,

'And that this meadow with its brook,
And bulrush, even as it appears
As I plunge by with hasty look,
Will stay the same a thousand years.'

Thus 'Wessex'. But a dubious ray
At times informs his steadfast eye,
Just for a trice, as though to say,
'Yet, will this pass, and pass shall I?'

THOMAS HARDY

The Stallion

A gigantic beauty of a stallion, fresh and responsive to my caresses,
Head high in the forehead, wide between the ears,
Limbs glossy and supple, tail dusting the ground,
Eyes full of sparkling wickedness, ears finely cut, flexibly moving.

His nostrils dilate as my heels embrace him,
His well-built limbs tremble with pleasure as we race around and return.

WALT WHITMAN

The Lizard

If on any warm day when you ramble around
Among moss and dead leaves, you should happen to see
A quick trembling thing dart and hide on the ground,
And you search in the leaves, you would uncover me.

THOMAS HARDY

The Crocodile

If you should meet a crocodile,
Don't take a stick and poke him;
Ignore the welcome in his smile,
Be careful not to stroke him.
For as he sleeps upon the Nile,
He thinner grows and thinner;
And whene'er you meet a crocodile
He's ready for his dinner.

ANONYMOUS

To a Mouse

Wee, sleekit, cowrin, tim'rous beastie,
O, what a panic's in thy breastie!
Thou need na start awa sae hasty,
    Wi' bickering brattle!
I wad be lathe to rin an' chase thee,
    Wi' murd'ring pattle!

84

I'm truly sorry man's dominion
Has broken Nature's social union,
An' justifies that ill opinion,
    Which makes thee startle,
At me, thy poor earth-born companion,
    An' fellow mortal!

But Mousie, thou are no thy lane,
In proving foresight may be vain:
The best laid schemes o' Mice an' Men
    Gang aft agley,
An' lea'e us nought but grief and pain,
    For promis'd joy.

Still thou art blest compar'd wi' me!
The present only toucheth thee:
But, Och! I backward cast my e'e,
    On prospects drear!
An' forward, tho' I canna see,
    I guess an' fear!

ROBERT BURNS

Sleekit: sleek   *pattle:* a stick
Wi' bickering brattle: With hasty scamper   *Gang aft a-gley:* often go wrong
Lathe: Loathe   *lea'e:* leave

Epitaph on a Hare

Here lies, whom hound did ne'er pursue,
  Nor swifter greyhound follow,
Whose foot ne'er tainted morning dew,
  Nor ear heard huntsman's 'hallo',

Old Tiney, surliest of his kind,
  Who, nurs'd with tender care,
And to domestic bounds confin'd,
  Was still a wild Jack-hare.

Though duly from my hand he took
  His pittance ev'ry night,
He did it with a jealous look,
  And, when he could, would bite.

His diet was of wheaten bread,
  And milk, and oats, and straw,
Thistles, or lettuces instead,
  With sand to scour his maw.

On twigs of hawthorn he regal'd,
  On pippins' russet peel;

And, when his juicy salads fail'd,
   Slic'd carrot pleas'd him well.

A Turkey carpet was his lawn,
   Whereon he lov'd to bound,
To skip and gambol like a fawn,
   And swing his rump around.

His frisking was at evening hours,
   For them he lost his fear;
But most before approaching show'rs,
   Or when a storm drew near.

Eight years and five round-rolling moons
   He thus saw steal away,
Dozing out all his idle noons,
   And ev'ry night at play.

I kept him for his humour's sake,
   For he would oft beguile
My heart of thoughts that made it ache,
   And force me to a smile.

But now, beneath this walnut-shade
   He finds his long, last home,
And waits in snug concealment laid,
   Till gentler Puss shall come.

He, still more aged, feels the shocks
   From which no care can save,
And, partner once of Tiney's box,
   Must soon partake his grave.

WILLIAM COWPER

To a Cat

Cat! who has pass'd thy grand climacteric,
   How many mice and rats hast in thy days
   Destroy'd? – How many tit bits stolen? Gaze
With those bright languid segments green, and prick
Those velvet ears – but pr'ythee do not stick
   Thy latent talons in me – and upraise
   Thy gentle mew – and tell me all thy frays
Of fish and mice, and rats and tender chick.
Nay, look not down, nor lick thy dainty wrists –
   For all the wheezy asthma, – and for all
Thy tail's tip is nick'd off – and though the fists
   Of many a maid have given thee many a maul,
Still is that fur as soft as when the lists
   In youth thou enter'dst on glass bottled wall.

JOHN KEATS

The Squirrel

The squirrel, flippant, pert, and full of play,
Drawn from his refuge in some lonely elm
That age or injury hath hollowed deep,
Where, on his bed of wool and matted leaves,
He has out-slept the winter, ventures forth
To frisk awhile, and bask in the warm sun:
He sees me, and at once, swift as a bird,
Ascends the neighbouring beech: there whisks his brush,
And perks his ears, and stamps, and cries aloud,
With all the prettiness of feigned alarm,
And anger insignificantly fierce.

WILLIAM COWPER

Ducks' Ditty

All along the backwater,
Through the rushes tall,
Ducks are a-dabbling,
   Up tails all!

Ducks' tails, drakes' tails,
Yellow feet a-quiver,
Yellow bills all out of sight
   Busy in the river!

Slushy green undergrowth
Where the roach swim –
Here we keep our larder
   Cool and full and dim!

Every one for what he likes!
We like to be
Heads down, tails up,
   Dabbling free!

High in the blue above
Swifts whirl and call –
We are down a-dabbling
   Up tails all!

KENNETH GRAHAME

Grizzly

Coward, – of heroic size,
In whose lazy muscles lies
Strength we fear and yet despise;
Savage, – whose relentless tusks
Are content with acorn husks;
Robber, – whose exploits ne'er soared
O'er the bee's or squirrel's hoard;
Whiskered chin and feeble nose,
Claws of steel on baby toes, –
Here, in solitude and shade,
Shambling, shuffling plantigrade,
Be thy courses undismayed!

Here, where Nature makes thy bed,
Let thy rude, half-human tread
    Point to hidden Indian springs,
Lost in ferns and fragrant grasses,
    Hovered o'er by timid wings,
Where the wood-duck lightly passes,
Where the wild bee holds her sweets, –
Epicurean retreats,
Fit for thee, and better than
Fearful spoils of dangerous man.

In thy fat jowled deviltry
Friar Tuck shall live in thee;
Thou mayst levy tithe and dole;
    Thou shalt spread the woodland cheer,
From the pilgrim taking toll;
    Match thy cunning with his fear;
Eat, and drink, and have thy fill;
Yet remain an outlaw still!   BRET HARTE

Stories in Verse

The Land of Story-books

R. L. STEVENSON
Illustrated by Jessie Wilcox Smith

At evening when the lamp is lit,
Around the fire my parents sit;
They sit at home and talk and sing,
And do not play at anything.

Now, with my little gun, I crawl
All in the dark along the wall,
And follow round the forest track
Away behind the sofa back.

There, in the night, where none can spy,
All in my hunter's camp I lie,
And play at books that I have read
Till it is time to go to bed.

These are the hills, these are the woods,
These are my starry solitudes;
And there the river by whose brink
The roaring lions come to drink.

I see the others far away
As if in firelit camp they lay,
And I, like to an Indian scout,
Around their party prowled about.

So, when my nurse comes in for me,
Home I return across the sea,
And go to bed with backward looks
At my dear land of Story-books.

The Fairies

WILLIAM ALLINGHAM

Up the airy mountain,
  Down the rushy glen,
We daren't go a-hunting
  For fear of little men;
Wee folk, good folk,
  Trooping all together;
Green jacket, red cap,
  And white owl's feather!

Down along the rocky shore
  Some make their home,
They live on crispy pancakes
  Of yellow tide-foam;
Some in the reeds
  Of the black mountain lake,
With frogs for their watch-dogs,
  All night awake.

High on the hill-top
  The old King sits;
He is now so old and grey
  He's nigh lost his wits.
With a bridge of white mist
  Columbkill he crosses,
On his stately journeys
  From Slieveleague to Rosses;
Or going up with music
  On cold starry nights

To sup with the Queen
    Of the gay Northern Lights.

They stole little Bridget
    For seven years long;
When she came down again
    Her friends were all gone.
They took her lightly back,
    Between the night and morrow,
They thought that she was fast asleep,
    But she was dead with sorrow.
They have kept her ever since
    Deep within the lake,
On a bed of flag-leaves,
    Watching till she wake.

By the craggy hill-side,
    Through the mosses bare,
They have planted thorn-trees
    For pleasure here and there.
Is any man so daring
    As dig them up in spite,
He shall find their sharpest thorns
    In his bed at night.

Up the airy mountain,
    Down the rushy glen,
We daren't go a-hunting
    For fear of little men;
Wee folk, good folk,
    Trooping all together;
Green jacket, red cap,
    And white owl's feather!

Casey Jones

WALLACE SAUNDERS

Come all you rounders for I want you to hear
The story of a brave engineer;
Casey Jones was the fellow's name,
A big eight-wheeler of a mighty fame.
Caller called Casey at half-past four,
He kissed his wife at the station door,
Mounted to the cabin with orders in his hand,
And took his farewell trip to the promised land.
  Casey Jones, he mounted to the cabin,
  Casey Jones, with his orders in his hand!
  Casey Jones, he mounted to the cabin,
  Took his farewell trip into the promised land.

Put in your water and shovel in your coal,
Put your head out the window, watch the drivers roll,
I'll run her till she leaves the rail,
'Cause we're eight hours late with the Western Mail!
He looked at his watch and his watch was slow,
Looked at the water and the water was low,
Turned to his fireboy and said,
'We'll get to 'Frisco, but we'll all be dead!'
  Casey Jones, he mounted to the cabin,
  Casey Jones, with his orders in his hand!
  Casey Jones, he mounted to the cabin,
  Took his farewell trip into the promised land.

Casey pulled up Reno Hill,
Tooted for the crossing with an awful shrill,
Snakes all knew by the engine's moans
That the hogger at the throttle was Casey Jones.
He pulled up short two miles from the place,
Number four stared him right in the face,
Turned to his fireboy, said 'You'd better jump,
'Cause there's two locomotives going to bump!'
    Casey Jones, he mounted to the cabin,
    Casey Jones, with his orders in his hand!
    Casey Jones, he mounted to the cabin,
    Took his farewell trip into the promised land.

Casey said, just before he died,
'There's two more roads I'd like to ride.'
Fireboy said, 'What can they be?'
'The Rio Grande and the Old S.P.'
Mrs. Jones sat on her bed a-sighing,
Got a pink that Casey was dying,
Said, 'Go to bed, children; hush your crying,
'Cause you'll get another papa on the Salt Lake line.'
    Casey Jones! Got another papa!
    Casey Jones, on the Salt Lake Line!
    Casey Jones! Got another papa!
    Got another papa on the Salt Lake Line!

The Jackdaw of Rheims

R. H. BARHAM
Illustrated by John Leech

The Jackdaw sat on the Cardinal's chair!
Bishop, and abbot, and prior were there;
    Many a monk, and many a friar,
    Many a knight, and many a squire,
With a great many more of lesser degree, –
In sooth a goodly company;
And they served the Lord Primate on bended knee.
    Never, I ween,
    Was a prouder seen,
Read of in books, or dreamt of in dreams,
Than the Cardinal Lord Archbishop of Rheims!

    In and out
    Through the motley rout,
That little Jackdaw kept hopping about;
    Here and there
    Like a dog in a fair,
    Over comfits and cates,
    And dishes and plates,
Cowl and cope, and rochet and pall,
Mitre and crosier! he hopp'd upon all!
    With saucy air,
    He perch'd on the chair
Where, in state, the great Lord Cardinal sat
In the great Lord Cardinal's great red hat;
    And he peer'd in the face
    Of his Lordship's Grace,

With a satisfied look, as if he would say,
'We two are the greatest folks here to-day!'
  And the priests, with awe,
  As such freaks they saw,
Said, 'The Devil must be in that little Jackdaw!'

The feast was over, the board was clear'd,
The flawns and the custards had all disappear'd,
And six little Singing-boys, – dear little souls!
In nice clean faces, and nice white stoles,
  Came, in order due,
  Two by two,
Marching that grand refectory through!
A nice little boy held a golden ewer,
Emboss'd and fill'd with water, as pure
As any that flows between Rheims and Namur,
Which a nice little boy stood ready to catch
In a fine golden hand-basin made to match.
Two nice little boys, rather more grown,
Carried lavender-water, and eau de Cologne;
And a nice little boy had a nice cake of soap,
Worthy of washing the hands of the Pope.
  One little boy more
  A napkin bore,
Of the best white diaper, fringed with pink,
And a Cardinal's Hat mark'd in 'permanent ink.'

The great Lord Cardinal turns at the sight
 Of these nice little boys dress'd all in white:
  From his finger he draws
  His costly turquoise;
And, not thinking at all about little Jackdaws,
  Deposits it straight
  By the side of his plate,

While the nice little boys on his Eminence wait;
Till, when nobody's dreaming of any such thing,
That little Jackdaw hops off with the ring!

There's a cry and a shout,
And a deuce of a rout,
And nobody seems to know what they're about,
But the Monks have their pockets all turn'd inside out.
The Friars are kneeling,
And hunting, and feeling
The carpet, the floor, and the walls, and the ceiling.
The Cardinal drew
Off each plum-colour'd shoe,
And left his red stockings exposed to the view;
He peeps, and he feels
In the toes and the heels;
They turn up the dishes, – they turn up the plates, –
They take up the poker and poke out the grates,
– They turn up the rugs,
They examine the mugs: –
But, no! – no such thing; –
They can't find THE RING!
And the Abbot declared that, 'when nobody twigg'd it,
Some rascal or other had popp'd in, and prigg'd it!'

The Cardinal rose with a dignified look,
He call'd for his candle, his bell, and his book!
In holy anger, and pious grief,
He solemnly cursed that rascally thief!
He cursed him at board, he cursed him in bed;
From the sole of his foot to the crown of his head;
He cursed him in sleeping, that every night
He should dream of the devil, and wake in a fright;
He cursed him in eating, he cursed him in drinking,

He cursed him in coughing, in sneezing, in winking;
He cursed him in sitting, in standing, in lying;
He cursed him in walking, in riding, in flying,
He cursed him in living, he cursed him in dying! –
Never was heard such a terrible curse!!
　　But what gave rise
　　To no little surprise,
Nobody seem'd one penny the worse!

　　The day was gone,
　　The night came on,
The Monks and the Friars they search'd till dawn; –
　　When the Sacristan saw,
　　On crumpled claw,
Come limping a poor little lame Jackdaw!
　　No longer gay,
　　As on yesterday;
His feathers all seem'd to be turn'd the wrong way;
His pinions droop'd – he could hardly stand, –
His head was as bald as the palm of your hand;
　　His eye so dim,
　　So wasted each limb,
That, heedless of grammar, they all cried, 'THAT'S HIM! –
That's the scamp that has done this scandalous thing!
That's the thief that has got my Lord Cardinal's Ring!'
　　The poor little Jackdaw,
　　When the Monks he saw,
Feebly gave vent to the ghost of a caw;
And turn'd his bald head, as much as to say,
'Pray, be so good as to walk this way!'
　　Slower and slower
　　He limp'd on before,
Till they came to the back of the belfry door,
　　Where the first thing they saw,

Come limping a poor little lame jackdaw

Midst the sticks and the straw,
Was the RING in the nest of that little Jackdaw!
Then the great Lord Cardinal call'd for his book,
And off that terrible curse he took;
　　The mute expression
　　Served in lieu of confession,

And, being thus coupled with full restitution,
The Jackdaw got plenary absolution!
   – When those words were heard,
    That poor little bird
Was so changed in a moment, 'twas really absurd.
    He grew sleek, and fat;
    In addition to that,   .
A fresh crop of feathers came thick as a mat!
    His tail waggled more
    Even than before;
But no longer it wagg'd with an impudent air,
No longer he perch'd on the Cardinal's chair.
    He hopp'd now about
    With a gait devout;
At Matins, at Vespers, he never was out;
And, so far from any more pilfering deeds,
He always seem'd telling the Confessor's beads.
If any one lied, – or if any one swore, –
Or slumber'd in pray'r-time and happen'd to snore,
    That good Jackdaw
    Would give a great 'Caw!'
As much as to say, 'Don't do so any more!'
While many remark'd, as his manners they saw,
That they 'never had known such a pious Jackdaw!'
    He long lived the pride
    Of that country side,
And at last in the odour of sanctity died;
    When, as words were too faint
    His merits to paint,
The Conclave determined to make him a Saint;
And on newly-made Saints and Popes, as you know,
It's the custom, at Rome, new names to bestow,
So they canonized him by the name of Jim Crow!

The Diverting History
of John Gilpin

WILLIAM COWPER
Illustrated by R. Caldecott

John Gilpin was a citizen
  Of credit and renown,
A train-band captain eke was he,
  Of famous London town.

John Gilpin's spouse said to her dear,
  'Though wedded we have been
These twice ten tedious years, yet we
  No holiday have seen.

'To-morrow is our wedding-day,
  And we will then repair
Unto the "Bell" at Edmonton,
  All in a chaise and pair.

'My sister, and my sister's child,
  Myself, and children three,
Will fill the chaise; so you must ride
  On horseback after we.'

He soon replied, 'I do admire
  Of womankind but one,
And you are she, my dearest dear,
  Therefore it shall be done.

'I am a linendraper bold,
　　As all the world doth know,
And my good friend the calender
　　Will lend his horse to go.'

Quoth Mrs. Gilpin, 'That's well said;
　　And for that wine is dear,
We will be furnished with our own,
　　Which is both bright and clear.'

John Gilpin kissed his loving wife;
　　O'erjoyed was he to find,
That though on pleasure she was bent,
　　She had a frugal mind.

The morning came, the chaise was brought,
　　But yet was not allowed
To drive up to the door, lest all
　　Should say that she was proud.

So three doors off the chaise was stayed,
　　Where they did all get in;
Six precious souls, and all agog
　　To dash through thick and thin.

Smack went the whip, round went the wheels,
　　Were never folks so glad!
The stones did rattle underneath,
　　As if Cheapside were mad.

John Gilpin at his horse's side
　　Seized fast the flowing mane,
And up he got, in haste to ride,
　　But soon came down again;

For saddletree scarce reached had he,
 His journey to begin,
When, turning round his head, he saw
 Three customers come in.

So down he came; for loss of time,
 Although it grieved him sore,
Yet loss of pence, full well he knew,
 Would trouble him much more.

'Twas long before the customers
 Were suited to their mind,
When Betty screaming came downstairs,
 'The wine is left behind!'

'Good lack!' quoth he, 'yet bring it me,
  My leathern belt likewise,
In which I bear my trusty sword
  When I do exercise.'

Now Mistress Gilpin (careful soul!)
  Had two stone bottles found,
To hold the liquor that she loved,
  And keep it safe and sound.

Each bottle had a curling ear,
  Through which the belt he drew,
And hung a bottle on each side,
  To make his balance true.

Then over all, that he might be
  Equipped from top to toe,
His long red cloak, well brushed and neat,
  He manfully did throw.

Now see him mounted once again
  Upon his nimble steed,
Full slowly pacing o'er the stones,
  With caution and good heed.

But finding soon a smoother road
  Beneath his well-shod feet,
The snorting beast began to trot,
  Which galled him in his seat.

'So, fair and softly!' John he cried,
  But John he cried in vain;
That trot became a gallop soon,
  In spite of curb and rein.

So stooping down, as needs he must
　Who cannot sit upright,
He grasped the mane with both his hands,
　And eke with all his might.

His horse, who never in that sort
　Had handled been before,
What thing upon his back had got,
　Did wonder more and more.

Away went Gilpin, neck or nought;
　Away went hat and wig;
He little dreamt, when he set out,
　Of running such a rig.

The wind did blow, the cloak did fly
　Like streamer long and gay,
Till, loop and button failing both,
　At last it flew away.

Then might all people well discern
   The bottles he had slung;
A bottle swinging at each side,
   As hath been said or sung.

The dogs did bark, the children screamed,
   Up flew the windows all;
And every soul cried out, 'Well done!'
   As loud as he could bawl.

Away went Gilpin – who but he?
   His fame soon spread around;
'He carries weight! he rides a race!
   'Tis for a thousand pound!'

And still as fast as he drew near,
   'Twas wonderful to view
How in a trice the turnpike-men
   Their gates wide open threw.

And now, as he went bowing down
  His reeking head full low,
The bottles twain behind his back
  Were shattered at a blow.

Down ran the wine into the road,
  Most piteous to be seen,
Which made the horse's flanks to smoke,
  As they had basted been.

But still he seemed to carry weight.
  With leathern girdle braced;
For all might see the bottle-necks
  Still dangling at his waist.

Thus all through merry Islington
  These gambols he did play,
Until he came unto the Wash
  Of Edmonton so gay;

And there he threw the wash about
  On both sides of the way,
Just like unto a trundling mop,
  Or a wild goose at play.

At Edmonton his loving wife
  From the balcony spied
Her tender husband, wondering much
  To see how he did ride.

'Stop, stop, John Gilpin! – Here's the house!'
  They all at once did cry;
'The dinner waits, and we are tired;'
  Said Gilpin – 'So am I!'

But yet his horse was not a whit
   Inclined to tarry there;
For why? – his owner had a house
   Full ten miles off, at Ware.

So like an arrow swift he flew,
   Shot by an archer strong;
So did he fly – which brings me to
   The middle of my song.

Away went Gilpin, out of breath,
   And sore against his will,
Till at his friend the calender's
   His horse at last stood still.

The calender, amazed to see
   His neighbour in such trim,
Laid down his pipe, flew to the gate,
   And thus accosted him:

'What news? what news? your tidings tell;
   Tell me you must and shall –
Say why bareheaded you are come,
   Or why you come at all?'

Now Gilpin had a pleasant wit,
   And loved a timely joke;
And thus unto the calender
   In merry guise he spoke:

'I came because your horse would come:
   And, if I well forbode,
My hat and wig will soon be here,
   They are upon the road.'

The calender, right glad to find
   His friend in merry pin,
Returned him not a single word,
   But to the house went in;

Whence straight he came with hat and wig,
   A wig that flowed behind,
A hat not much the worse for wear,
   Each comely in its kind.

He held them up, and in his turn
   Thus showed his ready wit:
'My head is twice as big as yours,
   They therefore needs must fit.'

'But let me scrape the dirt away,
 That hangs upon your face;
And stop and eat, for well you may
 Be in a hungry case.'

Said John, 'It is my wedding-day,
 And all the world would stare
If wife should dine at Edmonton,
 And I should dine at Ware.'

So turning to his horse, he said
 'I am in haste to dine;
'Twas for your pleasure you came here,
 You shall go back for mine.'

Ah! luckless speech, and bootless boast
 For which he paid full dear;
For while he spake, a braying ass
 Did sing most loud and clear;

Whereat his horse did snort, as he
 Had heard a lion roar,
And galloped off with all his might,
 As he had done before.

Away went Gilpin, and away
 Went Gilpin's hat and wig;
He lost them sooner than at first,
 For why? – they were too big.

Now Mistress Gilpin, when she saw
 Her husband posting down
Into the country far away,
 She pulled out half-a-crown;

And thus unto the youth she said
   That drove them to the 'Bell,'
'This shall be yours when you bring back
   My husband safe and well.'

The youth did ride, and soon did meet
   John coming back amain;
Whom in a trice he tried to stop,
   By catching at his rein.

But not performing what he meant,
   And gladly would have done,
The frighted steed he frighted more,
   And made him faster run.

Away went Gilpin, and away
   Went postboy at his heels,
The postboy's horse right glad to miss
   The lumbering of the wheels.

Six gentlemen upon the road,
    Thus seeing Gilpin fly,
With postboy scampering in the rear,
    They raised the hue and cry.

'Stop thief! stop thief! a highwayman!'
    Not one of them was mute;
And all and each that passed that way
    Did join in the pursuit.

And now the turnpike-gates again
    Flew open in short space;
The toll-man thinking, as before,
    That Gilpin rode a race.

And so he did, and won it too,
    For he got first to town;
Nor stopped till where he had got up,
    He did again get down.

Now let us sing, Long live the King,
    And Gilpin, long live he;
And when he next doth ride abroad,
    May I be there to see.

The Pied Piper of Hamelin

ROBERT BROWNING
Illustrated by Kate Greenaway

I

Hamelin Town's in Brunswick,
  By famous Hanover city;
The river Weser, deep and wide,
Washes its wall on the southern side;
A pleasanter spot you never spied;
  But, when begins my ditty,
Almost five hundred years ago,
To see the townsfolk suffer so
  From vermin, was a pity.

II

  Rats!
They fought the dogs and killed the cats,
  And bit the babies in the cradles,
And ate the cheeses out of the vats,
  And licked the soup from the cooks' own ladles,
Split open the kegs of salted sprats,
Made nests inside men's Sunday hats,
And even spoiled the women's chats
    By drowning their speaking
    With shrieking and squeaking
In fifty different sharps and flats.

III

At last the people in a body
  To the Town Hall came flocking:
' 'Tis clear,' cried they, 'Our Mayor's a noddy;
    'And as for our Corporation – shocking
'To think we buy gowns lined with ermine
'For dolts that can't or won't determine
'What's best to rid us of our vermin!
'You hope, because you're old and obese,
'To find in the furry civic robe ease?
'Rouse up, sirs! Give your brains a racking
'To find the remedy we're lacking,
  'Or, sure as fate, we'll send you packing!'
At this the Mayor and Corporation
Quaked with a mighty consternation.

*And licked the soup from
the cook's own ladles*

IV

An hour they sat in council,
  At length the Mayor broke silence:
'For a guilder I'd my ermine gown sell,
  'I wish I were a mile hence!
'It's easy to bid one rack one's brain –
'I'm sure my poor head aches again,
'I've scratched it so, and all in vain.
'Oh for a trap, a trap, a trap!'
Just as he said this, what should hap
At the chamber door but a gentle tap?
'Bless us,' cried the Mayor, 'what's that?'
(With the Corporation as he sat,
Looking little though wondrous fat,
Nor brighter was his eye, nor moister
Than a too-long-opened oyster,
Save when at noon his paunch grew mutinous
For a plate of turtle green and glutinous)
'Only a scraping of shoes on the mat?
'Anything like the sound of a rat
'Makes my heart go pit-a-pat!'

V

'Come in!' – the Mayor cried, looking bigger:
And in did come the strangest figure!
His queer long coat from heel to head
Was half of yellow and half of red,
And he himself was tall and thin,
With sharp blue eyes, each like a pin,
And light loose hair, yet swarthy skin,
No tuft on cheek nor beard on chin,
But lips where smiles went out and in;
There was no guessing his kith and kin:
And nobody could enough admire

The tall man and his quaint attire.
Quoth one: 'It's as my great-grandsire,
'Starting up at the Trump of Doom's tone,
'Had walked this way from his painted tomb-stone!'

VI

He advanced to the council-table:
And, 'Please your honours,' said he, 'I'm able,
'By means of a secret charm, to draw
    'All creatures living beneath the sun,
    'That creep or swim or fly or run,
'After me so as you never saw!
'And I chiefly use my charm
'On creatures that do people harm,
'The mole and toad and newt and viper;
'And people call me the Pied Piper.'
(And here they noticed round his neck
    A scarf of red and yellow stripe,
To match with his coat of the self-same cheque;
    And at the scarf's end hung a pipe;
And his fingers, they noticed, were ever straying
As if impatient to be playing
Upon this pipe, as low it dangled
Over his vesture so old-fangled.)
'Yet,' said he, 'poor piper as I am,
'In Tartary I freed the Cham,
    'Last June, from his huge swarms of gnats;
'I eased in Asia the Nizam
    'Of a monstrous brood of vampyre-bats:
'And as for what your brain bewilders,
    'If I can rid your town of rats
'Will you give me a thousand guilders?'
'One? fifty thousand!'– was the exclamation
Of the astonished Mayor and Corporation.

VII

Into the street the Piper stept,
  Smiling first a little smile,
As if he knew what magic slept
  In his quiet pipe the while;
Then, like a musical adept,

The Piper

To blow the pipe his lips he wrinkled,
And green and blue his sharp eyes twinkled,
Like a candle-flame where salt is sprinkled;
And ere three shrill notes the pipe uttered,
You heard as if an army muttered;
And the muttering grew to a grumbling;
And the grumbling grew to a mighty rumbling;
And out of the houses the rats came tumbling.
Great rats, small rats, lean rats, brawny rats,
Brown rats, black rats, grey rats, tawny rats,

Grave old plodders, gay young friskers,
  Fathers, mothers, uncles, cousins,
Cocking tails and pricking whiskers,
  Families by tens and dozens,
Brothers, sisters, husbands, wives –
Followed the Piper for their lives.
From street to street he piped advancing,
And step for step they followed dancing,
Until they came to the river Weser,
  Wherein all plunged and perished!
  – Save one who, stout as Julius Caesar,
Swam across and lived to carry
  (As he, the manuscript he cherished)
To Rat-land home his commentary:
Which was, 'At the first shrill notes of the pipe,
'I heard a sound as of scraping tripe,
'And putting apples, wondrous ripe,
'Into a cider-press's gripe:
'And a moving away of pickle-tub-boards,
'And a leaving ajar of conserve-cupboards,
'And a drawing the corks of train-oil-flasks,
'And a breaking the hoops of butter-casks:
'And it seemed as if a voice
  '(Sweeter far than bý harp or bý psaltery
'Is breathed) called out, "Oh rats, rejoice!
  '"The world is grown to one vast drysaltery!
'"So munch on, crunch on, take your nuncheon,
'"Breakfast, supper, dinner, luncheon!"
'And just as a bulky sugar-puncheon,
'All ready staved, like a great sun shone
'Glorious scarce an inch before me,
'Just as methought it said, "Come, bore me!"
'– I found the Weser rolling o'er me.'

VIII

You should have heard the Hamelin people
Ringing the bells till they rocked the steeple.
'Go,' cried the Mayor, 'and get long poles,
'Poke out the nests and block up the holes!
'Consult with carpenters and builders,
'And leave in our town not even a trace
'Of the rats!' – when suddenly, up the face
Of the Piper perked in the market-place,
With a, 'First, if you please, my thousand guilders!'

IX

A thousand guilders! The Mayor looked blue;
So did the Corporation too.
For council dinners made rare havoc
With Claret, Moselle, Vin-de-Grave, Hock;
And half the money would replenish
Their cellar's biggest butt with Rhenish.
To pay this sum to a wandering fellow
With a gipsy coat of red and yellow!
'Beside,' quoth the Mayor with a knowing wink,
'Our business was done at the river's brink;
'We saw with our eyes the vermin sink,
'And what's dead can't come to life, I think.
'So, friend, we're not the folks to shrink
'From the duty of giving you something for drink,
'And a matter of money to put in your poke;
'But as for the guilders, what we spoke
'Of them, as you very well know, was in joke.
'Beside, our losses have made us thrifty.
'A thousand guilders! Come, take fifty!'

X

The Piper's face fell, and he cried
'No trifling! I can't wait, beside!
'I've promised to visit by dinnertime
'Bagdat, and accept the prime
'Of the Head-Cook's pottage, all he's rich in,
'For having left, in the Caliph's kitchen,
'Of a nest of scorpions no survivor:
'With him I proved no bargain-driver,
'With you, don't think I'll bate a stiver!
'And folks who put me in a passion
'May find me pipe after another fashion.'

XI

'How?' cried the Mayor, 'd'ye think I brook
'Being worse treated than a Cook?
'Insulted by a lazy ribald
'With idle pipe and vesture piebald?
'You threaten us, fellow? Do your worst,
'Blow your pipe there till you burst!'

XII

Once more he stept into the street
    And to his lips again
    Laid his long pipe of smooth straight cane;
And ere he blew three notes (such sweet
Soft notes as yet musician's cunning
    Never gave the enraptured air)
There was a rustling that seemed like a bustling
Of merry crowds justling at pitching and hustling,
Small feet were pattering, wooden shoes clattering,
Little hands clapping and little tongues chattering,

And, like fowls in a farm-yard when barley is scattering,
Out came the children running.
All the little boys and girls,
With rosy cheeks and flaxen curls,
And sparkling eyes and teeth like pearls,
Tripping and skipping, ran merrily after
The wonderful music with shouting and laughter.

XIII

The Mayor was dumb, and the Council stood
As if they were changed into blocks of wood,
Unable to move a step, or cry
To the children merrily skipping by,
– Could only follow with the eye
That joyous crowd at the Piper's back.
But how the Mayor was on the rack,
And the wretched Council's bosoms beat,
As the Piper turned from the High Street
To where the Weser rolled its waters
Right in the way of their sons and daughters!
However he turned from South to West,
And to Koppelberg Hill his steps addressed,
And after him the children pressed;
Great was the joy in every breast.
'He never can cross that mighty top!
'He's forced to let the piping drop,
'And we shall see our children stop!'
When, lo, as they reached the mountain-side,
A wondrous portal opened wide,
As if a cavern was suddenly hollowed;
And the Piper advanced and the children followed,
And when all were in to the very last,
The door in the mountain-side shut fast.

Did I say, all? No! One was lame,
   And could not dance the whole of the way;
And in after years, if you would blame
   His sadness, he was used to say, –
'It's dull in our town since my playmates left!
'I can't forget that I'm bereft
'Of all the pleasant sights they see,
'Which the Piper also promised me.
'For he led us, he said, to a joyous land,
'Joining the town and just at hand,

One was lame

'Where waters gushed and fruit-trees grew
'And flowers put forth a fairer hue,
'And everything was strange and new;
'The sparrows were brighter than peacocks here,
'And their dogs outran our fallow deer,
'And honey-bees had lost their stings,
'And horses were born with eagles' wings:
'And just as I became assured
'My lame foot would be speedily cured,
'The music stopped and I stood still,
'And found myself outside the hill.
'Left alone against my will,
'To go now limping as before,
'And never hear of that country more!'

XIV

Alas, alas for Hamelin!
   There came into many a burgher's pate
   A text which says that heaven's gate
   Opes to the rich at as easy rate
As the needle's eye takes a camel in!
The Mayor sent East, West, North and South,
To offer the Piper, by word of mouth,
   Wherever it was men's lot to find him,
Silver and gold to his heart's content,
If he'd only return the way he went,
   And bring the children behind him.
But when they saw 'twas a lost endeavour,
And Piper and dancers were gone for ever,
They made a decree that lawyers never
   Should think their records dated duly
If, after the day of the month and year,
These words did not as well appear,

'And so long after what happened here
  'On the Twenty-second of July,
'Thirteen hundred and seventy-six:'
And the better in memory to fix
The place of the children's last retreat,
They called it, the Pied Piper's Street –
Where any one playing on pipe or tabor
Was sure for the future to lose his labour.
Nor suffered they hostelry or tavern
  To shock with mirth a street so solemn;
But opposite the place of the cavern
  They wrote the story on a column,
And on the great church-window painted
The same, to make the world acquainted
How their children were stolen away,
And there it stands to this very day.
And I must not omit to say
That in Transylvania there's a tribe
Of alien people who ascribe
The outlandish ways and dress
On which their neighbours lay such stress,
To their fathers and mothers having risen
Out of some subterraneous prison
Into which they were trepanned
Long time ago in a mighty band
Out of Hamelin town in Brunswick land,
But how or why, they don't understand.

XV

So, Willy, let me and you be wipers
Of scores out with all men – especially pipers!
And, whether they pipe us free fróm rats or fróm mice,
If we've promised them aught, let us keep our promise!

Paul Revere's Ride

HENRY WADSWORTH LONGFELLOW

*During the American War of Independence, Paul Revere received the news –
as he kept watch near the Old North Church in Boston – that a British force
was approaching. At once he mounted his horse and set off on a midnight ride to
warn the Revolutionary troops at Lexington and Concord.*

Listen, my children, and you shall hear
Of the midnight ride of Paul Revere,
On the eighteenth of April, in Seventy-five;
Hardly a man is now alive
Who remembers that famous day and year.

He said to his friend, 'If the British march
By land or sea from the town tonight,
Hang a lantern aloft in the belfry arch
Of the North Church tower as a signal light, –
One, if by land, and two, if by sea;
And I on the opposite shore will be,
Ready to ride and spread the alarm
Through every Middlesex village and farm,
For the country folk to be up and to arm.'

Then he said, 'Good night!' and with muffled oar
Silently rowed to the Charlestown shore,
Just as the moon rose over the bay,
Where swinging wide at her moorings lay
The Somerset, British man-of-war;
A phantom ship, with each mast and spar
Across the moon like a prison bar,

And a huge black hulk, that was magnified
By its own reflection in the tide.

Meanwhile, his friend, through alley and street,
Wanders and watches with eager ears,
Till in the silence around him he hears
The muster of men at the barrack door,
The sound of arms, and the tramp of feet,
And the measured tread of the grenadiers,
Marching down to their boats on the shore.

Then he climbed the tower of the Old North Church,
By the wooden stairs, with stealthy tread,
To the belfry-chamber overhead,
And startled the pigeons from their perch
On the sombre rafters, that round him made
Masses and moving shapes of shade, –
By the trembling ladder, steep and tall,
To the highest window in the wall,
Where he paused to listen and look down
A moment on the roofs of the town,
And the moonlight flowing over all.

Beneath, in the churchyard, lay the dead,
In their night-encampment on the hill,
Wrapped in silence so deep and still
That he could hear, like a sentinel's tread,
The watchful night-wind, as it went
Creeping along from tent to tent,
And seeming to whisper, 'All is well!'
A moment only he feels the spell
Of the place and the hour, and the secret dread
Of the lonely belfry and the dead;
For suddenly all his thoughts are bent

On a shadowy something far away,
Where the river widens to meet the bay, –
A line of black that bends and floats
On the rising tide, like a bridge of boats.

Meanwhile, impatient to mount and ride,
Booted and spurred, with a heavy stride
On the opposite shore walked Paul Revere.
Now he patted his horse's side,
Now gazed at the landscape far and near,
Then, impetuous, stamped the earth,
And turned and tightened his saddle-girth;
But mostly he watched with eager search
The belfry-tower of the Old North Church,
As it rose above the graves on the hill,
Lonely and spectral and sombre and still.
And lo! as he looks, on the belfry's height
A glimmer, and then a gleam of light!
He springs to the saddle, the bridle he turns,
But lingers and gazes, till full on his sight
A second lamp in the belfry burns!

A hurry of hoofs in a village street,
A shape in the moonlight, a bulk in the dark,
And beneath, from the pebbles, in passing, a spark
Struck out by a steed flying fearless and fleet:
That was all! And yet, through the gloom and the light,
The fate of a nation was riding that night:
And the spark struck out by that steed, in his flight,
Kindled the land into flame with its heat.

He has left the village and mounted the steep,
And beneath him, tranquil and broad and deep,
Is the Mystic, meeting the ocean tides;

And under the alders, that skirt its edge,
Now soft on the sand, now loud on the ledge,
Is heard the tramp of his steed as he rides.

It was twelve by the village clock
When he crossed the bridge into Medford town.
He heard the crowing of the cock,
And the barking of the farmer's dog,
And felt the damp of the river fog,
That rises after the sun goes down.

It was one by the village clock,
When he galloped into Lexington.
He saw the gilded weathercock
Swim in the moonlight as he passed,
And the meeting-house windows, blank and bare,
Gaze at him with a spectral glare,
As if they already stood aghast
At the bloody work they would look upon.

It was two by the village clock,
When he came to the bridge in Concord town.
He heard the bleating of the flock,
And the twitter of birds among the trees,
And felt the breath of the morning breeze
Blowing over the meadows brown.
And one was safe and asleep in his bed
Who at the bridge would be first to fall,
Who that day would be lying dead,
Pierced by a British musket–ball.

You know the rest. In the books you have read,
How the British Regulars fired and fled, –
How the farmers gave them ball for ball,

From behind each fence and farmyard wall,
Chasing the red-coats down the lane,
Then crossing the fields to emerge again
Under the trees at the turn of the road,
And only pausing to fire and load.

So through the night rode Paul Revere;
And so through the night went his cry of alarm
To every Middlesex village and farm, –
A cry of defiance and not of fear,
A voice in the darkness, a knock at the door,
And a word that shall echo for evermore!
For, borne on a night-wind of the Past,
Through all our history, to the last,
In the hour of darkness and peril and need,
The people will waken and listen to hear
The hurrying hoof-beats of that steed,
And the midnight message of Paul Revere.

Goblin Market

CHRISTINA ROSSETTI
Illustrated by D. G. Rossetti

Morning and evening
Maids heard the goblins cry.
'Come buy our orchard fruits,
Come buy, come buy:
Apples and quinces,
Lemons and oranges,
Plump unpecked cherries,
Melons and raspberries,
Bloom-down-cheeked peaches
Swart-headed mulberries,
Wild free-born cranberries,
Crab-apples, dewberries,
Pine-apples, blackberries,
Apricots, strawberries: –
All ripe together
In summer weather, –
Morns that pass by,
Fair eves that fly;
Come buy, come buy:
Our grapes fresh from the vine,
Pomegranates full and fine,
Dates and sharp bullaces,
Rare pears and greengages,
Damsons and bilberries,
Taste them and try:
Currants and gooseberries,
Bright-fire-like barberries,

Figs to fill your mouth,
Citrons from the South,
Sweet to tongue and sound to eye;
Come buy, come buy.'

Evening by evening
Among the brookside rushes,
Laura bowed her head to hear,
Lizzie veiled her blushes:
Crouching close together
In the cooling weather,
With clasping arms and cautioning lips,
With tingling cheeks and finger tips.
'Lie close,' Laura said,
Pricking up her golden head:
'We must not look at goblin men,
We must not buy their fruits:
Who knows upon what soil they fed
Their hungry thirsty roots?'
'Come buy,' call the goblins
Hobbling down the glen.
'Oh,' cried Lizzie, 'Laura, Laura,
You should not peep at goblin men.'
Lizzie covered up her eyes,
Covered close lest they should look;
Laura reared her glossy head,
And whispered like the restless brook:
'Look, Lizzie, look, Lizzie,
Down the glen tramp little men.
One hauls a basket,
One bears a plate,
One lugs a golden dish
Of many pounds weight.
How fair the vine must grow

Whose grapes are so luscious;
How warm the wind must blow
Through those fruit bushes.'
'No,' said Lizzie: 'No, no, no;
Their offers should not charm us,
Their evil gifts would harm us.'
She thrust a dimpled finger
In each ear, shut eyes and ran:
Curious Laura chose to linger
Wondering at each merchant man.
One had a cat's face,
One whisked a tail,
One tramped at a rat's pace,
One crawled like a snail,
One like a wombat prowled obtuse and furry,
One like a ratel tumbled hurry skurry.
She heard a voice like voices of doves
Cooing all together:
They sounded kind and full of loves
In the pleasant weather.

    Laura stretched her gleaming neck
Like a rush-imbedded swan,
Like a lily from the beck,
Like a moonlit poplar branch,
Like a vessel at the launch
When its last restraint is gone.

    Backwards up the mossy glen
Turned and trooped the goblin men,
With their shrill repeated cry,
'Come buy, come buy.'
When they reached where Laura was
They stood stock still upon the moss,

Leering at each other,
Brother with queer brother;
Signalling each other,
Brother with sly brother.
One set his basket down,
One reared his plate;
One began to weave a crown
Of tendrils, leaves, and rough nuts brown
(Men sell not such in any town);
One heaved the golden weight
Of dish and fruit to offer her:
'Come buy, come buy,' was still their cry.
Laura stared but did not stir,
Longed but had no money:
The whisk-tailed merchant bade her taste
In tones as smooth as honey,
The cat-faced purr'd,
The rat-paced spoke a word
Of welcome, and the snail-paced even was heard;
One parrot-voiced and jolly
Cried 'Pretty Goblin' still for 'Pretty Polly;' –
One whistled like a bird.

But sweet-tooth Laura spoke in haste:
'Good Folk, I have no coin;
To take were to purloin;
I have no copper in my purse,
I have no silver either,
And all my gold is on the furze
That shakes in windy weather
Above the rusty heather.'
'You have much gold upon your head,'
They answered all together:
'Buy from us with a golden curl.'

"Buy from us with a golden curl"

She clipped a precious golden lock,
She dropped a tear more rare than pearl,
Then sucked their fruit globes fair or red:
Sweeter than honey from the rock,
Stronger than man-rejoicing wine,
Clearer than water flowed that juice;
She never tasted such before,
How should it cloy with length of use?
She sucked and sucked and sucked the more

Fruits which that unknown orchard bore;
She sucked until her lips were sore;
Then flung the emptied rinds away
But gathered up one kernel stone,
And knew not was it night or day
As she turned home alone.

Lizzie met her at the gate
Full of wise upbraidings:
'Dear, you should not stay so late,
Twilight is not good for maidens;
Should not loiter in the glen
In the haunts of goblin men.
Do you not remember Jeanie,
How she met them in the moonlight,
Took their gifts both choice and many,
Ate their fruits and wore their flowers
Plucked from bowers
Where summer ripens at all hours?
But ever in the noonlight
She pined and pined away;
Sought them by night and day,
Found them no more, but dwindled and grew grey;
Then fell with the first snow,
While to this day no grass will grow
Where she lies low:
I planted daisies there a year ago
That never blow.
You should not loiter so.'
'Nay, hush,' said Laura:
'Nay, hush, my sister:
I ate and ate my fill,
Yet my mouth waters still;
To-morrow night I will

Buy more:' and kissed her:
'Have done with sorrow;
I'll bring you plums to-morrow
Fresh on their mother twigs,
Cherries worth getting;
You cannot think what figs
My teeth have met in,
What melons icy-cold
Piled on a dish of gold
Too huge for me to hold,
What peaches with a velvet nap,
Pellucid grapes without one seed:
Odorous indeed must be the mead
Whereon they grow, and pure the wave they drink
With lilies at the brink,
And sugar-sweet their sap.'

Golden head by golden head,
Like two pigeons in one nest
Folded in each other's wings,

"*Golden head by golden head*"

They lay down in their curtained bed:
Like two blossoms on one stem,
Like two flakes of new-fall'n snow,
Like two wands of ivory
Tipped with gold for awful kings.
Moon and stars gazed in at them,
Wind sang to them lullaby,
Lumbering owls forebore to fly.
Not a bat flapped to and fro
Round their rest:
Cheek to cheek and breast to breast
Locked together in one nest.

   Early in the morning
When the first cock crowed his warning,
Neat like bees, as sweet and busy,
Laura rose with Lizzie:
Fetched in honey, milked the cows,
Aired and set to rights the house,
Kneaded cakes of whitest wheat,
Cakes for dainty mouths to eat,
Next churned butter, whipped up cream,
Fed their poultry, sat and sewed;
Talked as modest maidens should:
Lizzie with an open heart,
Laura in an absent dream,
One content, one sick in part;
One warbling for the mere bright day's delight,
One longing for the night.

   At length slow evening came:
They went with pitchers to the reedy brook;
Lizzie most placid in her look,
Laura most like a leaping flame.

They drew the gurgling water from its deep;
Lizzie plucked purple and rich golden flags,
Then turning homeward said: 'The sunset flushes
Those furthest loftiest crags;
Come, Laura, not another maiden lags.
No wilful squirrel wags,
The beasts and birds are fast asleep.'
But Laura loitered still among the rushes
And said the bank was steep.

And said the hour was early still,
The dew not fall'n, the wind not chill;
Listening ever, but not catching
The customary cry,
'Come buy, come buy,'
With its iterated jingle
Of sugar-baited words:
Not for all her watching
Once discerning even one goblin
Racing, whisking, tumbling, hobbling;
Let alone the herds
That used to tramp along the glen,
In groups or single,
Of brisk fruit-merchant men.

Till Lizzie urged, 'O Laura, come;
I hear the fruit-call, but I dare not look:
You should not loiter longer at this brook:
Come with me home.
The stars rise, the moon bends her arc,
Each glowworm winks her spark,
Let us get home before the night grows dark:
For clouds may gather

Though this is summer weather,
Put out the lights and drench us through;
Then if we lost our way what should we do?'

Laura turned cold as stone
To find her sister heard that cry alone,
That goblin cry,
'Come buy our fruits, come buy.'
Must she then buy no more such dainty fruit?
Must she no more such succous pasture find,
Gone deaf and blind?
Her tree of life drooped from the root:
She said not one word in her heart's sore ache;
But peering thro' the dimness, nought discerning,
Trudged home, her pitcher dripping all the way;
So crept to bed, and lay
Silent till Lizzie slept;
Then sat up in a passionate yearning,
And gnashed her teeth for baulked desire, and wept
As if her heart would break.

Day after day, night after night,
Laura kept watch in vain
In sullen silence of exceeding pain.
She never caught again the goblin cry:
'Come buy, come buy;' –
She never spied the goblin men
Hawking their fruits along the glen:
But when the noon waxed bright
Her hair grew thin and grey;
She dwindled, as the fair full moon doth turn
To swift decay and burn
Her fire away.

One day remembering her kernel-stone
She set it by a wall that faced the south;
Dewed it with tears, hoped for a root
Watched for a waxing shoot,
But there came none;
It never saw the sun,
It never felt the trickling moisture run:
While with sunk eyes and faded mouth
She dreamed of melons, as a traveller sees
False waves in desert drouth
With shade of leaf-crowned trees,
And burns the thirstier in the sandful breeze.

She no more swept the house,
Tended the fowls or cows,
Fetched honey, kneaded cakes of wheat,
Brought water from the brook:
But sat down listless in the chimney-nook
And would not eat.

Tender Lizzie could not bear
To watch her sister's cankerous care
Yet not to share.
She night and morning
Caught the goblins' cry:
'Come buy our orchard fruits,
Come buy, come buy:' –
Beside the brook, along the glen,
She heard the tramp of goblin men,
The voice and stir
Poor Laura could not hear;
Longed to buy fruit to comfort her,
But feared to pay too dear.
She thought of Jeanie in her grave,

Who should have been a bride;
But who for joys brides hope to have
Fell sick and died
In her gay prime,
In earliest Winter time,
With the first glazing rime,
With the first snow-fall of crisp Winter time.

Till Laura dwindling
Seemed knocking at Death's door:
Then Lizzie weighed no more
Better and worse;
But put a silver penny in her purse,
Kissed Laura, crossed the heath with clumps of furze
At twilight, halted by the brook:
And for the first time in her life
Began to listen and look.

Laughed every goblin
When they spied her peeping:
Came towards her hobbling,
Flying, running, leaping,
Puffing and blowing,
Chuckling, clapping, crowing,
Clucking and gobbling,
Mopping and mowing,
Full of airs and graces,
Pulling wry faces,
Demure grimaces,
Cat-like and rat-like,
Ratel- and wombat-like,
Snail-paced in a hurry,
Parrot-voiced and whistler,
Helter skelter, hurry skurry,

Chattering like magpies,
Fluttering like pigeons,
Gliding like fishes, –
Hugged her and kissed her:
Squeezed and caressed her:
Stretched up their dishes,
Panniers, and plates:
'Look at our apples
Russet and dun,
Bob at our cherries,
Bite at our peaches,
Citrons and dates,
Grapes for the asking,
Pears red with basking
Out in the sun,
Plums on their twigs;
Pluck them and suck them,
Pomegranates, figs.' –

'Good folk,' said Lizzie,
Mindful of Jeanie:
'Give me much and many:' –
Held out her apron,
Tossed them her penny.
'Nay, take a seat with us,
Honour and eat with us,'
They answered grinning:
'Our feast is but beginning.
Night yet is early,
Warm and dew-pearly,
Wakeful and starry:
Such fruits as these
No man can carry;
Half their bloom would fly,

Half their dew would dry,
Half their flavour would pass by.
Sit down and feast with us,
Be welcome guest with us,
Cheer you and rest with us.' –
'Thank you,' said Lizzie: 'But one waits
At home alone for me:
So without further parleying,
If you will not sell me any
Of your fruits though much and many,
Give me back my silver penny
I tossed you for a fee.' –
They began to scratch their pates,
No longer wagging, purring,
But visibly demurring,
Grunting and snarling.
One called her proud,
Cross-grained, uncivil:
Their tones waxed loud,
Their looks were evil.
Lashing their tails
They trod and hustled her,
Elbowed and jostled her,
Clawed with their nails,
Barking, mewing, hissing, mocking,
Tore her gown and soiled her stocking,
Twitched her hair out by the roots,
Stamped upon her tender feet,
Held her hands and squeezed their fruits
Against her mouth to make her eat.

   White and golden Lizzie stood,
Like a lily in a flood, –
Like a rock of blue-veined stone

Lashed by tides obstreperously, –
Like a beacon left alone
In a hoary roaring sea,
Sending up a golden fire, –
Like a fruit-crowned orange-tree
White with blossoms honey-sweet
Sore beset by wasp and bee, –
Like a royal virgin town
Topped with gilded dome and spire
Close beleaguered by a fleet
Mad to tug her standard down.

   One may lead a horse to water,
Twenty cannot make him drink.
Though the goblins cuffed and caught her,
Coaxed and fought her,
Bullied and besought her,
Scratched her, pinched her black as ink,
Kicked and knocked her,
Mauled and mocked her,
Lizzie uttered not a word;
Would not open lip from lip
Lest they should cram a mouthful in:
But laughed in heart to feel the drip
Of juice that syrupped all her face,
And lodged in dimples of her chin,
And streaked her neck which quaked like curd.
At last the evil people,
Worn out by her resistance,
Flung back her penny, kicked their fruit
Along whichever road they took,
Not leaving root or stone or shoot;
Some writhed into the ground,
Some dived into the brook

With ring and ripple,
Some scudded on the gale without a sound,
Some vanished in the distance.

In a smart, ache, tingle,
Lizzie went her way;
Knew not was it night or day;
Sprang up the bank, tore thro' the furze,
Threaded copse and dingle,
And heard her penny jingle
Bouncing in her purse, —
Its bounce was music to her ear.
She ran and ran
As if she feared some goblin man
Dogged her with gibe or curse
Or something worse:
But not one goblin skurried after,
Nor was she pricked by fear;
The kind heart made her windy-paced
That urged her home quite out of breath with haste
And inward laughter.

She cried, 'Laura,' up the garden.
'Did you miss me?
Come and kiss me.
Never mind my bruises,
Hug me, kiss me, suck my juices
Squeezed from goblin fruits for you,
Goblin pulp and goblin dew.
Eat me, drink me, love me;
Laura, make much of me;
For your sake I have braved the glen
And had to do with goblin merchant men.'

Laura started from her chair,
Flung her arms up in the air,
Clutched her hair:
'Lizzie, Lizzie, have you tasted
For my sake the fruit forbidden?
Must your light like mine be hidden,
Your young life like mine be wasted.
Undone in mine undoing,
And ruined in my ruin,
Thirsty, cankered, goblin-ridden?' –
She clung about her sister,
Kissed and kissed and kissed her:
Tears once again
Refreshed her shrunken eyes,
Dropping like rain
After long sultry drouth;
Shaking with aguish fear, and pain,
She kissed and kissed her with a hungry mouth.

Her lips began to scorch,
That juice was wormwood to her tongue,
She loathed the feast:
Writhing as one possessed she leaped and sung,
Rent all her robe, and wrung
Her hands in lamentable haste,
And beat her breast.
Her locks streamed like the torch
Borne by a racer at full speed,
Or like the mane of horses in their flight,
Or like an eagle when she stems the light
Straight toward the sun,
Or like a caged thing freed,
Or like a flying flag when armies run.
Swift fire spread through her veins, knocked at her heart,

Met the fire smouldering there
And overbore its lesser flame;
She gorged on bitterness without a name:
Ah! fool, to choose such part
Of soul-consuming care!
Sense failed in the mortal strife:
Like the watch-tower of a town
Which an earthquake shatters down,
Like a lightning-stricken mast,
Like a wind-uprooted tree
Spun about
Like a foam-topped waterspout
Cast down headlong in the sea,
She fell at last;
Pleasure past and anguish past,
Is it death or is it life?

Life out of death.
That night long Lizzie watched by her,
Counted her pulse's flagging stir,
Felt for her breath,
Held water to her lips, and cooled her face
With tears and fanning leaves:
But when the first birds chirped about their eaves,
And early reapers plodded to the place
Of golden sheaves,
And dew-wet grass
Bowed in the morning winds so brisk to pass,
And new buds with new day
Opened of cup-like lilies on the stream,
Laura awoke as from a dream,
Laughed in the innocent old way,
Hugged Lizzie but not twice or thrice;
Her gleaming locks showed not one thread of grey

Her breath was sweet as May
And light danced in her eyes.

   Days, weeks, months, years
Afterwards, when both were wives
With children of their own;
Their mother-hearts beset with fears,
Their lives bound up in tender lives;
Laura would call the little ones
And tell them of her early prime,
Those pleasant days long gone
Of not-returning time:
Would talk about the haunted glen,
The wicked, quaint fruit-merchant men,
Their fruits like honey to the throat
But poison in the blood;
(Men sell not such in any town):
Would tell them how her sister stood
In deadly peril to do her good,
And win the fiery antidote:
Then joining hands to little hands
Would bid them cling together,
'For there is no friend like a sister
In calm or stormy weather;
To cheer one on the tedious way,
To fetch one if one goes astray,
To lift one if one totters down,
To strengthen whilst one stands.'

The Revenge

A BALLAD OF THE FLEET

―――――――――――――――――

ALFRED LORD TENNYSON

At Flores in the Azores Sir Richard Grenville lay,
And a pinnace, like a flutter'd bird, came flying from far away:
'Spanish ships of war at sea! we have sighted fifty-three!'
Then sware Lord Thomas Howard: ''Fore God I am no coward;
But I cannot meet them here, for my ships are out of gear,
And the half my men are sick. I must fly, but follow quick.
We are six ships of the line; can we fight with fifty-three?'

Then spake Sir Richard Grenville: 'I know you are no coward;
You fly them for a moment to fight with them again.
But I've ninety men and more that are lying sick ashore.
I should count myself the coward if I left them, my Lord Howard,
To these Inquisition dogs and the devildoms of Spain.'

So Lord Howard past away with five ships of war that day,
Till he melted like a cloud in the silent summer heaven;
But Sir Richard bore in hand all his sick men from the land
Very carefully and slow,
Men of Bideford in Devon,
And we laid them on the ballast down below;
For we brought them all aboard,
And they blest him in their pain, that they were not left to Spain,
To the thumbscrew and the stake, for the glory of the Lord.

He had only a hundred seamen to work the ship and to fight,
And he sailed away from Flores till the Spaniard came in sight,

With his huge sea-castles heaving upon the weather bow.
'Shall we fight or shall we fly?
Good Sir Richard, tell us now,
For to fight is but to die!
There'll be little of us left by the time this sun be set.'
And Sir Richard said again: 'We be all good English men.
Let us bang these dogs of Seville, the children of the devil,
For I never turn'd my back upon Don or devil yet.'

Sir Richard spoke and he laugh'd, and we roar'd a hurrah, and so
The little Revenge ran on sheer into the heart of the foe,
With her hundred fighters on deck, and her ninety sick below;
For half of their fleet to the right and half to the left were seen,
And the little Revenge ran on thro' the long sea-lane between.

Thousands of their soldiers look'd down from their decks and
  laugh'd,
Thousands of their seamen made mock at the mad little craft
Running on and on, till delay'd
By their mountain-like San Philip that, of fifteen hundred tons,
And up-shadowing high above us with her yawning tiers of guns,
Took the breath from our sails, and we stay'd.

And while now the great San Philip hung above us like a cloud
Whence the thunderbolt will fall
Long and loud,
Four galleons drew away
From the Spanish fleet that day,
And two upon the larboard and two upon the starboard lay,
And the battle-thunder broke from them all.

But anon the great San Philip, she bethought herself and went
Having that within her womb that had left her ill content;
And the rest they came aboard us, and they fought us hand to hand,

For a dozen times they came with their pikes and musqueteers,
And a dozen times we shook 'em off as a dog that shakes his ears
When he leaps from the water to the land.

And the sun went down, and the stars came out far over the summer
sea,
But never a moment ceased the fight of the one and the fifty-three.
Ship after ship, the whole night long, their high-built galleons came,
Ship after ship, the whole night long, with her battle-thunder and
flame;
Ship after ship, the whole night long, drew back with her dead and her
shame.
For some were sunk and many were shatter'd and so could fight us no
more –
God of battles, was ever a battle like this in the world before?

For he said 'Fight on! fight on!'
Tho' his vessel was all but a wreck;
And it chanced that, when half of the short summer night was gone,
With a grisly wound to be drest he had left the deck,
But a bullet struck him that was dressing it suddenly dead,
And himself he was wounded again in the side and the head,
And he said 'Fight on! fight on!'

And the night went down, and the sun smiled out far over the summer
sea,
And the Spanish fleet with broken sides lay round us all in a ring;
But they dared not touch us again, for they fear'd that we still could
sting,
So they watch'd what the end would be.
And we had not fought them in vain,
But in perilous plight were we,
Seeing forty of our poor hundred were slain,
And half of the rest of us maim'd for life

In the crash of the cannonades and the desperate strife;
And the sick men down in the hold were most of them stark and cold,
And the pikes were all broken or bent, and the powder was all of it
    spent;
And the masts and the rigging were lying over the side;
But Sir Richard cried in his English pride,
'We have fought such a fight for a day and a night
As may never be fought again!
We have won great glory, my men!
And a day less or more
At sea or ashore,
We die – does it matter when?
Sink me the ship, Master Gunner – sink her, split her in twain!
Fall into the hands of God, not into the hands of Spain!'

And the gunner said 'Ay, ay,' but the seamen made reply:
'We have children, we have wives,
And the Lord hath spared our lives.
We will make the Spaniard promise, if we yield, to let us go;
We shall live to fight again and to strike another blow.'
And the lion there lay dying, and they yielded to the foe.

And the stately Spanish men to their flagship bore him then,
Where they laid him by the mast, old Sir Richard caught at last,
And they praised him to his face with their courtly foreign grace;
But he rose upon their decks, and he cried:
'I have fought for Queen and Faith like a valiant man and true;
I have only done my duty as a man is bound to do:
With a joyful spirit I Sir Richard Grenville die!'
And he fell upon their decks, and he died.

And they stared at the dead that had been so valiant and true,
And had holden the power and glory of Spain so cheap
That he dared her with one little ship and his English few;

Was he devil or man? He was devil for aught they knew,
But they sank his body with honour down into the deep,
And they mann'd the Revenge with a swarthier alien crew,
And away she sail'd with her loss and long'd for her own;
When a wind from the lands they had ruin'd awoke from sleep,
And the water began to heave and the weather to moan,
And or ever that evening ended a great gale blew
And a wave like the wave that is raised by an earthquake grew,
Till it smote on their hulls and their sails and their masts and their flags,
And the whole sea plunged and fell on the shot-shatter'd navy of
   Spain,
And the little Revenge herself went down by the island crags
To be lost evermore in the main.

Fables

The Frog and the Ox

The Frog and the Ox

Illustrated by Charles Robinson

An Ox, grazing in a swampy meadow, chanced to set his foot among a whole family of young Frogs, and crushed nearly the whole brood to death. One that escaped ran off to his mother with the dreadful news.

'Oh Mother!' said he, 'it was a beast – such a big four-footed beast – that did it.'

'Big?' said the old Frog, 'How big? Was it as big' – and she puffed herself out to a great degree – 'as big as this?'

'Oh,' said the little one, 'a great deal bigger than that.'

'Well, was it so big?' and she swelled herself out yet more.

'Indeed, mother, it was much bigger; and if you were to burst yourself, you would never reach half its size.'

Wishing to prove that she could be as big as any other animal, the old Frog made one more trial, and burst herself like a balloon!

So men are ruined by trying to appear greater than they really are.

The Old Man and the Donkey

Illustrated by Charles Robinson

An old man and a little boy were driving a donkey before them to
sell in the market.

'What's this?' said an onlooker. 'You've got a donkey, yet you make
the little boy walk.' So the old man put the boy on the donkey's back
and tramped along beside them.

'What's this?' said someone else to the boy. 'You lazy fellow,
making your old father walk while you ride at your ease.' So the old
man lifted the boy down and got on the donkey's back himself.

But when a third man said what a shame it was that the little chap
had to walk whilst his father rode, the father set his son up behind him.

Finally, a fourth onlooker asked in amazement whether the donkey
really belonged to them, it was so over-loaded.

So the old man, no longer knowing what to do for the best, bound
the donkey's legs together with some cord and together he and his son
tried to bring it to market hanging on a pole which they carried on
their shoulders. Everyone laughed at such a ridiculous sight and so
upset the old man that in a rage he turned the donkey loose in a field
and went back home with his son.

And the moral of that is that if you try to please everyone you will
end up by pleasing no one, not even yourself.

The Old Man and the Donkey

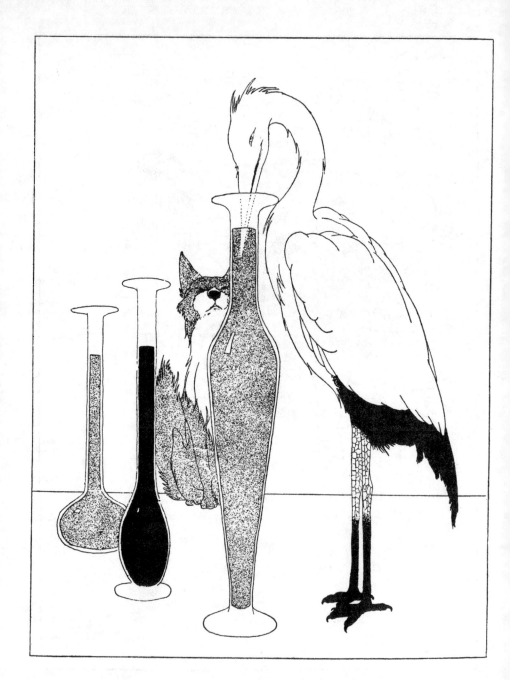

The Fox and the Stork

The Fox and the Stork

Illustrated by Charles Robinson

A Fox one day invited a Stork to dinner. Deciding to amuse himself at the expense of his guest, he provided nothing to eat but some thin soup in a shallow dish. The Fox lapped this up very readily, but the Stork, unable to gain a mouthful with her long narrow bill, was as hungry at the end of the dinner as when she began. The Fox meanwhile professed his regret at seeing her eat so sparingly, and feared that the dish was not seasoned to her taste. The Stork said little, but begged that the Fox would do her the honour of returning her visit; and he agreed to dine with her on the following day. He arrived true to his appointment, and the dinner was ordered. When it was served up, he found to his dismay that it was contained in a narrow-necked vessel. The Stork could reach in easily with her long neck and bill, but he was obliged to content himself with licking the neck of the jar. Unable to satisfy his hunger, he retired with as good a grace as he could, observing that he could hardly find fault with his entertainer, who had only paid him back in his own coin.

The Fox and the Crow

Illustrated by Charles Robinson

A Crow had snatched a large piece of cheese out of a window, and flew with it into a high tree, intending to enjoy her prize. A Fox spied the morsel, and craftily he planned his approach.

'Oh, Crow,' said he, 'how beautiful are thy wings, how bright thine eye! how graceful thy neck! thy breast is the breast of an eagle! thy claws – I beg pardon – thy talons, are a match for all the beasts of the field. Oh, that such a bird should be dumb, and lack only a voice!'

The Crow, pleased with this flattery, and chuckling to think how she would surprise the Fox with her caw, opened her mouth. Down dropped the cheese! The Fox snapped it up, observing as he walked away, that whatever he had remarked of her beauty, he had said nothing of her brains.

Men seldom flatter without some private end in view; and they who listen to such music may expect to have to pay the piper.

The Fox and the Crow

The Ant and the Grasshopper

The Ant and the Grasshopper

Illustrated by Charles Robinson

On a cold frosty day an Ant was dragging out some of the corn which he had laid up in summer time, to dry it. A Grasshopper, half-perished with hunger, begged the Ant to give him a morsel of it to preserve his life.

'What were you doing,' said the Ant, 'this last summer?'

'Oh,' said the Grasshopper, 'I was not idle. I kept singing all the summer long.'

The Ant, laughing and shutting up his granary, said,

'Since you could sing all summer, you may dance all winter.'

Winter finds out what Summer lays by.

The Lion and the Mouse

Illustrated by Charles Robinson

A Lion was sleeping in his lair, when a Mouse, not knowing where he was going, ran over the mighty beast's nose and awakened him. The Lion clapped his paw upon the frightened little creature, and was about to make an end of him in a moment.

The Mouse, in a pitiable tone, begged him to be merciful, and not stain his honourable paws with so small a prey. The Lion, smiling at his little prisoner's fright, generously let him go. Now it happened no long time after, that the Lion, while ranging the woods for his prey, fell into the nets of the hunters. Finding himself entangled without hope of escape, he set up a roar that filled the whole forest with its echo. The Mouse, recognising the voice of his former preserver, ran to the spot, and without more ado set to work to nibble through the cord that bound the Lion. In a short time he had set the noble beast at liberty. Thus we see that kindness is seldom thrown away, and that there is no creature so much below another but that he may have it in his power to return a good deed.

The Lion and the Mouse

The Horse and the Stag

The Horse and the Stag

Illustrated by Charles Robinson

A Horse lived happily by himself in a fertile meadow, until a Stag came into the neighbourhood and began to damage the pasture. The Horse, anxious to have his revenge, asked a Man if he could assist him in punishing the Stag.

'Yes,' said the Man, 'only let me put a bit in your mouth, and get upon your back, and I will find the weapons.'

The Horse agreed, and the Man mounted accordingly; but instead of getting his revenge, the Horse has been from that time forward the slave of Man.

Revenge is too dearly purchased at the price of liberty.

The Hare and the Tortoise

Illustrated by Charles Robinson

A Hare jeered at a Tortoise for the slowness of his pace. But the Tortoise laughed and said that he would run against her and beat her any day she would name.

'Come on,' said the Hare, 'you shall soon see what my feet are made of.' So it was agreed that they should start at once. The Tortoise went off jogging along, without a moment's stopping, at his usual steady pace. The Hare, treating the whole matter very lightly, said she would first take a little nap, and then she would easily overtake the Tortoise. Meanwhile the Tortoise plodded on. The Hare overslept, and when she finally woke and dashed for the finishing line she saw that the tortoise had arrived before her.

Slow and steady wins the race.

The Hare and the Tortoise

The Fisherman and the Little Fish

The Fisherman and the Little Fish

Illustrated by Charles Robinson

After fishing unsuccessfully all day, an angler finally caught a tiny little fish.

'Let me go,' said the fish. 'I'm so small that I won't be worth eating. If you put me back in the sea I shall go on growing and next time you catch me I shall be fit for a feast.'

But the fisherman was deaf to these entreaties.

'Better a fish in the hand, however small,' he said to himself, 'than any number of uncaught fishes in the sea.'

The Dog and his Shadow

Illustrated by Charles Robinson

A Dog had stolen a piece of meat out of a butcher's shop, and was crossing a river on his way home, when he saw his own shadow reflected in the stream below. Thinking that it was another dog with another piece of meat, he resolved to make himself master of that also; but in snapping at the supposed treasure, he dropped the bit he was carrying, and so lost all.

Grasp at the shadow and lose the substance – the common fate of those who risk losing a real blessing for some imaginary good.

The Dog and his Shadow

The Hen With the Golden Eggs

The Hen with the Golden Eggs

Illustrated by Charles Robinson

A certain woman had the good fortune to possess a Hen that laid her a Golden Egg every day. But dissatisfied with so slow an income, and wishing to seize the whole treasure at once, she killed the Hen; and, cutting her open, found no treasure at all! The Hen was just like any other bird.

So greed, always wanting more, loses what it has.

The Council Held by the Rats

Illustrated by Charles Robinson

Old Rodilard, a certain Cat,
　Such havoc of the Rats had made,
'Twas difficult to find a Rat
　With nature's debt unpaid.
The few that did remain,
　To leave their holes afraid,
From their usual food abstain,
　Not eating half their fill.
　And meantime, with a will,
Old Rodilard ne'er ceased to revel
As if he were a very devil.
Now, on a day, this dread Rat-eater,
Who had a wife, went out to meet her;
And while he held his caterwauling,
The unkill'd Rats, their chapter calling,
Discuss'd the point, in grave debate,
How they might shun impending fate.
　Their dean, a prudent Rat,
Thought best, and better soon than late,
　To bell the fatal Cat;
That, when he took his hunting round,
The Rats, well caution'd by the sound,
Might hide in safety under ground;
　Indeed he knew no other means.
　　And all the rest
　　At once confess'd
　Their minds were with the dean's.
No better plan, they all believed,

The Council Held by the Rats

Could possibly have been conceived,
No doubt the thing would work right well,
If any one would hang the bell.

Fairy Tales

Cinderella

CHARLES PERRAULT
Illustrated by Walter Crane

Once there was a gentleman whose wife died young. He was grief-stricken at first, but after a year he married again. His second wife was the haughtiest woman imaginable, and she had two plain daughters who were just as proud and ill-tempered as their mother. Now the gentleman had a young daughter of his own by his first wife; she was a good, sweet-tempered girl.

As soon as the ceremonies of the wedding were over, the step-mother began to show herself in her true colours. She could not bear the good qualities of her pretty stepdaughter, as her own daughters seemed all the more odious by comparison. Therefore, she set the girl to work at the meanest tasks. She had to scour the dishes and tables, clean Madam's chamber and those of the fine Misses, her daughters, and wash the clothes. She slept in a cold garret, on a wretched straw bed, while her step-sisters lay in fine rooms with deep carpets, soft beds of the very newest fashion, and looking-glasses so large that they could admire themselves from head to foot.

The poor girl bore all this patiently. She dared not complain to her father, who was often away, and did not know what was going on; he was quite dominated by his wife. When she had done her work, she used to go to the chimney-corner and sit down among the cinders and ashes to keep warm. So her sisters mockingly called her *Cinderella*. But even her mean clothes, and the ashes that smudged her face and hands, could not disguise Cinderella's beauty nor her goodness of heart. Her step-sisters saw this, and it made them dislike her all the more.

It happened that the King's son decided to give a ball, and invited all the wealthy people of the country. The young Misses were delighted when they received their invitations, and spent hours deciding what to wear. This meant more trouble for Cinderella, for it was she who had to wash and iron their dresses and mend their lace.

They talked of nothing but the ball, and their clothes, all day long.

'I will wear my red velvet gown with the French trimming,' decided the eldest.

'And I,' said the younger, 'will wear my gold-flowered dress and my diamond collar.'

Cinderella had to join in these discussions, because she had excellent taste and always gave good advice. She was deft with her hands, and a good hairdresser, so she had to stand for hours patiently curling and pinning up her sisters' hair. While she was doing this, they asked her,

'Cinderella, wouldn't you like to go to the ball?'

'You're making fun of me,' she replied sadly. 'How could *I* go to the palace?'

'Quite right,' they answered, laughing cruelly. 'The court would think it a fine joke if a grubby serving-maid like you appeared at a ball!'

Anyone but Cinderella would have burned their hair with the curling tongs in revenge for this unkind joke, but she kept her temper.

At last the time came; the sisters set off for the palace, and Cinderella watched them until they were out of sight. Then she began to cry bitterly.

Her godmother, who was a fairy, happened to be passing by and saw Cinderella in tears.

'My dear Cinderella, what is the matter?'

'I wish . . . I wish . . .' The poor girl was sobbing too hard to continue.

'You wish you could go to the ball – isn't that it?'

'Yes,' cried Cinderella, sighing.

'Well,' said her godmother, 'be a good girl and I will see to it that you *shall* go. Now, run into the garden, and bring me a pumpkin.'

Cinderella went immediately to pick the best pumpkin she could find, although she could not imagine how a pumpkin could help her to get to the ball. Her godmother scooped out all the flesh, leaving nothing but the rind; then she struck it with her wand, and the pumpkin was instantly turned into a fine golden coach.

She then went to the mouse-cage, where she found six white mice, and ordered Cinderella to lift them out. She gave each mouse in turn a little tap with her wand, and immediately the tiny creatures turned into six fine dapple-grey horses. But where was the coachman?

'I'll go and see if there is a rat in the rat-trap; you could make a coachman of him!' suggested Cinderella excitedly.

'That's a good idea,' replied her godmother, 'go and look.'

Cinderella brought the trap to her. In the cage were three fat rats who had been tempted in by the bait and could not get out again. The fairy chose the biggest of them and touched him with her wand; at once he turned into a fat, jolly coachman with the smartest whiskers you ever saw. After that, she said to Cinderella,

'Go into the garden again, and you'll find six lizards behind the watering-can. Bring them to me.'

As soon as she had done so, her fairy godmother turned them into six footmen in silver and gold livery, who skipped up behind the coach. The fairy then said to Cinderella,

'Well, you see here a coach fit to take you to the ball; aren't you pleased with it?'

Cinderella hung her head. 'Oh, yes . . . But must I go as I am, dressed in these nasty rags?'

Her godmother only just touched her with the magic wand, and in an instant her drab clothes turned into a dress of gold and silver all sparkling with jewels. This done, the fairy gave her a pair of the prettiest glass slippers for her feet, and then Cinderella was ready to jump up into her coach. Her godmother told her to enjoy herself, but on no account to stay later than midnight. At that time, if she stayed one moment longer, her coach would become a pumpkin again, her horses mice, her coachman a rat, her footmen lizards, and her fine clothes the grubby rags they had been before.

Cinderella promised to leave before midnight; then she drove away, hardly able to contain her joy. When she reached the palace the King's

The King's son led Cinderella to the place of honour

son himself, seeing the beautiful stranger arrive, ran out to receive her. He gave her his hand as she alighted from the coach, and led her into the ballroom. Silence fell; people stopped dancing, and the violins ceased to play. Nothing was heard but a confused muttering of,

'How beautiful she is! Who is she?'

The king himself, old as he was, could not help watching her, and said softly to the Queen that it was a long time since he had seen so beautiful and graceful a creature.

All the ladies were busy studying her clothes and hairstyle so that they could copy her finery themselves. It was a vain hope, however, for Cinderella's dress was made by magic.

The King's son led Cinderella to the place of honour, and afterwards asked her to dance with him. She danced so gracefully that everyone present admired her. Dinner was served, but the prince was too engrossed in gazing at Cinderella to eat a morsel.

Cinderella sat down by her sisters, and spoke to them civilly. They were astonished, for they little thought that this dazzling creature could be their slighted step-sister. While Cinderella was amusing herself in this way, she heard the clock strike a quarter to twelve; immediately she curtsied to the company and ran away as quickly as she could.

As soon as she reached home, panting and breathless, she rushed to find her godmother and thanked her for the marvellous evening. She asked shyly if she could go to the ball the next night, as the prince had begged her to be there. The fairy smiled and agreed.

While she was telling her godmother all about the ball, her sisters knocked at the door. Cinderella ran to open it.

'How late you are!' she exclaimed, yawning and rubbing her eyes as if she had been asleep, although she could not have felt more wide awake.

'If you had been at the ball you wouldn't be so sleepy!' her eldest sister cried, sweeping indoors. 'A beautiful princess from another country was there. She was *most* polite and friendly to us, and singled us out for her *special* attention.'

Cinderella pretended not to be very interested, but she asked if anyone knew the strange princess's identity.

'No, no-one has the least idea. But the prince is simply frantic, and would give half his father's kingdom to know who she is!'

Cinderella smiled mischievously at this, and replied,

'Indeed, she must be very beautiful. I should like to see her. Charlotte, do lend me your old yellow dress so that I can go to the ball tomorrow.'

'What!' cried Miss Charlotte. 'Lend my clothes to a dirty thing like you, all covered in cinders? I wouldn't dream of it. Now, come and unpin my hair.'

Cinderella had expected this reply, and indeed was very glad of the refusal; for she would have been in a pickle if her sister had agreed.

The next night the two sisters went to the ball, and so did Cinderella, dressed even more magnificently than before. The prince stayed by her side all evening, and never ceased complimenting her on her beauty. All this was so pleasant to Cinderella that she quite forgot her godmother's warning, and the clock was striking twelve before she even knew eleven o'clock had passed. She rose in horror and fled like a startled deer. In her wild flight she lost one of her glass slippers on the steps of the palace. The prince followed her, calling to her to stop, but he could not overtake her. Cinderella got home safely, but quite out of breath, and in her nasty old clothes, with nothing left of all her finery but one of the little glass slippers.

The guards at the palace gate were asked if they had seen a princess go out. They said they had seen nobody but a young girl, very meanly dressed, who looked more like a servant than a gentlewoman.

When the two sisters returned from the ball Cinderella asked them if they had enjoyed themselves, and if the fine lady had appeared.

They said yes, she had been there, but she had hurried away when it struck twelve, and in such haste that she dropped one of her pretty little glass slippers. The prince had picked it up, and had done nothing but look at it after she left. Most certainly he was very much in love with the beautiful owner of the glass slipper.

They were quite right; for the very next day the King's son issued a proclamation that he would marry the girl whose foot this slipper would just fit. The gentlemen he employed for the task began to try the slipper on the princesses at the court, then the duchesses, then the ladies-in-waiting, then the noblewomen of the city, but in vain. It was finally brought to the two sisters, who did all they possibly could to thrust their feet into the slipper; but they could scarcely fit in a big toe. Cinderella, who saw all this, and knew the slipper to be hers, said to them with a smile,

'Let me see if it will fit me.'

Her sisters burst out laughing at the very idea, but the gentleman who was sent to try the slipper looked earnestly at Cinderella. In spite of her ragged clothes he could see how pretty she was, and he said that it was only fair that she should try. After all, he had orders from the prince to let every girl in the kingdom make the attempt.

He led Cinderella politely to a chair and tried the slipper on her foot. It fitted perfectly! The step-sisters' astonishment knew no bounds when Cinderella pulled the other slipper out of her pocket and put it on her foot. Just at that moment in came her godmother, who touched Cinderella's dirty old frock with her wand and made it into a sparkling gown even 1richer and more magnificent than the dresses she had worn to the palace.

Now her sisters realised that the fine, beautiful lady whom they had seen at the ball was none other than Cinderella! They threw themselves to the ground in front of her to beg her pardon for all their ill-treatment. Kind-hearted Cinderella raised them to their feet and embraced them, saying that she forgave them for everything and would not neglect them in the midst of her good fortune.

Cinderella was conducted straight away to the palace, where the prince received her with joy. A few days later their wedding was celebrated amid great rejoicing.

Cinderella and her prince lived long and happily together. However, she was as kind as she was beautiful, and she did not forget her promise to her sisters. She gave them both lodgings at the palace and introduced them to two great lords of the court, to whom they were married soon after.

Little Red Riding Hood

CHARLES PERRAULT
Illustrated by Walter Crane

Once upon a time there lived in a certain village a little country girl, the prettiest creature that you ever saw. Her mother was excessively fond of her; and her grandmother doted on her still more. This good woman made the little girl a red cape and hood, which suited her so well that everybody called her Little Red Riding Hood.

One day her mother, who had made some custards, said to her, 'My dear, go and see how your grandmother is, for I hear she has been ill. Take her these custards, and a little pot of fresh butter.'

Little Red Riding Hood set out immediately to go to her grandmother, who lived in another village.

As she was going through the wood, she met Mr Wolf. He wanted very much to eat her up, but he dared not, because there were some woodcutters nearby in the forest. He asked her where she was going. The poor child, who did not know that it was dangerous to stay and hear a wolf talk, said to him,

'I am going to see my grandmamma and carry some custards and a little pot of butter from my mamma.'

'Does she live far off?' asked the Wolf.

'Oh, yes,' answered Little Red Riding Hood, 'it is beyond that mill you see there, at the first house in the village.'

'Well,' said the Wolf, 'I'll go and see her too. I'll go this way, and you go that, and we shall see who will be there soonest.'

The Wolf began to run as fast as he could, taking the shortest way; and the little girl went by the longest route, diverting herself by gathering nuts, running after butterflies, and making posies of wild flowers. It was not long before Mr Wolf got to the old woman's house. He knocked at the door – tap, tap.

'Who's there?'

'Your granddaughter, Little Red Riding Hood,' replied the Wolf, imitating the child's voice. 'I've brought you some custards and a little pot of butter which mamma has sent you.'

The good grandmother, who was in bed feeling ill, cried out, 'Pull the bobbin, and the latch will go up.'

The Wolf pulled the bobbin, and the door opened, and then at once he fell upon the good woman and ate her up in a moment! He then shut the door and got into the grandmother's bed, waiting for Little Red Riding Hood. Some time afterwards she arrived and knocked at the door – tap, tap.

'Who's there?'

Little Red Riding Hood, hearing the big voice of the Wolf, was afraid at first. But, believing that her grandmother had got a cold and was hoarse, she answered,

'It's your granddaughter, Little Red Riding Hood. I've brought you some custards and a little pot of butter which mamma has sent you.'

The Wolf cried out, softening his voice as much as he could, 'Pull the bobbin, and the latch will go up.'

Little Red Riding Hood pulled the bobbin, and the door opened.

The Wolf, seeing her come in, hid himself under the bedclothes and said to her,

'Put the custards and the little pot of butter upon the stool, and come and sit down with me.'

Little Red Riding Hood went and sat down on the bed. She was greatly amazed to see how her grandmother looked in her nightdress.

'Grandmamma, what great arms you have got!'

'All the better to hug you with, my dear.'

'Grandmamma, what great legs you have got!'

'All the better to run with, my child.'

'Grandmamma, what great ears you have got!'

'All the better to hear you with, my child.'

'Grandmamma, what great eyes you have got!'

'Come and sit down with me'

'All the better to see you with, my dear.'
'Grandmamma, what great teeth you have got!'
'All the better to eat you up!'
And, saying these words, the wicked wolf fell upon Little Red
Riding Hood and would have eaten her up in a moment! But just then

a woodcutter, who had heard the Wolf's growl, burst in. He struck the Wolf a great blow and forced him to open his big mouth up wide so that Red Riding Hood's grandmother could jump out. Then he chased the Wolf away into the deepest part of the forest.

Little Red Riding Hood and her grandmother rejoiced at their deliverance, and you may be sure that no wicked wolf ever tricked Little Red Riding Hood again.

The Tinder Box

HANS ANDERSEN
Illustrated by E.H. Wehnert

A soldier came marching along the high road – One, two! One, two! He had his rucksack on his back and his sword at his side, and he was on his way home from the wars.

As he marched along he met an ugly old woman.

'Good morning,' she croaked. 'You must be a strong fellow to carry that big rucksack. How would you like to earn yourself enough money to fill it?'

The soldier, who had only a few pennies in his pocket, shrugged his shoulders.

'What do I have to do?'

'Do you see that big tree?' The old woman pointed to the side of the road. 'It's hollow. If you climb to the top you can let yourself down inside the trunk. Then, when you shout, I'll pull you out with this rope.'

'What's inside the tree?' asked the soldier.

'Money!' she said, clenching her wrinkled hands. 'When you get to the bottom you'll find yourself in a large hall where a hundred lamps are burning. There are three doors in the hall. If you go through the first door you'll see a large box with a dog sitting on it. It has eyes as big as tea-cups, but don't be frightened of it. I'll give you my blue checked apron, and if you spread it out on the floor and put the dog on top of it, you can help yourself to the money. It's all copper. If you want silver you must go into the second room. A dog with eyes as big as cart-wheels is sitting there, but if you place it on my apron it will let you take as much money as you want. If you want gold, though, you must go into the third room. The dog that is seated on the money-box in there has eyes as big as the Round Tower of Copenhagen! But just put him on my apron, and he won't hurt you.'

'That sounds easy,' the soldier said. 'But what do *you* want from the money-boxes?'

'Not a penny,' the old woman said. 'Just bring me my grandmother's old tinder-box. She left it in there years ago.'

'All right, I'll do it,' the soldier agreed. He took the blue checked apron, tied the rope around his middle and climbed up the tree. He slipped down the hollow trunk and found himself in a large hall where a hundred lamps were burning, just as the old woman had said.

There were three doors in front of him. He opened the first door and, sure enough, there sat a dog with eyes as big as tea-cups. The soldier felt rather nervous of this odd creature, but bravely he picked it up and placed it on the old woman's apron. It watched him closely while he filled his pockets with copper coins. Then he lifted the dog back on to the box and went into the next room.

A great dog with eyes as big as cart-wheels was staring at him from the money-box.

'Don't look at me like that, or you'll strain your eyes,' the soldier said. He seated the dog on the apron and, when he saw the silver coins in the box, he threw away all his copper money and filled his pockets with the more valuable metal. Then he went into the third room, where the third dog was sitting. This dog's eyes were as large as the Round Tower of Copenhagen, and kept turning round in its head like catherine wheels.

The soldier had never seen such a strange animal in his life. However, he put it on the apron and opened the box. His mouth dropped open at what he saw. There were heaps and heaps of gold coins inside, more riches than he had ever imagined. He threw away the silver money and filled his rucksack, his pockets, his cap and even his boots with the glittering coins.

'Pull me up!' he shouted to the old woman.

'Have you got my tinder-box?' she demanded.

The soldier had completely forgotten about it. He hurried back and fetched it, jingling as he walked because of all the gold in his pockets.

When the old woman had pulled him out of the tree, the soldier asked her,

'What do you want this old tinder-box for, when there is all that money?'

'That's none of your business,' the old woman said crossly. 'You've got your gold – give me my tinder box.'

But the soldier was suspicious. 'I won't give you the tinder-box until you tell me what is so special about it.'

'No!' the old woman snapped.

The soldier started to draw his sword. The old woman shrieked in alarm and ran away, leaving the tinder-box behind. Shrugging his shoulders, the soldier put the box in his pocket and walked on to the nearest town.

It was a fine, large town, and the soldier went straight to the very grandest hotel. He moved into the best rooms, and ordered himself a splendid new suit of clothes, and glossy leather boots to replace his old travel-stained ones.

He soon made friends in the town. They all boasted to him about the loveliness of their Princess.

'She is the most beautiful Princess in the whole world!' they said.

'Really? How can I see her?' the soldier asked.

'You can't,' they all told him, shaking their heads. 'She's shut up in a brass tower surrounded by high walls and guards. No-one but the King and Queen can go inside. It has been foretold that she will marry an ordinary soldier, and the King is desperate to stop that happening. So he keeps her locked up where she cannot meet anyone.'

'I'd like to see her,' thought the soldier, but he could not think how to manage it.

He led a merry life in the city. He went to the theatre, wore the most expensive clothes, and dined out in the best restaurants: the King himself scarcely lived better. His new friends never tired of telling him what a fine fellow he was – especially when he paid for their theatre tickets. Still, the soldier did not forget how miserable it was to have no money, and he gave generously to the poor people in the city.

But, as he spent and spent, his supply of gold grew gradually smaller and smaller. At last he woke up one morning and found he had only one gold coin left. He had to leave his splendid suite in the hotel, and move into a grubby little attic room, where he cooked his own poor meals on a tiny stove. Strangely enough, his fine new friends, who had visited him every day in the hotel, did not come to see him now.

One evening he was sitting alone in his room. It was growing dark, and he had no money to buy a candle. He felt very miserable. Then he remembered that there was a small taper in the tinder-box which he had brought out of the hollow tree. He got out the flint and steel – but no sooner had he struck a spark than the dog with eyes as big as tea-cups stood before him. The soldier was astonished. The dog blinked twice, and said,

'I am here to serve you. What is your wish?'

The soldier realised why the old woman had wanted the box so badly. It was a *magic* tinder-box, and her grandmother must have been a witch.

'Quick,' he told the dog, 'fetch me some money!'

The dog disappeared in a flash, but before a minute had passed it was back again with a purse of money in its mouth.

The soldier knew now just how valuable the old tinder-box was. He discovered that if he struck the flint once, the dog that guarded the copper money appeared. If he struck it twice, the dog that guarded the silver answered the signal; and if he struck it three times, he could summon the dog that guarded the gold.

Now the soldier could have as much money as he liked. He moved back into the hotel, and his friends gave him a great welcome. But he could not stop thinking about the Princess.

'They say she is the most beautiful Princess in the world,' he mused, 'but she can never be seen. She must be lonely in the brass tower. I wonder if one of the magical dogs could show her to me?' He struck a

The dog was back again with the Princess

spark from the tinder-box, and instantly the dog with eyes like tea-cups appeared.

'I know it's the middle of the night,' the soldier said, 'but I'd like to see the Princess – just for a moment.'

The dog blinked twice and vanished. Before the soldier had time to look about him, it was back again with the Princess. She was lying on its back, fast asleep. She was so lovely that the soldier could not resist bending down and kissing her.

Then the dog sped away with the Princess, leaving the soldier deep in thought.

The next morning, when the King and Queen were at breakfast with their daughter, the Princess, she told them, 'I had the strangest dream last night! I dreamed that I rode on the back of a huge dog, and a soldier kissed me. At least, I think it was a dream. It seemed so real!'

The King was alarmed. He decided that the next night the Princess's old nurse, who had some magic powers, should sit by his daughter's bed and watch over her.

At midnight the dog appeared and ran off like lightning with the Princess. The old nurse was amazed; but she put on a pair of magic boots and followed them to the hotel. She waited outside until the dog took the Princess home, then she marked the door of the hotel with chalk and went to tell the King what she had seen.

The clever dog, however, had seen the chalk mark, so when the old lady had gone it took a piece of chalk in its mouth and put crosses on every single door in the town.

Early next day, the King, the Queen, the old nurse, and all the nobles of the court came to see where the Princess had been taken.

'Here it is!' the King said.

'No, over there!' said the Queen.

'Over here!' said a courtier.

'No, there!' shouted another.

The whole court was thrown into confusion, for wherever they looked there were crosses on all the doors. The King was furious.

The Queen, however, had a clever idea. She took her big golden scissors, cut up a piece of silk, and made a pretty little bag which she filled with flour and hung around the Princess's neck at bedtime. Then she cut a tiny hole in the bag so that the flour would dribble out and leave a trail wherever she went.

That night the dog came again, took the Princess on its back and carried her to the soldier. By now the soldier was very much in love with the beautiful Princess, and longed to marry her.

This time the dog did not notice the fine trail of flour that led from the castle to the soldier's window. The King and Queen could see plainly where their daughter had been, and at once the soldier was arrested and condemned to death.

The poor soldier had left his magic tinder-box at the hotel. What could he do?

As he was looking sadly out of his prison window, a little boy ran past kicking a ball. It bounced against the bars, not an inch from the soldier's nose.

'Here, you!' the soldier called. 'Run to my hotel and fetch my tinder-box, and I'll give you this gold coin.'

The boy did not wait to be asked twice. In ten minutes he was back with the precious box. The soldier took it joyfully and put it in his pocket. He had an idea.

That afternoon, thousands of people came to watch the execution. The King and Queen sat on their golden thrones with the royal guard lined up behind them. The soldier was led up to the gallows, where the hangman in his black mask stood.

'Your Majesty!' he called to the King, 'will you grant me one last wish? I'd like to smoke a pipe.'

The King agreed, so the soldier took out his pipe and his tinder-box and struck fire. One! Two! Three! Immediately the three dogs stood before him, one with eyes like tea-cups, one with eyes like cartwheels, and one with eyes like the Round Tower of Copenhagen.

'Help! Don't let them hang me!' shouted the soldier. The dogs blinked twice, and then sprang into action. One bounded into the ranks of soldiers and bowled them over like ninepins. The second carried off the hangman in his black mask, and the third lifted the King and Queen out of their thrones and shook them just as a puppy shakes a bone, growling like thunder.

'Help! Help! Call them off!' yelled the King, his voice wobbling because of the shaking he was receiving. 'You're pardoned! You can go!'

'And what about your daughter, the Princess? I want to marry her!'

'Yes! Yes! You can marry her, if she'll have you, and have half the kingdom!'

The soldier called off the dogs, and came down from the scaffold. He ordered the dog with eyes like teacups to fetch the Princess from her brass tower straight away. She was very happy to be released, and agreed at once to marry the soldier.

The marriage-feast lasted a whole week, and the dogs sat at the table with the other guests, rolling their eyes at everyone around them.

The Ugly Duckling

HANS ANDERSEN

Illustrated by E.H. Wehnert

It was a beautiful summer day in the country. The corn was golden, and the hay was stacked neatly in the meadow.

An old mansion, surrounded by a moat and a wall, stood bathed in the bright sunshine. In a quiet spot beside the moat a mother duck sat on her nest waiting for her eggs to hatch. She was feeling rather bored, for time passed slowly with no-one to talk to.

Suddenly there was a cracking sound from one of the eggs, and then another, and then another. One by one the little ducklings poked their heads out of the eggshells, chirping loudly. They stared about them, wide-eyed.

'The world is so big!' they said.

'*This* is not the whole world,' their mother said scornfully. 'Why, there's far more to the world than this – there are two more fields beyond the moat. But I've never been that far. Now, let me count you and make sure you are all here.'

She counted the fluffy little heads, and sighed. 'No, one of you isn't hatched yet. The biggest egg is still unbroken. I must wait a bit longer.'

Later that day an old duck came to see her.

'How are you getting on?' she asked.

'There's one egg that just *won't* hatch out,' the mother complained. 'But look at my other children. Aren't they the prettiest ducklings you ever saw?'

'Show me the egg,' the old duck said, interrupting her. 'You take my word for it, it's a turkey's egg. Someone played the same trick on me once. I had the most terrible trouble! The little one just would *not* get into the water. You take my advice – don't bother with it. Take your youngsters down for a swim.'

'I'll wait a bit longer,' the mother said, shaking her head. 'Another day or so won't hurt me.'

'Do what you like,' the other duck said sharply, and waddled off, muttering, 'No good will come of it, you'll see.'

At long last, the large egg burst and the duckling fell head-first out of the shell. He was so big and ugly that his mother hardly knew what to say.

'My goodness, perhaps it is a turkey after all! There's one way to find out. I'll take them all swimming tomorrow, and if he can't swim he can drown, and serve him right.'

The following day dawned bright and sunny, and the duck led her whole family down to the moat. Splash! She jumped into the water. One by one the little ducklings followed her, and all of them swam most beautifully. Even the ugly, grey latecomer paddled his feet and sailed along quite expertly.

'Well, that's that. He's not a turkey,' said the mother duck. 'He's a good swimmer, and he's not *that* bad-looking.'

She decided to take her family to the poultry-yard at once and present them to the other ducks.

'Keep close to me,' she told her children. 'Bow prettily when I introduce you to the Spanish Duck. She is in charge of the poultry-yard, and you must be very polite to her. Keep your feet turned out, and quack nicely!'

When they reached the yard the other ducks cried,

'Oh, look at that ugly duckling! We're not having him in the yard. What a monster!' One young drake even bit the poor youngster in the neck.

'Leave him alone,' exclaimed the mother angrily, spreading her wing over the ugly duckling.

The old Spanish Duck flapped her wings and all the others fell silent.

'Your children are very pretty,' she said to the mother duck. 'All except that one. I would keep *him* out of sight if I were you.'

The mother was upset by this, but she said as politely as she could, 'Well, he's not a beauty, but he swims well. He needs to fill out a bit, that's all.'

The Spanish Duck just smiled and said, 'Hmm. Well, make yourselves at home.' So the ducklings began their new life in the poultry-yard.

It was not a happy time for the ugly youngster. All the other birds made fun of him; his own brothers and sisters turned against him, and said, 'We hope the cat will catch you!' Even his mother sighed and shook her head as if she wished he had never been born. The ducks bit him, the chickens pecked him, and the girl who brought them their food in the morning kicked him with her muddy boots.

Finally the duckling could stand no more, and he decided to run away. Fluttering his weak wings, he half-flew and half-scrambled over the wall and set off across the fields.

By evening he reached a swamp, surrounded by woods, where many wild ducks and geese lived. Too tired to go on, the duckling tucked his head under his wing and spent the night hiding in some rushes.

Early next morning, at the first glimmer of daylight, the wild ducks flew up into the warm summer air to stretch their wings. They saw the stranger, and flew down beside him.

'What an ugly-looking bird! Where did you come from?'

The little duckling bowed to them very humbly. The wild ducks were pleased by his politeness, and said to him,

'Well, you can stay here if you like – as long as you don't marry into our family.'

The duckling had no thought of marrying – he simply wanted somewhere quiet to live where he would not be mocked and bullied. He thanked the wild birds for their kindness. But, just at that moment – Bang! Bang! Shots rang out from the trees, and the wild ducks flew away in alarm. Hunters had crept up through the woods and were firing at the frightened birds. The smoke from their guns rose up in a cloud above the marsh, and with loud splashes the hunting dogs sprang into the water to fetch the birds which had been shot.

Terrified, the duckling cowered under the reeds, hoping no-one would see him. But an enormous dog, teeth bared, came crashing through the reed-beds towards him. The duckling gave himself up for lost. At the very last moment, however, the dog decided not to bother with this scrawny prey, and bounded off.

'Poor me!' the duckling sobbed. 'I'm so ugly that even a dog won't touch me.'

He stayed hidden in the reeds until the hunters had gone, then fled from the swamp as fast as he could go.

A strong wind was blowing, and the little duckling had difficulty struggling along. Late in the evening he reached a cottage. It was old and tumbledown, but it offered some shelter from the wind. The duckling squeezed inside through a crack in the door.

An old woman lived in the cottage with her tom-cat and her hen. The cat caught mice, and purred loudly when the old woman stroked his back; the hen laid a fine egg every day. The old woman loved both of them as if they were her own children.

It was not long before they discovered the duckling hiding in a corner of the room.

'What's this?' said the old woman. Her eyesight was bad, and she thought the skinny duckling was a fat duck. 'Good, now I'll have duck's eggs – that is, if the silly creature isn't a drake. We'll give it a trial and see.'

So the duckling was allowed to stay. The hen and the cat, however, did not exactly make him welcome.

'Can you lay eggs?' asked the hen.

'No.'

'Then don't bother me. *I've* got important things to do.'

'Can you purr, or catch mice?' asked the tom-cat, flexing his sharp claws.

'No.'

'Then what use are you? Keep quiet and stay out of the way.'

The ugly duckling felt sadder than ever. He could not help thinking about the fresh air and sparkling water outside the cottage, and longed to go swimming again.

'Swimming?' clucked the hen. 'You must be mad. Ask the cat if he likes to go splashing about in the water. Ask our mistress! She's the wisest person in the world, and you wouldn't catch *her* getting herself soaking wet in the river. Why don't you learn to do something useful, like purring, or laying eggs?'

'You don't understand me,' the duckling sighed. 'It's so wonderful to swim in the clear water, and live in the open air.'

'Live there then,' the hen said rudely, 'and good riddance!'

So the duckling went on his way. He was happy to be free again to swim on the river, and dive for fish, but gradually he grew lonely. None of the other river birds would speak to him, and he was all alone.

Autumn came. The leaves were blown from the trees by the wind, and it grew colder and colder. The poor duckling shivered as he sat amongst the reeds.

One frosty evening, just as the fiery red sun was setting, a flock of magnificent swans swept by. The ugly duckling thought that he had never seen any birds so beautiful. Their feathers were white, as white as snow, and as they flew they uttered a strange whistling cry which made the little duckling want to stretch out his neck and answer them. After they disappeared from view, he stared up at the sky for hours, longing for the wonderful birds to return.

Autumn turned into winter, and the weather became so bitterly cold that the ugly duckling had to swim round and round in circles to stop the water from freezing over. Night after night the circle of water grew smaller until finally, exhausted, the duckling found himself frozen tight into the ice.

Luckily for the little bird, early next morning a farmer came by and saw what had happened. He was a kind-hearted man, and he took pity on the duckling. Breaking the ice with his stick, he carried the bird home to his children.

In the warm kitchen of the farmhouse the duckling soon recovered his strength. The farmer's children wanted to play with him, but the

In his fright he fluttered into a milk pan

poor duckling was afraid of them and tried to run away. In his fright
he fluttered into a milk-pan, knocking it over. Then he waddled
through the butter-dish; and as the laughing children gave chase, he
finally fell backwards into the flour-tub. He did look a sight! The flour
clung to his feathers like a sticky white coat. In panic, the duckling

waddled towards the door. Luckily it was open, and the little bird took his chance and scuttled outside. It was pandemonium in the kitchen, and nobody saw where he went. He rolled in the snow to get rid of his sticky covering, and then hid himself among the rushes in the marsh where no-one could find him.

It was a cold, hard winter, but at last the sun began to shine again and the snow melted away. The larks began to sing; spring had arrived.

The young drake flapped his wings to stretch them. They had grown much stronger over the winter months, and almost before he knew it he was flying high above the ground. It felt wonderful to soar through the air. Presently he saw below him a beautiful garden, and he flew down to have a closer look.

It was a lovely place. The fruit trees were in blossom, and a weeping willow trailed its graceful branches in the cool water of a stream. As the duckling looked about him in delight, three splendid swans came sailing along the water towards him. The duckling made up his mind at once to go and meet them.

'Even if they kill me for my boldness,' he thought, 'it doesn't matter. I'd rather be killed than go on like this any longer.'

He bent his head, waiting for the swans to approach, and saw his reflection in the still water. But what did he see? Not an ugly, scrawny grey duckling, but – a wonderful snow-white swan!

At last the truth dawned on him. The mother duck had hatched a swan's egg by mistake. He, the ugly duckling, was a swan!

Joyfully he lifted his head and greeted the other swans. They welcomed him lovingly, stroking his neck with their bills.

The young swan could hardly believe his good fortune. From the depths of his heart he said,

'I never dreamed of such happiness when I was the Ugly Duckling!'

Puss in Boots

CHARLES PERRAULT

Illustrated by Walter Crane

Once upon a time there was a miller who had three sons. When he died he left them nothing but his mill, his donkey and his cat. This poor patrimony was soon divided. The eldest son had the mill, the second the donkey, and the youngest nothing but the cat. The youngest brother felt very sorry for himself.

'Together, my brothers can earn a good living with the mill and the donkey,' he said. 'But what on earth can I do with a cat, unless I eat it and make a fur collar out of its skin?'

The cat, who was sitting nearby washing his fur, heard this. With a grave and serious air he said,

'Do not worry, master. All you have to do is give me a leather bag, and have a pair of boots made for me to protect my paws from the mud and the brambles. Then you will see that I can be more help to you than you think.'

The young man was doubtful about this. However, he knew that Puss was a very clever cat, who often used the most cunning tricks to catch rats and mice. Sometimes he would hang by his feet, and sometimes hide in the grain and pretend to be dead. So the young man gave the cat what he asked, and hoped for the best.

The cat looked very dashing when he put on his new boots. However, he wasted no time admiring himself. He filled the leather bag with bran and carrots and hung it around his neck. Then he went to a warren where a great many rabbits lived and stretched out on the ground as if he were dead. He lay quite still, not moving a whisker, but he kept tight hold of the strings of the bag.

He had been there scarcely five minutes when an unwary young rabbit, smelling the tasty carrots, hopped into the bag. Quick as lightning Puss sprang up and pulled the bag shut with the foolish rabbit inside. Then, proud of his catch, he took it to the palace and asked to speak to the King. He was shown into the royal apartment, where he made a deep bow.

'Your Majesty, I have brought you a tender young rabbit, a gift from my master, the Lord Marquis of Carabas.' (Puss had invented this fine-sounding title as he walked to the palace.)

'Tell your master I thank him,' said the King, 'and I am very pleased with his gift.'

The next day the cat hid himself amongst the corn in the cornfield, holding his bag open in front of him. When two fine partridges ran into it, he drew the strings tight and caught them both. He presented these to the King also, with the compliments of the Lord Marquis of Carabas. The King was delighted, and rewarded the cat with some gold coins.

For two or three weeks the cat continued to take the King presents. Each time, he pretended that they had been sent by the Lord Marquis of Carabas.

Then, one day, the cat heard that the King was going for a drive in his coach along the river-bank. His daughter, the most beautiful Princess in the world, was to go with him. The cat hurried to his master and said,

'Quick – do as I tell you and your fortune is made. Undress and go for a swim in the river, just by those two willow-trees. Leave the rest to me.'

The young man did as the cat told him, without knowing why. As he was swimming to and fro, the King's coach passed by, and the cat began to cry out,

'Help! Help! My Lord Marquis of Carabas is going to be drowned!'

The King put his head out of the window, wondering what all this noise was about. He recognised the cat, and straight away he commanded his guards to run to the assistance of his Lordship the Marquis of Carabas. While they pulled the dripping young man out of the river, the cat ran to the coach. He told the King that some thieves had stolen the Marquis's clothes while he was washing, though the cat had cried out, 'Thieves! Thieves!' as loud as he could.

(In fact, the cunning cat had hidden his master's clothes under a rock).

At once the King commanded that one of his own suits should be brought for the Lord Marquis of Carabas.

The King and his daughter made a great fuss of the young man, and invited him to come into the coach and drive with them. The young man looked very handsome in his borrowed clothes, and he spoke so courteously and gently that the beautiful Princess soon began to fall in love with him.

The cat was overjoyed to see his plan succeeding so well. He marched on ahead of the coach, until he met with some countrymen who were mowing a meadow. He said to them fiercely,

'The King is driving this way. If you don't tell him that this meadow you are mowing belongs to my Lord Marquis of Carabas, something terrible will happen to you!'

As the King passed by, he asked the mowers to whom the meadow belonged. The cat's threats had frightened them, so they said, 'To my Lord Marquis of Carabas.'

'Yes,' said the Marquis, joining in the pretence, 'we always have a good harvest from this meadow.'

The cat went on ahead, and soon he met some reapers.

'You people,' he said to them, 'listen! The King is driving this way. Tell him that this field you are reaping belongs to the Marquis of Carabas, or something terrible will happen to you.'

A few minutes later the King passed by, and he asked to whom all that corn belonged. 'To my Lord Marquis of Carabas,' the reapers replied. The King congratulated the Marquis.

The cat, who ran ahead of the coach all the way, said the same words to everyone he met, and the King was astonished at the vast estates of my Lord Marquis of Carabas.

Puss came at last to a great castle. In it lived an ogre. He was ugly

The ogre received him civilly

and cruel, but very rich. All the land that the King had seen on his drive really belonged to this ogre.

The cat knocked on the great door. He said that he could not pass by without paying his respects to the owner of the castle, and he was duly invited in.

The ogre received him as civilly as an ogre could do, and invited him to sit down.

'I have been told,' said the cat, 'that you have the magic power of turning yourself into any animal you like. People say you can turn yourself into an elephant – or a lion – or whatever you wish.'

'It's true,' the ogre replied. 'Watch!'

And poor Puss found himself staring into the enormous snarling jaws of a lion. Thoroughly alarmed, he sprang out of the window and on to the roof. (It wasn't at all easy, for his boots kept slipping on the tiles.) There was a loud roaring from below, which soon became a roar of ogre-ish laughter. Puss peeked down, and saw the ogre back in his natural shape. He climbed down, feeling rather foolish, and admitted that he had had a bad fright.

'That was very clever of you,' said the cat, 'but I've also been told that you can turn yourself into something as tiny as a mouse. I must say, I don't believe you can do *that*.'

'Oh, can't I!' bellowed the ogre. 'You just look at this!' Instantly, he transformed himself into a tiny grey mouse, and began to scamper about the floor.

In a flash the cat pounced on him and ate him up!

Meanwhile, the King's coach was approaching the castle. Hearing it clatter across the draw-bridge, Puss ran to meet it.

'Your Majesty,' he called out, 'welcome to the castle of the Lord Marquis of Carabas!' He winked at the Marquis, who did his best not to look surprised.

The King was impressed.

'Does this magnificent castle belong to you too? I've never seen such a fine building. May we go in?'

The King, the Princess and the Marquis followed the cat into the great dining-hall, where a splendid feast was laid out. (The ogre had invited all his friends to a special dinner that night, and the food was laid out ready. However, when the guests heard that the ogre had disappeared, and saw that the King's coach was outside the castle, they dared not go in.)

The King was completely charmed by the good qualities of the Lord Marquis of Carabas, and the Princess adored him already. After five or six glasses of wine, the King drank a toast to the Marquis and said,

'I could not imagine a better son-in-law than you, my Lord Marquis. If you were to ask for the hand of my daughter in marriage, I should be honoured.'

The Marquis was not slow to take advantage of this hint, as you can imagine. He and the Princess were married the very next day, and lived happily ever after in the ogre's castle.

Puss became a great lord, and never ran after mice any more except for his own amusement.

Pinocchio

CARLO COLLODI

This is an extract from Pinocchio, *an Italian children's novel first published in 1883. It describes what happens when an old carpenter, Geppetto, makes a wooden puppet to keep him company.*

Geppetto lived in a small ground-floor room that was only lighted from the staircase. The furniture could not have been simpler – a bad chair, a poor bed, and a broken-down table. At the end of the room there was a fireplace with a lighted fire; but the fire was painted, and by the fire was a painted saucepan that was boiling cheerfully, and sending out a cloud of smoke that looked exactly like real smoke.

As soon as he reached home Geppetto took his tools and set to work to cut out and model his puppet.

'What name shall I give him?' he said to himself; 'I think I will call him Pinocchio. It is a name that will bring him luck. I once knew a whole family so called. There was Pinocchio the father, Pinocchia the mother, and Pinocchi the children, and all of them did well. The richest of them was a beggar.'

Having found a name for his puppet he began to work in good earnest, and he first made his hair, then his forehead, and then his eyes.

The eyes being finished, imagine his astonishment when he perceived that they moved and looked fixedly at him.

Geppetto seeing himself stared at by those two wooden eyes took it almost in bad part, and said in an angry voice:

'Wicked wooden eyes, why do you look at me?'

No one answered.

He then proceeded to carve the nose; but no sooner had he made it than it began to grow. And it grew, and grew, and grew, until in a few minutes it had become an immense nose that seemed as if it would never end.

Poor Geppetto tired himself out with cutting it off; but the more he cut and shortened it, the longer did that impertinent nose become!

The mouth was not even completed when it began to laugh and deride him.

'Stop laughing!' said Geppetto, provoked; but he might as well have spoken to the wall.

'Stop laughing, I say!' he roared in a threatening tone.

The mouth then ceased laughing, but put out its tongue as far as it would go.

Geppetto, not to spoil his handiwork, pretended not to see, and continued his labours. After the mouth he fashioned the chin, then the throat, then the shoulders, the stomach, the arms and the hands.

The hands were scarcely finished when Geppetto felt his wig snatched from his head. He turned round, and what did he see? He saw his yellow wig in the puppet's hand.

'Pinocchio! . . . Give me back my wig instantly!'

But Pinocchio, instead of returning it, put it on his own head, and was in consequence nearly smothered.

Geppetto at this insolent and derisive behaviour felt sadder and more melancholy than he had ever been in his life before; and turning to Pinocchio he said to him:

'You young rascal! You are not yet completed, and you are already beginning to show want of respect to your father! That is bad, my boy, very bad!'

And he dried a tear.

The legs and the feet remained to be done.

When Geppetto had finished the feet he received a kick on the point of his nose.

'I deserve it!' he said to himself; 'I should have thought of it sooner! Now it is too late!'

He then took the puppet under the arms and placed him on the floor to teach him to walk.

Pinocchio's legs were stiff and he could not move, but Geppetto led him by the hand and showed him how to put one foot before the other.

When his legs became flexible Pinocchio began to walk by himself and to run about the room; until, having gone out of the house door, he jumped into the street and escaped.

Poor Geppetto rushed after him but was not able to overtake him, for that rascal Pinocchio leapt in front of him like a hare, and knocking his wooden feet together against the pavement made as much clatter as twenty pairs of peasants' clogs.

'Stop him! stop him!' shouted Geppetto; but the people in the street, seeing a wooden puppet running like a racehorse, stood still in astonishment to look at it, and laughed, and laughed, and laughed, until it beats description.

At last, as good luck would have it, a policeman arrived who, hearing the uproar, imagined that a colt had escaped from his master. Planting himself courageously with his legs apart in the middle of the road, he waited with the determined purpose of stopping him, and thus preventing the chance of worse disasters.

When Pinocchio, still at some distance, saw the policeman barricading the whole street, he endeavoured to take him by surprise and to pass between his legs. But he failed signally.

The policeman without disturbing himself in the least caught him cleverly by the nose – it was an immense nose of ridiculous proportions that seemed made on purpose to be laid hold of by policemen – and consigned him to Geppetto. Wishing to punish him, Geppetto intended to pull his ears at once. But imagine his feelings when he could not succeed in finding them. And do you know the reason? It was that, in his hurry to model him, he had forgotten to make them.

He then took him by the collar, and as he was leading him away he said to him, shaking his head threateningly:

'We will go home at once, and as soon as we arrive we will regulate our accounts, never doubt it.'

At this announcement Pinocchio threw himself on the ground and would not take another step. In the meanwhile a crowd of idlers and inquisitive people began to assemble and to make a ring round them.

Some of them said one thing, some another.

'Poor puppet!' said several, 'he is right not to wish to return home! Who knows how Geppetto, that bad old man, will beat him! . . .'

And the others added maliciously:

'Geppetto seems a good man! but with boys he is a regular tyrant! If that poor puppet is left in his hands he is quite capable of tearing him in pieces! . . .'

It ended in so much being said and done that the policeman at last set Pinocchio at liberty and conducted Geppetto to prison. The poor man not being ready with words to defend himself cried like a calf, and as he was being led away to prison sobbed out:

'Wretched boy! And to think how I have laboured to make him a well-conducted puppet! But it serves me right! I should have thought of it sooner! . . .'

Aladdin and the Wonderful Lamp

ANDREW LANG

Illustrated by Walter Crane

This version of the famous story comes from The Arabian Nights Entertainments *(1898)*

There once lived a poor tailor, who had a son called Aladdin, a careless, idle boy who would do nothing but play all day long in the streets with little idle boys like himself. This so grieved the father that he died; yet, in spite of his mother's tears and prayers, Aladdin did not mend his ways. One day, when he was playing in the streets as usual, a stranger asked him his age, and if he were not the son of Mustapha the tailor.

'I am, sir,' replied Aladdin; 'but he died a long while ago.'

On this the stranger, who was a famous African magician, fell on his neck and kissed him, saying: 'I am your uncle, and knew you from your likeness to my brother. Go to your mother and tell her I am coming.'

Aladdin ran home, and told his mother of his newly found uncle.

'Indeed, child,' she said, 'your father had a brother, but I always thought he was dead.'

However, she prepared supper, and bade Aladdin seek his uncle, who came laden with wine and fruit. He presently fell down and kissed the place where Mustapha used to sit, bidding Aladdin's mother not to be surprised at not having seen him before, as he had been forty years out of the country. He then turned to Aladdin, and asked him his trade, at which the boy hung his head, while his mother burst into tears. On learning that Aladdin was idle and would learn no trade, he offered to take a shop for him and stock it with merchandise. Next day he bought Aladdin a fine suit of clothes, and took him all over the city, showing him the sights, and brought him home at nightfall to his mother, who was overjoyed to see her son so fine.

Next day the magician led Aladdin into some beautiful gardens a long way outside the city gates. They sat down by a fountain, and the magician pulled a cake from his girdle, which he divided between them. They then journeyed onwards till they almost reached the mountains. Aladdin was so tired that he begged to go back, but the magician entertained him with pleasant stories, and led him on in spite of himself.

At last they came to two mountains divided by a narrow valley.

'We will go no farther,' said the false uncle. 'I will show you something wonderful; you gather up some sticks while I kindle a fire.'

When it was lit the magician threw on it a powder he had about him, at the same time saying some magical words. The earth trembled a little and opened in front of them, disclosing a square flat stone with a brass ring in the middle to raise it by. Aladdin tried to run away, but the magician caught him and gave him a blow that knocked him down.

'What have I done, uncle?' he said piteously; whereupon the magician said more kindly: 'Fear nothing, but obey me. Beneath this stone lies a treasure which is to be yours, and no one else may touch it, so you must do exactly as I tell you.'

At the word treasure, Aladdin forgot his fears, and grasped the ring as he was told, saying the names of his father and grandfather. The stone came up quite easily and some steps appeared.

'Go down,' said the magician; 'at the foot of those steps you will find an open door leading into three large halls. Tuck up your gown and go through them without touching anything, or you will die instantly. These halls lead into a garden of fine fruit trees. Walk on till you come to a niche in a terrace where stands a lighted lamp. Pour out the oil it contains and bring it to me.' He drew a ring from his finger and gave it to Aladdin, bidding him prosper.

Aladdin found the lamp

Aladdin found everything as the magician had said, gathered some fruit off the trees, and, having got the lamp, arrived at the mouth of the cave. The magician cried out in a great hurry:

'Make haste and give me the lamp.' This Aladdin refused to do until he was out of the cave. The magician flew into a terrible passion, and throwing some more powder on the fire, he said something, and the stone rolled back into its place.

The magician left Persia for ever, which plainly showed that he was no uncle of Aladdin's, but a cunning magician who had read in his magic books of a wonderful lamp, which would make him the most powerful man in the world. Though he alone knew where to find it, he could only receive it from the hand of another. He had picked out the foolish Aladdin for this purpose, intending to get the lamp and kill him afterwards.

For two days Aladdin remained in the dark, crying and lamenting. At last he clasped his hands in prayer, and in so doing rubbed the ring, which the magician had forgotten to take from him. Immediately an enormous and frightful genie rose out of the earth, saying:

'What wouldst thou with me? I am the Slave of the Ring, and will obey thee in all things.'

Aladdin fearlessly replied: 'Deliver me from this place!' whereupon the earth opened, and he found himself outside. As soon as his eyes could bear the light he went home, but fainted on the threshold. When he came to himself he told his mother what had passed, and showed her the lamp and the fruits he had gathered in the garden, which were in reality precious stones. He then asked for some food.

'Alas! child,' she said, 'I have nothing in the house, but I have spun a little cotton and will go and sell it.'

Aladdin bade her keep her cotton, for he would sell the lamp instead. As it was very dirty she began to rub it, that it might fetch a higher price. Instantly a hideous genie appeared, and asked what she would have. She fainted away, but Aladdin, snatching the lamp, said boldly:

'Fetch me something to eat!'

The genie returned with a silver bowl, twelve silver plates containing rich meats, two silver cups, and two bottles of wine. Aladdin's mother, when she came to herself, said:

'Whence comes this splendid feast?'

'Ask not, but eat,' replied Aladdin.

So they sat at breakfast till it was dinner-time, and Aladdin told his mother about the lamp. She begged him to sell it, and have nothing to do with devils.

'No,' said Aladdin, 'since chance has made us aware of its virtues, we will use it and the ring likewise, which I shall always wear on my finger.' When they had eaten all the genie had brought, Aladdin sold one of the silver plates, and so on till none were left. He then had recourse to the genie, who gave him another set of plates, and thus they lived for many years.

One day Aladdin heard an order from the Sultan proclaiming that everyone was to stay at home and close his shutters while the princess, his daughter, went to and from the bath. Aladdin was seized by a desire to see her face, which was very difficult, as she always went veiled. He hid himself behind the door of the bath, and peeped through a chink. The princess lifted her veil as she went in, and looked so beautiful that Aladdin fell in love with her at first sight. He went home so changed that his mother was frightened. He told her he loved the princess so deeply that he could not live without her, and meant to ask her in marriage of her father. His mother, on hearing this, burst out laughing, but Aladdin at last prevailed upon her to go before the Sultan and carry his request. She fetched a napkin and laid in it the magic fruits from the enchanted garden, which sparkled and shone like the most beautiful jewels. She took these with her to please the Sultan, and set out, trusting in the lamp. The grand-vizir and the lords of council had just gone in as she entered the hall and placed herself in front of the Sultan. He, however, took no notice of her. She went every day for a week, and stood in the same place.

When the council broke up on the sixth day the Sultan said to his vizir: 'I see a certain woman in the audience-chamber every day carrying something in a napkin. Call her next time, that I may find out what she wants.'

Next day, at a sign from the vizir, she went up to the foot of the throne, and remained kneeling till the Sultan said to her: 'Rise, good woman, and tell me what you want.'

She hesitated, so the Sultan sent away all but the vizir, and bade her speak freely, promising to forgive her beforehand for anything she might say. She then told him of her son's violent love for the princess.

'I prayed him to forget her,' she said, 'but in vain; he threatened to do some desperate deed if I refused to go and ask your Majesty for the hand of the princess. Now I pray you to forgive not me alone, but my son Aladdin.'

The Sultan asked her kindly what she had in the napkin, whereupon she unfolded the jewels and presented them.

He was thunderstruck, and turning to the vizir said: 'What sayest thou? Ought I not to bestow the princess on one who values her at such a price?'

The vizir, who wanted her for his own son, begged the Sultan to withhold her for three months, in the course of which he hoped his son would contrive to make him a richer present. The Sultan granted this, and told Aladdin's mother that, though he consented to the marriage, she must not appear before him again for three months.

Aladdin waited patiently for nearly three months, but after two had elapsed his mother, going into the city to buy oil, found every one rejoicing, and asked what was going on.

'Do you not know,' was the answer, 'that the son of the grand-vizir is to marry the Sultan's daughter tonight?'

Breathless, she ran and told Aladdin, who was overwhelmed at first, but presently bethought him of the lamp. He rubbed it, and the genie appeared, saying: 'What is thy will?'

Aladdin replied: 'The Sultan, as thou knowest, has broken his promise to me, and the vizir's son is to have the princess.

My command is that to-night you bring hither the bride and bridegroom.'

'Master, I obey,' said the genie.

Aladdin then went to his chamber, where, sure enough, at midnight the genie transported the bed containing the vizir's son and the princess.

'Take this new-married man,' he said, 'and put him outside in the cold, and return at daybreak.'

Whereupon the genie took the vizir's son out of bed, leaving Aladdin with the princess.

'Fear nothing,' Aladdin said to her; 'you are my wife, promised to me by your unjust father, and no harm shall come to you.'

The princess was too frightened to speak, and passed the most miserable night of her life, while Aladdin lay down beside her and slept soundly. At the appointed hour the genie fetched the shivering bridegroom, laid him in his place, and transported the bed back to the palace.

Presently the Sultan came to wish his daughter good-morning. The unhappy vizir's son jumped up and hid himself, while the princess would not say a word, and was very sorrowful.

The Sultan sent her mother to her, who said: 'How comes it, child, that you will not speak to your father? What has happened?'

The princess sighed deeply, and at last told her mother how, during the night, the bed had been carried into some strange house, and what had passed there. Her mother did not believe her in the least, but bade her rise and consider it an idle dream.

The following night exactly the same thing happened, and next morning, on the princess's refusing to speak, the Sultan threatened to cut off her head. She then confessed all, bidding him ask the vizir's son if it were not so. The Sultan told the vizir to ask his son, who owned the truth, adding that, dearly as he loved the princess, he had rather die than go through another such fearful night, and wished to be separated from her. His wish was granted, and there was an end of feasting and rejoicing.

When the three months were over, Aladdin sent his mother to remind the Sultan of his promise. She stood in the same place as before, and the Sultan, who had forgotten Aladdin, at once remembered him, and sent for her. On seeing her poverty the Sultan felt less inclined than ever to keep his word, and asked the vizir's advice, who counselled him to set so high a value on the princess that no man living could come up to it.

The Sultan then turned to Aladdin's mother, saying: 'Good woman, a Sultan must remember his promises, and I will remember mine, but your son must first send me forty basins of gold brimful of jewels, carried by forty black slaves, led by as many white ones, splendidly dressed. Tell him that I await his answer.' The mother of Aladdin bowed low and went home, thinking all was lost.

She gave Aladdin the message, adding: 'He may wait long enough for your answer!'

'Not so long, mother, as you think,' her son replied. 'I would do a great deal more than that for the princess.' He summoned the genie, and in a few moments the eighty slaves arrived, and filled up the small house and garden.

Aladdin made them set out to the palace, two and two, followed by his mother. They were so richly dressed, with splendid jewels in their girdles, that everyone crowded to see them and the basins of gold they carried on their heads.

They entered the palace, and, after kneeling before the Sultan, stood in a half-circle round the throne with their arms crossed, while Aladdin's mother presented them to the Sultan.

He hesitated no longer, but said: 'Good woman, return and tell your son that I wait for him with open arms.'

She lost no time in telling Aladdin, bidding him make haste. But Aladdin first called the genie.

'I want a scented bath,' he said, 'a richly embroidered habit, a horse surpassing the Sultan's, and twenty slaves to attend me.

Besides this, six slaves, beautifully dressed, to wait on my mother; and lastly, ten thousand pieces of gold in ten purses.'

No sooner said than done. Aladdin mounted his horse and passed through the streets, the slaves strewing gold as they went. Those who had played with him in his childhood knew him not, he had grown so handsome.

When the Sultan saw him he came down from his throne, embraced him, and led him into a hall where a feast was spread, intending to marry him to the princess that very day.

But Aladdin refused, saying, 'I must build a palace fit for her,' and took his leave.

Once home he said to the genie: 'Build me a palace of the finest marble, set with jasper, agate, and other precious stones. In the middle you shall build me a large hall with a dome, its four walls of massy gold and silver, each side having six windows, whose lattices, all except one, which is to be left unfinished, must be set with diamonds and rubies. There must be stables and horses and grooms and slaves; go and see about it!'

The palace was finished by next day, and the genie carried him there and showed him all his orders faithfully carried out, even to the laying of a velvet carpet from Aladdin's palace to the Sultan's. Aladdin's mother then dressed herself carefully, and walked to the palace with her slaves, while he followed her on horseback. The Sultan sent musicians with trumpets and cymbals to meet them, so that the air resounded with music and cheers. She was taken to the princess, who saluted her and treated her with great honour. At night the princess said good-bye to her father, and set out on the carpet for Aladdin's palace, with his mother at her side, and followed by the hundred slaves. She was charmed at the sight of Aladdin, who ran to receive her.

'Princess,' he said, 'blame your beauty for my boldness if I have displeased you.'

She told him that, having seen him, she willingly obeyed her father in this matter. After the wedding had taken place Aladdin led her into the hall, where a feast was spread, and she supped with him, after which they danced till midnight.

Next day Aladdin invited the Sultan to see the palace. On entering the hall with the four-and-twenty windows, with their rubies, diamonds, and emeralds, he cried:

'It is a world's wonder! There is only one thing that surprises me. Was it by accident that one window was left unfinished?'

'No, sir, by design,' returned Aladdin. 'I wished your Majesty to have the glory of finishing this palace.'

The Sultan was pleased, and sent for the best jewellers in the city. He showed them the unfinished window, and bade them fit it up like the others.

'Sir,' replied their spokesman, 'we cannot find jewels enough.'

The Sultan had his own fetched, which they soon used, but to no purpose, for in a month's time the work was not half done. Aladdin, knowing that their task was vain, bade them undo their work and carry the jewels back, and the genie finished the window at his command. The Sultan was surprised to receive his jewels again and visited Aladdin, who showed him the window finished. The Sultan embraced him, the envious vizir meanwhile hinting that it was the work of enchantment.

Aladdin had won the hearts of the people by his gentle bearing. He was made captain of the Sultan's armies, and won several battles for him, but remained modest and courteous as before, and lived thus in peace and content for several years.

But far away in Africa the magician remembered Aladdin, and by his magic arts discovered that Aladdin, instead of perishing miserably in the cave, had escaped, and had married a princess, with whom he was living in great honour and wealth. He knew that the poor tailor's son could only have accomplished this by means of the lamp, and travelled night and day till he reached the capital of China, bent on Aladdin's ruin. As he passed through the town he heard people talking everywhere about a marvellous palace.

'Forgive my ignorance,' he asked, 'what is this palace you speak of?'

'Have you not heard of Prince Aladdin's palace,' was the reply, 'the greatest wonder of the world? I will direct you if you have a mind to see it.'

The magician thanked him who spoke, and having seen the palace knew that it had been raised by the genie of the lamp, and became half mad with rage. He determined to get hold of the lamp, and again plunge Aladdin into the deepest poverty.

Unluckily, Aladdin had gone a-hunting for eight days, which gave the magician plenty of time. He bought a dozen copper lamps, put them into a basket, and went to the palace, crying: 'New lamps for old!' followed by a jeering crowd.

The princess, sitting in the hall of four-and-twenty windows, sent a slave to find out what the noise was about, who came back laughing, so that the princess scolded her.

'Madam,' replied the slave, 'who can help laughing to see an old fool offering to exchange fine new lamps for old ones?'

Another slave, hearing this, said: 'There is an old one on the cornice there which he can have.'

Now this was the magic lamp, which Aladdin had left there, as he could not take it out hunting with him. The princess, not knowing its value, laughingly bade the slave take it and make the exchange.

She went and said to the magician: 'Give me a new lamp for this.'

He snatched it and bade the slave take her choice, amid the jeers of the crowd. Little he cared, but left off crying his lamps, and went out of the city gates to a lonely place, where he remained till nightfall, when he pulled out the lamp and rubbed it. The genie appeared, and at the magician's command carried him, together with the palace and the princess in it, to a lonely place in Africa.

Next morning the Sultan looked out of the window towards Aladdin's palace and rubbed his eyes, for it was gone. He sent for the vizir, and asked what had become of the palace. The vizir looked out too, and was lost in astonishment. He again put it down to enchantment, and this time the Sultan believed him, and sent thirty men on horseback to fetch Aladdin in chains. They met him riding home, bound him, and forced him to go with them on foot. The people, however, who loved him, followed, armed, to see that he came to no harm. He was carried before the Sultan, who ordered the executioner to cut off his head. The executioner made Aladdin kneel down, bandaged his eyes, and raised his scimitar to strike. At that instant the vizir, who saw that the crowd had forced their way into the courtyard and were scaling the walls to rescue Aladdin, called to the executioner to stay his hand. The people, indeed, looked so threatening that the Sultan gave way and ordered Aladdin to be unbound, and pardoned him in the sight of the crowd.

Aladdin now begged to know what he had done.

'False wretch!' said the Sultan, 'come hither,' and showed him from the window the place where his palace had stood.

Aladdin was so amazed that he could not say a word.

'Where is my palace and my daughter?' demanded the Sultan. 'For the first I am not so deeply concerned, but my daughter I must have, and you must find her or lose your head.'

Aladdin begged for forty days in which to find her, promising if he failed to return and suffer death at the Sultan's pleasure. His prayer was granted, and he went forth sadly from the Sultan's presence. For three days he wandered about like a madman, asking everyone what had become of his palace, but they only laughed and pitied him. He came to the banks of a river, and knelt down to say his prayers before throwing himself in. In so doing he rubbed the magic ring he still wore.

The genie he had seen in the cave appeared, and asked his will.

'Save my life, genie,' said Aladdin, 'and bring my palace back.'

'That is not in my power,' said the genie; 'I am only the slave of the ring; you must ask the slave of the lamp.'

'Even so,' said Aladdin, 'but thou canst take me to the palace, and set me down under my dear wife's window.' He at once found himself in Africa, under the window of the princess, and fell asleep out of sheer weariness.

He was awakened by the singing of the birds, and his heart was lighter. He saw plainly that all his misfortunes were owing to the loss of the lamp, and vainly wondered who had robbed him of it.

That morning the princess rose earlier than she had done·since she had been carried into Africa by the magician, whose company she was forced to endure once a day. She, however, treated him so harshly that he dared not live there altogether. As she was dressing, one of her women looked out and saw Aladdin. The princess ran and opened the window, and at the noise she made Aladdin looked up. She called to him to come to her, and great was the joy of these lovers at seeing each other again.

After he had kissed her Aladdin said: 'I beg of you, Princess, in God's name, before we speak of anything else, for your own sake and mine, tell me what has become of an old lamp I left on the cornice in the hall of four-and-twenty windows, when I went a-hunting.'

'Alas!' she said, 'I am the innocent cause of our sorrows,' and told him of the exchange of the lamp.

'Now I know,' cried Aladdin, 'that we have to thank the African magician for this! Where is the lamp?'

'He carries it about with him,' said the princess, 'I know, for he pulled it out of his breast to show me. He wishes me to break my faith with you and marry him, saying that you were beheaded by my father's command. He is for ever speaking ill of you, but I only reply by my tears. If I persist, I doubt not but he will use violence.'

Aladdin comforted her, and left her for a while. He changed clothes with the first person he met in the town, and having bought a certain powder returned to the princess, who let him in by a little side door.

'Put on your most beautiful dress,' he said to her, 'and receive the magician with smiles, leading him to believe that you have forgotten me. Invite him to sup with you, and say you wish to taste the wine of his country. He will go for some, and while he is gone I will tell you what to do.'

She listened carefully to Aladdin, and when he left her arrayed herself gaily for the first time since she left China. She put on a girdle and head-dress of diamonds, and seeing in a glass that she looked more

beautiful than ever, received the magician, saying to his great amazement: 'I have made up my mind that Aladdin is dead, and that all my
tears will not bring him back to me, so I am resolved to mourn no
more, and have therefore invited you to sup with me; but I am tired of
the wines of China, and would fain taste those of Africa.'

The magician flew to his cellar, and the princess put the powder,
Aladdin had given her in her cup. When he returned she asked him to
drink her health in the wine of Africa, handing him her cup in
exchange for his as a sign she was reconciled to him.

Before drinking the magician made her a speech in praise of her
beauty, but the princess cut him short, saying:

'Let me drink first, and you shall say what you will afterwards.' She
set her cup to her lips and kept it there, while the magician drained his
to the dregs and fell back lifeless.

The princess then opened the door to Aladdin, and flung her arms
round his neck; but Aladdin put her away, bidding her to leave him, as
he had more to do. He then went to the dead magician, took the lamp
out of his vest, and bade the genie carry the palace and all in it back to
China. This was done, and the princess in her chamber only felt two
little shocks, and little thought she was at home again.

The Sultan, who was sitting in his closet, mourning for his lost
daughter, happened to look up, and rubbed his eyes, for there stood
the palace as before! He hastened thither, and Aladdin received him in
the hall of the four-and-twenty windows, with the princess at his side.
Aladdin told him what had happened, and showed him the dead body
of the magician, that he might believe. A ten days' feast was proclaimed, and it seemed as if Aladdin might now live the rest of his life
in peace; but it was not to be.

The African magician had a younger brother, who was, if possible,
more wicked and more cunning than himself. He travelled to China to
avenge his brother's death, and went to visit a pious woman called
Fatima, thinking she might be of use to him. He entered her cell and
clapped a dagger to her breast, telling her to rise and do his bidding on
pain of death. He changed clothes with her, coloured his face like hers,

put on her veil and murdered her, that she might tell no tales. Then he went towards the palace of Aladdin, and all the people thinking he was the holy woman, gathered round him, kissing his hands and begging his blessing. When he got to the palace there was such a noise going on round him that the princess bade her slave look out of the window and ask what was the matter. The slave said it was the holy woman, curing people by her touch of their ailments, whereupon the princess, who had long desired to see Fatima, sent for her. On coming to the princess the magician offered up a prayer for her health and prosperity. When he had done the princess made him sit by her, and begged him to stay with her always. The false Fatima, who wished for nothing better, consented, but kept his veil down for fear of discovery. The princess showed him the hall, and asked him what he thought of it.

'It is truly beautiful,' said the false Fatima. 'In my mind it wants but one thing.'

'And what is that?' said the princess.

'If only a roc's egg,' replied he, 'were hung up from the middle o' this dome, it would be the wonder of the world.'

After this the princess could think of nothing but a roc's egg, and when Aladdin returned from hunting he found her in a very ill humour. He begged to know what was amiss, and she told him that all her pleasure in the hall was spoilt for the want of a roc's egg hanging from the dome.

'If that is all,' replied Aladdin, 'you shall soon be happy.'

He left her and rubbed the lamp, and when the genie appeared commanded him to bring a roc's egg. The genie gave such a loud and terrible shriek that the hall shook.

'Wretch!' he cried, 'is it not enough that I have done everything for you, but you must command me to bring my master and hang him up in the midst of this dome? You and your wife and your palace deserve to be burnt to ashes; but this request does not come from you, but from the brother of the African magician whom you destroyed. He is now in your palace disguised as the holy woman – whom he murdered. He it was who put that wish into your wife's head. Take care of yourself, for he means to kill you.' So saying the genie disappeared.

Aladdin went back to the princess, saying his head ached, and requesting that the holy Fatima should be fetched to lay her hands on it. But when the magician came near, Aladdin seizing his dagger, pierced him to the heart.

'What have you done?' cried the princess. 'You have killed the holy woman!'

'Not so,' replied Aladdin, 'but a wicked magician,' and told her of how she had been deceived.

After this Aladdin and his wife lived in peace. He succeeded the Sultan when he died, and reigned for many years, leaving behind him a long line of kings.

The Happy Prince

OSCAR WILDE

Illustrated by Walter Crane

High above the city, on a tall column, stood the statue of the
Happy Prince. He was gilded all over with thin leaves of fine
gold, for eyes he had two bright sapphires, and a large red ruby
glowed on his sword-hilt.

He was very much admired indeed. 'He is as beautiful as a weathercock,' remarked one of the Town Councillors who wished to gain a
reputation for having artistic tastes; 'only not quite so useful,' he
added, fearing lest people should think him unpractical, which he
really was not.

'Why can't you be like the Happy Prince?' asked a sensible mother
of her little boy who was crying for the moon. 'The Happy Prince
never dreams of crying for anything.'

'I am glad there is some one in the world who is quite happy,'
muttered a disappointed man as he gazed at the wonderful statue.

'He looks just like an angel,' said the Charity Children as they came
out of the cathedral in their bright scarlet cloaks and their clean white
pinafores.

'How do you know?' said the Mathematical Master, 'you have
never seen one.'

'Ah! but we have, in our dreams,' answered the children; and the
Mathematical Master frowned and looked very severe, for he did not
approve of children dreaming.

One night there flew over the city a little Swallow. His friends had
gone away to Egypt six weeks before, but he had stayed behind, for he
was in love with the most beautiful Reed. He had met her early in the
spring as he was flying down the river after a big yellow moth, and had

been so attracted by her slender waist that he had stopped to talk to her.

'Shall I love you?' said the Swallow, who liked to come to the point at once, and the Reed made him a low bow. So he flew round and round her, touching the water with his wings, and making silver ripples. This was his courtship, and it lasted all through the summer.

'It is a ridiculous attachment,' twittered the other Swallows; 'she has no money, and far too many relations;' and indeed the river was quite full of Reeds. Then, when the autumn came they all flew away.

After they had gone he felt lonely, and began to tire of his lady-love. 'She has no conversation,' he said, 'and I am afraid that she is a coquette, for she is always flirting with the wind.' And certainly, whenever the wind blew, the Reed made the most graceful curtseys. 'I admit that she is domestic,' he continued, 'but I love travelling, and my wife, consequently, should love travelling also.'

'Will you come away with me?' he said finally to her, but the Reed shook her head, she was so attached to her home.

'You have been trifling with me,' he cried. 'I am off to the Pyramids. Good-bye!' and he flew away.

All day long he flew, and at night-time he arrived at the city. 'Where shall I put up?' he said; 'I hope the town has made preparations.'

Then he saw the statue on the tall column.

'I will put up there,' he cried; 'it is a fine position, with plenty of fresh air.' So he alighted just between the feet of the Happy Prince.

'I have a golden bedroom,' he said softly to himself as he looked round, and he prepared to go to sleep; but just as he was putting his head under his wing a large drop of water fell on him. 'What a curious thing!' he cried; 'there is not a single cloud in the sky, the stars are quite clear and bright, and yet it is raining. The climate in the north of Europe is really dreadful. The Reed used to like the rain, but that was merely her selfishness.'

Then another drop fell.

'What is the use of a statue if it cannot keep the rain off?' he said; 'I must look for a good chimney-pot,' and he determined to fly away.

But before he had opened his wings, a third drop fell, and he looked up, and saw – Ah! what did he see?

The eyes of the Happy Prince were filled with tears, and tears were running down his golden cheeks. His face was so beautiful in the moonlight that the little Swallow was filled with pity.

'Who are you?' he said.

'I am the Happy Prince.'

'Why are you weeping then?' asked the Swallow; 'you have quite drenched me.'

'When I was alive and had a human heart,' answered the statue, 'I did not know what tears were, for I lived in the Palace of Sans-Souci, where sorrow is not allowed to enter. In the daytime I played with my companions in the garden, and in the evening I led the dance in the Great Hall. Round the garden ran a very lofty wall, but I never cared to ask what lay beyond it, everything about me was so beautiful. My courtiers called me the Happy Prince, and happy indeed I was, if pleasure be happiness. So I lived, and so I died. And now that I am dead they have set me up here so high that I can see all the ugliness and all the misery of my city, and though my heart is made of lead yet I cannot choose but weep.'

'What! is he not solid gold?' said the Swallow to himself. He was too polite to make any personal remarks out loud.

'Far away,' continued the statue in a low musical voice, 'far away in a little street there is a poor house. One of the windows is open, and through it I can see a woman seated at a table. Her face is thin and worn, and she has coarse, red hands, all pricked by the needle, for she is a seamstress. She is embroidering passion-flowers on a satin gown for the loveliest of the Queen's maids-of-honour to wear at the next Court-ball. In a bed in the corner of the room her little boy is lying ill. He has a fever, and is asking for oranges. His mother has nothing to give him but river water, so he is crying. Swallow, Swallow, little Swallow, will you not bring her the ruby out of my sword-hilt? My feet are fastened to this pedestal and I cannot move.'

'I am waited for in Egypt,' said the Swallow. 'My friends are flying up and down the Nile, and talking to the large lotus-flowers. Soon they will go to sleep in the tomb of the great King. The King is there himself in his painted coffin. He is wrapped in yellow linen, and embalmed with spices. Round his neck is a chain of pale green jade, and his hands are like withered leaves.'

'Swallow, Swallow, little Swallow,' said the Prince, 'will you not stay with me for one night, and be my messenger? The boy is so thirsty, and the mother so sad.'

'I don't think I like boys,' answered the Swallow. 'Last summer, when I was staying on the river, there were two rude boys, the miller's sons, who were always throwing stones at me. They never hit me, of course; we swallows fly far too well for that, and besides, I come of a family famous for its agility; but still, it was a mark of disrespect.'

But the Happy Prince looked so sad that the little Swallow was sorry. 'It is very cold here,' he said; 'but I will stay with you for one night, and be your messenger.'

'Thank you, little Swallow,' said the Prince.

So the Swallow picked out the great ruby from the Prince's sword, and flew away with it in his beak over the roofs of the town.

He passed by the cathedral tower, where the white marble angels were sculptured. He passed by the palace and heard the sound of dancing. A beautiful girl came out on the balcony with her lover. 'How wonderful the stars are,' he said to her, 'and how wonderful is the power of love!'

'I hope my dress will be ready in time for the State-ball,' she answered; 'I have ordered passion-flowers to be embroidered on it; but the seamstresses are so lazy.'

He passed over the river, and saw the lanterns hanging to the masts of the ships. He passed over the Ghetto, and saw the old Jews bargaining with each other, and weighing out money in copper scales. At last he came to the poor house and looked in. The boy was tossing feverishly on his bed, and the mother had fallen asleep, she was so tired. In he hopped, and laid the great ruby on the table beside the woman's thimble. Then he flew gently round the bed, fanning the

The Happy Prince

boy's forehead with his wings. 'How cool I feel!' said the boy, 'I must be getting better:' and he sank into a delicious slumber.

Then the Swallow flew back to the Happy Prince, and told him what he had done. 'It is curious,' he remarked, 'but I feel quite warm now, although it is so cold.'

'That is because you have done a good action,' said the Prince. And the little Swallow began to think, and then he fell asleep. Thinking always made him sleepy.

When day broke he flew down to the river and had a bath. 'What a remarkable phenomenon!' said the Professor of Ornithology as he was passing over the bridge. 'A swallow in winter!' And he wrote a long letter about it to the local newspaper. Every one quoted it, it was full of so many words that they could not understand.

'To-night I go to Egypt,' said the Swallow, and he was in high spirits at the prospect. He visited all the public monuments, and sat a long time on top of the church steeple. Wherever he went the Sparrows chirruped, and said to each other, 'What a distinguished stranger!' so he enjoyed himself very much.

When the moon rose he flew back to the Happy Prince. 'Have you any commissions for Egypt?' he cried; 'I am just starting.'

'Swallow, Swallow, little Swallow,' said the Prince, 'will you not stay with me one night longer?'

'I am waited for in Egypt,' answered the Swallow. 'To-morrow my friends will fly up to the Second Cataract. The river-horse couches there among the bulrushes, and on a great granite throne sits the God Memnon. All night long he watches the stars, and when the morning star shines he utters one cry of joy, and then he is silent. At noon the yellow lions come down to the water's edge to drink. They have eyes like green beryls, and their roar is louder than the roar of the cataract.'

'Swallow, Swallow, little Swallow,' said the Prince, 'far away across the city I see a young man in a garret. He is leaning over a desk covered with papers, and in a tumbler by his side there is a bunch of withered violets. His hair is brown and crisp, and his lips are red as a pomegranate, and he has large and dreamy eyes. He is trying to finish a play for the Director of the Theatre, but he is too cold to write any more. There is no fire in the grate, and hunger has made him faint.'

'I will wait with you one night longer,' said the Swallow, who really had a good heart. 'Shall I take him another ruby?'

'Alas! I have no ruby now,' said the Prince; 'my eyes are all that I have left. They are made of rare sapphires, which were brought out of India a thousand years ago. Pluck out one of them and take it to him. He will sell it to the jeweller, and buy firewood, and finish his play.'

'Dear Prince,' said the Swallow, 'I cannot do that'; and he began to weep.

'Swallow, Swallow, little Swallow,' said the Prince, 'do as I command you.'

So the Swallow plucked out the Prince's eye, and flew away to the student's garret. It was easy enough to get in, as there was a hole in the roof. Through this he darted, and came into the room. The young man had his head buried in his hands, so he did not hear the flutter of the bird's wings, and when he looked up he found the beautiful sapphire lying on the withered violets.

'I am beginning to be appreciated,' he cried; 'this is from some great admirer. Now I can finish my play,' and he looked quite happy.

The next day the Swallow flew down to the harbour. He sat on the mast of a large vessel and watched the sailors hauling big chests out of the hold with ropes. 'Heave a-hoy!' they shouted as each chest came up. 'I am going to Egypt!' cried the Swallow, but nobody minded, and when the moon rose he flew back to the Happy Prince.

'I am come to bid you good-bye,' he cried.

'Swallow, Swallow, little Swallow,' said the Prince, 'will you not stay with me one night longer?'

'It is winter,' answered the Swallow, 'and the chill snow will soon be here. In Egypt the sun is warm on the green palm-trees, and the crocodiles lie in the mud and look lazily about them. My companions are building a nest in the Temple of Baalbec, and the pink and white doves are watching them, and cooing to each other. Dear Prince, I must leave you, but I will never forget you, and next spring I will bring you back two beautiful jewels in place of those you have given away. The ruby shall be redder than a rose, and the sapphire shall be as blue as the great sea.'

'In the square below,' said the Happy Prince, 'there stands a little match-girl. She has let her matches fall in the gutter, and they are all spoiled. Her father will beat her if she does not bring home some money, and she is crying. She has no shoes or stockings, and her little head is bare. Pluck out my other eye, and give it to her, and her father will not beat her.'

'I will stay with you one night longer,' said the Swallow, 'but I cannot pluck out your eye. You would be quite blind then.'

'Swallow, Swallow, little Swallow,' said the Prince, 'do as I command you.'

So he plucked out the Prince's other eye, and darted down with it. He swooped past the match-girl, and slipped the jewel into the palm of her hand. 'What a lovely bit of glass!' cried the little girl; and she ran home, laughing.

Then the Swallow came back to the Prince. 'You are blind now,' he said, 'so I will stay with you always.'

'No, little Swallow,' said the poor prince, 'you must go away to Egypt.'

'I will stay with you always,' said the Swallow, and he slept at the Prince's feet.

All the next day he sat on the Prince's shoulder, and told him stories of what he had seen in strange lands. He told him of the red ibises, who stand in long rows on the banks of the Nile, and catch goldfish in their beaks; of the Sphinx, who is as old as the world itself, and lives in the desert, and knows everything; of the merchants, who walk slowly by the side of their camels and carry amber beads in their hands; of the King of the Mountains of the Moon, who is as black as ebony, and worships a large crystal; of the great green snake that sleeps in a palm-tree, and has twenty priests to feed it with honey-cakes; and of the pygmies who sail over a big lake on large flat leaves, and are always at war with the butterflies.

'Dear little Swallow,' said the Prince, 'you tell me of marvellous things, but more marvellous than anything is the suffering of men and of women. There is no Mystery so great as Misery. Fly over my city, little Swallow, and tell me what you see there.'

So the Swallow flew over the great city, and saw the rich making merry in their beautiful houses, while the beggars were sitting at the gates. He flew into dark lanes, and saw the white faces of starving children looking out listlessly at the black streets. Under the archway of a bridge two little boys were lying in one another's arms to try and keep themselves warm. 'How hungry we are!' they said. 'You must not lie here,' shouted the watchman, and they wandered out into the rain.

Then he flew back and told the Prince what he had seen.

'I am covered with fine gold,' said the Prince, 'you must take it off, leaf by leaf, and give it to my poor; the living always think that gold can make them happy.'

Leaf after leaf of the fine gold the Swallow picked off, till the Happy Prince looked quite dull and grey. Leaf after leaf of the fine gold he brought to the poor, and the children's faces grew rosier, and they laughed and played games in the street. 'We have bread now!' they cried.

Then the snow came, and after the snow the frost. The streets looked as if they were made of silver, they were so bright and glistening; long icicles like crystal daggers hung down from the eaves of the houses, everybody went about in furs, and the little boys wore scarlet caps and skated on the ice.

The poor little Swallow grew colder and colder, but he would not leave the Prince, he loved him too well. He picked up crumbs outside the baker's door when the baker was not looking, and tried to keep himself warm by flapping his wings.

But at last he knew that he was going to die. He had just enough strength to fly up to the Prince's shoulder once more. 'Good-bye, dear Prince!' he murmured, 'will you let me kiss your hand?'

'I am glad that you are going to Egypt at last, little Swallow,' said the Prince, 'you have stayed too long here; but you must kiss me on the lips, for I love you.'

'It is not to Egypt that I am going,' said the Swallow. 'I am going to the House of Death. Death is the brother of Sleep, is he not?'

And he kissed the Happy Prince on the lips, and fell down dead at his feet.

At that moment a curious crack sounded inside the statue, as if something had broken. The fact is that the leaden heart had snapped right in two. It certainly was a dreadfully hard frost.

Early the next morning the Mayor was walking in the square below in company with the Town Councillors. As they passed the column he looked up at the statue: 'Dear me! how shabby the Happy Prince looks!' he said.

'How shabby, indeed!' cried the Town Councillors, who always agreed with the Mayor; and they went up to look at it.

'The ruby has fallen out of his sword, his eyes are gone, and he is golden no longer,' said the Mayor; 'in fact, he is little better than a beggar!'

'Little better than a beggar,' said the Town Councillors.

'And here is actually a dead bird at his feet!' continued the Mayor. 'We must really issue a proclamation that birds are not to be allowed to die here.' And the Town Clerk made a note of the suggestion.

So they pulled down the statue of the Happy Prince. 'As he is no longer beautiful he is no longer useful,' said the Art Professor at the University.

Then they melted the statue in a furnace, and the Mayor held a meeting of the Corporation to decide what was to be done with the metal. 'We must have another statue, of course,' he said, 'and it shall be a statue of myself.'

'Of myself,' said each of the Town Councillors, and they quarrelled. When I last heard of them they were quarrelling still.

'What a strange thing!' said the overseer of the workmen at the foundry. 'This broken lead heart will not melt in the furnace. We must throw it away.' So they threw it on a dust-heap where the dead Swallow was also lying.

'Bring me the two most precious things in the city,' said God to one of His Angels; and the Angel brought Him the leaden heart and the dead bird.

'You have rightly chosen,' said God, 'for in my garden of Paradise this little bird shall sing for evermore, and in my city of gold the Happy Prince shall praise me.'

Myths and Legends

King Arthur

JANE IVES

Illustrated by Howard Pyle

There are many legends about King Arthur, Merlin and the Knights of the Round Table. This one tells of Arthur's birth and how he became King of Britain.

Long ago, when the green land of Britain was covered with great forests, and wolves and bears roamed wild in the countryside, there lived a powerful king. His name was Uther Pendragon and he was the bravest of all the kings of Britain. His closest friend and advisor was an old man called Merlin.

Now Merlin was no ordinary man. In the days when the old magic had not died there were many great wizards and Merlin was the greatest wizard who had ever lived. Because he knew so many magical spells and was so very wise in the ways of the world, King Uther Pendragon always asked Merlin for advice and help. King Uther's wife was the beautiful Ingerne, Duchess of Tintagel, and when they had been married for about two years, Ingerne gave birth to a baby boy. They named him Arthur and Merlin was present at his christening.

'Sire,' said Merlin, holding the baby in his arms. 'This child will grow up to be the greatest king that Britain has ever known. Would you allow me to bring him up to be a good and wise king?'

'We can bring him up ourselves,' said Ingerne, for she did not want to lose her baby.

'To be raised in a royal household is not always the best training for kingship,' Merlin told them. 'What will your child know of the people he will one day reign over if all he sees are castles and palaces? How will he know how ordinary people live, what they need and what they

265

lack if he always has everything he wants? Let me take him and put him where he will learn all he needs.'

So Uther Pendragon and Ingerne agreed, for they knew that Merlin was the best person to help their son to learn to rule wisely and well. Thus Merlin took the baby away and for many years no more was heard of little Prince Arthur.

In those days, the country of Britain was made up of many different kingdoms, each ruled by a different king. Uther Pendragon was the most powerful of all the kings, but his lands were often threatened by the people of the North who were greedy for Uther's lands and possessions. When Uther fell ill the men of the North formed a huge army and sailed southwards round the coast of Britain to overthrow the dying monarch.

Merlin went to Uther and advised him.

'Sire, only you can lead your armies into battle,' he told Uther. 'The soldiers trust you and will fight fiercely if you are there, but if you are not, then they will surely be overthrown.'

Uther left his sickbed and rallied his men round him. He knew that he had only a few weeks to live but even so he was determined that his men should not know how near he was to death. The two great armies met at a place just outside St Albans, a town close to London. The Northmen believing that Uther's army had lost heart without their king to lead them were amazed when they were met with fierce opposition. The battle was short but decisive – the Northmen were soundly beaten and fled back to the north. Almost the last thing that Uther heard was the cheering of his soldiers and the joyful sound of victory trumpets.

The king was dying. He sent for Merlin and made his last wishes clear. His son Arthur was to become king and Merlin was to be chief advisor to the crown. But where was Arthur? He was a young man by now and almost old enough to rule, yet no one knew where he was, and Merlin would tell no one what had become of the heir to the throne. When he was asked he would answer,

'All will be made clear in time,' and he would say no more.

The winter after the death of Uther Pendragon a strange stone appeared outside one of the largest churches in London. Buried in this stone, so that only the richly carved hilt could be seen, was a great broad sword, and carved round the stone in clear letters was the legend: WHOSOEVER PULLS THE SWORD FROM THE STONE IS THE RIGHTFUL KING OF BRITAIN.

'But Arthur is the rightful king of Britain,' the people said. 'Why does he not pull the sword from the stone?

Months passed and still Arthur did not appear. People began to believe that like his father, he was dead.

Many knights came to London to try to take the sword from the stone, but none succeeded and strife began to break out in the land. There was no one to rule and some of the knights tried to take the crown by force, but they failed.

The following summer, a great tournament was held in London and knights and soldiers came from all over Britain to take part. One of these knights was Sir Hector, who brought his two sons with him. Sir Hector's elder son was Kay, a young man of eighteen. The younger son, who was only just sixteen, was not yet allowed to carry arms, although he was fully trained in the arts of horsemanship and combat. Because he was not allowed to join in, the younger son was acting as squire to Kay and Sir Hector. He looked after their horses and took care of their armour and weapons. Sir Hector and Kay took part in many of the tournaments, particularly the single combat contests where two men fought each other on foot with swords and shields. During the first contest, Kay's sword broke and Kay sent his brother to fetch his other sword.

The young lad darted away as fast as he could, for the place where they were staying was a long way away from the tournament ground, and he did not want his brother to miss any of the contests. As he ran through the streets he passed the churchyard where the magic stone stood. The young man did not stop to read the inscription; all he saw was a sword that no one seemed to want. He vaulted over the churchyard wall and took hold of the hilt of the sword. With one smooth pull he drew the sword from the stone.

It was a beautiful sword, as sharp as a razor and well balanced. Kay's brother ran back to the tournament as fast as he could, pleased that he could return so quickly. He was in such a hurry that he did not notice the amazed look on the faces of the people who had seen what he had done.

'He must be the rightful king . . .' said one man.

'But he seemed not to know what the stone said . . .' said another.

'The inscription said that only the rightful king could take the sword,' said another.

The news spread through London and people began to make their way to the tournament ground to see the boy who had pulled the sword from the stone and proclaim him their king.

Sir Hector and Kay were just as amazed when they saw the sword.

'Where did you find this?' they asked. 'Don't you know what this sword is?'

Sir Hector fell to his knees before his younger son.

'Sire . . .' he said.

'Oh get up, father,' said his son, 'don't be silly . . .'

'Arthur,' said Sir Hector, for that was the boy's name, 'the time has come for me to tell you the secret that I have kept in my heart for nearly sixteen years. Although you have always thought that I was your father, you are not, in fact, my real son. When you were a tiny baby, the wizard Merlin brought you to me. He would not tell me who your real parents were, but he asked me to bring you up as if you were my own child. He told me that you must be taught all the arts of a knight as well as honesty and duty. He said that you must be treated as any other boy even though you had a high destiny to fulfil. I see now that Merlin knew all along that you were the rightful heir to the throne of Britain.'

'And so I did,' said a deep voice.

Turning round, Arthur saw a tall, white-haired man. It was the wizard Merlin.

'Your real parents were Uther Pendragon and Ingerne, King and Queen of Britain,' said Merlin. 'You are truly the rightful king. It was only in this way that I could ensure that you would gain the throne. If the people of Britain did not believe you to be the king, they would not allow you to rule them. Now all can see that you, and only you, could draw the sword from the stone. Other men have tried and failed; other men have tried to take the crown and have failed. You will not fail, for you are the true son of your father.'

A great cheer rose up above the tournament ground, and the people there fell to their knees and hailed Arthur as king.

And so Arthur took the crown and led his people into battle. He had ruled for several years when the sword vanished. It had gone as mysteriously as it had arrived.

That evening Merlin took Arthur to a quiet and secret lake, high up in the Welsh mountains. A small rowing boat was moored at its edge but there were no oars.

'Get into the boat,' Merlin told King Arthur, 'and do not be afraid of anything that may happen to you.'

Arthur did as he was told and as he seated himself, the boat began to move smoothly out into the lake. When it reached the centre of the lake it stopped. All around Arthur the lake shimmered in the moonlight, as still as a mirror. Then, without a sound, and without causing a ripple, a slender white hand rose from the waters. The hand held a sword.

'Take the sword,' Merlin's voice whispered.

Arthur reached down and took the sword. Faintly through the water he thought he could see the face of a beautiful woman, but as he grasped the sword the hand sank back under the lake again and the face disappeared. The little boat moved back to the shore bearing Arthur and his precious gift.

'This is the sword Excalibur,' Merlin told the king. 'It is a magical sword and may only be carried by you. It will protect you in battle and while you wear it you will never be wounded.'

A slender white hand rose from the waters

'Who was the beautiful woman I saw under the water?' asked Arthur.

'That was the Lady of the Lake,' answered Merlin.

All his life Arthur carried the sword Excalibur, and as Merlin had said, he was never wounded.

Some years later, Arthur married the beautiful daughter of King Laodegan. Guinevere was said to be the loveliest lady in Britain and for many years she and Arthur were happy together. When the wedding was celebrated, knights and kings came from all over the kingdom bearing rich gifts for the happy couple. Of all the wedding presents that Arthur and Guinevere received, the most wonderful was a huge wooden table, richly carved and painted. The table was completely round and could seat one hundred and fifty knights. It was a present from Queen Guinevere's father Laodegan, and with it came one hundred knights, all sworn to the service of King Arthur.

This table became famous as the round table of legend. Only the bravest and noblest knight was allowed to sit there and because the table had no top or bottom, no knight could claim that he was more important than the others. When Arthur had decided who was to be allowed to sit at the round table, he held a great feast and for the first time the knights were all seated together. Suddenly, during the feast, the room became dark and on the back of the chairs where each knight was sitting, their names appeared in golden letters. Sir Lancelot of the Lake, Sir Gawain, Sir Bors, Sir Hector, Sir Perceval, Sir Galahad, Sir Pinel, Sir Kay, Sir Bedivere: these and all the other knights saw their names written in glowing letters and knew then that many adventures awaited them.

Thor, Loki and the Enchanter

JANE IVES

The Norsemen (Scandinavians) of ancient times have passed down to us many tales of gods and heroes. The Norsemen believed that their gods lived high above the Earth in a kingdom called Asgard. However, they often descended to Earth to seek adventure or meddle in the affairs of men. The king of the gods was called Odin or Woden (he gave his name to our Wednesday or Woden's Day). This story concerns two of Odin's sons: Thor, the god of thunder, and Loki the spirit of trouble and mischief.

Thor was the favourite son of the great god Odin. Even when he was young he showed such strength that his mother had had to make him a teething ring of iron because he chewed through his silver one as soon as it was put into his mouth – and that was before his teeth had even started to grow! When Thor reached full adulthood his power was legendary, as was his most famous possession, a magical stone hammer. This hammer was called Mjöllnir and never missed anything that it was hurled at. What was even stranger, it always returned to the hand of Thor and then shrank until it was tiny enough to hide in Thor's sleeve. Yet the moment Thor drew it out, it grew to its full size immediately, ready to be hurled at the next god or mortal who angered Thor. Not that many gods or mortals dared to anger this god of thunder, since his temper was as legendary as his strength.

Thor had a brother called Loki and hardly ever have two brothers been born who were so different. Where Thor was burly and tall, Loki was slender and of middle height. Where Thor was open-faced and ruddy-cheeked, Loki's face had a closed and secretive look and his cheeks were pale. Where Thor's voice was loud and jolly, Loki always spoke softly and hissed like a snake when he said words with an 's' in them. Where Thor was fast to act but sometimes slow to think, Loki had a quicksilver mind and weighed up everything he did before he acted. Nevertheless, the two brothers were fond of each other, and often, when Thor needed advice, it was to Loki that he turned. And when Loki needed the help of his brother's huge strength, he turned to Thor.

One day, Thor felt the need for adventure. He and Loki left Asgard and came down the Bifrost bridge* to earth. There they met two young peasants.

'We are off to seek an adventure,' Thor told the young men in his jolly booming voice, 'would you like to come with us?'

The two young men, who had no idea that Thor and Loki were gods, agreed and the four of them set off for Niflheim and the land of the giants. They marched along at a good pace and soon came to an enormous forest. This forest was so huge that even after three days of travelling they had still not come through it. On the third night Thor decided that they should rest and the two peasants were delighted, for they were amazed at the strength of their companions and had not liked to complain of tiredness.

'We must find shelter,' said Thor, 'for we shall be cold when we stop marching.'

He looked around and saw a house just ahead of them in a large clearing. A very strange house to be sure, but it seemed empty and would give them shelter.

They entered the house through its enormous doorway and found that there were five long narrow rooms leading off the central chamber.

'This will be fine,' boomed Thor. 'There is a room for each of us and one for our sacks of food.' Each of them made themselves comfortable and settled down to sleep. But sleep was difficult that night, for all through the hours of darkness they heard rumblings and groaning and the earth shook and quivered.

'How did you sleep?' Thor asked the others in the morning. 'I had a

*The Bifrost bridge is the rainbow.

most disturbed night. Perhaps we should go on and find somewhere quieter to rest.'

They picked up their sacks of food and set off through the forest again. They had not gone very far when they came across the biggest giant any of them had ever seen. Although all of them had seen many giants in their time they were each amazed that anyone so big could live on the earth.

The giant was lying on his back snoring and wheezing and they understood now where the strange sounds that had kept them awake the night before had come from. They walked all round the giant and marvelled. Just as Thor was about to tap the giant lightly with his hammer to wake him up the giant stirred and stretched and stood up. He towered over them.

'Good morning,' he said, and his voice made the trees shake and the grass flatten as if in a gale. 'I am the giant Skrymir. I recognize you,' he said, pointing at Thor. 'You are Thor, the god of thunder.'

The two peasants were as amazed by this as they had been by the giant.

'No wonder they needed no rest in three days' marching,' one whispered to the other. 'We have been journeying with the gods!'

Skrymir stretched again and then looked around him.

'Where is my glove?' he asked. 'I must have dropped it.'

The four travellers then realized that they had spent the night inside the giant's glove. They led him to it and Skrymir asked if he might join them on their journey.

'Indeed you may,' answered Thor. 'But we shall stop early tonight, for we are all tired. You may carry our food sacks.'

They marched on and on and when night came Skrymir immediately lay down and fell asleep. Thor and his companions tried to open the sack of food, but Skrymir had tied it so tightly that even Thor could not loosen the drawstring that held the neck of the sack closed. This irritated Thor so much that he picked up his hammer and hit the sleeping giant on the head as hard as he could. Skrymir stirred in his sleep. 'The flies round here are very irritating,' he said and fell asleep again. This made Thor even angrier and again he swung his hammer at the giant's head, almost snapping the handle with the force of his blow.

'Mmmmm . . .' mumbled the giant. 'The night moths seem to be alighting on me.'

Again Thor swung his hammer and this time the hammer sank into Skrymir's head.

'Mngngngng . . .' muttered the giant, 'bird's eggs must be dropping out of the trees. I think I shall never get any sleep here.'

The giant rose and said to Thor and his companions, 'I shall be off now but if you go on to the castle over there, you will find giants far stronger than me. I am but a babe compared to them.'

The giant left and Thor, Loki and the two peasants journeyed on to the castle. The castle gateway towered over them and by the side of the gate was a vast iron bell. Thor rang it and demanded entrance.

A great voice boomed out at them.

'Whoever enters here must first prove his strength,' the voice roared. 'We will have no weaklings here.'

The voice belonged to Utgardaloki, the master of the castle and one of the most powerful magicians of that place.

'It is Thor, the god of thunder, and Loki, his brother, who rings,' Thor bellowed back. 'We will match our strength with any of you.'

Loki stepped forward. 'Throughout Asgard I am known as the mightiest eater of the gods,' he announced. 'I challenge any one of you to an eating match.'

At that a thin, red-headed giant called Logi stepped out and behind him two giants each carrying an enormous plate heaped high with joints of meat. There must have been meat from at least sixteen oxen on each plate. Loki sat down and started to eat and in no time had emptied the plate, leaving only the clean bones. Imagine his surprise when he looked at his opponent's plate and found that the thin red-haired man had eaten not only the meat but the bones and plate as well.

'I am the fastest runner on earth,' announced one of the peasants who had been journeying with Thor and Loki. 'I am Thjalfi the swift. Match me with one of your clumsy giants.'

At this another giant stepped out. His name was Hugi and he looked so weak and frail that Thor began to laugh. Utgardaloki gave the signal and Thjalfi and Hugi began to race. Although the peasant ran as fast as the wind he could not catch up with Hugi.

'And now it is my turn,' announced Thor. 'First I challenge anyone to outdrink me.' For Thor could drink more than any god or human.

An enormous drinking horn was brought out of the castle and Thor took a deep breath and raised it to his lips. He took three great gulps from the horn but to his amazement, when he put it down the level in the horn was only a little lower than before.

'I am also the strongest of all the gods,' he boasted, 'give me another test.'

'If you can lift my cat up, then I shall believe that you are the strongest,' said Utgardaloki. He whistled and a small grey cat slunk out of the castle. Thor grinned and bent down to lift the little animal, but no matter how hard he tried he could only lift one paw of the cat from the ground.

'One last test,' Thor demanded, 'and then I shall admit defeat.'

'Very well,' said Utgardaloki. 'You must wrestle with my old nurse Elli and we shall see who wins.'

An old, wrinkled woman came slowly out of the castle and stood before Thor.

'Are you afraid to wrestle with an old woman?' she demanded. 'No, by the Bifrost Bridge!' retorted Thor, and rushed at her. They grappled together and slowly but surely, Elli forced Thor to his knees.

Thor and Loki were ashamed and amazed.

'Never have I been beaten before,' said Thor. 'These are indeed mighty giants.' They turned to go when Utgardaloki stopped them.

'Stay a moment,' he said. 'I will explain why you were defeated. I would never dare to let you in, for you are truly the strongest gods of all. When you met Skrymir in the forest it was none other than myself.

When I lay down I covered my head with mountains to protect myself. You may see what damage you did.'

Thor looked at the mountain range in the distance and saw huge trenches and valleys had been gouged out of it.

'When Loki tried to outeat Logi, he failed because Logi is none other than fire, and fire consumes everything. Thjalfi has been beaten by Hugi because Hugi is thought, which runs faster than anything. The drinking horn that Thor could not empty is always full because the other end is dipped into the sea, and by lowering the level of the horn, Thor has caused the first tides to appear. The cat is none other than the serpent Midgard, which is coiled round the centre of the earth and by lifting one paw, Thor has caused gigantic earthquakes. Finally the old nurse, Elli, is really old age, and no one can defeat age. So you see, your strength is amazing.'

Thor was furious when he found out that he had been tricked. With a mighty war cry he rushed at Utgardaloki and raised his hammer to smash him into the ground. But the magician was too quick for him and in a twinkling the castle and the giants disappeared, leaving only the sighing trees of the forest and the rushing winds of the plain.

The Voyage of Ulysses

ANDREW LANG
Illustrated by H. J. Ford

The adventures of Ulysses (or Odysseus, as he is also called) were first related by the ancient Greek poet Homer. Andrew Lang's version appeared in Tales of Troy and Greece *in 1907.*

In this extract, Ulysses and his men are sailing home from the Trojan War. They have been blown off course by a storm and have already survived encounters with the cyclops (a fearsome one-eyed giant) and the man-eating Laestrygonians.

I

CIRCE'S ISLAND

On they sailed till they came to an island, and there they landed. What the place was they did not know, but it was called Aeaea, and here lived Circe, the enchantress.

For two days Ulysses and his men lay on land beside their ship, which they anchored in a bay of the island. On the third morning Ulysses took his sword and spear, and climbed to the top of a high hill, whence he saw the smoke rising out of the wood where Circe had her palace. He thought of going to the house, but it seemed better to return to his men and send some of them to spy out the place. Since the adventure of the Cyclops Ulysses did not care to risk himself among unknown people, and for all that he knew there might be man-eating giants on the island. So he went back, and, as he came to the bank of the river, he found a great red deer drinking under the shadow of the green boughs. He speared the stag, and, tying his feet together, slung the body from his neck, and so, leaning on his spear, he came to his fellows. Glad they were to see fresh venison, which they cooked, and so dined with plenty of wine.

Next morning Ulysses divided his men into two companies, Eurylochus led one company and he himself the other. Then they put two marked pieces of wood, one for Eurylochus, one for Ulysses, in a helmet, to decide who should go to the house in the wood. They shook the helmet, and the lot of Eurylochus leaped out, and, weeping for fear, he led his twenty-two men away into the forest. Ulysses and the other twenty-two waited, and, when Eurylochus came back alone, he was weeping, and unable to speak for sorrow. At last he told his story: they had come to the beautiful house of Circe, within the wood, and tame wolves and lions were walking about in front of the house. They wagged their tails, and jumped up, like friendly dogs, round the men of Ulysses, who stood in the gateway and heard Circe singing in a sweet voice, as she went up and down before the loom at which she was weaving. Then one of the men of Ulysses called to her, and she came out, a beautiful lady in white robes covered with jewels of gold. She opened the doors and bade them come in, but Eurylochus hid himself and watched, and saw Circe and her maidens mix honey and wine for the men, and bid them sit down on chairs at tables, but, when they had drunk of her cup, she touched them with her wand. Then they were all changed into swine, and Circe drove them out and shut them up in the styes.

When Ulysses heard that he slung his sword-belt round his shoulders, seized his bow, and bade Eurylochus come back with him to the house of Circe; but Eurylochus was afraid. Alone went Ulysses through the woods, and in a dell he met a most beautiful young man, who took his hand and said, 'Unhappy one! how shalt thou free thy friends from so great an enchantress?' Then the young man plucked a plant from the ground; the flower was as white as milk, but the root was black: it is a plant that men may not dig up, but to the Gods all things are easy, and the young man was the cunning God Hermes, whom Autolycus, the grandfather of Ulysses, used to worship. 'Take this herb of grace,' he said, 'and when Circe has made thee drink of the

Then they were all changed into swine

cup of her enchantments the herb will so work that they shall have no
power over thee. Then draw thy sword, and rush at her, and make her
swear that she will not harm thee with her magic.'

    Then Hermes departed, and Ulysses went to the house of Circe, and
she asked him to enter, and seated him on a chair, and gave him the
enchanted cup to drink, and then smote him with her wand and bade

him go to the styes of the swine. But Ulysses drew his sword, and Circe, with a great cry, fell at his feet, saying, 'Who art thou on whom the cup has no power? Truly thou art Ulysses of Ithaca, for the God Hermes has told me that he should come to my island on his way from Troy. Come now, fear not; let us be friends!'

Then the maidens of Circe came to them, fairy damsels of the wells and woods and rivers. They threw covers of purple silk over the chairs, and on the silver tables they placed golden baskets, and mixed wine in a silver bowl, and heated water, and bathed Ulysses in a polished bath, and clothed him in new raiment, and led him to the table and bade him eat and drink. But he sat silent, neither eating nor drinking, in sorrow for his company, till Circe called them out from the styes and disenchanted them. Glad they were to see Ulysses, and they embraced him, and wept for joy.

So they went back to their friends at the ship, and told them how Circe would have them all to live with her; but Eurylochus tried to frighten them, saying that she would change them into wolves and lions. Ulysses drew his sword to cut off the head of Eurylochus for his cowardice, but the others prayed that he might be left alone to guard the ship. So Ulysses left him; but Eurylochus had not the courage to be alone, and slunk behind them to the house of Circe. There she welcomed them all, and gave them a feast, and there they dwelt for a whole year, and then they wearied for their wives and children, and longed to return to Ithaca. Therefore, they took their leave of Circe and set off in their ship once again.

II

THE WHIRLPOOL, THE SEA MONSTER,
AND THE CATTLE OF THE SUN

They had not sailed far when they heard the sea roaring, and saw a great wave, over which hung a thick shining cloud of spray. They had drifted to a place where the sea narrowed between two high black rocks: under the rock on the left was a boiling whirlpool in which no ship could live; the opposite rock showed nothing dangerous, but Ulysses had been warned by Circe that here too lay great peril. We may ask, Why did Ulysses pass through the narrows between these two rocks? why did he not steer on the outer side of one or the other? The reason seems to have been that, on the outer side of these cliffs, were the tall reefs which men called the Rocks Wandering. Between them the sea water leaped in high columns of white foam, and the rocks themselves rushed together, grinding and clashing, while fire flew out of the crevices and crests as from a volcano.

Circe had told Ulysses about the Rocks Wandering, which do not even allow flocks of doves to pass through them; every one of the doves is always caught and crushed, and no ship of men escapes that tries to pass that way, and the bodies of the sailors and the planks of the ships are confusedly tossed by the waves of the sea and the storms of ruinous fire. Of all ships that ever sailed the sea only 'Argo', the ship of Jason, has escaped the Rocks Wandering. For these reasons Ulysses was forced to steer between the rock of the whirlpool and the rock which seemed harmless. In the narrows between these two cliffs the sea ran like a rushing river, and the men, in fear, ceased to hold the oars, and down the stream the oars plashed in confusion. But Ulysses, whom Circe had told of this new danger, bade them grasp the oars again and row hard. He told the man at the helm to steer under the great rocky cliff, on the right, and to keep clear of the whirlpool and the cloud of spray on the left. Well he knew the danger of the rock on the right, for within it was a deep cave, where a monster named Scylla lived, yelping with a shrill voice out of her six hideous heads. Each head hung down from a long, thin, scaly neck, and in each mouth were three rows of greedy teeth, and twelve long feelers, with claws at the ends of them, dropped down, ready to catch at men. There in her cave Scylla sits, fishing with her feelers for dolphins and other great fish, and for men, if any men sail by that way. Against this deadly thing none may fight, for she cannot be slain with the spear.

Scylla

All this Ulysses knew, for Circe had warned him. But he also knew
that on the other side of the strait, where the sea spray for ever flew
high above the rock, was a whirlpool, called Charybdis, which would
swallow up his ship if it came within the current, while Scylla could
only catch some of his men. For this reason he bade the helmsman to
steer close to the rock of Scylla, and he did not tell the sailors that she
lurked there with her body hidden in her deep cave. He himself put on
his armour, and took two spears, and went and stood in the raised half

deck at the front of the ship, thinking that, at least, he would have a stroke at Scylla. Then they rowed down the swift sea stream, while the wave of the whirlpool now rose up, till the spray hid the top of the rock, and now fell, and bubbled with black sand. They were watching the whirlpool, when out from the hole in the cliff sprang the six heads of Scylla, and up into the air went six of Ulysses' men, each calling to him, as they were swept within her hole in the rock, where she devoured them. 'This was the most pitiful thing,' Ulysses said, 'that my eyes have seen, of all my sorrows in searching out the paths of the sea.'

The ship swept through the roaring narrows between the rock of Scylla and the whirlpool of Charybdis, into the open sea, and the men, weary and heavy of heart, bent over their oars, and longed for rest.

Now a place of rest seemed near at hand, for in front of the ship lay a beautiful island, and the men could hear the bleating of sheep and the lowing of cows as they were being herded into their stalls. But Ulysses remembered that, in the Land of the Dead, the ghost of the blind prophet had warned him of one thing. If his men killed and ate the cattle of the Sun, in the sacred island of Thrinacia, they would all perish. So Ulysses told his crew of this prophecy, and bade them row past the island. Eurylochus was angry and said that the men were tired, and could row no further, but must land, and take supper, and sleep comfortably on shore. On hearing Eurylochus, the whole crew shouted and said that they would go no further that night, and Ulysses had no power to compel them. He could only make them swear not to touch the cattle of the Sun God, which they promised readily enough, and so went ashore, took supper, and slept.

In the night a great storm arose: the clouds and driving mist blinded the face of the sea and sky, and for a whole month the wild south wind hurled the waves on the coast, and no ship of these times could venture out in the tempest. Meanwhile the crew ate up all the stores in the ship, and finished the wine, so that they were driven to catch sea birds and fishes, of which they took but few, the sea being so rough upon the rocks. Ulysses went up into the island alone, to pray to the Gods, and when he had prayed he found a sheltered place, and there he fell asleep.

Eurylochus took the occasion, while Ulysses was away, to bid the crew seize and slay the sacred cattle of the Sun God, which no man might touch, and this they did, so that, when Ulysses wakened, and came near the ship, he smelled the roast meat, and knew what had been done. He rebuked the men, but, as the cattle were dead, they kept eating them for six days; and then the storm ceased, the wind fell, the sun shone, and they set the sails, and away they went. But this evil deed was punished, for when they were out of sight of land, a great thunder cloud over-shadowed them, the wind broke the mast, which crushed the head of the helmsman, the lightning struck the ship in the centre; she reeled, the men fell overboard, and the heads of the crew floated a moment, like cormorants, above the waves.

But Ulysses had kept hold of a rope, and, when the vessel righted, he walked the deck till a wave stripped off all the tackling, and loosened the sides from the keel. Ulysses had only time to lash the broken mast with a rope to the keel, and sit on this raft with his feet in the water, while the South Wind rose again furiously, and drove the raft back till it came under the rock where was the whirlpool of Charybdis. Here Ulysses would have been drowned, but he caught at the root of a fig tree that grew on the rock, and there he hung, clinging with his toes to the crumbling stones till the whirlpool boiled up again, and up came the timbers. Down on the timbers Ulysses dropped, and so sat rowing with his hands, and the wind drifted him at last to a shelving beach of an island.

This island belonged to a kind fairy called Calypso, who took pity on Ulysses and cared for him. However, Ulysses was still far from home and more adventures awaited him before he reached Ithaca once more.

King Midas

NATHANIEL HAWTHORNE
Illustrated by Walter Crane

This ancient Greek legend was re-told by Nathaniel Hawthorne in Tangle-wood Tales *(1853). (This is a slightly shortened version).*

Once upon a time there lived a very rich man, and a king besides, whose name was Midas; and he had a little daughter, whom nobody but myself ever heard of, and whose name I either never knew, or have entirely forgotten. So, because I love odd names for little girls, I choose to call her Marygold.

This King Midas was fonder of gold than of anything else in the world. He valued his royal crown chiefly because it was composed of that precious metal. If he loved anything better, or half so well, it was the one little maiden who played so merrily around her father's footstool. But the more Midas loved his daughter, the more did he desire and seek for wealth. He thought, foolish man! that the best thing he could possibly do for this dear child would be to bequeath her the biggest pile of yellow, glistening coin that had ever been heaped together since the world was made.

And yet in his earlier days, before he was so entirely possessed of this insane desire for riches, King Midas had shown a great taste for flowers. He had planted a garden, in which grew the biggest and loveliest and sweetest roses that any mortal ever saw or smelt. These roses were still growing in the garden, as large, as lovely, and as fragrant as when Midas used to pass whole hours in gazing at them, and inhaling their perfume. But now, if he looked at them at all, it was only to calculate how much the garden would be worth, if each of the innumerable rose-petals were a thin plate of gold.

He made it his custom, therefore, to pass a large portion of every day in a dark and dreary apartment under ground, at the basement of his palace. It was here that he kept his wealth. To this dismal hole – for it was little better than a dungeon – Midas betook himself whenever he wanted to be particularly happy. Here, after carefully locking the door, he would take a bag of gold coin, or a gold cup as big as a wash-bowl, or a heavy golden bar, or a peck measure of gold-dust, and bring them from the obscure corners of the room into the one bright and narrow sunbeam that fell from the dungeon-like window. He valued the sunbeam for no other reason but that his treasure would not shine without its help. And then would he reckon over the coins in the bag; toss up the bar, and catch it as it came down; sift the gold-dust through his fingers; look at the funny image of his own face, as reflected in the burnished circumference of the cup; and whisper to himself, 'O Midas, rich King Midas, what a happy man art thou!' But it was laughable to see how the image of his face kept grinning at him out of the polished surface of the cup. It seemed to be aware of his foolish behaviour, and to have a naughty inclination to make fun of him.

Midas called himself a happy man, but felt that he was not yet quite so happy as he might be. The very tiptop of enjoyment would never be reached, unless the whole world were to become his treasure-room, and be filled with yellow metal which should be all his own.

★   ★   ★   ★

Midas was enjoying himself in his treasure-room one day as usual, when he perceived a shadow fall over the heaps of gold; and, looking suddenly up, what should he behold but the figure of a stranger, standing in the bright and narrow sunbeam! It was a young man, with a cheerful and ruddy face.

As Midas knew that he had carefully turned the key in the lock, and that no mortal strength could possibly break into his treasure-room, he of course concluded that his visitor must be something more than mortal. It is no matter about telling you who he was. In those days, when the earth was comparatively a new affair, it was supposed to be

A stranger was standing in the sunbeam

often the resort of beings endowed with supernatural power, and who used to interest themselves in the joys and sorrows of men, women, and children, half playfully and half seriously. Midas had met such beings before now, and was not sorry to meet one of them again. The stranger's aspect, indeed, was so good-humoured and kindly, if not beneficent, that it would have been unreasonable to suspect him of intending any mischief. It was far more probable that he came to do Midas a favour. And what could that favour be, unless to multiply his heaps of treasure?

The stranger gazed about the room; and when his lustrous smile had glistened upon all the golden objects that were there, he turned again to Midas.

'You are a wealthy man, friend Midas!' he observed. 'I doubt whether any other four walls on earth contain so much gold as you have contrived to pile up in this room.'

'I have done pretty well – pretty well,' answered Midas in a discontented tone. 'But, after all, it is but a trifle, when you consider that it has taken me my whole life to get it together. If one could live a thousand years, he might have time to grow rich!'

'What!' exclaimed the stranger. 'Then you are not satisfied?'

Midas shook his head.

'And pray what would satisfy you?' asked the stranger. 'Merely for the curiosity of the thing, I should be glad to know.'

A bright idea occurred to King Midas. It seemed really as bright as the glistening metal which he loved so much.

Raising his head, he looked the lustrous stranger in the face.

'Well, Midas,' observed his visitor, 'I see that you have at length hit upon something that will satisfy you. Tell me your wish.'

'It is only this,' replied Midas. 'I am weary of collecting my treasures with so much trouble, and beholding the heap so diminutive, after I have done my best. I wish everything that I touch to be changed to gold!'

The stranger's smile grew so very broad, that it seemed to fill the room like an outburst of the sun, gleaming into a shadowy dell, where the yellow autumnal leaves – for so looked the lumps and particles of gold – lie strewn in the glow of light.

'The Golden Touch!' exclaimed he. 'You certainly deserve credit, friend Midas, for striking out so brilliant a conception. But are you quite sure that this will satisfy you?'

'How could it fail?' said Midas.

'And will you never regret the possession of it?'

'What could induce me?' asked Midas. 'I ask nothing else to render me perfectly happy.'

'Be it as you wish, then,' replied the stranger, waving his hand in token of farewell. 'To-morrow, at sunrise, you will find yourself gifted with the Golden Touch.'

★　　★　　★　　★

Whether Midas slept as usual that night, the story does not say. Asleep or awake, however, his mind was probably in the state of a child's, to whom a beautiful new plaything has been promised in the morning. At any rate, day had hardly peeped over the hills, when King Midas was broad awake, and, stretching his arms out of bed, began to touch the objects that were within reach. He was anxious to prove whether the Golden Touch had really come, according to the stranger's promise. So he laid his finger on a chair by the bedside, and on various other things, but was grievously disappointed to perceive that they remained of exactly the same substance as before. Indeed, he felt very much afraid that he had only dreamed about the lustrous stranger, or else that the latter had been making game of him. And what a miserable affair would it be, if, after all his hopes, Midas must content himself with what little gold he could scrape together by ordinary means, instead of creating it by a touch!

All this while it was only the grey of morning, with a hot streak of brightness along the edge of the sky, where Midas could not see it. He lay in a very disconsolate mood, regretting the downfall of his hopes, and kept growing sadder and sadder, until the earliest sunbeam shone through the window, and gilded the ceiling over this head. It seemed to Midas that this bright yellow sunbeam was reflected in rather a singular way on the white covering of the bed. Looking more closely, what was his astonishment and delight, when he found that this linen fabric had been transmuted to what seemed a woven texture of the purest and brightest gold! The Golden Touch had come to him with the first sunbeam!

Midas started up in a kind of joyful frenzy, and ran about the room, grasping at everything that happened to be in his way. He seized one of the bed-posts, and it became immediately a fluted golden pillar. He pulled aside a window curtain, in order to admit a clear spectacle of the wonders which he was performing, and the tassel grew heavy in his hand, – a mass of gold. He took up a book from the table. At his first touch it assumed the appearance of such a splendidly bound and gilt-edged volume as one often meets with now-a-days; but, on running his fingers through the leaves, behold! it was a bundle of thin golden plates, in which all the wisdom of the book had grown illegible. He hurriedly put on his clothes, and was enraptured to see himself in a magnificent suit of gold cloth, which retained its flexibility and softness, although it burdened him a little with its weight. He drew out his handkerchief, which little Marygold had hemmed for him. That was likewise gold, with the dear child's neat and pretty stitches running all along the border in gold thread!

Somehow or other this last transformation did not quite please King Midas. He would rather that his little daughter's handiwork should have remained just the same as when she climbed his knee and put it into his hand.

But it was not worth while to vex himself about a trifle. Wise King Midas was so exalted by his good fortune, that the palace seemed not sufficiently spacious to contain him. He therefore went down-stairs, and smiled on observing that the balustrade of the staircase became a bar of burnished gold as his hand passed over it in his descent. He lifted the door-latch (it was brass only a moment ago, but golden when his fingers quitted it), and emerged into the garden. Here, as it happened, he found a great number of beautiful roses in full bloom, and others in all the stages of lovely bud and blossom. Very delicious was their fragrance in the morning breeze. Their delicate blush was one of the fairest sights in the world; so gentle, so modest, and so full of sweet tranquillity did these roses seem to be.

But Midas knew a way to make them far more precious, according to his way of thinking, than roses had ever been before. So he took great pains in going from bush to bush, and exercised his magic touch most indefatigably, until every individual flower and bud, and even the worms at the heart of them, were changed to gold. By the time this good work was completed, King Midas was summoned to breakfast; and as the morning air had given him an excellent appetite, he made haste back to the palace.

★　★　★　★

Little Marygold had not yet made her appearance. Her father ordered her to be called, and, seating himself at table, awaited the child's coming, in order to begin his own breakfast. To do Midas justice, he really loved his daughter, and loved her so much the more this morning, on account of the good fortune which had befallen him. It was not a great while before he heard her coming along the passage-way crying bitterly. This circumstance surprised him, because Marygold was one of the cheerfullest little people whom you would see in a summer's day, and hardly shed a thimbleful of tears in a twelvemonth. When Midas heard her sobs, he determined to put little Marygold into better spirits by an agreeable surprise; so, leaning across the table, he touched his daughter's bowl (which was a china one, with pretty figures all around it), and transmuted it to gleaming gold.

Meanwhile Marygold slowly and disconsolately opened the door, and showed herself with her apron at her eyes, still sobbing as if her heart would break.

'How now, my little lady!' cried Midas. 'Pray what is the matter with you, this bright morning?'

Marygold, without taking the apron from her eyes, held out her hand, in which was one of the roses which Midas had so recently transmuted.

'Beautiful!' exclaimed her father. 'And what is there in this magnificent golden rose to make you cry?'

'Ah, dear father!' answered the child, as well as her sobs would let her, 'it is not beautiful, but the ugliest flower that ever grew! As soon as I was dressed, I ran into the garden to gather some roses for you, because I know you like them, and like them the better when gathered by your little daughter. But, O dear, dear me! what do you think has happened? Such a misfortune! All the beautiful roses, that smelled so sweetly and had so many lovely blushes, are blighted and spoilt! They are grown quite yellow, as you see this one, and have no longer any fragrance! What can have been the matter with them?'

'Pooh, my dear little girl! pray don't cry about it!' said Midas, who was ashamed to confess that he himself had wrought the change which so greatly afflicted her. 'Sit down and eat your bread and milk! You will find it easy enough to exchange a golden rose like that (which will last hundreds of years) for an ordinary one which would wither in a day.'

'I don't care for such roses as this!' cried Marygold, tossing it contemptuously away. 'It has no smell, and the hard petals prick my nose!'

The child now sat down to table, but was so occupied with her grief for the blighted roses, that she did not even notice the wonderful transmutation of her china bowl. Perhaps this was all the better; for Marygold was accustomed to take pleasure in looking at the queer figures, and strange trees and houses, that were painted on the circumference of the bowl; and these ornaments were now entirely lost in the yellow hue of the metal.

Midas, meanwhile, had poured out a cup of coffee; and, as a matter of course, the coffee-pot, whatever metal it may have been when he took it up, was gold when he set it down. He thought to himself that it was rather an extravagant style of splendour, in a king of his simple habits, to breakfast off a service of gold, and began to be puzzled with the difficulty of keeping his treasures safe. The cupboard and the kitchen would no longer be a secure place of deposit for articles so valuable as golden bowls and coffee-pots.

Amid these thoughts he lifted a spoonful of coffee to his lips, and, sipping it, was astonished to perceive that, the instant his lips touched the liquid, it became molten gold, and the next moment hardened into a lump!

'Ha!' exclaimed Midas, rather aghast.

'What is the matter, father?' asked little Marygold, gazing at him with the tears still standing in her eyes.

'Nothing, child, nothing!' said Midas. 'Eat your bread and milk before it gets quite cold.'

He took one of the nice little trouts on his plate, and, by way of experiment, touched its tail with his finger. To his horror, it was immediately transmuted from an admirably fried brook trout into a gold fish, though not one of those gold fishes which people often keep in glass globes as ornaments for the parlour. No; but it was really a metallic fish, and looked as if it had been very cunningly made by the cleverest goldsmith in the world.

'Well, this is a quandary!' thought he, leaning back in his chair, and looking quite enviously at little Marygold, who was now eating her bread and milk with great satisfaction. 'Such a costly breakfast before me, and nothing that can be eaten!'

Hoping that, by dint of great despatch, he might avoid what he now felt to be a considerable inconvenience, King Midas next snatched a hot potato, and attempted to cram it into his mouth, and swallow it in a hurry. But the Golden Touch was too nimble for him. He found his mouth full, not of mealy potato, but of solid metal, which so burnt his tongue that he roared aloud, and, jumping up from the table, began to dance and stamp about the room, both with pain and affright.

'Father, dear father!' cried little Marygold, who was a very affectionate child, 'pray what is the matter? Have you burnt your mouth?'

'Ah, dear child,' groaned Midas dolefully, 'I don't know what is to become of your poor father!'

And truly, did you ever hear of such a pitiable case in all your lives? Here was literally the richest breakfast that could be set before a king and its very richness made it absolutely good for nothing. The poorest labourer, sitting down to his crust of bread and cup of water, was far better off than King Midas, whose delicate food was really worth its weight in gold. And what was to be done? Already, at breakfast, Midas was excessively hungry. Would he be less so by dinnertime? And how ravenous would be his appetite for supper, which must undoubtedly consist of the same sort of indigestible dishes as those now before him! How many days, think you, would he survive a continuance of this rich fare?

These reflections so troubled wise King Midas, that he began to doubt whether, after all, riches are the one desirable thing in the world, or even the most desirable. But this was only a passing thought. So fascinated was Midas with the glitter of the yellow metal, that he would still have refused to give up the Golden Touch for so paltry a consideration as a breakfast.

'It would be quite too dear,' thought Midas.

Nevertheless, so great was his hunger and the perplexity of his situation, that he again groaned aloud, and very grievously too. Our pretty Marygold could endure it no longer. She sat a moment gazing at her father, and trying, with all the might of her little wits, to find out what was the matter with him. Then, with a sweet and sorrowful impulse to comfort him, she started from her chair, and, running to Midas, threw her arms affectionately about his knees. He bent down and kissed her. He felt that his little daughter's love was worth a thousand times more than he had gained by the Golden Touch.

'My precious, precious Marygold!' cried he.

But Marygold made no answer.

Alas, what had he done? How fatal was the gift which the stranger bestowed! The moment the lips of Midas touched Marygold's forehead, a change had taken place. Her sweet, rosy face, so full of

Little Marygold was a golden statue

affection as it had been, assumed a glittering yellow colour, with yellow tear-drops congealing on her cheeks. Her beautiful brown ringlets took the same tint. Her soft and tender little form grew hard and inflexible within her father's encircling arms. Oh, terrible misfortune! The victim of his insatiable desire for wealth, little Marygold was a human child no longer, but a golden statue!

It had been a favourite phrase of Midas, whenever he felt particularly fond of the child, to say that she was worth her weight in gold. And now the phrase had become literally true. And now at last, when it was too late, he felt how infinitely a warm and tender heart, that loved him, exceeded in value all the wealth that could be piled up betwixt the earth and sky!

It would be too sad a story if I were to tell you how Midas, in the fulness of all his gratified desires, began to wring his hands and bemoan himself; and how he could neither bear to look at Marygold, nor yet to look away from her. Except when his eyes were fixed on the image, he could not possibly believe that she was changed to gold. But, stealing another glance, there was the precious little figure, with a yellow tear-drop on its yellow cheek, and a look so piteous and tender, that it seemed as if that very expression must needs soften the gold, and make it flesh again. This, however, could not be. So Midas had only to wring his hands, and to wish that he were the poorest man in the wide world, if the loss of all his wealth might bring back the faintest rose-colour to his dear child's face.

While he was in this tumult of despair, he suddenly beheld a stranger standing near the door. Midas bent down his head without speaking, for he recognised the same figure which had appeared to him the day before in the treasure-room, and had bestowed on him this disastrous faculty of the Golden Touch. The stranger's countenance still wore a smile, which seemed to shed a yellow lustre all about the room, and gleamed on little Marygold's image, and on the other objects that had been transmuted by the touch of Midas.

'Well, friend Midas,' said the stranger, 'pray how do you succeed with the Golden Touch?'

Midas shook his head.

'I am very miserable,' said he.

'Very miserable! Indeed!' exclaimed the stranger. 'And how happens that? Have I not faithfully kept my promise to you? Have you not everything that your heart desired?'

'Gold is not everything,' answered Midas. 'And I have lost all that my heart really cared for.'

'Ah! So you have made a discovery since yesterday?' observed the stranger. 'Let us see, then. Which of these two things do you think is really worth the most, – the gift of the Golden Touch, or one cup of clear cold water?'

'O blessed water!' exclaimed Midas. 'It will never moisten my parched throat again!'

'The Golden Touch,' continued the stranger, 'or a crust of bread?'

'A piece of bread,' answered Midas, 'is worth all the gold on earth!'

'The Golden Touch,' asked the stranger, 'or your own little Marygold, warm, soft, and loving, as she was an hour ago?'

'O my child, my dear child!' cried poor Midas, wringing his hands. 'I would not have given that one small dimple in her chin for the power of changing this whole big earth into a solid lump of gold!'

'You are wiser than you were, King Midas!' said the stranger, looking seriously at him. 'Your own heart, I perceive, has not been entirely changed from flesh to gold. Were it so, your case would indeed be desperate. But you appear to be still capable of understanding that the commonest things, such as lie within everybody's grasp, are more valuable than the riches which so many mortals sigh and struggle after. Tell me now, do you sincerely desire to rid yourself of this Golden Touch?'

'It is hateful to me!' replied Midas.

A fly settled on his nose, but immediately fell to the floor; for it, too, had become gold. Midas shuddered.

'Go, then,' said the stranger, 'and plunge into the river that glides past the bottom of your garden. Take likewise a vase of the same water, and sprinkle it over any object that you may desire to change back again from gold into its former substance. If you do this in earnestness and sincerity, it may possibly repair the mischief which your avarice has occasioned.'

King Midas bowed low; and when he lifted his head, the lustrous stranger had vanished.

★   ★   ★   ★

You will easily believe that Midas lost no time in snatching up a great earthen pitcher (but, alas me! it was no longer earthen after he touched it), and hastening to the river side. As he scampered along, and forced his way through the shubbery, it was positively marvellous to see how the foliage turned yellow behind him, as if the autumn had been there, and nowhere else. On reaching the river's brink, he plunged headlong in, without waiting so much as to pull off his shoes.

'Poof! poof! poof!' snorted King Midas as his head emerged out of the water. 'Well, this is really a refreshing bath, and I think it must have quite washed away the Golden Touch. And now for filling my pitcher!'

As he dipped the pitcher into the water, it gladdened his very heart to see it change from gold into the same good, honest earthen vessel which it had been before he touched it. He was conscious, also, of a change within himself. A cold, hard, and heavy weight seemed to have gone out of his bosom. No doubt his heart had been gradually losing its human substance, and transmuting itself into insensible metal, but had now softened back again into flesh. Perceiving a violet that grew on the bank of the river, Midas touched it with his finger, and was overjoyed to find that the delicate flower retained its purple hue, instead of undergoing a yellow blight. The curse of the Golden Touch had therefore really been removed from him.

King Midas hastened back to the palace; and, I suppose, the servants knew not what to make of it when they saw their royal master so carefully bringing home an earthen pitcher of water. But that water, which was to undo all the mischief that his folly had wrought, was more precious to Midas than an ocean of molten gold could have been. The first thing he did, as you need hardly be told, was to sprinkle it by handfuls over the golden figure of little Marygold.

No sooner did it fall on her than you would have laughed to see how the rosy colour came back to the dear child's cheek! – and how she began to sneeze and sputter! – and how astonished she was to find herself dripping wet, and her father still throwing more water over her!

'Pray do not, dear father!' cried she. 'See how you have wet my nice frock, which I put on only this morning!'

For Marygold did not know that she had been a little golden statue; nor could she remember anything that had happened since the moment when she ran with outstretched arms to comfort poor King Midas.

Her father did not think it necessary to tell his beloved child how very foolish he had been, but contented himself with showing how much wiser he had now grown. For this purpose he led little Marygold into the garden, where he sprinkled all the remainder of the water over the rose-bushes, and with such good effect, that above five thousand roses recovered their beautiful bloom. There were two circumstances, however, which, as long as he lived, used to put King Midas in mind of the Golden Touch. One was, that the sands of the river sparkled like gold; the other, that little Marygold's hair had now a golden tinge, which he had never observed in it before she had been transmuted by the effect of his kiss. This change of hue was really an improvement, and made Marygold's hair richer than in her babyhood.

When King Midas had grown quite an old man, and used to trot Marygold's children on his knee, he was fond of telling them this marvellous story, pretty much as I have now told it to you. And then would he stroke their glossy ringlets, and tell them that their hair likewise had a rich shade of gold, which they had inherited from their mother.

'And, to tell you the truth, my precious little folks,' quoth King Midas, diligently trotting the children all the while, 'ever since that morning, I have hated the very sight of all other gold, save this!'

The Story of Robin Hood

ANDREW LANG
Illustrated by H. J. Ford

Robin Hood is one of the most popular folk heroes of Britain, and is said to have lived in Sherwood Forest during the reigns of King Richard the Lionheart and King John.

I
ROBIN HOOD'S ENGLAND

Many hundreds of years ago, when the Plantagenets were kings, England was so covered with woods that a squirrel was said to be able to hop from tree to tree from the Severn to the Humber. It must have been very different to look at from the country we travel through now; but still there were roads that ran from north to south and from east to west, for the use of those that wished to leave their homes, and at certain times of the year these roads were thronged with people. Pilgrims going to some holy shrine passed along, merchants taking their wares to Court, fat Abbots and Bishops ambling by on palfreys nearly as fat as themselves, to bear their part in the King's Council, and, more frequently still, a solitary Knight, seeking adventures.

Besides the broad roads there were small tracks and little green paths, and these led to clumps of low huts, where dwelt the peasants, charcoal-burners, and ploughmen, and here and there some larger clearing than usual told that the house of a yeoman was near. Now and then as you passed through the forest you might ride by a splendid abbey, and catch a glimpse of monks in long black or white gowns, fishing in the streams and rivers that abound in this part of England, or casting nets in the fish ponds which were in the midst of the abbey gardens. Or you might chance to see a castle with round turrets and high battlements, circled by strong walls, and protected by a moat full of water.

This was the sort of England into which the famous Robin Hood was born. We do not know anything about him, who he was, or where he lived, or what evil deed he had done to put him beyond the King's grace. For he was an outlaw, and any man might kill him and never pay penalty for it. But, outlaw or not, the poor people loved him and looked on him as their friend, and many a stout fellow came to join him, and led a merry life in the greenwood, with moss and fern for bed, and for meat the King's deer, which it was death to slay. Peasants of all sorts, tillers of the land, yeomen, and as some say Knights, went on their ways freely, for of them Robin took no toll; but lordly churchmen with money-bags well filled, or proud Bishops with their richly dressed followers, trembled as they drew near to Sherwood Forest – who was to know whether behind every tree there did not lurk Robin Hood or one of his men?

II

THE COMING OF LITTLE JOHN

One day Robin was walking alone in the wood, and reached a river which was spanned by a very narrow bridge, over which one man only could pass. In the midst stood a stranger, and Robin bade him go back and let him go over. 'I am no man of yours,' was all the answer Robin got, and in anger he drew his bow and fitted an arrow to it. 'Would you shoot a man who has no arms but a staff?' asked the stranger in scorn; and with shame Robin laid down his bow, and unbuckled an oaken stick at his side. 'We will fight till one of us falls into the water,' he said; and fight they did, till the stranger planted a blow so well that Robin rolled over into the river. 'You are a brave soul,' said he, when he had waded to land, and he blew a blast with his horn which brought fifty good fellows, clad in green, to the little bridge. 'Have you fallen into the river that your clothes are wet?' asked one; and Robin made answer, 'No, but this stranger, fighting on the bridge, got the better of me, and tumbled me into the stream.'

At this the foresters seized the stranger, and would have ducked him had not their leader bade them stop, and begged the stranger to stay with them and make one of themselves. 'Here is my hand,' replied the stranger, 'and my heart with it. My name, if you would know it, is John Little.'

'That must be altered,' cried Will Scarlett; 'we will call a feast, and henceforth, because he is full seven feet tall and round the waist at least an ell, he shall be called Little John.'

And thus it was done; but at the feast Little John, who always liked to know exactly what work he had to do, put some questions to Robin Hood. 'Before I join hands with you, tell me first what sort of life is this you lead? How am I to know whose goods I shall take, and whose I shall leave? Whom I shall beat, and whom I shall refrain from beating?'

And Robin answered: 'Look that you harm not any tiller of the ground, nor any yeoman of the greenwood – no, nor no Knight nor Squire, unless you have heard him ill spoken of. But if Bishops or Archbishops come your way, see that you spoil *them*, and mark that you always hold in your mind the High Sheriff of Nottingham.'

This being settled, Robin Hood declared Little John to be second in command to himself among the brotherhood of the forest, and the new outlaw never forgot to 'hold in his mind' the High Sheriff of Nottingham, who was the bitterest enemy the foresters had.

III

HOW LITTLE JOHN BECAME THE SHERIFF'S SERVANT

Meanwhile the High Sheriff of Nottingham proclaimed a great shooting-match in a broad open space, and Little John was minded to try his skill with the rest. He rode through the forest, whistling gaily to himself, for well he knew that not one of Robin Hood's men could send an arrow as straight as he, and he felt little fear of anyone else. When he reached the trysting place he found a large company assembled, the Sheriff with them, and the rules of the match were read out: where they were to stand, how far the mark was to be, and how that three tries should be given to every man.

Some of the shooters shot near the mark, some of them even touched it, but none but Little John split the slender wand of willow with every arrow that flew from his bow. And at this sight the Sheriff of Nottingham swore a great oath that Little John was the best archer that ever he had seen, and asked him who he was and where he was born, and vowed that if he would enter his service he would give twenty marks a year to so good a bowman.

Little John, who did not wish to confess that he was one of Robin Hood's men and an outlaw, said his name was Reynold Greenleaf, and that he was in the service of a Knight, whose leave he must get before he became the servant of any man. This was given heartily by the Knight, and Little John bound himself to the Sheriff for the space of twelve months, and was given a good white horse to ride on whenever he went abroad. But for all that he did not like his bargain, and made up his mind to do the Sheriff, who was hated of the outlaws, all the mischief he could.

His chance came on a Wednesday when the Sheriff always went hunting and Little John lay in bed till noon, when he grew hungry. Then he got up, and told the steward that he wanted some dinner. The steward answered he should have nothing till the Sheriff came home, so Little John grumbled and left him, and sought out the butler. Here he was no more successful than before; the butler just went to the buttery door and locked it, and told Little John that he would have to make himself happy till his lord returned.

Rude words mattered nothing to Little John, who was not accustomed to be baulked by trifles, so he gave a mighty kick which burst open the door, and then ate and drank as much as he would, and when he had finished all there was in the buttery, he went down into the kitchen.

Now the Sheriff's cook was a strong man and a bold one, and had no mind to let another man play the king in his kitchen; so he gave Little John three smart blows, which were returned heartily. 'Thou art a brave man and hardy,' said Little John, 'and a good fighter. I have a sword, take you another, and let us see which is the better man of us twain.'

The cook did as he was bid, and for two hours they fought, neither of them harming the other. 'Fellow,' said Little John at last, 'you are one of the best swordsmen that I ever saw – and if you could shoot as well with the bow I would take you back to the merry greenwood, and Robin Hood would give you twenty marks a year and two changes of clothing.'

'Put up your sword,' said the cook, and I will go with you. But first we will have some food in my kitchen, and carry off a little of the gold that is in the Sheriff's treasure house.'

They ate and drank till they wanted no more, then they broke the locks of the treasure house, and took of the silver as much as they could carry, three hundred pounds and more, and departed unseen by anyone to Robin in the forest.

'Welcome! Welcome!' cried Robin when he saw them, 'welcome, too, to the fair yeoman you bring with you. What tidings from Nottingham, Little John?'

'The proud Sheriff greets you, and sends you by my hand his cook and his silver vessels, and three hundred pounds and three also.'

Robin shook his head, for he knew better than to believe Little John's tale. 'It was never by his good will that you brought such treasure to me,' he answered, and Little John, fearing that he might be ordered to take it back again, slipped away into the forest to carry out a plan that had just come into his head.

He ran straight on for five miles, till he came up with the

Sheriff, who was still hunting, and flung himself on his knees before him.

'Reynold Greenleaf,' cried the Sheriff, 'what are you doing here, and where have you been?'

'I have been in the forest, where I saw a fair hart of a green colour, and sevenscore deer feeding hard by.'

'That sight would I see too,' said the Sheriff.

'Then follow me,' answered Little John, and he ran back the way he came, the Sheriff following on horseback, till they turned a corner of the forest, and found themselves in Robin Hood's presence. 'Sir, here is the master-hart,' said Little John.

> Still stood the proud Sheriff,
> A sorry man was he,
> 'Woe be to you, Reynold Greenleaf,
> Thou hast betrayed me!'

'It was not my fault,' answered Little John, 'but the fault of your servants, master. For they would not give me my dinner,' and he went away to see to the supper.

It was spread under the greenwood tree, and they sat down to it, hungry men all. But when the Sheriff saw himself served from his own vessels, his appetite went from him.

'Take heart, man,' said Robin Hood, 'and think not we will poison you. For charity's sake, and for the love of Little John, your life shall be granted you. Only for twelve months you shall dwell with me, and learn what it is to be an outlaw.'

To the Sheriff this punishment was worse to bear than the loss of gold or silver dishes, and earnestly he begged Robin Hood to set him free, vowing he would prove himself the best friend that ever the foresters had.

Neither Robin nor any of his men believed him, but he took a great oath that he would never seek to do them harm, and that if he found any of them in evil plight he would deliver them out of it. With that Robin let him go.

IV

HOW ROBIN MET FRIAR TUCK

In many ways life in the forest was dull in the winter, and often the days passed slowly; but in summer, when the leaves grew green, and flowers and ferns covered all the woodland, Robin Hood and his men would come out of their warm resting places, like the rabbits and the squirrels, and would play too. Races they ran, to stretch their legs, or leaping matches were arranged, or they would shoot at a mark. Anything was pleasant, when the grass was soft once more under their feet.

'Who can kill a hart of grace five hundred paces off?'

So said Robin to his men in the bright May time; and they went into the wood and tried their skill, and in the end it was Little John who brought down the 'hart of grace,' to the great joy of Robin Hood. 'I would ride my horse a hundred miles to find one who could match with thee,' he said to Little John, and Will Scarlett, who was perhaps rather jealous of this mighty deed, answered with a laugh, 'There lives a friar in Fountains Abbey who would beat both him and you.'

Now Robin Hood did not like to be told that any man could shoot better than himself or his foresters, so he swore lustily that he would neither eat nor drink till he had seen that friar. Leaving his men where they were, he put on a coat of mail and a steel cap, took his shield and sword, slung his bow over his shoulder, and filled his quiver with arrows. Thus armed, he set forth to Fountains Dale.

By the side of the river a friar was walking, armed like Robin, but without a bow. At this sight Robin jumped from his horse, which he tied to a thorn, and called to the friar to carry him over the water or it would cost him his life.

The friar said nothing, but hoisted Robin on his broad back and marched into the river. Not a word was spoken till they reached the other side, when Robin leaped lightly down, and was going on his way when the friar stopped him. 'Not so fast, my fine fellow,' said he. 'It is my turn now, and you shall take me across the river, or woe will betide you.' So Robin carried him, and when they had reached the side from which they had started he set down the friar and jumped for the second time on his back, and bade him take him whence he had come. The friar strode into the stream with his burden, but as soon as they got to the middle he bent his head and Robin fell into the water. 'Now you can sink or swim as you like,' said the friar, as he stood and laughed.

Robin Hood swam to a bush of golden broom, and pulled himself out of the water, and while the friar was scrambling out Robin fitted an arrow to his bow and let fly at him. But the friar quickly held up his shield, and the arrow fell harmless.

'Shoot on, my fine fellow, shoot on all day if you like,' shouted the friar, and Robin shot till his arrows were gone, but always missed his mark. Then they took their swords, and at four of the afternoon they were still fighting.

By this time Robin's strength was wearing, and he felt he could not fight much more. 'A boon, a boon!' cried he. 'Let me but blow three blasts on my horn, and I will thank you on my bended knees for it.'

The friar told him to blow as many blasts as he liked, and in an instant the forest echoed with his horn; it was but a few minutes before half a hundred yeomen were racing over the lea. The friar stared when he saw them; then turning to Robin, he begged of him a boon also, and leave being granted he gave three whistles, which were followed by the noise of a great crashing through the trees, as fifty great dogs bounded towards him.

'Here's a dog for each of your men,' said the friar, 'and I myself for you'; but the dogs did not listen to his words, for two of them rushed at Robin, and tore his mantle of Lincoln green from off his back. His men were too busy defending themselves to take heed of their master's plight, for every arrow shot at a dog was caught and held in the creature's mouth.

Robin's men were not used to fight with dogs, and felt they were getting beaten. At last Little John bade the friar call off his dogs, and as he did not do so at once he let fly some arrows, which this time left half a dozen dead on the ground.

'Hold, hold, my good fellow,' said the friar, 'till your master and I can come to a bargain,' and when the bargain was made this was how it ran. That the friar was to forswear Fountains Abbey and join Robin Hood, and that he should be paid a golden noble every Sunday throughout the year, besides a change of clothes on each holy day.

> This Friar had kept Fountains Dale
>   Seven long years or more,
> There was neither Knight, nor Lord, nor Earl
>   Could make him yield before.

But now he became one of the most famous members of Robin Hood's men under the name of Friar Tuck.

V

HOW THE KING VISITED ROBIN HOOD

Now the King had no mind that Robin Hood should do as he willed, and called his Knights to follow him to Nottingham, where they would lay plans how best to take captive the felon. Here they heard sad tales of Robin's misdoings, and how of the many herds of wild deer that had been wont to roam the forest in some places scarce one remained. This was the work of Robin Hood and his merry men, on whom the King swore vengeance with a great oath.

'I would I had this Robin Hood in my hands,' cried he, 'and an end should soon be put to his doings.' So spake the King; but an old Knight, full of days and wisdom, answered him and warned him that the task of taking Robin Hood would be a sore one, and best let alone. The King, who had seen the vanity of his hot words the moment that he had uttered them, listened to the old man, and resolved to bide his time, if perchance some day Robin should fall into his power.

All this time and for six weeks later that he dwelt in Nottingham the King could hear nothing of Robin, who seemed to have vanished into the earth with his merry men, though one by one the deer were vanishing too!

At last one day a forester came to the King, and told him that if he would see Robin he must come with him and take five of his best Knights. The King eagerly sprang up to do his bidding, and the six men clad in monks' clothes mounted their palfreys and rode down to the Abbey, the King wearing an Abbot's broad hat over his crown and singing as he passed through the greenwood.

Suddenly at the turn of a path Robin and his archers appeared before them.

'By your leave, Sir Abbot,' said Robin, seizing the King's bridle, 'you will stay a while with us. Know that we are yeomen, who live upon the King's deer, and other food have we none. Now you have abbeys and churches, and gold in plenty; therefore give us some of it, in the name of holy charity.'

'I have no more than forty pounds with me,' answered the King, 'but sorry I am it is not a hundred, for you should have had it all.'

So Robin took the forty pounds, and gave half to his men, and then told the King he might go on his way. 'I thank you,' said the King, 'but I would have you know that our liege lord has bid me bear you his seal, and pray you to come to Nottingham.'

At this message Robin bent his knee. 'I love no man in all the world so well as I do my King', he cried, 'and Sir Abbot, for thy tidings, which fill my heart with joy, to-day thou shalt dine with me, for love of my King.' Then he led the King into an open place, and Robin took a horn and blew it loud, and at its blast seven score of young men came speedily to do his will.

'They are quicker to do his bidding than my men are to do mine,' said the King to himself.

Speedily the foresters set out the dinner, venison, and white bread, and the good red wine, and Robin and Little John served the King. 'Make good cheer,' said Robin, 'Abbot, for charity, and

There is pith in your arm said ROBIN HOOD

then you shall see what sort of life we lead, that so you may tell our King.'

When he had finished eating the archers took their bows, and hung rose-garlands up with a string, and every man was to shoot through the garland. If he failed, he should have a buffet on the head from Robin.

Good bowmen as they were, few managed to stand the test. Little John and Will Scarlett, and Much, all shot wide of the mark, and at length no one was left in but Robin himself and Gilbert of the White Hand. Then Robin fired his last bolt, and it fell three fingers from the garland. 'Master,' said Gilbert, 'you have lost, stand forth and take your punishment.'

'I will take it,' answered Robin, 'but, Sir Abbot, I pray you that I may suffer it at your hands.'

The King hesitated. 'It did not become him,' he said, 'to smite such a stout yeoman,' but Robin bade him smite on; so he turned up his sleeve, and gave Robin such a buffet on the head that he rolled upon the ground.

'There is pith in your arm,' said Robin. 'Come, shoot a main with me.' And the King took up a bow, and in so doing his hat fell back and Robin saw his face.

'My lord the King of England, now I know you well,' cried he, and he fell on his knees and all the outlaws with him. 'Mercy I ask, my lord the King, for my men and me.'

'Mercy I grant,' then said the King, 'and therefore I came hither, to bid you and your men leave the greenwood and dwell in my Court with me.'

'So shall it be,' answered Robin, 'I and my men will come to your Court, and see how your service pleases us.'

VI

ROBIN AT COURT

'Have you any green cloth,' asked the King, 'that you could sell to me?' and Robin brought out thirty yards and more, and clad the King and his men in coats of Lincoln green. 'Now we will all ride to Nottingham,' said he, and they went merrily, shooting by the way.

The people of Nottingham saw them coming, and trembled as they watched the dark mass of Lincoln green drawing near over the fields. 'I fear lest our King be slain,' whispered one to another, 'and if Robin Hood gets into the town there is not one of us whose life is safe'; and every man, woman, and child made ready to fly.

The King laughed out when he saw their fright, and called them back. Right glad were they to hear his voice, and they feasted and made merry. A few days later the King returned to London, and Robin dwelt in his Court for twelve months. By that time he had spent a hundred pounds, for he gave largely to the Knights and Squires he met, and great renown he had for his open-handedness.

But his men, who had been born under the shadow of the forest, could not live amid streets and houses. One by one they slipped away, till only Little John and Will Scarlett were left. Then Robin himself grew home-sick, and at the sight of some young men shooting thought upon the time when he was accounted the best archer in all England, and went straightway to the King and begged for leave to go on a pilgrimage to Bernisdale.

'I may not say you nay,' answered the King, 'seven nights you may be gone and no more.' And Robin thanked him, and that evening set out for the greenwood.

It was early morning when he reached it at last, and listened thirstily to the notes of singing birds, great and small.

'It seems long since I was here,' he said to himself; 'it would give me great joy if I could bring down a deer once more'; and he shot a great hart, and blew his horn, and all the outlaws of the forest came flocking round him. 'Welcome,' they said, 'our dear master, back to the greenwood tree,' and they threw off their caps and fell on their knees before him in delight at his return.

VII

THE DEATH OF ROBIN HOOD

For two and twenty years Robin Hood dwelt in Sherwood Forest after he had run away from Court, and naught that the King could say would tempt him back again. At the end of that time he fell ill; he neither ate nor drank, and had no care for the things he loved. 'I must go to merry Kirkley,' said he, 'and have my blood let.'

But Will Scarlett, who heard his words, spoke roundly to him. 'Not by *my* leave, nor without a hundred bowmen at your back. For there abides an evil man, who is sure to quarrel with you, and you will need us badly.'

'If you are afraid, Will Scarlett, you may stay at home, for me,' said Robin, 'and in truth no man will I take with me, save Little John only, to carry my bow.'

'Bear your bow yourself, master, and I will bear mine, and we will shoot for a penny as we ride.'

'Very well, let it be so,' said Robin, and they went on merrily enough till they came to some women weeping sorely near a stream.

'What is the matter, good wives?' said Robin Hood.

'We weep for Robin Hood and his dear body, which to-day must let blood,' was their answer.

'Pray why do you weep for me?' asked Robin; 'the Prioress is the daughter of my aunt, and my cousin, and well I know she would not do me harm for all the world.' And he passed on, with Little John at his side.

Soon they reached the Priory, where they were let in by the Prioress herself, who bade them welcome heartily, and not the less because Robin handed her twenty pounds in gold as payment for his stay, and told her if he cost her more she was to let him know of it. Then she began to bleed him, and for long Robin said nothing, giving her credit for kindness and for knowing her art, but at length so much blood came from him that he suspected treason. He tried to open the door, for she had left him alone in the room, but it was locked fast, and while

ROBIN HOOD SHOOTS HIS LAST ARROW

the blood was still flowing he could not escape from the casement. So he lay down for many hours, and none came near him, and at length the blood stopped. Slowly Robin uprose and staggered to the lattice-window, and blew thrice on his horn; but the blast was so low, and so little like what Robin was wont to give, that Little John, who was watching for some sound, felt that his master must be nigh to death.

At this thought he started to his feet, and ran swiftly to the Priory. He broke the locks of all the doors that stood between him and Robin Hood, and soon entered the chamber where his master lay, white, with nigh all his blood gone from him.

'I crave a boon of you, dear master,' cried Little John.

'And what is that boon,' said Robin Hood, 'which Little John begs of me?' And Little John answered, 'It is to burn fair Kirkley Hall, and all the nunnery.'

But Robin Hood, in spite of the wrong that had been done him, would not listen to Little John's cry for revenge. 'I never hurt a woman in all my life,' he said, 'nor a man that was in her company. But now my time is done, that know I well; so give me my bow and a broad arrow, and wheresoever it falls there shall my grave be dug. Lay a green sod under my head and another at my feet, and put beside me my bow, which ever made sweetest music to my ears, and see that green and gravel make my grave. And, Little John, take care that I have length enough and breadth enough to lie in.' So he loosened his last arrow from the string and then died, and where the arrow fell Robin was buried.

Comic Stories

A Mad Tea-Party

LEWIS CARROLL
Illustrated by John Tenniel

This is one of the chapters from Alice's Adventures in Wonderland *(1865). Its author, whose real name was the Rev. C. L. Dodgson, lectured in mathematics at Oxford University when he was not writing children's stories.*

There was a table set out under a tree in front of the house, and the March Hare and the Hatter were having tea at it: a Dormouse was sitting between them, fast asleep, and the other two were using it as a cushion, resting their elbows on it, and talking over its head. 'Very uncomfortable for the Dormouse,' thought Alice; 'only as it's asleep, I suppose it doesn't mind.'

The table was a large one, but the three were all crowded together at one corner of it. 'No room! No room!' they cried out when they saw Alice coming. 'There's *plenty* of room!' said Alice indignantly, and she sat down in a large arm-chair at one end of the table.

'Have some wine,' the March Hare said in an encouraging tone.

Alice looked all round the table, but there was nothing on it but tea. 'I don't see any wine,' she remarked.

'There isn't any,' said the March Hare.

'Then it wasn't very civil of you to offer it,' said Alice angrily.

'It wasn't very civil of you to sit down without being invited,' said the March Hare.

'I didn't know it was *your* table,' said Alice: 'it's laid for a great many more than three.'

'Your hair wants cutting,' said the Hatter. He had been looking at Alice for some time with great curiosity, and this was his first speech.

'You should learn not to make personal remarks,' Alice said with some severity: 'it's very rude.'

The Hatter opened his eyes very wide on hearing this; but all he *said* was 'Why is a raven like a writing-desk?'

'Come, we shall have some fun now!' thought Alice. 'I'm glad they've begun asking riddles – I believe I can guess that,' she added aloud.

'Do you mean that you think you can find out the answer to it,' said the March Hare.

'Exactly so,' said Alice.

'Then you should say what you mean,' the March Hare went on.

'I do,' Alice hastily replied; 'at least – at least I mean what I say – that's the same thing, you know.'

'Not the same thing a bit!' said the Hatter. 'Why, you might just as well say that "I see what I eat" is the same thing as "I eat what I see"!'

'You might just as well say,' added the March Hare, 'that "I like what I get" is the same thing as "I get what I like"!'

'You might just as well say,' added the Dormouse, which seemed to be talking in its sleep, 'that "I breathe when I sleep" is the same thing as "I sleep when I breathe"!'

'It *is* the same thing with you,' said the Hatter, and here the conversation dropped, and the party sat silent for a minute, while Alice thought over all she could remember about ravens and writing-desks, which wasn't much.

The Hatter was the first to break the silence. 'What day of the month is it?' he said, turning to Alice: he had taken his watch out of his pocket, and was looking at it uneasily, shaking it every now and then, and holding it to his ear.

Alice considered a little, and then said, 'The fourth.'

'Two days wrong!' sighed the Hatter. 'I told you butter wouldn't suit the works!' he added, looking angrily at the March Hare.

'It was the *best* butter,' the March Hare meekly replied.

'Yes, but some crumbs must have got in as well,' the Hatter grumbled: 'you shouldn't have put it in with the bread-knife.'

The March Hare took the watch and looked at it gloomily; then he dipped it into his cup of tea, and looked at it again: but he could think of nothing better to say than his first remark, 'It was the *best* butter, you know.'

Alice had been looking over his shoulder with some curiosity. 'What a funny watch!' she remarked. 'It tells the day of the month, and doesn't tell what o'clock it is!'

'Why should it?' muttered the Hatter. 'Does *your* watch tell you what year it is?'

'Of course not,' Alice replied very readily: 'but that's because it stays the same year for such a long time together.'

'Which is just the case with *mine*,' said the Hatter.

Alice felt dreadfully puzzled. The Hatter's remark seemed to her to have no sort of meaning in it, and yet it was certainly English. 'I don't quite understand you,' she said, as politely as she could.

'The Dormouse is asleep again,' said the Hatter, and he poured a little hot tea upon its nose.

The Dormouse shook its head impatiently, and said, without opening its eyes, 'Of course, of course: just what I was going to remark myself.'

'Have you guessed the riddle yet?' the Hatter said, turning to Alice again.

'No, I give it up,' Alice replied. 'What's the answer?'

'I haven't the slightest idea,' said the Hatter.

'Nor I,' said the March Hare.

Alice sighed wearily. 'I think you might do something better with the time,' she said, 'than wasting it in asking riddles that have no answers.'

'If you knew Time as well as I do,' said the Hatter, 'you wouldn't talk about wasting *it*. It's *him*.'

'I don't know what you mean,' said Alice.

'Of course you don't,' the Hatter said, tossing his head contemptuously. 'I dare say you never spoke to Time!'

'Perhaps not,' Alice cautiously replied, 'but I know I have to beat time when I learn music.'

'Ah! That accounts for it,' said the Hatter. 'He wo'n't stand beating. Now, if you only kept on good terms with him, he'd do almost anything you liked with the clock. For instance, suppose it were nine o'clock in the morning, just time to begin lessons: you'd only have to whisper a hint to Time, and round goes the clock in a twinkling! Half-past one, time for dinner!'

('I only wish it was,' the March Hare said to itself in a whisper.)

'That would be grand, certainly,' said Alice thoughtfully; 'but then – I shouldn't be hungry for it, you know.'

'Not at first, perhaps,' said the Hatter: 'but you could keep it to half-past one as long as you liked.'

'Is that the way *you* manage?' Alice asked.

The Hatter shook his head mournfully. 'Not I!' he replied. 'We quarrelled last March – just before *he* went mad, you know—' (pointing with his teaspoon at the March Hare), '—it was at the great concert given by the Queen of Hearts, and I had to sing

Twinkle, twinkle, little bat!
How I wonder what you're at!

You know the song, perhaps?'

'I've heard something like it,' said Alice.

'It goes on, you know,' the Hatter continued, 'in this way:–

Up above the world you fly,
Like a tea-tray in the sky.
Twinkle, twinkle—'

Here the Dormouse shook itself and began singing in its sleep *'Twinkle, twinkle, twinkle, twinkle—'* and went on so long that they had to pinch it to make it stop.

'Well, I'd hardly finished the first verse,' said the Hatter, 'when the Queen bawled out, "He's murdering the time! Off with his head!"'

'How dreadfully savage!' exclaimed Alice.

'And ever since that,' the Hatter went on in a mournful tone, 'he won't do a thing I ask! It's always six o'clock now.'

A bright idea came into Alice's head. 'Is that the reason so many tea-things are put out here?' she asked.

'Yes, that's it,' said the Hatter with a sigh: 'it's always tea-time, and we've no time to wash the things between whiles.'

'Then you keep moving round, I suppose?' said Alice.

'Exactly so,' said the Hatter: 'as the things get used up.'

'But what happens when you come to the beginning again?' Alice ventured to ask.

'Suppose we change the subject,' the March Hare interrupted, yawning. 'I'm getting tired of this. I vote the young lady tells us a story.'

'I'm afraid I don't know one,' said Alice, rather alarmed at the proposal.

'Then the Dormouse shall!' they both cried. 'Wake up, Dormouse!' And they pinched it on both sides at once.

The Dormouse slowly opened its eyes. 'I wasn't asleep,' it said in a hoarse, feeble voice, 'I heard every word you fellows were saying.'

'Tell us a story!' said the March Hare.

'Yes, please do!' pleaded Alice.

'And be quick about it,' added the Hatter, 'or you'll be asleep again before it's done.'

'Once upon a time there were three little sisters,' the Dormouse began in a great hurry; 'and their names were Elsie, Lacie, and Tillie; and they lived at the bottom of a well—'

'What did they live on?' said Alice, who always took a great interest in questions of eating and drinking.

'They lived on treacle,' said the Dormouse, after thinking a minute or two.

'They couldn't have done that, you know,' Alice gently remarked. 'They'd have been ill.'

'So they were,' said the Dormouse; '*very* ill.'

Alice tried a little to fancy to herself what such an extraordinary way of living would be like, but it puzzled her too much: so she went on: 'But why did they live at the bottom of a well?'

'Take some more tea,' the March Hare said to Alice, earnestly.

'I've had nothing yet,' Alice replied in an offended tone: 'so I ca'n't take more.'

'You mean you ca'n't take *less*,' said the Hatter: 'it's very easy to take *more* than nothing.'

'Nobody asked *your* opinion,' said Alice.

'Who's making personal remarks now?' the Hatter asked triumphantly.

Alice did not quite know what to say to this: so she helped herself to some tea and bread-and-butter, and then turned to the Dormouse, and repeated her question. 'Why did they live at the bottom of a well?'

The Dormouse again took a minute or two to think about it, and then said 'It was a treacle-well.'

'There's no such thing!' Alice was beginning very angrily, but the Hatter and the March Hare went 'Sh! Sh!' and the Dormouse sulkily remarked 'If you ca'n't be civil, you'd better finish the story for yourself.'

'No, please go on!' Alice said very humbly. 'I wo'n't interrupt you again. I dare say there may be *one*.'

'One, indeed!' said the Dormouse indignantly. However, he consented to go on. 'And so these three little sisters – they were learning to draw, you know—'

'What did they draw?' said Alice, quite forgetting her promise.

'Treacle,' said the Dormouse, without considering at all, this time.

'I want a clean cup,' interrupted the Hatter: 'let's all move one place on.'

He moved on as he spoke, and the Dormouse followed him: the March Hare moved into the Dormouse's place, and Alice rather unwillingly took the place of the March Hare. The Hatter was the only one who got any advantage from the change; and Alice was a good deal worse off than before, as the March Hare had just upset the milk-jug into his plate.

Alice did not wish to offend the Dormouse again, so she began very cautiously: 'But I don't understand. Where did they draw the treacle from?'

'You can draw water out of a water-well,' said the Hatter; 'so I should think you could draw treacle out of a treacle-well – eh, stupid?'

'But they were *in* the well,' Alice said to the Dormouse, not choosing to notice this last remark.

'Of course they were,' said the Dormouse: 'well in.'

This answer so confused poor Alice, that she let the Dormouse go on for some time without interrupting it.

'They were learning to draw,' the Dormouse went on, yawning and rubbing its eyes, for it was getting very sleepy; 'and they drew all manner of things – everything that begins with an M—'

'Why with an M?' said Alice.

'Why not?' said the March Hare.

Alice was silent.

The Dormouse had closed its eyes by this time, and was going off into a doze; but, on being pinched by the Hatter, it woke up again with a little shriek, and went on: '—that begins with an M, such as mouse-traps, and the moon, and memory, and muchness – you know you say things are "much of a muchness" – did you ever see such a thing as a drawing of a muchness?'

'Really, now you ask me,' said Alice, very much confused, 'I don't think—'

'Then you shouldn't talk,' said the Hatter.

This piece of rudeness was more than Alice could bear: she got up in great disgust, and walked off: the Dormouse fell asleep instantly, and neither of the others took the least notice of her going, though she looked back once or twice, half hoping that they would call after her: the last time she saw them, they were trying to put the Dormouse into the teapot.

'At any rate I'll never go *there* again!' said Alice, as she picked her way through the wood. 'It's the stupidest tea-party I ever was at in all my life!'

Whitewashing

_____

MARK TWAIN
Illustrated by Ian Beck

This is a chapter from The Adventures of Tom Sawyer _(1876)._

Saturday morning was come, and all the summer world was bright
and fresh, and brimming with life. There was a song in every
heart; and if the heart was young the music issued at the lips. There
was cheer in every face, and a spring in every step. The locust trees
were in bloom, and the fragrance of the blossoms filled the air.

Cardiff Hill, beyond the village and above it, was green with
vegetation, and it lay just far enough away to seem a Delectable Land,
dreamy, reposeful, and inviting.

Tom appeared on the side-walk with a bucket of white-wash and a
long-handled brush. He surveyed the fence, and the gladness went out
of nature, and a deep melancholy settled down upon his spirit. Thirty
yards of board fence nine feet high! It seemed to him that life was
hollow, and existence but a burden. Sighing he dipped his brush and
passed it along the topmost plank; repeated the operation; did it again;
compared the insignificant whitewashed streak with the far-reaching
continent of unwhitewashed fence, and sat down on a tree-box
discouraged. Jim came skipping out at the gate with a tin pail, and
singing _Buffalo Gals_. Bringing water from the town pump had always
been hateful work in Tom's eyes before, but now it did not strike him
so. He remembered that there was company at the pump. White,
mulatto, and Negro boys and girls were always there waiting their
turns, resting, trading playthings, quarrelling, fighting, skylarking.
And he remembered that although the pump was only a hundred and
fifty yards off Jim never got back with a bucket of water under an
hour; and even then somebody generally had to go after him. Tom said:

'Say, Jim; I'll fetch the water if you'll whitewash some.'

Jim shook his head, and said:

'Can't, Ma'rs Tom. Ole missis she tole me I got to go an' git dis water an' not stop foolin' 'roun' wid anybody. She say she spec' Ma'rs Tom gwyne to ax me to whitewash, an' so she tole me go 'long an' 'tend to my own business – she 'lowed *she'd* 'tend to de whitewashin'.'

'Oh, never you mind what she said, Jim. That's the way she always talks. Gimme the bucket – I won't be gone only a minute. *She* won't ever know.'

'Oh, I dasn't, Ma'rs Tom. Ole missis she'd take an' tar de head off'n me. 'Deed she would.'

'*She*! she never licks anybody – whacks 'em over the head with her thimble, and who cares for that, I'd like to know? She talks awful, but talk don't hurt – anyways, it don't if she don't cry. Jim, I'll give you a marble. I'll give you a white alley!'

Jim began to waver.

'White alley, Jim; and it's a bully taw.'

'My: dat's a mighty gay marvel, *I* tell you. But, Ma'rs Tom, I's powerful 'fraid ole missis.'

'And besides, if you will, I'll show you my sore toe.'

But Jim was only human – this attraction was too much for him. He put down his pail, took the white alley. In another minute he was flying down the street with his pail and a tingling rear. Tom was whitewashing with vigour, and Aunt Polly was retiring from the field with a slipper in her hand and triumph in her eye.

But Tom's energy did not last. He began to think of the fun he had planned for this day, and his sorrows multiplied. Soon the free boys would come tripping along on all sorts of delicious expeditions, and they would make a world of fun of him for having to work – the very thought of it burnt him like fire. He got out his worldly wealth and examined it – bits of toys, marbles, and trash; enough to buy an exchange of work maybe, but not enough to buy so much as half an hour of pure freedom. So he returned his straitened means to his pocket, and gave up the idea of trying to buy the boys. At this dark and hopeless moment an inspiration burst upon him. Nothing less than a great, magnificent inspiration.

He took up his brush and went tranquilly to work. Ben Rogers hove in sight presently; the very boy of all boys whose ridicule he had been dreading. Ben's gait was the hop, skip, and jump – proof enough that his heart was light and his anticipations high. He was eating an apple, and giving a long melodious whoop at intervals, followed by a deep-toned ding dong dong, ding dong dong, for he was personating a steamboat! As he drew near he slackened speed, took the middle of the street, leaned far over to starboard, and rounded-to ponderously, and with laborious pomp and circumstance, for he was personating the *Big Missouri*, and considered himself to be drawing nine feet of water. He was boat, and captain, and engine-bells combined, so he had to imagine himself standing on his own hurricane-deck giving the orders and executing them.

'Stop her, sir! Ling-a-ling-ling.' The headway ran almost out, and he drew up slowly towards the side-walk. 'Ship up to back! Ling-a-ling-ling!' His arms straightened and stiffened down his sides. 'Set her back on the stabboard! Ling-a-ling-ling! Chow! ch-chow-wow-chow!' his right hand meantime describing stately circles, for it was representing a forty-foot wheel. 'Let her go back on the labboard! Ling-a-ling-ling! Chow-ch-chow-chow!' The left hand began to describe circles.

'Stop the stabboard! Ling-a-ling-ling! Stop the labboard! Come ahead on the stabboard! Stop her! Let your outside turn over slow! Ling-a-ling-ling! Chow-ow-ow! Get out that head-line! Lively, now! Come – out with your spring-line – what're you about there? Take a turn round that stump with the bight of it! Stand by that stage now – let her go! Done with the engines, sir! Ling-a-ling-ling!'

'Sht! s'sht! sht!' (Trying the gauge-cocks.)

Tom went on whitewashing – paid no attention to the steamer. Ben stared a moment, and then said:

'Hi-yi! You're up a stump, ain't you?'

No answer. Tom surveyed his last touch with the eye of an artist;

then he gave his brush another gentle sweep, and surveyed the result as before. Ben ranged up alongside of him. Tom's mouth watered for the apple, but he stuck to his work. Ben said:

'Hello, old chap; you got to work, hey?'

'Why, it's you, Ben! I warn't noticing.'

'Say, I'm going in a swimming, I am. Don't you wish you could? But of course, you'd druther work, wouldn't you? 'Course you would!'

Tom contemplated the boy a bit, and said:

'What do you call work?'

'Why, ain't that work?'

Tom resumed his whitewashing, and answered carelessly:

'Well, maybe it is, and maybe it ain't. All I know is, it suits Tom Sawyer.'

'Oh, come now, you don't mean to let on that you like it?'

The brush continued to move.

'Like it? Well, I don't see why I oughtn't to like it. Does a boy get a chance to whitewash a fence every day?'

That put the thing in a new light. Ben stopped nibbling his apple. Tom swept his brush daintily back and forth – stepped back to note the effect – added a touch here and there – criticized the effect again, Ben watching every move, and getting more and more interested, more and more absorbed. Presently he said:

'Say, Tom, let me whitewash a little.'

Tom considered; was about to consent; but he altered his mind: 'No, no; I reckon it wouldn't hardly do, Ben. You see, Aunt Polly's awful particular about this fence – right here on the street, you know – but if it was the back fence I wouldn't mind, and she wouldn't.. Yes she's awful particular about this fence: it's got to be done very careful: I reckon there ain't one boy in a thousand, maybe two thousand, that can do it the way it's got to be done.'

'No – is that so? Oh, come now; lemme just try, only just a little. I'd let you, if you was me, Tom.'

'Ben, I'd like to, honest injun; but Aunt Polly – well, Jim wanted to

The retired artist sat on a barrel in the shade

do it, but she wouldn't let him. Sid wanted to do it, but she wouldn't let Sid. Now, don't you see how I am fixed? If you was to tackle this fence, and anything was to happen to it—'

'Oh, shucks; I'll be just as careful. Now lemme try. Say – I'll give you the core of my apple.'

'Well, here. No, Ben; now don't; I'm afeard—'

'I'll give you all of it!'

Tom gave up the brush with reluctance in his face, but alacrity in his heart. And while the late steamer *Big Missouri* worked and sweated in the sun, the retired artist sat on a barrel in the shade close by, dangled his legs, munched his apple, and planned the slaughter of more innocents. There was no lack of material; boys happened along every little while; they came to jeer, but remained to whitewash. By the time Ben was fagged out, Tom had traded the next chance to Billy Fisher for a kite in good repair; and when he played out, Johnny Miller bought in for a dead rat and a string to swing it with; and so on, and so on, hour after hour. And when the middle of the afternoon came, from being a poor poverty-stricken boy in the morning Tom was literally rolling in wealth. He had besides the things I have mentioned, twelve marbles, part of a jew's harp, a piece of blue bottle-glass to look through, a spool-cannon, a key that wouldn't unlock anything, a fragment of chalk, a glass stopper of a decanter, a tin soldier, a couple of tadpoles, six fire-crackers, a kitten with only one eye, a brass door-knob, a dog-collar – but no dog – the handle of a knife, four pieces of orange-peel, and a dilapidated old window-sash. He had had a nice, good, idle time all the while – plenty of company – and the fence had three coats of whitewash on it! If he hadn't run out of whitewash he would have bankrupted every boy in the village.

Tom said to himself that it was not such a hollow world after all. He had discovered a great law of human action, without knowing it, namely, that, in order to make a man or a boy covet a thing, it is only necessary to make the thing difficult to attain. If he had been a great and wise philosopher, like the writer of this book, he would now have comprehended that work consists of whatever a body is obliged to do, and that play consists of whatever a body is not obliged to do. And this would help him to understand why constructing artificial flowers, or performing on a treadmill, is work, whilst rolling nine-pins or climbing Mont Blanc is only amusement. There are wealthy gentlemen in England who drive four-horse passenger-coaches twenty or thirty miles on a daily line, in the summer, because the privilege costs them considerable money; but if they were offered wages for the service that would turn it into work, then they would resign.

Rip Van Winkle

WASHINGTON IRVING

Illustrated by Gordon Browne

Whoever has made a voyage up the Hudson must remember the Kaatskill mountains. They are a dismembered branch of the great Appalachian family, and are seen away to the west of the river, swelling up to a noble height, and lording it over the surrounding country. Every change of season, every change of weather, indeed, every hour of the day, produces some change in the magical hues and shapes of these mountains, and they are regarded by all the good wives, far and near, as perfect barometers. When the weather is fair and settled, they are clothed in blue and purple, and print their bold outlines on the clear evening sky; but sometimes, when the rest of the landscape is cloudless, they will gather a hood of grey vapours about their summits, which, in the last rays of the setting sun, will glow and light up like a crown of glory.

At the foot of these fairy mountains, the voyager may have descried the light smoke curling up from a village, whose shingle-roofs gleam among the trees, just where the blue tints of the upland melt away into the fresh green of the nearer landscape. It is a little village, of great antiquity, having been founded by some of the Dutch colonists, in the early times of the province, just about the beginning of the govern-ment of the good Peter Stuyvesant (may he rest in peace!) and there were some of the houses of the original settlers standing within a few years, built of small yellow bricks brought from Holland, having latticed windows and gable fronts, surmounted with weathercocks.

In that same village and in one of these very houses (which, to tell the precise truth, was sadly time-worn and weather-beaten), there lived many years since, while the country was yet a province of Great Britain, a simple good-natured fellow, of the name of Rip Van

Winkle. He was a descendant of the Van Winkles who figured so gallantly in the chivalrous days of Peter Stuyvesant, and accompanied him to the siege of Fort Christina. He inherited, however, but little of the martial character of his ancestors. I have observed that he was a simple good-natured man; he was, moreover, a kind neighbour, and an obedient hen-pecked husband. Indeed, to the latter circumstance might be owing that meekness of spirit which gained him such universal popularity; for those men are most apt to be obsequious and conciliating abroad, who are under the discipline of shrews at home. Their tempers, doubtless, are rendered pliant and malleable in the fiery furnace of domestic tribulation, and a curtain lecture is worth all the sermons in the world for teaching the virtues of patience and long-suffering. A termagant wife may, therefore, in some respects, be considered a tolerable blessing; and if so, Rip Van Winkle was thrice blessed.

Certain it is that he was a great favourite among all the good wives of the village, who, as usual with the amiable sex, took his part in all family squabbles; and never failed, whenever they talked those matters over in their evening gossipings, to lay all the blame on Dame Van Winkle. The children of the village, too, would shout with joy whenever he approached. He assisted at their sports, made their playthings, taught them to fly kites and shoot marbles, and told them long stories of ghosts, witches, and Indians. Whenever he went dodging about the village, he was surrounded by a troop of them hanging on his skirts, clambering on his back, and playing a thousand tricks on him with impunity; and not a dog would bark at him throughout the neighbourhood.

The great error in Rip's composition was an insuperable aversion to all kinds of profitable labour. It could not be from the want of assiduity or perseverance; for he would sit on a wet rock, with a rod as long and heavy as a Tartar's lance, and fish all day without a murmur, even though he should not be encouraged by a single nibble. He would carry a fowling-piece on his shoulder for hours together, trudging through woods and swamps, and up hill and down dale, to shoot a few squirrels or wild pigeons. He would never refuse to assist a neighbour even in the roughest toil, and was a foremost man at all country frolics for husking Indian corn, or building stone fences; the women of the village, too, used to employ him to run their errands, and to do such little odd jobs as their less obliging husbands would not do for them. In a word, Rip was ready to attend to anybody's business but his own; but as to doing family duty, and keeping his farm in order, he found it impossible.

In fact, he declared it was of no use to work on his farm; it was the most pestilent little piece of ground in the whole country; everything about it went wrong, and would go wrong, in spite of him. His fences were continually falling to pieces; his cow would either go astray, or get among the cabbages; weeds were sure to grow quicker in his fields than anywhere else; the rain always made a point of setting in just as he had some out-door work to do; so that though his patrimonial estate had dwindled away under his management, acre by acre, until there was little more left than a mere patch of Indian corn and potatoes, yet it was the worst conditioned farm in the neighbourhood.

His children, too, were as ragged and wild as if they belonged to nobody. His son Rip, an urchin begotten in his own likeness, promised to inherit the habits, with the old clothes, of his father. He was generally seen trooping like a colt at his mother's heels, equipped in a pair of his father's cast-off galligaskins, which he had much ado to hold up with one hand, as a fine lady does her train in bad weather.

Rip Van Winkle, however, was one of those happy mortals, of foolish, well-oiled dispositions, who take the world easy, eat white bread or brown, whichever can be got with least thought or trouble, and would rather starve on a penny than work for a pound. If left to himself, he would have whistled life away in perfect contentment; but his wife kept continually dinning in his ears about his idleness, his carelessness, and the ruin he was bringing on his family. Morning, noon, and night, her tongue was incessantly going, and everything he said or did was sure to produce a torrent of household eloquence. Rip had but one way of replying to all lectures of the kind, and that, by frequent use, had grown into a habit. He shrugged his shoulders, shook his head, cast up his eyes, but said nothing. This, however, always provoked a fresh volley from his wife; so that he was fain to draw off his forces, and take to the outside of the house – the only side which, in truth, belongs to a hen-pecked husband.

Rip's sole domestic adherent was his dog Wolf, who was as much hen-pecked as his master; for Dame Van Winkle regarded them as companions in idleness, and even looked upon Wolf with an evil eye, as the cause of his master's going so often astray. True it is, in all points of spirit befitting an honourable dog, he was as courageous an animal as ever scoured the woods – but what courage can withstand the ever-during and all-besetting terrors of a woman's tongue? The moment Wolf entered the house, his crest fell, his tail drooped to the ground, or curled between his legs, he sneaked about with a gallows air, casting many a side-long glance at Dame Van Winkle, and at the least flourish of a broomstick or ladle, he would fly to the door with yelping precipitation.

Times grew worse and worse with Rip Van Winkle as years of matrimony rolled on; a tart temper never mellows with age, and a sharp tongue is the only edged tool that grows keener with constant use. For a long while he used to console himself, when driven from home, by frequenting a kind of perpetual club of the sages, philosophers, and other idle personages of the village; which held its sessions on a bench before a small inn, designated by a rubicund portrait of His Majesty George the Third. Here they used to sit in the shade through a long lazy summer's day, talking listlessly over village gossip, or telling endless sleepy stories about nothing. But it would have been worth any statesman's money to have heard the profound discussions that sometimes took place, when by chance an old newspaper fell into their hands from some passing traveller. How solemnly they would listen to the contents, as drawled out by Derrick Van Bummel, the school-master, a dapper learned little man, who was not to be daunted by the most gigantic word in the dictionary; and how sagely they would deliberate upon public events some months after they had taken place.

The opinions of this junto were completely controlled by Nicholas Vedder, a patriarch of the village, and landlord of the inn, at the door of which he took his seat from morning till night, just moving sufficiently to avoid the sun and keep in the shade of a large tree; so that the neighbours could tell the hour by his movements as accurately as by a sundial. It is true he was rarely heard to speak, but smoked his pipe incessantly. His adherents, however (for every great man has his adherents), perfectly understood him, and knew how to gather his opinions. When anything that was read or related displeased him, he was observed to smoke his pipe vehemently, and to send forth short, frequent, and angry puffs, but when pleased he would inhale the smoke slowly and tranquilly, and emit it in light and placid clouds; and sometimes, taking the pipe from his mouth, and letting the fragrant vapour curl about his nose, would gravely nod his head in token of perfect approbation.

From even this stronghold the unlucky Rip was at length routed by his termagant wife, who would break in upon the tranquillity of the assemblage and call the members all to naught; nor was that august personage, Nicholas Vedder himself, sacred from the daring tongue of this terrible virago, who charged him outright with encouraging her husband in habits of idleness.

Poor Rip was at last reduced almost to despair; and his only alternative, to escape from the labour of the farm and clamour of his wife, was to take gun in hand and stroll away into the woods. Here he would sometimes seat himself at the foot of a tree, and share the contents of his wallet with Wolf, with whom he sympathized as a fellow-sufferer in persecution. 'Poor Wolf,' he would say, 'thy mistress leads thee a dog's life of it; but never mind, my lad, whilst I live thou shalt never want a friend to stand by thee!' Wolf would wag his tail, look wistfully in his master's face, and if dogs can feel pity, I verily believe he reciprocated the sentiment with all his heart.

In a long ramble of the kind on a fine autumnal day, Rip had unconsciously scrambled to one of the highest parts of the Kaatskill mountains. He was after his favourite sport of squirrel-shooting, and the still solitudes had echoed and re-echoed with the reports of his gun. Panting and fatigued, he threw himself, late in the afternoon, on a green knoll, covered with mountain herbage, that crowned the brow of a precipice. From an opening between the trees he could overlook all the lower country for many a mile of rich woodland. He saw at a distance the lordly Hudson, far, far below him, moving on its silent but majestic course, with the reflection of a purple cloud, or the sail of a lagging bark, here and there sleeping on its glassy bosom, and at last losing itself in the blue highlands.

On the other side he looked down into a deep mountain glen, wild, lonely, and shagged, the bottom filled with fragments from the impending cliffs, and scarcely lighted by the reflected rays of the setting sun. For some time Rip lay musing on this scene; evening was gradually advancing; the mountains began to throw their long blue shadows over the valleys; he saw that it would be dark long before he could reach the village, and he heaved a heavy sigh when he thought of encountering the terrors of Dame Van Winkle.

As he was about to descend, he heard a voice from a distance, hallooing, 'Rip Van Winkle! Rip Van Winkle!' He looked round, but could see nothing but a crow winging its solitary flight across the mountain. He thought his fancy must have deceived him, and turned again to descend, when he heard the same cry ring through the still evening air: 'Rip Van Winkle! Rip Van Winkle!' – at the same time Wolf bristled up his back, and, giving a loud growl, skulked to his master's side, looking fearfully down into the glen. Rip now felt a vague apprehension stealing over him; he looked anxiously in the same direction, and perceived a strange figure slowly toiling up the rocks, and bending under the weight of something he carried on his back. He was surprised to see any human being in this lonely and unfrequented place; but supposing it to be some one of the neighbour-hood in need of his assistance, he hastened down to yield it.

On nearer approach he was still more surprised at the singularity of the stranger's appearance. He was a short, square-built old fellow, with thick bushy hair and a grizzled beard. His dress was of the antique Dutch fashion – a cloth jerkin, strapped round the waist – several pair of breeches, the outer one of ample volume, decorated with rows of buttons down the sides, and bunches at the knees. He bore on his shoulder a stout keg, that seemed full of liquor, and made signs for Rip to approach and assist him with the load. Though rather shy and distrustful of his new acquaintance, Rip complied with his usual alacrity; and mutually relieving each other, they clambered up a narrow gully, apparently the dry bed of a mountain torrent. As they ascended, Rip every now and then heard long rolling peals, like distant thunder, that seemed to issue out of a deep ravine, or rather cleft, between lofty rocks, toward which their rugged path conducted. He paused for an instant, but supposing it to be the muttering of one of those transient thundershowers which often take place in mountain heights, he proceeded. Passing through the ravine, they came to a hollow, like a small amphitheatre, surrounded by perpendicular precipices, over the brinks of which impending trees shot their branches, so that you only caught glimpses of the azure sky and the bright evening cloud. During the whole time Rip and his companion had laboured on in silence, for though the former marvelled greatly what could be the object of carrying a keg of liquor up this wild mountain; yet there was something strange and incomprehensible about the unknown, that inspired awe and checked familiarity.

On entering the amphitheatre, new objects of wonder presented themselves. On a level spot in the centre was a company of odd-looking personages playing at ninepins. They were dressed in a quaint outlandish fashion; some wore short doublets, others jerkins, with long knives in their belts, and most of them had enormous breeches, of similar style with that of the guide's. Their visages, too, were peculiar; one had a large head, broad face, and small piggish eyes; the face of another seemed to consist entirely of nose, and was surmounted by a white sugar-loaf hat, set off with a little red cock's tail. They all had beards, of various shapes and colours. There was one

Rip Van Winkle asleep

who seemed to be the commander. He was a stout old gentleman, with a weather-beaten countenance; he wore a laced doublet, broad belt and hanger, high-crowned hat and feather, red stockings, and high-heeled shoes, with roses in them. The whole group reminded Rip of the figure in an old Flemish painting, in the parlour of Dominie Van Shaick, the village parson, and which had been brought over from Holland at the time of the settlement.

What seemed particularly odd to Rip was, that though these folks were evidently amusing themselves, yet they maintained the gravest faces, the most mysterious silence, and were, withal, the most melancholy party of pleasure he had ever witnessed. Nothing interrupted the stillness of the scene but the noise of the balls, which, whenever they were rolled, echoed along the mountains like rumbling peals of thunder.

As Rip and his companion approached them, they suddenly desisted from their play, and stared at him with such fixed, statue-like gaze, and such strange, uncouth, lack-lustre countenances, that his heart turned within him, and his knees smote together. His companion now emptied the contents of the keg into large flagons, and made signs to him to wait upon the company. He obeyed with fear and trembling; they quaffed the liquor in profound silence, and then returned to their game.

By degrees Rip's awe and apprehension subsided. He even ventured when no eye was fixed upon him, to taste the beverage, which he found had much of the flavour of excellent Hollands. He was naturally a thirsty soul, and was soon tempted to repeat the draught. One taste provoked another; and he reiterated his visits to the flagon so often, that at length his senses were overpowered, his eyes swam in his head, gradually declined, and he fell into a deep sleep.

On waking, he found himself on the green knoll whence he had first seen the old man of the glen. He rubbed his eyes – it was a bright sunny morning. The birds were hopping and twittering among the bushes, and the eagle was wheeling aloft, and breasting the pure mountain breeze. 'Surely,' thought Rip, 'I have not slept here all night.' He recalled the occurrences before he fell asleep. The strange man with a keg of liquor – the mountain ravine – the wild retreat among the rocks – the woe-begone party at ninepins – the flagon— 'Oh! that flagon! that wicked flagon!' thought Rip; 'what excuse shall I make to Dame Van Winkle?'

He looked round for his gun, but in place of the clean well-oiled fowling-piece, he found an old firelock lying by him, the barrel encrusted with rust, the lock falling off, and the stock worm-eaten. He now suspected that the grave roysters of the mountain had put a trick upon him, and having dosed him with liquor, had robbed him of his gun. Wolf, too, had disappeared, but he might have strayed away after a squirrel or partridge. He whistled after him, and shouted his name, but all in vain; the echoes repeated his whistle and shout, but no dog was to be seen.

He determined to revisit the scene of the last evening's gambol, and, if he met with any of the party, to demand his dog and gun. As he rose to walk he found himself stiff in the joints, and wanting in his usual activity. 'These mountain beds do not agree with me,' thought Rip; 'and if this frolic should lay me up with a fit of the rheumatism, I shall have a blessed time with Dame Van Winkle.' With some difficulty he got down into the glen: he found the gully up which he and his companion had ascended the preceding evening; but, to his astonishment, a mountain stream was now foaming down it – leaping from rock to rock, and filling the glen with babbling murmurs. He, however, made shift to scramble up its sides, working his toilsome way through thickets of birch, sassafras, and witch-hazel, and sometimes tripped up or entangled by the wild grape-vines that twisted their coils or tendrils from tree to tree, and spread a kind of network in his path.

At length he reached to where the ravine had opened through the cliffs to the amphitheatre; but no traces of such opening remained. The rocks presented a high impenetrable wall, over which the torrent came tumbling in a sheet of feathery foam, and fell into a broad deep basin, black from the shadows of the surrounding forest. Here, then, poor

Rip was brought to a stand. He again called and whistled after his dog; he was only answered by the cawing of a flock of idle crows, sporting high in air about a dry tree that overhung a sunny precipice; and who, secure in their elevation, seemed to look down and scoff at the poor man's perplexities. What was to be done? – the morning was passing away, and Rip felt famished for want of his breakfast. He grieved to give up his dog and his gun; he dreaded to meet his wife; but it would not do to starve among the mountains. He shook his head, shouldered the rusty firelock, and, with a heart full of trouble and anxiety, turned his steps homeward.

As he approached the village he met a number of people, but none whom he knew, which somewhat surprised him, for he had thought himself acquainted with everyone in the country round. Their dress, too, was of a different fashion from that to which he was accustomed. They all stared at him with equal marks of surprise, and, whenever they cast their eyes upon him, invariably stroked their chins. The constant recurrence of this gesture induced Rip, involuntarily, to do the same – when, to his astonishment, he found his beard had grown a foot long!

He had now entered the skirts of the village. A troop of strange children ran at his heels, hooting after him, and pointing at his grey beard. The dogs, too, not one of which he recognised for an old acquaintance, barked at him as he passed. The very village was altered; it was larger and more populous. There were rows of houses which he had never seen before, and those which had been his familiar haunts had disappeared. Strange names were over the doors – strange faces at the windows – everything was strange. His mind now misgave him; he began to doubt whether both he and the world around him were not bewitched. Surely this was his native village, which he had left but the day before. There stood the Kaatskill mountains – there ran the silver Hudson at a distance – there was every hill and dale precisely as it had always been. Rip was sorely perplexed. 'That flagon last night,' thought he, 'has addled my poor head sadly!'

It was with some difficulty that he found the way to his own house, which he approached with silent awe, expecting every moment to hear the shrill voice of Dame Van Winkle. He found the house gone to decay – the roof fallen in, the windows shattered, and the doors off the hinges. A half-starved dog that looked like Wolf was skulking about it. Rip called him by name, but the cur snarled, showed his teeth, and passed on. This was an unkind cut indeed – 'My very dog,' sighed poor Rip, 'has forgotten me!'

He entered the house, which, to tell the truth, Dame Van Winkle had always kept in neat order. It was empty, forlorn and apparently abandoned. The desolateness overcame all his connubial fears – he called loudly for his wife and children – the lonely chambers rang for a moment with his voice, and then all again was silence.

He now hurried forth, and hastened to his old resort, the village inn – but it too was gone. A large, rickety, wooden building stood in its place, with great gaping windows, some of them broken and mended with old hats and petticoats, and over the door was painted, 'The Union Hotel, by Jonathan Doolittle'. Instead of the great tree that used to shelter the quiet little Dutch inn of yore, there was now reared a naked pole, with something on the top that looked like a red nightcap, and from it was fluttering a flag, on which was a singular assemblage of stars and stripes – all this was strange and incomprehensible. He recognized on the sign, however, the ruby face of King George, under which he had smoked so many a peaceful pipe; but even this was singularly metamorphosed. The red coat was changed for one of blue and buff, a sword was held in the hand instead of a sceptre, the head was decorated with a cocked hat, and underneath was painted in large characters, GENERAL WASHINGTON.

There was, as usual, a crowd of folks about the door, but none that Rip recollected. The very character of the people seemed changed. There was a busy, bustling, disputatious tone about it, instead of the accustomed phlegm and drowsy tranquillity. He looked in vain for the sage Nicholas Vedder, with his broad face, double chin, and fair long pipe, uttering clouds of tabacco-smoke instead of idle speeches; or Van Bummel, the schoolmaster, doling forth the contents of an

Rip Van Winkle returns

ancient newspaper. In place of these, a lean, bilious-looking fellow, with his pockets full of hand-bills, was haranguing vehemently about rights of citizens – elections – members of Congress – liberty – Bunker Hill – heroes of seventy-six – and other words, which were a perfect Babylonish jargon to the bewildered Van Winkle.

The appearance of Rip, with his long grizzled beard, his rusty fowling-piece, his uncouth dress, and an army of women and children at his heels, soon attracted the attention of the tavern politicians. They crowded round him, eyeing him from head to foot with great curiosity. The orator bustled up to him, and, drawing him partly aside, inquired 'on which side he voted?' Rip stared in vacant stupidity. Another short but busy little fellow pulled him by the arm, and, rising on tiptoe, inquired in his ear, 'Whether he was Federal or Democrat?' Rip was equally at a loss to comprehend the question; when a knowing, self-important gentleman, in a sharp cocked hat, made his way through the crowd, putting them to the right and left with his elbows as he passed, and planting himself before Van Winkle, with one arm akimbo, the other resting on his cane, his keen eyes and sharp hat penetrating, as it were, into his very soul, demanded in an austere tone, 'What brought him to the election with a gun on his shoulder, and a mob at his heels, and whether he meant to breed a riot in the village?' – 'Alas! gentlemen,' cried Rip, somewhat dismayed, 'I am a poor quiet man, a native of the place, and a loyal subject of the king, God bless him!'

Here a general shout burst from the bystanders— 'A tory! a tory! a spy! a refugee! hustle him! away with him!' It was with great difficulty that self-important man in the cocked hat restored order; and, having assumed a tenfold austerity of brow, demanded again of the unknown culprit, what he came there for, and whom he was seeking? The poor man humbly assured him that he meant no harm, but merely came there in search of his neighbours, who used to keep about the tavern.

'Well – who are they? – name them.'

Rip bethought himself a moment, and inquired, 'Where's Nicholas Vedder?'

There was a silence for a little while, when an old man replied in a thin piping voice, 'Nicholas Vedder! why, he is dead and gone these eighteen years! There was a wooden tombstone in the churchyard that used to tell all about him, but that's rotten and gone too.'

'Where's Brom Dutcher?'

'Oh, he went off to the army in the beginning of the war; some say he was killed at the storming of Stony Point – others say he was drowned in a squall at the foot of Antony's Nose. I don't know – he never came back again,'

'Where's Van Bummel, the schoolmaster?'

'He went off to the wars too, was a great militia general, and is now in Congress.'

Rip's heart died away at hearing of these sad changes in his home and friends, and finding himself thus alone in the world. Every answer puzzled him too, by treating of such enormous lapses of time, and of matters which he could not understand; war – Congress – Stony Point; – he had no courage to ask after any more friends, but cried out in despair, 'Does nobody here know Rip Van Winkle?'

'Oh, Rip Van Winkle!' exclaimed two or three. 'Oh, to be sure! that's Rip Van Winkle yonder, leaning against the tree.'

Rip looked, and beheld a precise counterpart of himself, as he went up the mountain: apparently as lazy, and certainly as ragged. The poor fellow was now completely confounded. He doubted his own identity, and whether he was himself or another man. In the midst of his bewilderment, the man in the cocked hat demanded who he was, and what was his name?

'God knows,' exclaimed he, at his wits' end; 'I'm not myself – I'm somebody else – that's me yonder – no – that's somebody else got into my shoes – I was myself last night, but I fell asleep on the mountain, and they've changed my gun, and everything's changed, and I'm changed, and I can't tell what's my name, or who I am!'

The bystanders began now to look at each other, nod, wink significantly, and tap their fingers against their foreheads. There was a whisper, also, about securing the gun, and keeping the old fellow from doing mischief, at the very suggestion of which the self-important man in the cocked hat retired with some precipitation. At this critical moment a fresh, comely woman pressed through the throng to get a peep at the grey-bearded man. She had a chubby child in her arms, which, frightened at his looks, began to cry. 'Hush, Rip,' cried she, 'hush, you little fool; the old man won't hurt you.' The name of the child, the air of the mother, the tone of her voice, all awakened a train of recollections in his mind.

'What is your name, my good woman?' asked he.

'Judith Gardenier.'

'And your father's name?'

'Ah, poor man, Rip Van Winkle was his name, but it's twenty years since he went away from home with his gun, and never has been heard of since – his dog came home without him; but whether he shot himself, or was carried away by the Indians, nobody can tell. I was then but a little girl.'

Rip had but one question more to ask; but he put it with a faltering voice:

'Where's your mother?'

'Oh, she too had died but a short time since; she broke a bloodvessel in a fit of passion at a New-England pedlar.'

There was a drop of comfort, at least, in this intelligence. The honest man could contain himself no longer. He caught his daughter and her child in his arms. 'I am your father!' cried he – 'Young Rip Van Winkle once – old Rip Van Winkle now! – Does nobody know poor Rip Van Winkle?'

All stood amazed, until an old woman, tottering out from among the crowd, put her hand to her brow, and peering under it in his face for moment, exclaimed, 'Sure enough! it is Rip Van Winkle – it is himself! Welcome home again, old neighbour – Why, where have you been these twenty long years?

Rip's story was soon told, for the whole twenty years had been to him but one night. The neighbours stared when they heard it; some were seen to wink at each other, and put their tongues in their cheeks:

and the self-important man in the cocked hat, who, when the alarm was over, had returned to the field, screwed down the corners of his mouth, and shook his head – upon which there was a general shaking of the head throughout the assemblage.

It was determined, however, to take the opinion of old Peter Vanderdonk, who was seen slowly advancing up the road. He was a descendant of the historian of that name, who wrote one of the earliest accounts of the province. Peter was the most ancient inhabitant of the village, and well versed in all the wonderful events and traditions of the neighbourhood. He recollected Rip at once, and corroborated his story in the most satisfactory manner. He assured the company that it was a fact, handed down from his ancestor the historian, that the Kaatskill mountains had always been haunted by strange beings. That it was affirmed that the great Hendrick Hudson, the first discoverer of the river and the country, kept a kind of vigil there every twenty years, with his crew of the *Half-moon*; being permitted in this way to revisit the scenes of his enterprise, and keep a guardian eye upon the river, and the great city called by his name. That his father had once seen them in their old Dutch dresses playing at ninepins in a hollow of the mountain; and that he himself had heard, one summer afternoon, the sound of their balls, like distant peals of thunder.

To make a long story short, the company broke up, and returned to the more important concerns of the election. Rip's daughter took him home to live with her; she had a snug, well-furnished house, and a stout cheery farmer for her husband, whom Rip recollected for one of the urchins that used to climb upon his back. As to Rip's son and heir, who was the ditto of himself, seen leaning against the tree, he was employed to work on the farm; but evinced an hereditary disposition to attend to anything else but his business.

Rip now resumed his old walks and habits; he soon found many of his former cronies, though all rather the worse for the wear and tear of time, and preferred making friends among the rising generation, with whom he soon grew into great favour.

Having nothing to do at home, and being arrived at that happy age when a man can be idle with impunity, he took his place once more on the bench at the inn door, and was reverenced as one of the patriarchs of the village, and a chronicle of the old times 'before the war'. It was some time before he could get into the regular track of gossip, or could be made to comprehend the strange events that had taken place during his torpor. How that there had been a revolutionary war – that the country had thrown off the yoke of Old England – and that, instead of being a subject of His Majesty George the Third, he was now a free citizen of the United States. Rip, in fact, was no politician; the changes of states and empires made but little impression on him; but there was one species of despotism under which he had long groaned, and that was – petticoat government. Happily that was at an end; he had got his neck out of the yoke of matrimony, and could go in and out whenever he pleased without dreading the tyranny of Dame Van Winkle. Whenever her name was mentioned, however, he shook his head, shrugged his shoulders, and cast up his eyes; which might pass either for an expression of resignation to his fate, or joy at his deliverance.

He used to tell his story to every stranger that arrived at Mr Doolittle's Hotel. He was observed at first to vary on some points every time he told it, which was, doubtless, owing to his having so recently awakened. It at last settled down precisely to the tale I have related, and not a man, woman or child in the neighbourhood but knew it by heart. Some always pretended to doubt the reality of it, and insisted that Rip had been out of his head, and that this was one point on which he always remained flighty. The old Dutch inhabitants, however, almost universally gave it full credit. Even to this day they never hear a thunder-storm of a summer afternoon about the Kaatskill, but they say Hendrick Hudson and his crew are at their game of ninepins; and it is a common wish of all henpecked husbands in the neighbourhood, when life hangs heavy on their hands, that they might have a quieting draught out of Rip Van Winkle's flagon.

Baron Munchausen

R. E. RASPE
Illustrated by J. B. Clark

Rudolph Erich Raspe came from Hanover in Germany. In danger of arrest there, he flew to England where he published (1785) an account of the incredible adventures of the boastful Baron Munchausen.

Some years before my beard announced approaching manhood, or, in other words, when I was neither man nor boy, but between both, I expressed in repeated conversations a strong desire of seeing the world, from which I was discouraged by my parents, though my father had been no inconsiderable traveller himself, as will appear before I have reached the end of my singular, and, I may add, interesting adventures. A cousin, by my mother's side, took a liking to me, often said I was a fine forward youth, and was much inclined to gratify my curiosity. His eloquence had more effect than mine, for my father consented to my accompanying him in a voyage to the island of Ceylon, where his uncle had resided as governor many years.

We sailed from Amsterdam with despatches from their High Mightinesses the States of Holland. The only circumstances which happened on our voyage worth relating was the wonderful effects of a storm, which had torn up by the roots a great number of trees of enormous bulk and height, in an island where we lay at anchor to take in wood and water; some of these trees weighed many tons, yet they were carried by the wind so amazingly high, that they appeared like the feathers of small birds floating in the air, for they were at least five miles above the earth: however, as soon as the storm subsided they all fell perpendicularly into their respective places, and took root again, except the largest, which happened, when it was blown into the air, to have a man and his wife, a very honest old couple, upon its branches, gathering cucumbers (in this part of the globe that useful vegetable grows upon trees): the weight of this couple, as the tree descended, over-balanced the trunk, and brought it down in a horizontal position: it fell upon the chief man of the island, and killed him on the spot; he had quitted his house in the storm, under an apprehension of its falling upon him, and was returning through his own garden when this fortunate accident happened. The word fortunate, here, requires some explanation. This chief was a man of a very avaricious and oppressive disposition, and though he had no family, the natives of the island were half-starved by his oppressive and infamous impositions.

The very goods which he had thus taken from them were spoiling in his stores, while the poor wretches from whom they were plundered were pining in poverty. Though the destruction of this tyrant was accidental, the people chose the cucumber-gatherers for their governors, as a mark of their gratitude for destroying, though accidentally, their late tyrant.

After we had repaired the damages we sustained in this remarkable storm, and taken leave of the new governor and his lady, we sailed with a fair wind for the object of our voyage.

In about six weeks we arrived at Ceylon, where we were received with great marks of friendship and true politeness.

After we had resided at Ceylon about a fortnight I accompanied one of the governor's brothers upon a shooting party. He was a strong, athletic man, and being used to that climate (for he had resided there sone years), he bore the violent heat of the sun much better than I could; in our excursion he had made a considerable progress through a thick wood when I was only at the entrance.

Near the banks of a large piece of water, which had engaged my attention, I thought I heard a rustling noise behind; on turning about I was almost petrified (as who would not be?) at the sight of a lion, which was evidently approaching with the intention of satisfying his appetite with my poor carcase, and that without asking my consent. What was to be done in this horrible dilemma? I had not even a moment for reflection; my piece was only charged with swan-shot, and I had no other about me: however, though I could have no idea of killing such an animal with that weak kind of ammunition, yet I had some hopes of frightening him by the report, and perhaps of wounding him also. I immediately let fly, without waiting till he was within reach, and the report did but enrage him, for he now quickened his pace, and seemed to approach me full speed: I attempted to escape, but that only added (if an addition could be made) to my distress; for the moment I turned about I found a large crocodile, with his mouth extended almost ready to receive me. On my right hand was the piece of water before mentioned, and on my left a deep precipice, said to have, as I have since learned, a receptacle at the bottom for venomous creatures; in short I gave myself up as lost, for the lion was now upon his hind-legs, just in the act of seizing me; I fell involuntarily to the ground with fear, and, as it afterwards appeared, he sprang over me. I lay some time in a situation which no language can describe, expecting to feel his teeth or talons in some part of me every moment: after waiting in this prostrate situation a few seconds I heard a violent but unusual noise, different from any sound that had ever before assailed my ears; nor is it at all to be wondered at, when I inform you from whence it proceeded: after listening for some time, I ventured to raise my head and look round, when, to my unspeakable joy, I perceived the lion had, by the eagerness with which he sprung at me, jumped forward, as I fell, into the crocodile's mouth! which, as before observed, was wide open; the head of the one stuck in the throat of the other! and they were struggling to extricate themselves! I fortunately recollected my *couteau de chasse*, which was by my side; with this instrument I severed the lion's head at one blow, and the body fell at my feet! I then, with the butt-end of my fowling-piece, rammed the head farther into the throat of the crocodile, and destroyed him by suffocation, for he could neither gorge nor eject it.

Soon after I had thus gained a complete victory over my two powerful adversaries, my companion arrived in search of me; for finding I did not follow him into the wood, he returned, apprehending I had lost my way, or met with some accident.

The crocodile swallows the lion

After mutual congratulations, we measured the crocodile, which was just forty feet in length.

As soon as we had related this extraordinary adventure to the governor, he sent a waggon and servants, who brought home the two carcases. The lion's skin was properly preserved, with its hair on, after which it was made into tobacco-pouches, and presented by me, upon our return to Holland, to the burgomasters, who, in return, requested my acceptance of a thousand ducats.

The skin of the crocodile was stuffed in the usual manner, and makes a capital article in their public museum at Amsterdam, where the exhibitor relates the whole story to each spectator, with such additions as he thinks proper. Some of his variations are rather extravagant; one of them is, that the lion jumped quite through the crocodile, and was making his escape at the back door, when, as soon as his head appeared, Monsieur the Great Baron (as he is pleased to call me) cut it off, and three feet of the crocodile's tail along with it; nay, so little attention has this fellow to the truth, that he sometimes adds, as soon as the crocodile missed his tail, he turned about, snatched the *couteau de chasse* out of Monsieur's hand, and swallowed it with such eagerness that it pierced his heart and killed him immediately!

The little regard which this impudent knave has to veracity makes me sometimes apprehensive that my *real facts* may fall under suspicion, by being found in company with his confounded inventions.

The White Knight

LEWIS CARROLL

Illustrated by John Tenniel

This is a chapter from Through the Looking Glass *(1872), the sequel to* Alice in Wonderland *(see page 321). In* Looking Glass Land, *Alice finds herself taking part in a living chess game. She begins as a pawn, and must find her way to the eighth square to become a queen.*

At this moment Alice's thoughts were interrupted by a loud shouting of 'Ahoy! Ahoy! Check!' and a Knight, dressed in crimson armour, came galloping down upon her, brandishing a great club. Just as he reached her, the horse stopped suddenly: 'You're my prisoner!' the Knight cried, as he tumbled off his horse.

Startled as she was, Alice was more frightened for him than for herself at the moment, and watched him with some anxiety as he mounted again. As soon as he was comfortably in the saddle, he began once more, 'You're my—' but here another voice broke in 'Ahoy! Ahoy! Check!' and Alice looked round in some surprise for the new enemy.

This time it was a White Knight. He drew up at Alice's side, and tumbled off his horse just as the Red Knight had done: then he got on again, and the two Knights sat and looked at each other for some time without speaking. Alice looked from one to the other in some bewilderment.

'She's *my* prisoner, you know!' the Red Knight said at last.

'Yes, but then *I* came and rescued her!' the White Knight replied.

'Well, we must fight for her then,' said the Red Knight, as he took up his helmet (which hung from the saddle, and was something the shape of a horse's head) and put it on.

'You will observe the Rules of Battle, of course?' the White Knight remarked, putting on his helmet too.

The White Knight

'I always do,' said the Red Knight, and they began banging away at each other with such fury that Alice got behind a tree to be out of the way of the blows.

'I wonder, now, what the Rules of Battle are,' she said to herself, as she watched the fight, timidly peeping out from her hiding-place. 'One Rule seems to be, that if one Knight hits the other, he knocks him off his horse; and, if he misses, he tumbles off himself – and another Rule seems to be that they hold their clubs with their arms, as if they were Punch and Judy – What a noise they make when they tumble! Just like a whole set of fire-irons falling into the fender! And how quiet the horses are! They let them get on and off them just as if they were tables!'

Another Rule of Battle, that Alice had not noticed, seemed to be that they always fell on their heads; and the battle ended with their both falling in this way, side by side. When they got up again, they shook hands, and then the Red Knight mounted and galloped off.

'It was a glorious victory, wasn't it?' said the White Knight, as he came up panting.

'I don't know,' Alice said doubtfully. 'I don't want to be anybody's prisoner. I want to be a Queen.'

'So you will, when you've crossed the next brook,' said the White Knight. 'I'll see you safe to the end of the wood – and then I must go back, you know. That's the end of my move.'

'Thank you very much,' said Alice. 'May I help you off with your helmet?' It was evidently more than he could manage by himself: however she managed to shake him out of it at last.

'Now one can breathe more easily,' said the Knight, putting back his shaggy hair with both hands, and turning his gentle face and large mild eyes to Alice. She thought she had never seen such a strange-looking soldier in all her life.

He was dressed in tin armour, which seemed to fit him very badly, and he had a queer-shaped little deal box fastened across his shoulders, upside-down, and with the lid hanging open. Alice looked at it with great curiosity.

'I see you're admiring my little box,' the Knight said in a friendly tone. 'It's my own invention – to keep clothes and sandwiches in. You see I carry it upside-down, so that the rain ca'n't get in.'

'But the things can get *out*,' Alice gently remarked. 'Do you know the lid's open?'

'I didn't know it,' the Knight said, a shade of vexation passing over his face. 'Then all the things must have fallen out! And the box is no use without them.' He unfastened it as he spoke, and was just going to throw it into the bushes, when a sudden thought seemed to strike him, and he hung it carefully on a tree. 'Can you guess why I did that?' he said to Alice.

Alice shook her head.

'In hopes some bees may make a nest in it – then I should get the honey.'

'But you've got a beehive – or something like one – fastened to the saddle,' said Alice.

'Yes, it's a very good beehive,' the Knight said in a discontented tone, 'one of the best kind. But not a single bee has come near it yet. And the other thing is a mouse-trap. I suppose the mice keep the bees out – or the bees keep the mice out, I don't know which.'

'I was wondering what the mouse-trap was for,' said Alice. 'It isn't very likely there would be any mice on the horse's back.'

'Not very likely, perhaps,' said the Knight; 'but, if they *do* come, I don't choose to have them running all about.'

'You see,' he went on after a pause, 'it's as well to be provided for *everything*. That's the reason the horse has all those anklets round his feet.'

'But what are they for?' Alice asked in a tone of great curiosity.

'To guard against the bites of sharks,' the Knight replied. 'It's an invention of my own. And now help me on. I'll go with you to the end of the wood – What's that dish for?'

'It's meant for plum cake,' said Alice.

'We'd better take that with us,' the Knight said. 'It'll come in handy if we find any plum cake. Help me to get it into this bag.'

This took a long time to manage, though Alice held the bag open very carefully, because the Knight was so *very* awkward in putting in the dish; the first two or three times that he tried he fell in himself instead. 'It's rather a tight fit, you see,' he said, as they got it in at last; 'there are so many candlesticks in the bag.' And he hung it to the saddle, which was already loaded with bunches of carrots, and fire-irons, and many other things.

'I hope you've got your hair well fastened on?' he continued, as they set off.

'Only in the usual way,' Alice said, smiling.

'That's hardly enough,' he said, anxiously. 'You see the wind is so *very* strong here. It's as strong as soup.'

'Have you invented a plan for keeping the hair from being blown off?' Alice enquired.

'Not yet,' said the Knight. 'But I've got a plan for keeping it from *falling* off.'

'I should like to hear it, very much.'

'First you take an upright stick,' said the Knight. 'Then you make your hair creep up it, like a fruit-tree. Now the reason hair falls off is because it hangs *down* – things never fall *upwards*, you know. It's a plan of my own invention. You may try it if you like.'

It didn't sound a comfortable plan, Alice thought, and for a few minutes she walked on in silence, puzzling over the idea, and every now and then stopping to help the poor Knight, who certainly was *not* a good rider.

Whenever the horse stopped (which it did very often), he fell off in front; and, whenever it went on again (which it generally did rather suddenly), he fell off behind. Otherwise he kept on pretty well, except that he had a habit of now and then falling off sideways; and, as he generally did this on the side on which Alice was walking, she soon found that it was the best plan not to walk *quite* close to the horse.

'I'm afraid you've not had much practice in riding,' she ventured to say, as she was helping him up from his fifth tumble.

The Knight looked very surprised, and a little offended at the remark. 'What makes you say that?' he asked, as he scrambled back into the saddle, keeping hold of Alice's hair with one hand, to save himself from falling over on the other side.

'Because people don't fall off quite so often, when they've had much practice!'

'I've had plenty of practice,' the Knight said very gravely: 'plenty of practice!'

Alice could think of nothing better to say than 'Indeed?' but she said it as heartily as she could. They went on a little way in silence after this, the Knight with his eyes shut, muttering to himself, and Alice watching anxiously for the next tumble.

'The great art of riding,' the Knight suddenly began in a loud voice, waving his right arm as he spoke, 'is to keep—' Here the sentence ended as suddenly as it had begun, as the Knight fell heavily on top of his head exactly in the path where Alice was walking. She was quite frightened this time, and said in an anxious tone, as she picked him up, 'I hope no bones are broken?'

'None to speak of,' the Knight said, as if he didn't mind breaking two or three of them. 'The great art of riding, as I was saying, is – to keep your balance properly. Like this, you know—'

He let go the bridle, and stretched out both his arms to show Alice what he meant, and this time he fell flat on his back, right under the horse's feet.

'Plenty of practice!' he went on repeating, all the time that Alice was getting him on his feet again. 'Plenty of practice!'

'It's too ridiculous!' cried Alice, losing all her patience this time. 'You ought to have a wooden horse on wheels, that you ought!'

'Does that kind go smoothly?' the Knight asked in a tone of great interest, clasping his arms round the horse's neck as he spoke, just in time to save himself from tumbling off again.

'Much more smoothly than a live horse,' Alice said, with a little scream of laughter, in spite of all she could do to prevent it.

'I'll get one,' the Knight said thoughtfully to himself. 'One or two – several.'

There was a short silence after this, and then the Knight went on again. 'I'm a great hand at inventing things. Now, I daresay you noticed, the last time you picked me up, that I was looking rather thoughtful?'

'You *were* a little grave,' said Alice.

'Well, just then I was inventing a new way of getting over a gate – would you like to hear it?'

'Very much indeed,' Alice said politely.

'I'll tell you how I came to think of it,' said the Knight. 'You see, I said to myself, "The only difficulty is with the feet: the *head* is high enough already." Now, first I put my head on the top of the gate – then the head's high enough – then I stand on my head – then the feet are high enough, you see – then I'm over, you see.'

'Yes, I suppose you'd be over when that was done,' Alice said thoughtfully: 'but don't you think it would be rather hard?'

'I haven't tried it yet,' the Knight said, gravely, 'so I ca'n't tell for certain – but I'm afraid it *would* be a little hard.'

He looked so vexed at the idea, that Alice changed the subject hastily. 'What a curious helmet you've got!' she said cheerfully. 'Is that your invention too?'

The Knight looked down proudly at his helmet which hung from the saddle. 'Yes,' he said; 'but I've invented a better one than that – like a sugar-loaf. When I used to wear it, if I fell off the horse, it always touched the ground directly. So I had a *very* little way to fall, you see – But there *was* the danger of falling *into* it, to be sure. That happened to me once – and the worst of it was, before I could get out again, the other White Knight came and put it on. He thought it was his own helmet.'

The Knight looked so solemn about it that Alice did not dare to laugh. 'I'm afraid you must have hurt him,' she said in a trembling voice, 'being on the top of his head.'

'I had to kick him, of course,' the Knight said, very seriously. 'And then he took the helmet off again – but it took hours and hours to get me out. I was as fast as – as lightning, you know.'

'But that's a different kind of fastness,' Alice objected.

The Knight shook his head. 'It was all kinds of fastness with me, I can assure you!' he said. He raised his hands in some excitement as he said this, and indignantly rolled out of the saddle, and fell headlong into a deep ditch.

Alice ran to the side of the ditch to look for him. She was rather startled by the fall, as for some time he had kept on very well, and she

was afraid that he really *was* hurt this time. However, though she could see nothing but the soles of his feet, she was much relieved to hear that he was talking on in his usual tone. 'All kinds of fastness,' he repeated: 'but it was careless of him to put another man's helmet on – with the man in it, too.'

'How can you go on talking so quietly, head downwards?' Alice asked, as she dragged him out by the feet, and laid him in a heap on the bank.

The Knight looked surprised at the question. 'What does it matter where my body happens to be?' he said. 'My mind goes on working all the same. In fact, the more head-downwards I am, the more I keep inventing new things.'

'Now the cleverest thing of the sort that I ever did,' he went on after a pause, 'was inventing a new pudding during the meat-course.'

'In time to have it cooked for the next course?' said Alice. 'Well, that *was* quick work, certainly!'

'Well, not the *next* course,' the Knight said in a slow thoughtful tone: 'no, certainly not the next *course*.'

'Then it would have to be the next day. I suppose you wouldn't have two pudding-courses in one dinner?'

'Well, not the *next* day,' the Knight repeated as before: 'not the next *day*. In fact,' he went on, holding his head down, and his voice getting lower and lower, 'I don't believe that pudding ever *was* cooked! In fact, I don't believe that pudding ever *will* be cooked! And yet it was a very clever pudding to invent.'

'What did you mean it to be made of?' Alice asked, hoping to cheer him up, for the poor Knight seemed quite low-spirited about it.

'It began with blotting-paper,' the Knight answered with a groan.

'That wouldn't be very nice, I'm afraid—'

'Not very nice *alone*,' he interrupted, quite eagerly: 'but you've no idea what a difference it makes, mixing it with other things – such as gunpowder and sealing-wax. And here I must leave you.' They had just come to the end of the wood.

Alice could only look puzzled: she was thinking of the pudding.

'You are sad,' the Knight said in an anxious tone: 'let me sing you a song to comfort you.'

'Is it very long?' Alice asked, for she had heard a good deal of poetry that day.

'It's long,' said the Knight, 'but it's very, *very* beautiful. Everybody that hears me sing it – either it brings the *tears* into their eyes, or else—'

'Or else what?' said Alice, for the Knight had made a sudden pause.

'Or else it doesn't, you know. The name of the song is called *"Haddock's Eyes"*.'

'Oh, that's the name of the song, is it?' Alice said, trying to feel interested.

'No, you don't understand,' the Knight said, looking a little vexed. 'That's what the name is *called*. The name really is *"The Aged Aged Man"*.'

'Then I ought to have said "That's what the *song* is called"?' Alice corrected herself.

'No, you oughtn't: that's quite another thing! The *song* is called *"Ways and Means"*: but that's only what it's *called*, you know!'

'Well, what *is* the song then?' said Alice, who was by this time completely bewildered.

'I was coming to that,' the Knight said. 'The song really *is "A-sitting on A Gate"*: and the tune's my own invention.'

So saying, he stopped his horse and let the reins fall on its neck: then, slowly beating time with one hand, and with a faint smile lighting up his gentle foolish face, as if he enjoyed the music of his song, he began.

Of all the strange things Alice saw in her journey Through the Looking Glass, this was the one that she always remembered most clearly. Years afterwards she could bring the whole scene back again, as if it had been only yesterday – the mild blue eyes and kindly smile of the Knight –the setting sun gleaming through his hair, and shining on his armour in a blaze that quite dazzled her – the horse quietly moving about, with the reins hanging loose on his neck, cropping the grass at her feet – and the black shadows of the forest behind – all this she took in like a picture, as, with one hand shading her eyes, she leant against a tree watching the strange pair, and listening, in a half-dream, to the melancholy music of the song.

'But the tune *isn't* his own invention,' she said to herself: 'it's *"I give thee all, I can no more"*.' She stood and listened very attentively, but no tears came into her eyes.

> *I'll tell thee everything I can:*
> *There's little to relate.*
> *I saw an aged aged man,*
> *A-sitting on a gate.*
> *'Who are you, aged man?' I said.*
> *'And how is it you live?'*
> *And his answer trickled through my head,*
> *Like water through a sieve.*
>
> *He said, 'I look for butterflies*
> *That sleep among the wheat:*
> *I make them into mutton-pies,*
> *And sell them in the street.*
> *I sell them unto men,' he said,*
> *'Who sail on stormy seas;*
> *And that's the way I get my bread –*
> *A trifle, if you please.'*
>
> *But I was thinking of a plan*
> *To dye one's whiskers green,*
> *And always use so large a fan*
> *That they could not be seen.*
> *So, having no reply to give*
> *To what the old man said,*
> *I cried 'Come, tell me how you live!'*
> *And thumped him on the head.*
>
> *His accents mild took up the tale:*
> *He said 'I go my ways,*
> *And when I find a mountain-rill,*
> *I set it in a blaze;*
> *And thence they make a stuff they call*
> *Rowland's Macassar-Oil –*

Yet twopence-halfpenny is all
They give me for my toil.'

But I was thinking of a way
To feed oneself on batter,
And so go on from day to day
Getting a little fatter.
I shook him well from side to side,
Until his face was blue:
'Come, tell me how you live,' I cried,
'And what it is you do!'

He said, 'I hunt for haddocks' eyes
Among the heather bright,
And work them into waistcoat-buttons
In the silent night.
And these I do not sell for gold

Or coin of silvery shine,
But for a copper halfpenny,
And that will purchase nine.

'I sometimes dig for buttered rolls,
Or set limed twigs for crabs:
I sometimes search the grassy knolls
For wheels of Hansom-cabs.
And that's the way' (he gave a wink)
'By which I get my wealth –
And very gladly will I drink
Your Honour's noble health.'

I heard him then, for I had just
Completed my design
To keep the Menai bridge from rust
By boiling it in wine.
I thanked him much for telling me
The way he got his wealth,
But chiefly for his wish that he
Might drink my noble health.

And now, if e'er by chance I put
My fingers into glue,
Or madly squeeze a right-hand foot
Into a left-hand shoe,
Or if I drop upon my toe
A very heavy weight,
I weep, for it reminds me so
Of that old man I used to know –
Whose look was mild, whose speech was slow,
Whose hair was whiter than the snow,
Whose face was very like a crow,
With eyes, like cinders, all aglow,
Who seemed distracted with his woe,
Who rocked his body to and fro,
And muttered mumblingly and low,
As if his mouth were full of dough,

Who snorted like a buffalo—
That summer evening long ago,
A-sitting on a gate.

As the Knight sang the last words of the ballad, he gathered up the reins, and turned his horse's head along the road by which they had come. 'You've only a few yards to go,' he said, 'down the hill and over that little brook, and then you'll be a Queen— But you'll stay and see me off first?' he added as Alice turned with an eager look in the direction to which he pointed. 'I sha'n't be long. You'll wait and wave your handkerchief when I get to that turn in the road! I think it'll encourage me, you see.'

'Of course I'll wait,' said Alice: 'and thank you very much for coming so far – and for the song – I liked it very much.'

'I hope so,' the Knight said doubtfully: 'but you didn't cry so much as I thought you would.'

So they shook hands, and then the Knight rode slowly away into the forest. 'It won't take long to see him *off*, I expect,' Alice said to herself, as she stood watching him. 'There he goes! Right on his head as usual! However, he gets on again pretty easily – that comes of having so many things hung round the horse—' So she went on talking to herself, as she watched the horse walking leisurely along the road, and the Knight tumbling off, first on one side then on the other. After the fourth or fifth tumble he reached the turn, and then she waved her handkerchief to him, and waited till he was out of sight.

'I hope it encouraged him,' she said, as she turned to run down the hill: 'and now for the last brook, and to be a Queen! How grand it sounds!' A very few steps brought her to the edge of the brook. 'The Eighth Square at last!' she cried as she bounded across, and threw herself down to rest on a lawn as soft as moss, with little flower-beds dotted about it here and there. 'Oh, how glad I am to get here! And what *is* this on my head?' she exclaimed in a tone of dismay, as she put her hands up to something very heavy, that fitted tight all round her head.

'But how *can* it have got there without my knowing it?' she said to herself, as she lifted it off, and set it on her lap to make out what it could possibly be.

It was a golden crown.

How Brigadier Gerard Saved an Army

SIR ARTHUR CONAN DOYLE

Brigadier Gerard was a vain and boastful bombadier in Napoleon's army. His adventures were described by Sir Arthur Conan Doyle in The Exploits *and* The Adventures of Brigadier Gerard *(1895 and 1903).*

I have told you, my friends, how we held the English shut up for six months, from October, 1810, to March, 1811, within their lines of Torres Vedras. It was during this time that I hunted the fox in their company, and showed them that amidst all their sportsmen there was not one who could outride a Hussar of Conflans. When I galloped back into the French lines with the blood of the creature still moist upon my blade, the outposts who had seen what I had done raised a frenzied cry in my honour, whilst these English hunters still yelled behind me, so that I had the applause of both armies. It made the tears rise to my eyes to feel that I had won the admiration of so many brave men. These English are generous foes. That very evening there came a packet under a white flag addressed, 'To the Hussar officer who cut down the fox.' Within I found the fox itself in two pieces, as I had left it. There was a note also, short, but hearty as the English fashion is, to say that as I had slaughtered the fox it only remained for me to eat it. They could not know that it was not our French custom to eat foxes, and it showed their desire that he who had won the honours of the chase should also partake of the game. It is not for a Frenchman to be outdone in politeness, and so I returned it to these brave hunters, and begged them to accept it as a side-dish for their next *dejeuner de la chasse*. It is thus that chivalrous opponents make war.

I had brought back with me from my ride a clear plan of the English lines, and this I laid before Massena that very evening.

I had hoped that it would lead him to attack, but all the marshals were at each other's throats, snapping and growling like so many hungry hounds. Ney hated Massena, and Massena hated Junot, and Soult hated them all. For this reason nothing was done. In the meantime food grew more and more scarce, and our beautiful cavalry was ruined for want of fodder. With the end of the winter we had swept the whole country bare, and nothing remained for us to eat, although we sent our forage parties far and wide. It was clear even to the bravest of us that the time had come to retreat. I was myself forced to admit it.

But retreat was not so easy. Not only were the troops weak and exhausted from want of supplies, but the enemy had been much encouraged by our long inaction. Of Wellington we had no great fear. We had found him to be brave and cautious, but with little enterprise. Besides, in that barren country his pursuit could not be rapid. But on our flanks and in our rear there had gathered great numbers of Portuguese militia, of armed peasants, and of guerillas. These people had kept a safe distance all the winter, but now that our horses were foundered they were as thick as flies all round our outposts, and no man's life was worth a sou when once he fell into their hands. I could name a dozen officers of my own acquaintance who were cut off during that time, and the luckiest was he who received a ball from behind a rock through his head or his heart. There were some whose deaths were so terrible that no report of them was ever allowed to reach their relatives. So frequent were these tragedies, and so much did they impress the imagination of the men, that it became very difficult to induce them to leave the camp. There was one especial scoundrel, a guerilla chief named Manuelo, 'The Smiler,' whose exploits filled our men with horror. He was a large, fat man of jovial aspect, and he lurked with a fierce gang among the mountains which lay upon our left flank. A volume might be written of this fellow's cruelties and brutalities, but he was certainly a man of power, for he organised his brigands in a manner which made it almost impossible for us to get through his country. This he did by imposing a severe discipline upon them and enforcing it by cruel penalties, a policy by which he made them formidable, but which had some unexpected results, as I will show you in my story. Had he not flogged his own lieutenant – but you will hear of that when the time comes.

There were many difficulties in connection with a retreat, but it was very evident that there was no other possible course, and so Massena began to quickly pass his baggage and his sick from Torres Novas, which was his headquarters, to Coimbra, the first strong post on his line of communications. He could not do this unperceived, however, and at once the guerillas came swarming closer and closer upon our flanks. One of our divisions, that of Clausel, with a brigade of Montbrun's cavalry, was far to the south of the Tagus, and it became very necessary to let them know that we were about to retreat, for otherwise they would be left unsupported in the very heart of the enemy's country. I remember wondering how Massena would accomplish this, for simple couriers could not get through, and small parties would be certainly destroyed. In some way an order to fall back must be conveyed to these men, or France would be the weaker by fourteen thousand men. Little did I think that it was I, Colonel Gerard, who was to have the honour of a deed which might have formed the crowning glory of any other man's life, and which stands high among those exploits which have made my own so famous.

★　★　★　★

At that time I was serving on Massena's staff, and he had two other aides-de-camp, who were also very brave and intelligent officers. The name of one was Cortex and of the other Duplessis. They were senior to me in age, but junior in every other respect. Cortex was a small, dark man, very quick and eager. He was a fine soldier, but he was ruined by his conceit. To take him at his own valuation, he was the first man in the army. Duplessis was a Gascon, like myself, and he was a very fine fellow, as all Gascon gentlemen are. We took it in turn, day about, to do duty, and it was Cortex who was in attendance upon the morning of which I speak. I saw him at breakfast, but afterwards neither he nor his horse was to be seen. All day Massena was in his usual gloom, and he spent much of his time staring with his telescope at the English lines and at the shipping in the Tagus. He said nothing of the mission upon which he had sent our comrade, and it was not for us to ask him any questions.

That night, about twelve o'clock, I was standing outside the Marshal's headquarters when he came out and stood motionless for half an hour, his arms folded upon his breast, staring through the darkness towards the east. So rigid and intent was he that you might have believed the muffled figure and the cocked hat to have been the statue of the man. What he was looking for I could not imagine; but at last he gave a bitter curse, and, turning on his heel, he went back into the house, banging the door behind him.

Next day the second aide-de-camp, Duplessis, had an interview with Massena in the morning, after which neither he nor his horse was seen again. That night, as I sat in the ante-room, the Marshal passed me, and I observed him through the window standing and staring to the east exactly as he had done before. For fully half an hour he remained there, a black shadow in the gloom. Then he strode in, the door banged, and I heard his spurs and his scabbard jingling and clanking through the passage. At the best he was a savage old man, but when he was crossed I had almost as soon face the Emperor himself. I heard him that night cursing and stamping above my head, but he did not send for me, and I knew him too well to go unsought.

Next morning it was my turn, for I was the only aide-de-camp left. I was his favourite aide-de-camp. His heart went out always to a smart soldier. I declare that I think there were tears in his black eyes when he sent for me that morning.

'Gerard!' said he. 'Come here!'

With a friendly gesture he took me by the sleeve and he led me to the open window which faced the east. Beneath us was the infantry camp, and beyond that the lines of the cavalry with the long rows of picketed horses. We could see the French outposts, and then a stretch of open country, intersected by vineyards. A range of hills lay beyond, with one well-marked peak towering above them. Round the base of these hills was a broad belt of forest. A single road ran white and clear, dipping and rising until it passed through a gap in the hills.

'This,' said Massena, pointing to the mountain, 'is the Sierra de Merodal. Do you perceive anything upon the top?'

I answered that I did not.

'Now?' he asked, and he handed me his field-glass.

With its aid I perceived a small mound or cairn upon the crest.

'What you see,' said the Marshal, 'is a pile of logs which was placed there as a beacon. We laid it when the country was in our hands, and now, although we no longer hold it, the beacon remains undisturbed. Gerard, that beacon must be lit tonight. France needs it, the Emperor needs it, the army needs it. Two of your comrades have gone to light it, but neither has made his way to the summit. Today it is your turn, and I pray that you may have better luck.'

It is not for a soldier to ask the reason for his orders, and so I was about to hurry from the room, but the Marshal laid his hand upon my shoulder and held me.

'You shall know all, and so learn how high is the cause for which you risk your life,' said he. 'Fifty miles to the south of us, on the other side of the Tagus, is the army of General Clausel. His camp is situated near a peak named the Sierra d'Ossa. On the summit of this peak is a beacon, and by this beacon he has a picket. It is agreed between us that when at midnight he shall see our signal fire he shall light his own as an answer, and shall then at once fall back upon the main army. If he does not start at once I must go without him. For two days I have endeavoured to send him his message. It must reach him today, or his army will be left behind and destroyed.'

Ah, my friends, how my heart swelled when I heard how high was the task which fortune had assigned to me! If my life were spared, here was one more splendid new leaf for my laurel crown. If, on the other hand, I died, then it would be a death worthy of such a career. I said nothing, but I cannot doubt that all the noble thoughts that were in me shone in my face, for Massena took my hand and wrung it.

'There is the hill and there the beacon,' said he. 'There is only this guerilla and his men between you and it. I cannot detach a large party for the enterprise, and a small one would be seen and destroyed. Therefore to you alone I commit it. Carry it out in your own way, but at twelve o'clock this night let me see the fire upon the hill.'

'If it is not there,' said I, 'then I pray you, Marshal Massena, to see that my effects are sold and the money sent to my mother.' So I raised my hand to my busby and turned upon my heel, my heart glowing at the thought of the great exploit which lay before me.

I sat in my own chamber for some little time considering how I had best take the matter in hand. The fact that neither Cortex nor Duplessis, who were very zealous and active officers, had succeeded in reaching the summit of the Sierra de Merodal showed that the country was very closely watched by the guerillas. I reckoned out the distance upon a map. There were ten miles of open country to be crossed before reaching the hills. Then came a belt of forest on the lower slopes of the mountain, which may have been three or four miles wide. And then there was the actual peak itself, of no very great height, but without any cover to conceal me. Those were the three stages of my journey.

It seemed to me that once I had reached the shelter of the wood all would be easy, for I could lie concealed within its shadows and climb upwards under the cover of night. From eight till twelve would give me four hours of darkness in which to make the ascent. It was only the first stage, then, which I had seriously to consider.

Over that flat country there lay the inviting white road, and I remembered that my comrades had both taken their horses. That was clearly their ruin, for nothing could be easier than for the brigands to keep watch upon the road, and to lay an ambush for all who passed along it. It would not be difficult for me to ride across country, and I was well horsed at that time, for I had not only Violette and Rataplan, who were two of the finest mounts in the army, but I had the splendid black English hunter which I had taken from Sir Cotton. However, after much thought, I determined to go upon foot, since I should then be in a better state to take advantage of any chance which might offer. As to my dress, I covered my Hussar uniform with a long cloak, and I put a grey forage cap upon my head. You ask me why I did not dress as a peasant, but I answer that a man of honour has no desire to die the death of a spy. It is one thing to be murdered, and it is another to be justly executed by the laws of war. I would not run the risk of such an end.

★ ★ ★ ★

In the late afternoon I stole out of the camp and passed through the line of our pickets. Beneath my cloak I had a field-glass and a pocket pistol as well as my sword. In my pocket were tinder, flint, and steel.

For two or three miles I kept under cover of the vineyards, and made such good progress that my heart was high within me, and I thought to myself that it only needed a man of some brains to take the matter in hand to bring it easily to success. Of course, Cortex and Duplessis galloping down the high road would be easily seen, but the intelligent Gerard lurking among the vines was quite another person. I dare say I had got as far as five miles before I met any check. At that point there is a small winehouse, round which I perceived some carts and a number of people, the first that I had seen. Now that I was well outside the lines I knew that every person was my enemy, so I crouched lower while I stole along to a point from which I could get a better view of what was going on. I then perceived that these people were peasants, who were loading two waggons with empty wine-casks. I failed to see how they could either help or hinder me, so I continued upon my way.

But soon I understood that my task was not so simple as had appeared. As the ground rose the vineyards ceased, and I came upon a stretch of open country studded with low hills. Crouching in a ditch I examined them with a glass, and I very soon perceived that there was a watcher upon every one of them, and that these people had a line of pickets and outposts thrown forward exactly like our own. I had heard of the discipline which was practised by this scoundrel whom they called 'The Smiler', and this, no doubt, was an example of it. Between the hills there was a cordon of sentries, and, though I worked some distance round to the flank, I still found myself faced by the enemy. It was a puzzle what to do. There was so little cover that a rat could hardly cross without being seen. Of course, it would be easy enough to slip through at night, as I had done with the English at Torres Vedras; but I was still far from the mountain, and I could not in that case reach it in time to light the midnight beacon. I lay in my ditch and I made a thousand plans, each more dangerous than the last. And then suddenly I had that flash of light which comes to the brave man who refuses to despair.

You remember I have mentioned that two waggons were loading up with empty casks at the inn. The heads of the oxen were turned to the east, and it was evident that those waggons were going in the direction which I desired. Could I only conceal myself upon one of them, what better and easier way could I find of passing through the lines of the guerillas? So simple and so good was the plan that I could not restrain a cry of delight as it crossed my mind, and I hurried away instantly in the direction of the inn. There, from behind some bushes, I had a good look at what was going on upon the road.

There were three peasants with red montero caps loading the barrels, and they had completed one waggon and the lower tier of the other. A number of empty barrels still lay outside the winehouse waiting to be put on. Fortune was my friend – I have always said that she is a woman and cannot resist a dashing young Hussar. As I watched, the three fellows went into the inn, for the day was hot, and they were thirsty after their labour. Quick as a flash I darted out from my hiding-place, climbed on to the waggon, and crept into one of the empty casks. It had a bottom but no top, and it lay upon its side with the open end inwards. There I crouched like a dog in its kennel, my knees drawn up to my chin; for the barrels were not very large and I am a well-grown man. As I lay there out came the three peasants again, and presently I heard a crash upon the top of me, which told that

I had another barrel above me. They piled them upon the cart until I could not imagine how I was ever to get out again. However, it is time to think of crossing the Vistula when you are over the Rhine, and I had no doubt that if chance and my own wits had carried me so far they would carry me farther.

Soon, when the waggon was full, they set forth upon their way, and I within my barrel chuckled at every step, for it was carrying me whither I wished to go. We travelled slowly, and the peasants walked beside the waggons. This I knew, because I heard their voices close to me. They seemed to me to be very merry fellows, for they laughed heartily as they went. What the joke was I could not understand. Though I speak their language fairly well I could not hear anything comic in the scraps of their conversation which met my ear.

I reckoned that at the rate of walking of a team of oxen we covered about two miles an hour. Therefore, when I was sure that two and a half hours had passed – such hours, my friends, cramped, suffocated, and nearly poisoned with the fumes of the lees – when they had passed, I was sure that the dangerous open country was behind us, and that we were upon the edge of the forest and the mountain. So now I had to turn my mind upon how I was to get out of my barrel. I had thought of several ways, and was balancing one against the other, when the question was decided for me in a very simple but unexpected manner.

The waggon stopped suddenly with a jerk, and I heard a number of gruff voices in excited talk. 'Where, where?' cried one. 'On our cart,' said another. 'Who is he?' said a third. 'A French officer; I saw his cap and his boots.' They all roared with laughter. 'I was looking out of the window of the *posada* and I saw him spring into the cask like a toreador with a Seville bull at his heels.' 'Which cask, then?' 'It was this one,' said the fellow, and, sure enough, his fist struck the wood beside my head.

What a situation, my friends, for a man of my standing! I blush now, after forty years, when I think of it. To be trussed like a fowl and to listen helplessly to the rude laughter of these boors – to know, too, that my mission had come to an ignominious and even ridiculous end.

I would have blessed the man who would have sent a bullet through the cask and freed me from my misery.

I heard the crashing of the barrels as they hurled them off the waggon, and then a couple of bearded faces and the muzzles of two guns looked in at me. They seized me by the sleeves of my coat, and they dragged me out into the daylight. A strange figure I must have looked as I stood blinking and gaping in the blinding sunlight. My body was bent like a cripple's, for I could not straighten my stiff joints, and half my coat was as red as an English soldier's from the lees in which I had lain. They laughed and laughed, these dogs, and as I tried to express by my bearing and gestures the contempt in which I held them, their laughter grew all the louder. But even in these hard circumstances I bore myself like the man I am, and as I cast my eye slowly round I did not find that any of the laughers were very ready to face it.

That one glance round was enough to tell me exactly how I was situated. I had been betrayed by these peasants into the hands of an outpost of guerillas. There were eight of them, savage-looking, hairy creatures, with cotton handkerchiefs under their sombreros, and many-buttoned jackets with coloured sashes round the waist. Each had a gun and one or two pistols stuck in his girdle. The leader, a great bearded ruffian, held his gun against my ear while the others searched my pockets, taking from me my overcoat, my pistol, my glass, my sword, and, worst of all, my flint and steel and tinder. Come what might I was ruined, for I had no longer the means of lighting the beacon even if I should reach it.

Eight of them, my friend, with three peasants, and I unarmed! Was Etienne Gerard in despair? Did he lose his wits? Ah, you know me too well; but they did not know me yet, these dogs of brigands. Never have I made so supreme and astounding an effort as at this very instant when all seemed lost. Yet you might guess many times before you would hit upon the device by which I escaped them. Listen and I will tell you.

They had dragged me from the waggon when they searched me,

and I stood, still twisted and warped, in the midst of them. But the stiffness was wearing off, and already my mind was very actively looking out for some methods of breaking away. It was a narrow pass in which the brigands had their outpost. It was bounded on the one hand by a steep mountain side. On the other the ground fell away in a very long slope, which ended in a bushy valley many hundreds of feet below. These fellows, you understand, were hardy mountaineers, who could travel either up hill or down very much quicker than I. They wore abarcas, or shoes of skin, tied on like sandals, which gave them a foothold everywhere. A less resolute man would have despaired. But in an instant I saw and used the strange chance which Fortune had placed in my way. On the very edge of the slope was one of the wine-barrels. I moved slowly towards it, and then with a tiger spring I dived into it feet foremost, and with a roll of my body I tipped it over the side of the hill.

Shall I ever forget that dreadful journey – how I bounded and crashed and whizzed down that terrible slope? I had dug in my knees and elbows, bunching my body into a compact bundle so as to steady it; but my head projected from the end, and it was a marvel that I did not dash out my brains. There were long, smooth slopes and then came steeper scarps where the barrel ceased to roll, and sprang into the air like a goat, coming down with a rattle and crash which jarred every bone in my body. How the wind whistled in my ears, and my head turned and turned until I was sick and giddy and nearly senseless! Then, with a swish and a great rasping and crackling of branches, I reached the bushes which I had seen so far below me. Through them I broke my way, down a slope beyond, and deep into another patch of underwood, where striking a sapling my barrel flew to pieces. From amid a heap of staves and hoops I crawled out, my body aching in every inch of it, but my heart singing loudly with joy and my spirit high within me, for I knew how great was the feat which I had accomplished, and I already seemed to see the beacon blazing on the hill.

A horrible nausea had seized me from the tossing which I had undergone, and I felt as I did upon the ocean when first I experienced those movements of which the English have taken so perfidious an advantage. I had to sit for a few moments with my head upon my hands beside the ruins of my barrel. But there was no time for rest. Already I heard shouts above me which told that my pursuers were descending the hill. I dashed into the thickest part of the underwood, and I ran and ran until I was utterly exhausted. Then I lay panting and listened with all my ears, but no sound came to them. I had shaken off my enemies.

★　★　★　★

When I had recovered my breath I travelled swiftly on, and waded knee-deep through several brooks, for it came into my head that they might follow me with dogs. On gaining a clear place and looking round me, I found to my delight that in spite of my adventures I had not been much out of my way. Above me towered the peak of Merodal, with its bare and bold summit shooting out of the groves of dwarf oaks which shrouded its flanks. These groves were the continuation of the cover under which I found myself, and it seemed to me that I had nothing to fear now until I reached the other side of the forest. At the same time I knew that every man's hand was against me, that I was unarmed, and that there were many people about me. I saw no one, but several times I heard shrill whistles, and once the sound of a gun in the distance.

It was hard work pushing one's way through the bushes, and so I was glad when I came to the larger trees and found a path which led between them. Of course, I was too wise to walk upon it, but I kept near it and followed its course. I had gone some distance, and had, as I imagined, nearly reached the limit of the wood, when a strange, moaning sound fell upon my ears. At first I thought it was the cry of some animals, but then there came words, of which I only caught the French exclamation, 'Mon Dieu!' With great caution I advanced in the direction from which the sound proceeded, and this is what I saw.

On a couch of dried leaves there was stretched a man dressed in the same grey uniform which I wore myself. He was evidently horribly wounded, for he held a cloth to his breast which was crimson with his blood. A pool had formed all round his couch, and he lay in a haze of flies, whose buzzing and droning would certainly have called my attention if his groans had not come to my ear. I lay for a moment, fearing some trap, and then, my pity and loyalty rising above all other feelings, I ran forward and knelt by his side. He turned a haggard face upon me, and it was Duplessis, the man who had gone before me. It needed but one glance at his sunken cheeks and glazing eyes to tell me that he was dying.

'Gerard!' said he; 'Gerard!'

I could but look my sympathy, but he, though the life was ebbing swiftly out of him, still kept his duty before him, like the gallant gentleman he was.

'The beacon, Gerard! You will light it?'

'Have you flint and steel?'

'It is here.'

'Then I will light it tonight.'

'I die happy to hear you say so. They shot me, Gerard. But you will tell the Marshal that I did my best.'

'And Cortex?'

'He was less fortunate. He fell into their hands and died horribly. If you see that you cannot get away, Gerard, put a bullet into your own heart. Don't die as Cortex did.'

I could see that his breath was failing, and I bent low to catch his words.

'Can you tell me anything which can help me in my task?' I asked.

'Yes, yes; De Pombal. He will help you. Trust De Pombal.' With the words his head fell back and he was dead.

'Trust De Pombal. It is good advice.' To my amazement a man was standing at the very side of me. So absorbed had I been in my comrade's words and intent on his advice that he had crept up without my observing him. Now I sprang to my feet and faced him. He was a tall, dark fellow, black-haired, black-eyed, black-bearded, with a long, sad face. In his hand he had a winebottle and over his shoulder was slung one of the trebucos, or blunderbusses, which these fellows bear. He made no effort to unsling it, and I understood that this was the man to whom my dead friend had commended me.

'Alas, he is gone!' said he, bending over Duplessis. 'He fled into the wood after he was shot, but I was fortunate enough to find where he had fallen and to make his last hours more easy. This couch was my making, and I had brought this wine to slake his thirst.'

'Sir,' said I, 'in the name of France I thank you. I am but a colonel of light cavalry, but I am Etienne Gerard, and the name stands for something in the French army. May I ask—'

'Yes, sir, I am Aloysius de Pombal, younger brother of the famous nobleman of that name. At present I am the first lieutenant in the band of the guerilla chief who is usually known as Manuelo, "The Smiler".'

My word, I clapped my hand to the place where my pistol should have been, but the man only smiled at the gesture.

'I am his first lieutenant, but I am also his deadly enemy,' said he. He slipped off his jacket and pulled up his shirt as he spoke. 'Look at this!' he cried, and he turned upon me a back which was all scored and lacerated with red and purple weals. 'This is what "The Smiler" has done to me, a man with the noblest blood of Portugal in my veins. What I will do to "The Smiler" you have still to see.'

There was such fury in his eyes and in the grin of his white teeth that I could no longer doubt his truth, with that clotted and oozing back to corroborate his words.

'I have ten men sworn to stand by me,' said he. 'In a few days I hope to join your army, when I have done my work here. In the meanwhile—' A strange change came over his face, and he suddenly slung his musket to the front: 'Hold up your hands, you French hound!' he yelled. 'Up with them, or I blow your head off!'

You start, my friends! You stare! Think, then, how I stared and started at this sudden ending of our talk. There was the black muzzle, and there the dark, angry eyes behind it. What could I do? I was helpless. I raised my hands in the air. At the same moment voices sounded from all parts of the wood, there were crying and calling and rushing of many feet. A swarm of dreadful figures broke through the green bushes, a dozen hands seized me, and I, poor, luckless, frenzied I, was a prisoner once more. Thank God, there was no pistol which I could have plucked from my belt and snapped at my own head. Had I been armed at that moment I should not be sitting here in this café and telling you these old-world tales.

With grimy, hairy hands clutching me on every side I was led along the pathway through the wood, the villain De Pombal giving directions to my captors. Four of the brigands carried up the dead body of Duplessis. The shadows of evening were already falling when we cleared the forest and came out upon the mountainside. Up this I was driven until we reached the headquarters of the guerillas, which lay in a cleft close to the summit of the mountain. There was the beacon which had cost me so much, a square stack of wood, immediately above our heads. Below were two or three huts which had belonged, no doubt, to goatherds, and which were now used to shelter these rascals. Into one of these I was cast, bound and helpless, and the dead body of my poor comrade was laid beside me.

I was lying there with one thought still consuming me, how to wait a few hours and to get at that pile of faggots above my head, when the door of my prison opened and a man entered. Had my hands been free I should have flown at his throat, for it was none other than De Pombal. A couple of brigands were at his heels, but he ordered them back and closed the door behind him.

'You villain!' said I.

'Hush!' he cried, 'Speak low, for I do not know who may be listening, and my life is at stake. I have some words to say to you, Colonel Gerard; I wish well to you, as I did to your dead companion. As I spoke to you beside his body I saw that we were surrounded, and that your capture was unavoidable. I should have shared your fate had I hesitated. I instantly captured you myself, so as to preserve the confidence of the band. Your own sense will tell you that there was nothing else for me to do. I do not know now whether I can save you, but at least I will try.'

This was a new light upon the situation. I told him that I could not tell how far he spoke the truth, but that I would judge him by his actions.

'I ask nothing better,' said he. 'A word of advice to you! The chief will see you now. Speak him fair, or he will have you sawn between two planks. Contradict nothing he says. Give him such information he wants. It is your only chance. If you can gain time something may come in our favour. Now, I have no more time. Come at once, or suspicion may be awakened.' He helped me to rise and then, opening the door, he dragged me out very roughly, and with the aid of the fellows outside he brutally pushed and thrust me to the place where the guerilla chief was seated, with his rude followers gathered round him.

A remarkable man was Manuelo, 'The Smiler.' He was fat and florid and comfortable, with a big, clean-shaven face and a bald head, the very model of a kindly father of a family. As I looked at his honest smile I could scarcely believe that this was, indeed, the infamous ruffian whose name was a horror through the English Army as well as our own. It is well known that Trent, who was a British officer, afterwards had the fellow hanged for his brutalities. He sat upon a boulder and he beamed upon me like one who meets an old acquaintance. I observed, however, that one of his men leaned upon a long saw, and the sight was enough to cure me of all delusions.

'Good evening, Colonel Gerard,' said he. 'We have been highly honoured by General Massena's staff: Major Cortex one day, Colonel Duplessis the next, and now Colonel Gerard. Possibly the Marshal himself may be induced to honour us with a visit. You have seen Duplessis, I understand. Cortex you will find nailed to a tree down yonder. It only remains to be decided how we can best dispose of yourself.'

It was not a cheering speech; but all the time his fat face was wreathed in smiles, and he lisped out his words in the most mincing and amiable fashion. Now, however, he suddenly leaned forward, and I read a very real intensity in his eyes.

'Colonel Gerard,' said he, 'I cannot promise you your life, for it is not our custom, but I can give you an easy death or I can give you a terrible one. Which shall it be?'

'What do you wish me to do in exchange?'

'If you would die easy I ask you to give me truthful answers to the questions which I ask.'

A sudden thought flashed through my mind.

'You wish to kill me,' said I; 'it cannot matter to you how I die. If I answer your questions, will you let me choose the manner of my death?'

'Yes, I will,' said he, 'so long as it is before midnight tonight.'

'Swear it!' I cried.

'The word of a Portuguese gentleman is sufficient,' said he.

'Not a word will I say until you have sworn it.'

He flushed with anger and his eyes swept round towards the saw. But he understood from my tone that I meant what I said, and that I was not a man to be bullied into submission. He pulled a cross from under his zammara or jacket of black sheepskin.

'I swear it,' said he.

Oh, my joy as I heard the words! What an end – what an end for the first swordsman of France! I could have laughed with delight at the thought.

'Now, your questions!' said I.

'You swear in turn to answer them truly?'

'I do, upon the honour of a gentleman and a soldier.' It was, as you perceive, a terrible thing that I promised, but what was it compared to what I might gain by compliance?

'This is a very fair and a very interesting bargain,' said he, taking a notebook from his pocket. 'Would you kindly turn your gaze towards the French camp?'

Following the direction of his gesture, I turned and looked down upon the camp in the plain beneath us. In spite of the fifteen miles, one could in that clear atmosphere see every detail with the utmost distinctness. There were the long squares of our tents and our huts, with the cavalry lines and the dark patches which marked the ten batteries of artillery. How sad to think of my magnificent regiment waiting down yonder, and to know that they would never see their colonel again! With one squadron of them I could have swept all these cut-throats off the face of the earth. My eager eyes filled with tears as I looked at the corner of the camp where I knew that there were eight hundred men, anyone of whom would have died for his colonel. But my sadness vanished when I saw behind the tents the plumes of smoke which marked the headquarters at Torres Novas. There was Massena, and, please God, at the cost of my life his mission would that night be done. A spasm of pride and exultation filled my breast. I should have liked to have had a voice of thunder that I might call to them, 'Behold it is I, Etienne Gerard, who will die in order to save the army of Clausel!' It was, indeed, sad to think that so noble a deed should be done, and that no one should be there to tell the tale.

'Now,' said the brigand chief, 'you see the camp and you see also the road which leads to Coimbra. It is crowded with your fourgons and your ambulances. Does this mean that Massena is about to retreat?'

One could see the dark moving lines of waggons with an occasional flash of steel from the escort. There could, apart from my promise, be no indiscretion in admitting that which was already obvious.

'He will retreat,' said I.

'By Coimbra?'

'I believe so.'

'But the army of Clausel?'

I shrugged my shoulders.

'Every path to the south is blocked. No message can reach them. If Massena falls back the army of Clausel is doomed.'

'It must take its chance,' said I.

'How many men has he?'

'I should say about fourteen thousand.'

'How much cavalry?'

'One brigade of Montbrun's Division.'

'What regiments?'

'The 4th Chasseurs, the 9th Hussars, and a regiment of Cuirassiers.'

'Quite right,' said he, looking at his notebook. 'I can tell you speak the truth, and Heaven help you if you don't.' Then, division by division, he went over the whole army, asking the composition of each brigade. Need I tell you that I would have had my tongue torn out before I would have told him such things had I not a greater end in view? I would let him know all if I could save the army of Clausel.

At last he closed his notebook and replaced it in his pocket. 'I am obliged to you for this information, which shall reach Lord Wellington tomorrow,' said he. 'You have done your share of the bargain; it is for me now to perform mine. How would you wish to die? As a soldier you would, no doubt, prefer to be shot, but some think that a jump over the Merodal precipice is really an easier death. A good few have taken it, but we were, unfortunately, never able to get an opinion from them afterwards. There is the saw, too, which does not appear to be popular. We could hang you, no doubt, but it would involve the inconvenience of going down to the wood. However, a promise is a promise, and you seem to be an excellent fellow, so we will spare no pains to meet your wishes.'

'You said,' I answered, 'that I must die before midnight. I will choose, therefore, just one minute before that hour.'

'Very good,' said he. 'Such clinging to life is rather childish, but your wishes shall be met.'

'As to the method,' I added, 'I love a death which all the world can see. Put me on yonder pile of faggots and burn me alive, as saints and martyrs have been burned before me. That is no common end, but one which an Emperor might envy.'

The idea seemed to amuse him very much.

'Why not?' said he. 'If Massena has sent you to spy upon us, he may guess what the fire upon the mountains means.'

'Exactly,' said I. 'You have hit upon my very reason. He will guess, and all will know, that I have died a soldier's death.'

'I see no objection whatever,' said the brigand, with his abominable smile. 'I will send some goat's flesh and wine into your hut. The sun is sinking, and it is nearly eight o'clock. In four hours be ready for your end.'

It was a beautiful world to be leaving. I looked at the golden haze below, where the last rays of the sinking sun shone upon the blue waters of the winding Tagus and gleamed upon the white sails of the English transports. Very beautiful it was, and very sad to leave; but there are things more beautiful than that. The death that is died for the sake of others, honour, and duty, and loyalty, and love – these are the beauties far brighter than any which the eye can see. My breast was filled with admiration for my own most noble conduct, and with wonder whether any soul would ever come to know how I had placed myself in the heart of the beacon which saved the army of Clausel. I hoped so and I prayed so, for what a consolation it would be to my mother, what an example to the army, what a pride to my Hussars! When De Pombal came at last into my hut with the food and the wine, the first request I made him was that he would write an account of my death and send it to the French camp. He answered not a word, but I ate my supper with a better appetite from the thought that my glorious fate would not be altogether unknown.

★   ★   ★   ★

I had been there about two hours when the door opened again, and the chief stood looking in. I was in darkness, but a brigand with a torch stood beside him, and I saw his eyes and his teeth gleaming as he peered at me.

'Ready?' he asked.

'It is not yet time.'

'You stand out for the last minute?'

'A promise is a promise.'

'Very good. Be it so. We have a little justice to do among ourselves, for one of my fellows has been misbehaving. We have a strict rule of our own which is no respecter of persons, as De Pombal here could tell you. Do you truss him and lay him on the faggots, De Pombal, and I will return to see him die.'

De Pombal and the man with the torch entered, while I heard the steps of the chief passing away. De Pombal closed the door.

'Colonel Gerard,' said he, 'you must trust this man, for he is one of my party. It is neck or nothing. We may save you yet. But I take a great risk, and I want a definite promise. If we save you, will you guarantee that we have a friendly reception in the French camp and that all the past will be forgotten?'

'I do guarantee it.'

'And I trust your honour. Now, quick, quick, there is not an instant to lose! If this monster returns we shall die horribly, all three.'

I stared in amazement at what he did. Catching up a long rope he wound it round the body of my dead comrade, and he tied a cloth round his mouth so as to almost cover his face.

'Do you lie there!' he cried, and he laid me in the place of the dead body. 'I have four of my men waiting, and they will place this upon the beacon.' He opened the door and gave an order. Several of the brigands entered and bore out Duplessis. For myself I remained upon the floor, with my mind in a turmoil of hope and wonder.

Five minutes later De Pombal and his men were back.

'You are laid upon the beacon,' said he; 'I defy any one in the world to say it is not you, and you are so gagged and bound that no one can expect you to speak or move. Now, it only remains to carry forth the body of Duplessis and to toss it over the Merodal precipice.'

Two of them seized me by the head and two by the heels and carried me, stiff and inert, from the hut. As I came into the open air I could have cried out in my amazement. The moon had risen, above the beacon, and there, clear outlined against its silver light, was the figure of the man stretched upon the top. The brigands were either in their camp or standing round the beacon, for none of them stopped or questioned our little party. De Pombal led them in the direction of the precipice. At the brow we were out of sight, and there I was allowed to use my feet once more. De Pombal pointed to a narrow, winding track.

'This is the way down,' said he, and then, suddenly, 'Dios mio, what is that?'

A terrible cry had risen out of the woods beneath us. I saw that De Pombal was shivering like a frightened horse.

'It is that devil,' he whispered. 'He is treating another as he treated me. But on, on, for Heaven help us if he lays his hands upon us!'

One by one we crawled down the narrow goat track. At the bottom of the cliff we were back in the woods once more. Suddenly a yellow glare shone above us, and the black shadows of the tree-trunks started out in front. They had fired the beacon behind us. Even from where we stood we could see that impassive body amid the flames, and the black figures of the guerillas as they danced, howling like cannibals, round the pile. Ha! how I shook my fist at them, the dogs, and how I vowed that one day my Hussars and I would make the reckoning level!

De Pombal knew how the outposts were placed and all the paths which led through the forest. But to avoid these villains we had to plunge among the hills and walk for many a weary mile. And yet how gladly would I have walked those extra leagues if only for one sight which they brought to my eyes! It may have been two o'clock in the morning when we halted upon the bare shoulder of a hill over which our path curled. Looking back we saw the red glow of the embers of the beacon as if volcanic fires were bursting from the tall peak of Merodal. And then, as I gazed, I saw something else – something which caused me to shriek with joy and to fall upon the ground, rolling in my delight. For, far away upon the southern horizon, there winked and twinkled one great yellow light, throbbing and flaming, the light of no house, the light of no star, but the answering beacon of Mount d'Ossa, which told that the army of Clausel knew what Etienne Gerard had been sent to tell them.

Animal Stories

The Elephant's Child

RUDYARD KIPLING

Just So Stories for Little Children (1902) is the name of the famous collection of animal stories in which 'The Elephant's Child' first appeared. Rudyard Kipling, its author, drew his own illustrations.

In the High and Far-Off Times the Elephant, O Best Beloved, had no trunk. He had only a blackish, bulgy nose, as big as a boot, that he could wriggle about from side to side; but he couldn't pick up things with it. But there was one Elephant – a new Elephant – an Elephant's Child – who was full of 'satiable curtiosity, and that means he asked ever so many questions. *And* he lived in Africa, and he filled all Africa with his 'satiable curtiosities. He asked his tall aunt, the Ostrich, why her tail-feathers grew just so, and his tall aunt the Ostrich spanked him with her hard, hard claw. He asked his tall uncle, the Giraffe, what made his skin spotty, and his tall uncle, the Giraffe, spanked him with his hard, hard hoof. And still he was full of 'satiable curtiosity! He asked his broad aunt, the Hippopotamus, why her eyes were red, and his broad aunt, the Hippopotamus, spanked him with her broad, broad hoof; and he asked his hairy uncle, the Baboon, why melons tasted just so, and his hairy uncle, the Baboon, spanked him with his hairy, hairy paw. And *still* he was full of 'satiable curtiosity! He asked questions about everything that he saw or heard, or felt, or smelt, or touched, and all his uncles and his aunts spanked him. And still he was full of 'satiable curtiosity!

One fine morning in the middle of the Precession of the Equinoxes this 'satiable Elephant's Child asked a new fine question that he had never asked before. He asked, 'What does the Crocodile have for dinner?' Then everybody said, 'Hush!' in a loud and dretful tone, and they spanked him immediately and directly, without stopping, for a long time.

By and by, when that was finished, he came upon Kolokolo Bird sitting in the middle of a wait-a-bit thorn-bush, and he said, 'My father has spanked me, and my mother has spanked me; all my aunts and uncles have spanked me for my 'satiable curtiosity; and *still* I want to know what the Crocodile has for dinner!'

Then Kolokolo Bird said, with a mournful cry, 'Go to the banks of the great grey-green, greasy Limpopo River, all set about with fever-trees, and find out.'

That very next morning, when there was nothing left of the Equinoxes, because the Precession had preceded according to precedent, this 'satiable Elephant's Child took a hundred pounds of bananas (the little short red kind), and a hundred pounds of sugar-cane (the long purple kind), and seventeen melons (the greeny-crackly kind), and said to all his dear families, 'Good-bye. I am going to the great grey-green, greasy Limpopo River, all set about with fever-trees, to find out what the Crocodile has for dinner.' And they all spanked him once more for luck, though he asked them most politely to stop.

Then he went away, a little warm, but not at all astonished, eating melons, and throwing the rind about, because he could not pick it up.

He went from Graham's Town to Kimberley, and from Kimberley to Khama's Country, and from Khama's Country he went east by north, eating melons all the time, till at last he came to the banks of the great grey-green, greasy Limpopo River, all set about with fever-trees, precisely as Kolokolo Bird had said.

Now you must know and understand, O Best Beloved, that till that very week, and day, and hour, and minute, this 'satiable Elephant's Child had never seen a Crocodile, and did not know what one was like. It was all his 'satiable curtiosity.

The first thing that he found was a Bi-Coloured-Python-Rock-Snake curled round a rock.

''Scuse me,' said the Elephant's Child most politely, 'but have you seen such a thing as a Crocodile in these promiscuous parts?'

'*Have* I seen a Crocodile?' said the Bi-Coloured-Python-Rock-Snake, in a voice of dretful scorn. 'What will you ask me next?'

''Scuse me,' said the Elephant's Child, 'but could you kindly tell me what he has for dinner?'

Then the Bi-Coloured-Python-Rock-Snake uncoiled himself very quickly from the rock, and spanked the Elephant's Child with his scalesome, flailsome tail.

'That is odd,' said the Elephant's Child, 'because my father and my mother, and my uncle and my aunt, not to mention my other aunt, the Hippopotamus, and my other uncle, the Baboon, have all spanked me for my 'satiable curtiosity – and I suppose this is the same thing.'

So he said good-bye very politely to the Bi-Coloured-Python-Rock-Snake, and helped to coil him up on the rock again, and went on, a little warm, but not at all astonished, eating melons, and throwing the rind about, because he could not pick it up, till he trod on what he thought was a log of wood at the very edge of the great grey-green, greasy Limpopo River, all set about with fever-trees.

But it was really the Crocodile, O Best Beloved, and the Crocodile winked one eye – like this!

''Scuse me,' said the Elephant's Child most politely, 'but do you happen to have seen a Crocodile in these promiscuous parts?'

Then the Crocodile winked the other eye, and lifted half his tail out of the mud; and the Elephant's Child stepped back most politely, because he did not wish to be spanked again.

'Come hither, Little One,' said the Crocodile. 'Why do you ask such things?'

''Scuse me,' said the Elephant's Child most politely, 'but my father has spanked me, my mother has spanked me, not to mention my tall aunt, the Ostrich, and my tall uncle, the Giraffe, who can kick ever so hard, as well as my broad aunt, the Hippopotamus, and my hairy uncle, the Baboon, *and* including the Bi-Coloured-Python-Rock-Snake, with the scalesome, flailsome tail, just up the bank, who spanks harder than any of them; and *so*, if it's quite all the same to you, I don't want to be spanked any more.'

'Come hither, Little One,' said the Crocodile, 'for I am the Crocodile,' and he wept crocodile-tears to show it was quite true.

Then the Elephant's Child grew all breathless, and panted, and kneeled down on the bank and said, 'You are the very person I have been looking for all these long days. Will you please tell me what you have for dinner?'

'Come hither, Little One,' said the Crocodile, 'and I'll whisper.'

Then the Elephant's Child put his head down close to the Crocodile's musky, tusky mouth, and the Crocodile caught him by his little nose, which up to that very week, day, hour, and minute, had been no bigger than a boot, though much more useful.

'I think,' said the Crocodile – and he said it between his teeth, like this – 'I think to-day I will begin with Elephant's Child!'

At this, O Best Beloved, the Elephant's Child was much annoyed, and he said, speaking through his nose, like this, 'Led go! You are hurtig be!'

Then the Bi-Coloured-Python-Rock-Snake scuffled down from the bank and said, 'My young friend, if you do not now, immediately and instantly, pull as hard as ever you can, it is my opinion that your acquaintance in the large-pattern leather ulster' (and by this he meant the Crocodile) 'will jerk you into yonder limpid stream before you can say Jack Robinson.'

This is the way Bi-Coloured-Python-Rock-Snakes always talk.

Then the Elephant's Child sat back on his little haunches, and pulled, and pulled, and pulled, and his nose began to stretch. And the Crocodile floundered into the water, making it all creamy with great sweeps of his tail, and *he* pulled, and pulled, and pulled.

And the Elephant's Child's nose kept on stretching; and the Elephant's Child spread all his little four legs and pulled, and pulled, and pulled, and his nose kept on stretching; and the Crocodile threshed his tail like an oar, and *he* pulled, and pulled, and pulled, and at each pull the Elephant's Child's nose grew longer and longer – and it hurt him hijjus!

Then the Elephant's Child felt his legs slipping, and he said through his nose, which was now nearly five feet long, 'This is too butch for be!'

Then the Bi-Coloured-Python-Rock-Snake came down from the bank, and knotted himself in a double-clove-hitch round the Elephant's Child's hind-legs, and said, 'Rash and inexperienced traveller, we will now seriously devote ourselves to a little high tension, because if we do not, it is my impression that yonder self-propelling man-of-war with the armour-plated upper deck' (and by this, O Best Beloved, he meant the Crocodile) 'will permanently vitiate your future career.'

That is the way all Bi-Coloured-Python-Rock-Snakes always talk.

So he pulled, and the Elephant's Child pulled, and the Crocodile pulled; but the Elephant's Child and the Bi-coloured-Python-Rock-Snake pulled hardest; and at last the Crocodile let go of the Elephant's Child's nose with a plop that you could hear all up and down the Limpopo.

Then the Elephant's Child sat down most hard and sudden; but first he was careful to say 'Thank you' to the Bi-Coloured-Python-Rock-Snake; and next he was kind to his poor pulled nose, and wrapped it all up in cool banana leaves, and hung it in the great grey-green, greasy Limpopo to cool.

'What are you doing that for?' said the Bi-Coloured-Python-Rock-Snake.

''Scuse me,' said the Elephant's Child, 'but my nose is badly out of shape, and I am waiting for it to shrink.'

'Then you will have to wait a long time,' said the Bi-Coloured-Python-Rock-Snake. 'Some people do not know what is good for them.'

The Elephant's Child sat there for three days waiting for his nose to shrink. But it never grew any shorter, and, besides, it made him squint. For, O Best Beloved, you will see and understand that the Crocodile had pulled it out into a really truly trunk same as all Elephants have to-day.

At the end of the third day a fly came and stung him on the shoulder, and before he knew what he was doing he lifted up his trunk and hit that fly dead with the end of it.

''Vantage number one!' said the Bi-Coloured-Python-Rock-Snake. 'You couldn't have done that with a mere-smear nose. Try and eat a little now.'

Before he thought what he was doing the Elephant's Child put out his trunk and plucked a large bundle of grass, dusted it clean against his fore-legs, and stuffed it into his own mouth.

''Vantage number two!' said the Bi-Coloured-Python-Rock-Snake. 'You couldn't have done that with a mere-smear nose. Don't you think the sun is very hot here?'

'It is,' said the Elephant's Child, and before he thought what he was doing he schlooped up a schloop of mud from the banks of the great grey-green, greasy Limpopo, and slapped it on his head, where it made a cool schloopy-sloshy mud-cap all trickly behind his ears.

''Vantage number three!' said the Bi-Coloured-Python-Rock-Snake. 'You couldn't have done that with a mere-smear nose. Now how do you feel about being spanked again?'

''Scuse me,' said the Elephant's Child, 'but I should not like it at all.'

'How would you like to spank somebody?' said the Bi-Coloured-Python-Rock-Snake.

'I should like it very much indeed,' said the Elephant's Child.

Opposite: This is the Elephant's Child having his nose pulled by the Crocodile. He is much surprised and astonished and hurt, and he is talking through his nose and saying, 'Led go! You are hurtig be!' He is pulling very hard, and so is the Crocodile; but the Bi-Coloured-Python-Rock-Snake is hurrying through the water to help the Elephant's Child. All that black stuff is the banks of the great grey-green, greasy Limpopo River (but I am not allowed to paint these pictures), and the bottly-tree with the twisty roots and the eight leaves is one of the fever trees that grow there.

Underneath the truly picture are shadows of African animals walking into an African ark. There are two lions, two ostriches, two oxen, two camels, two sheep, and two other things that look like rats, but I think they are rock-rabbits. They don't mean anything. I put them in because I thought they looked pretty. They would look very fine if I were allowed to paint them.

'Well', said the Bi-Coloured-Python-Rock-Snake, 'you will find that new nose of yours very useful to spank people with.'

'Thank you,' said the Elephant's Child, 'I'll remember that; and now I think I'll go home to all my dear families and try.'

So the Elephant's Child went home across Africa frisking and whisking his trunk. When he wanted fruit to eat he pulled fruit down from a tree, instead of waiting for it to fall as he used to do. When he wanted grass he plucked grass up from the ground, instead of going on his knees as he used to do. When the flies bit him he broke off the branch of a tree and used it as a fly-whisk; and he made himself a new, cool, slushy-squshy mud-cap whenever the sun was hot. When he felt lonely walking through Africa he sang to himself down his trunk, and the noise was louder than several brass bands. He went especially out of his way to find a broad Hippopotamus (she was no relation of his), and he spanked her very hard, to make sure that the Bi-Coloured-Python-Rock-Snake had spoken the truth about his new trunk. The rest of the time he picked up the melon rinds that he had dropped on his way to the Limpopo – for he was a Tidy Pachyderm.

One dark evening he came back to all his dear families, and he coiled up his trunk and said, 'How do you do?' They were very glad to see him, and immediately said, 'Come here and be spanked for your 'satiable curtiosity.'

'Pooh,' said the Elephant's Child. 'I don't think you peoples know anything about spanking; but *I* do, and I'll show you.'

Then he uncurled his trunk and knocked two of his dear brothers head over heels.

Opposite: This is just a picture of the Elephant's Child going to pull bananas off a banana-tree after he had got his fine new long trunk. I don't think it is a very nice picture; but I couldn't make it any better, because elephants and bananas are hard to draw. The streaky things behind the Elephant's Child mean squoggy marshy country somewhere in Africa. The Elephant's Child made most of his mud-cakes out of the mud that he found there. I think it would look better if you painted the banana tree green and the Elephant's Child red.

'O Bananas!' said they, 'where did you learn that trick, and what have you done to your nose?'

'I got a new one from the Crocodile on the banks of the great grey-green, greasy Limpopo River,' said the Elephant's Child. 'I asked him what he had for dinner, and he gave me this to keep.'

'It looks very ugly,' said his hairy uncle, the Baboon.

'It does,' said the Elephant's Child. 'But it's very useful,' and he picked up his hairy uncle, the Baboon, by one hairy leg, and hove him into a hornet's nest.

Then that bad Elephant's Child spanked all his dear families for a long time, till they were very warm and greatly astonished. He pulled out his tall Ostrich aunt's tail-feathers; and he caught his tall uncle, the Giraffe, by the hind-leg, and dragged him through a thorn-bush; and he shouted at his broad aunt, the Hippopotamus, and blew bubbles into her ear when she was sleeping in the water after meals; but he never let any one touch Kolokolo Bird.

At last things grew so exciting that his dear families went off one by one in a hurry to the banks of the great grey-green, greasy Limpopo River, all set about with fever-trees, to borrow new noses from the Crocodile. When they came back nobody spanked anybody any more; and ever since that day, O Best Beloved, all the Elephants you will ever see, besides all those that you won't, have trunks precisely like the trunk of the 'satiable Elephant's Child.

Toad of Toad Hall

KENNETH GRAHAME

Mr Toad is the boastful, badly-behaved hero of The Wind in the Willows *(1908), a story in which the other characters are all animals who live near the banks of a river.*

It was a bright morning in the early part of summer; the river had resumed its wonted banks and its accustomed pace, and a hot sun seemed to be pulling everything green and bushy and spiky up out of the earth towards him, as if by strings. The Mole and the Water Rat had been up since dawn, very busy on matters connected with boats and the opening of the boating season; painting and varnishing, mending paddles, repairing cushions, hunting for missing boat-hooks, and so on; and were finishing breakfast in their little parlour and eagerly discussing their plans for the day, when a heavy knock sounded at the door.

'Bother!' said the Rat, all over egg. 'See who it is, Mole, like a good chap, since you've finished.'

The Mole went to attend the summons, and the Rat heard him utter a cry of surprise. Then he flung the parlour door open, and announced with much importance, 'Mr. Badger!'

This was a wonderful thing, indeed, that the Badger should pay a formal call on them, or indeed on anybody. He generally had to be caught, if you wanted him badly, as he slipped quietly along a hedgerow of an early morning or a late evening, or else hunted up in his own house in the middle of the wood, which was a serious undertaking.

The Badger strode heavily into the room, and stood looking at the two animals with an expression full of seriousness. The Rat let his egg-spoon fall on the table-cloth, and sat open-mouthed.

'The hour has come!' said the Badger at last with great solemnity.

'What hour?' asked the Rat uneasily, glancing at the clock on the mantelpiece.

'*Whose* hour, you should rather say,' replied the Badger. 'Why, Toad's hour! The hour of Toad! I said I would take him in hand as soon as the winter was well over, and I'm going to take him in hand to-day!'

'Toad's hour, of course!' cried the Mole delightedly. 'Hooray! I remember now! *We'll* teach him to be a sensible Toad!'

'This very morning,' continued the Badger, taking an arm-chair, 'as I learnt last night from a trustworthy source, another new and exceptionally powerful motor-car will arrive at Toad Hall on approval or return. At this very moment, perhaps, Toad is busy arraying himself in those singularly hideous habiliments so dear to him, which transform him from a (comparatively) good-looking Toad into an Object which throws any decent-minded animal that comes across it into a violent fit. We must be up and doing, ere it is too late. You two animals will accompany me instantly to Toad Hall, and the work of rescue shall be accomplished.'

'Right you are!' cried the Rat, starting up. 'We'll rescue the poor unhappy animal! We'll convert him! He'll be the most converted Toad that ever was before we've done with him!'

They set off up the road on their mission of mercy, Badger leading the way. Animals when in company walk in a proper and sensible manner, in single file, instead of sprawling all across the road and being of no use or support to each other in case of sudden trouble or danger.

They reached the carriage-drive of Toad Hall to find, as the Badger had anticipated, a shiny new motor-car, of great size, painted a bright red (Toad's favourite colour), standing in front of the house. As they neared the door it was flung open, and Mr. Toad, arrayed in goggles, cap, gaiters, and enormous overcoat, came swaggering down the steps, drawing on his gauntleted gloves.

'Hullo! come on, you fellows!' he cried cheerfully on catching sight of them. 'You're just in time to come with me for a jolly – to come for a jolly – for a – er – jolly—'

His hearty accents faltered and fell away as he noticed the stern unbending look on the countenances of his silent friends, and his invitation remained unfinished.

The Badger strode up the steps. 'Take him inside,' he said sternly to his companions. Then, as Toad was hustled through the door, struggling and protesting, he turned to the *chauffeur* in charge of the new motor-car.

'I'm afraid you won't be wanted to-day,' he said. 'Mr. Toad has changed his mind. He will not require the car. Please understand that this is final. You needn't wait.' Then he followed the others inside and shut the door.

'Now, then!' he said to the Toad, when the four of them stood together in the hall, 'first of all, take those ridiculous things off!'

'Shan't!' replied Toad, with great spirit. 'What is the meaning of this gross outrage? I demand an instant explanation.'

'Take them off him, then, you two,' ordered the Badger briefly.

They had to lay Toad out on the floor, kicking and calling all sorts of names, before they could get to work properly. Then the Rat sat on him, and the Mole got his motor-clothes off him bit by bit, and they stood him up on his legs again. A good deal of his blustering spirit seemed to have evaporated with the removal of his fine panoply. Now that he was merely Toad, and no longer the Terror of the Highway, he giggled feebly and looked from one to the other appealingly, seeming quite to understand the situation.

'You knew it must come to this, sooner or later, Toad,' the Badger explained severely. 'You've disregarded all the warnings we've given you, you've gone on squandering the money your father left you, and you're getting us animals a bad name in the district by your furious driving and your smashes and your rows with the police. Independence is all very well, but we animals never allow our friends to make fools of themselves beyond a certain limit; and that limit you've reached. Now, you're a good fellow in many respects, and I don't want to be too hard on you. I'll make one more effort to bring you to reason. You will come with me into the smoking-room, and there you will hear some facts about yourself; and we'll see whether you come out of that room the same Toad that you went in.'

He took Toad firmly by the arm, led him into the smoking-room, and closed the door behind them.

'*That's* no good!' said the Rat comtemptuously. '*Talking* to Toad'll never cure him. He'll *say* anything.'

They made themselves comfortable in armchairs and waited patiently. Through the closed door they could just hear the long continuous drone of the Badger's voice, rising and falling in waves of oratory; and presently they noticed that the sermon began to be punctuated at intervals by long-drawn sobs, evidently proceeding from the bosom of Toad, who was a soft-hearted and affectionate fellow, very easily converted – for the time being – to any point of view.

After some three-quarters of an hour the door opened, and the Badger reappeared, solemnly leading by the paw a very limp and dejected Toad. His skin hung baggily about him, his legs wobbled, and his cheeks were furrowed by the tears so plentifully called forth by the Badger's moving discourse.

'Sit down there, Toad,' said the Badger kindly, pointing to a chair. 'My friends,' he went on, 'I am pleased to inform you that Toad has at last seen the error of his ways. He is truly sorry for his misguided conduct in the past, and he has undertaken to give up motor-cars entirely and for ever. I have his solemn promise to that effect.'

'That is very good news,' said the Mole gravely.

'Very good news indeed,' observed the Rat dubiously, 'if only – *if* only—'

He was looking very hard at Toad as he said this, and could not help thinking he perceived something vaguely resembling a twinkle in that animal's still sorrowful eye.

'There's only one thing more to be done,' continued the gratified Badger. 'Toad, I want you solemnly to repeat, before your friends here, what you fully admitted to me in the smoking-room just now. First, you are sorry for what you've done, and you see the folly of it all?'

There was a long, long pause. Toad looked desperately this way and that, while the other animals waited in grave silence. At last he spoke.

'No!' he said a little sullenly, but stoutly; 'I'm *not* sorry. And it wasn't folly at all! It was simply glorious!'

'What?' cried the Badger, greatly scandalised. 'You backsliding animal, didn't you tell me just now, in there—'

'O, yes, yes, in *there,*' said Toad impatiently. 'I'd have said anything in *there*. You're so eloquent, dear Badger, and so moving, and so convincing, and put all your points so frightfully well – you can do what you like with me in *there,* and you know it. But I've been searching in my mind since, and going over things in it, and I find that I'm not a bit sorry or repentant really, so it's no earthly good saying I am; now, is it?'

'Then you don't promise,' said the Badger, 'never to touch a motor-car again?'

'Certainly not!' replied Toad emphatically. 'On the contrary, I faithfully promise that the very first motor-car I see, poop-poop! off I go in it!'

'Told you so, didn't I?' observed the Rat to the Mole.

'Very well, then,' said the Badger firmly, rising to his feet. 'Since you won't yield to persuasion, we'll try what force can do. I feared it would come to this all along. You've often asked us three to come and stay with you, Toad, in this handsome house of yours; well, now we're going to. When we've converted you to a proper point of view we may quit, but not before. Take him upstairs, you two, and lock him up in his bedroom, while we arrange matters between ourselves.'

'It's for your own good, Toady, you know,' said the Rat kindly, as Toad, kicking and struggling, was hauled up the stairs by his two faithful friends. 'Think what fun we shall all have together, just as we used to, when you've quite got over this – this painful attack of yours!'

'We'll take great care of everything for you till you're well, Toad,' said the Mole; 'and we'll see your money isn't wasted, as it has been.'

'No more of those regrettable incidents with the police, Toad,' said the Rat, as they thrust him into his bedroom.

'And no more weeks in hospital, being ordered about by female nurses, Toad,' added the Mole, turning the key on him.

They descended the stair, Toad shouting abuse at them through the keyhole; and the three friends then met in conference on the situation.

'It's going to be a tedious business,' said the Badger, sighing. 'I've never seen Toad so determined. However, we will see it out. He must never be left an instant unguarded. We shall have to take it in turns to be with him, till the poison has worked itself out of his system.'

They arranged watches accordingly. Each animal took it in turns to sleep in Toad's room at night, and they divided the day up between them. At first Toad was undoubtedly very trying to his careful guardians. When his violent paroxysms possessed him he would arrange bedroom chairs in rude resemblance of a motor-car and would crouch on the foremost of them, bent forward and staring fixedly ahead, making uncouth and ghastly noises, till the climax was reached, when, turning a complete somersault, he would lie prostrate amidst the ruins of the chairs, apparently completely satisfied for the moment. As time passed, however, these painful seizures grew gradually less frequent, and his friends strove to divert his mind into fresh channels. But his interest in other matters did not seem to revive, and he grew apparently languid and depressed.

One fine morning the Rat, whose turn it was to go on duty, went upstairs to relieve Badger, whom he found fidgeting to be off and stretch his legs in a long ramble round his wood and down his earths and burrows. 'Toad's still in bed,' he told the Rat, outside the door. 'Can't get much out of him, except, "O, leave him alone, he wants nothing, perhaps he'll be better presently, it may pass off in time, don't be unduly anxious," and so on. Now, you look out, Rat! When Toad's quiet and submissive, and playing at being the hero of a

Sunday-school prize, then he's at his artfullest. There's sure to be something up. I know him. Well, now I must be off.'

'How are you to-day, old chap?' inquired the Rat cheerfully, as he approached Toad's bedside.

He had to wait some minutes for an answer. At last a feeble voice replied, 'Thank you so much, dear Ratty! So good of you to inquire! But first tell me how you are yourself, and the excellent Mole?'

'O, *we're* all right,' replied the Rat. 'Mole', he added incautiously, 'is going out for a run round with Badger. They'll be out till luncheon-time, so you and I will spend a pleasant morning together, and I'll do my best to amuse you. Now jump up, there's a good fellow, and don't lie moping there on a fine morning like this!'

'Dear, kind Rat,' murmured Toad, 'how little you realise my condition, and how very far I am from "jumping up" now – if ever! But do not trouble about me. I hate being a burden to my friends, and I do not expect to be one much longer. Indeed, I almost hope not.'

'Well, I hope not, too,' said the Rat heartily. 'You've been a fine bother to us all this time, and I'm glad to hear it's going to stop. And in weather like this, and the boating season just beginning! It's too bad of you, Toad! It isn't the trouble we mind, but you're making us miss such an awful lot.'

'I'm afraid it *is* the trouble you mind, though,' replied the Toad languidly. 'I can quite understand it. It's natural enough. You're tired of bothering about me. I mustn't ask you to do anything further. I'm a nuisance, I know.'

'You are, indeed,' said the Rat. 'But I tell you, I'd take any trouble on earth for you, if only you'd be a sensible animal.'

'If I thought that, Ratty,' murmured Toad, more feebly than ever, 'then I would beg you – for the last time, probably – to step round to the village as quickly as possible – even now it may be too late – and fetch the doctor. But don't you bother. It's only a trouble, and perhaps we may as well let things take their course.'

'Why, what do you want a doctor for?' inquired the Rat, coming closer and examining him. He certainly lay very still and flat, and his voice was weaker and his manner much changed.

'Surely you have noticed of late—' murmured Toad. 'But no – why should you? Noticing things is only a trouble. To-morrow, indeed, you may be saying to yourself, "O, if only I had noticed sooner! If only I had done something!" But no; it's a trouble. Never mind – forget that I asked.'

'Look here, old man,' said the Rat, beginning to get rather alarmed, 'of course I'll fetch a doctor to you, if you really think you want him. But you can hardly be bad enough for that yet. Let's talk about something else.'

'I fear, dear friend,' said Toad, with a sad smile, 'that "talk" can do little in a case like this – or doctors either, for that matter; still, one must grasp at the slightest straw. And, by the way – while you are about it – I *hate* to give you additional trouble, but I happen to remember that you will pass the door – would you mind at the same time asking the lawyer to step up? It would be a convenience to me, and there are moments – perhaps I should say there is *a* moment – when one must face disagreeable tasks, at whatever cost to exhausted nature!'

'A lawyer! O, he must be really bad!' the affrighted Rat said to himself, as he hurried from the room, not forgetting, however, to lock the door carefully behind him.

Outside, he stopped to consider. The other two were far away, and he had no one to consult.

'It's best to be on the safe side,' he said, on reflection. 'I've known Toad fancy himself frightfully bad before, without the slightest reason; but I've never heard him ask for a lawyer! If there's nothing really the matter, the doctor will tell him he's an old ass, and cheer him up; and that will be something gained. I'd better humour him and go; it won't take very long.' So he ran off to the village on his errand of mercy.

The Toad, who had hopped lightly out of bed as soon as he heard the key turned in the lock, watched him eagerly from the window till he disappeared down the carriage-drive. Then, laughing heartily, he dressed as quickly as possible in the smartest suit he could lay hands on at the moment, filled his pockets with cash which he took from a small drawer in the dressing-table, and next, knotting the sheets from his bed together and tying one end of the improvised rope round the central mullion of the handsome Tudor window which formed such a feature of his bedroom, he scrambled out, slid lightly to the ground, and, taking the opposite direction to the Rat, marched off light-heartedly, whistling a merry tune.

It was a gloomy luncheon for Rat when the Badger and the Mole at length returned, and he had to face them at table with his pitiful and unconvincing story. The Badger's caustic, not to say brutal, remarks may be imagined, and therefore passed over; but it was painful to the Rat that even the Mole, though he took his friend's side as far as possible, could not help saying, 'You've been a bit of a duffer this time, Ratty! Toad, too, of all animals!'

'He did it awfully well,' said the crestfallen Rat.

'He did *you* awfully well!' rejoined the Badger hotly. 'However, talking won't mend matters. He's got clear away for the time, that's certain; and the worst of it is, he'll be so conceited with what he'll think is his cleverness that he may commit any folly. One comfort is, we're free now, and needn't waste any more of our precious time doing sentry-go. But we'd better continue to sleep at Toad Hall for a while longer. Toad may be brought back at any moment – on a stretcher, or between two policemen.'

So spoke the Badger, not knowing what the future held in store, or how much water, and of how turbid a character, was to run under bridges before Toad should sit at ease again in his ancestral Hall.

Buck: A Sled Dog

JACK LONDON
Illustrated by Caroline Holmes-Smith

In this chapter from Jack London's The Call of the Wild *(1903) Buck wins a bet for his master, John Thornton, from his fellow miners during the Klondike Gold Rush in Alaska.*

That winter, at Dawson, Buck performed an exploit that put his name high on the totem-pole of Alaskan fame. This exploit was particularly gratifying to the three men; for they stood in need of the outfit which it furnished, and were enabled to make a long-desired trip into the virgin East, where miners had not yet appeared. It was brought about by a conversation in the Eldorado Saloon, in which men waxed boastful of their favourite Dogs. Buck, because of his record, was the target for these men, and Thornton was driven stoutly to defend him. At the end of half an hour, one man stated that his Dog could start a sled with five hundred pounds and walk off with it; a second bragged six hundred for his Dog; and a third, seven hundred.

'Pooh! pooh!' said John Thornton; 'Buck can start a thousand pounds.'

'And break it out? and walk off with it for a hundred yards?' demanded Matthewson, a Bonanza King, he of the seven hundred vaunt.

'And break it out, and walk off with it for a hundred yards,' John Thornton said coolly.

'Well,' Matthewson said, slowly and deliberately, so that all could hear, 'I've got a thousand dollars that says he can't. And there it is.' So saying, he slammed a sack of gold dust of the size of a bologna sausage down upon the bar.

Nobody spoke. Thornton's bluff, if bluff it was, had been called.

He could feel a flush of warm blood creeping up his face. His tongue had tricked him. He did not know whether Buck could start a thousand pounds. Half a ton! The enormousness of it appalled him. He had great faith in Buck's strength, and had often thought him capable of starting such a load; but never, as now, had he faced the possibility of it, the eyes of a dozen men fixed upon him, silent and waiting. Further, he had no thousand dollars; nor had Hans or Pete.

'I've got a sled standing outside now, with twenty fifty-pound sacks of flour on it,' Matthewson went on with brutal directness; 'so don't let that hinder you.'

Thornton did not reply. He did not know what to say. He glanced from face to face in the absent way of a man who has lost the power of thought and is seeking somewhere to find the thing that will start it going again. The face of Jim O'Brien, a Mastodon King and old-time comrade, caught his eyes. It was as a cue to him, seeming to rouse him to do what he could never have dreamed of doing.

'Can you lend me a thousand?' he asked, almost in a whisper.

'Sure,' answered O'Brien, thumping down a plethoric sack by the side of Matthewson's. 'Though it's little faith I'm having, John, that the beast can do the trick.'

The Eldorado emptied its occupants into the street to see the test. The tables were deserted, and the dealers and gamekeepers came forth to see the outcome of the wager and to lay odds. Several hundred men, furred and mittened, banked around the sled within easy distance. Matthewson's sled, loaded with a thousand pounds of flour, had been standing for a couple of hours, and in the intense cold (it was sixty below zero) the runners had frozen fast to the hard-packed snow. Men offered odds of two to one that Buck could not budge the sled. A quibble arose concerning the phrase 'break out.' O'Brien contended it was Thornton's privilege to knock the runners loose, leaving Buck to 'break it out' from a dead stand-still. Matthewson insisted that the phrase included breaking the runners from the frozen grip of the snow. A majority of the men who had witnessed the making of the bet decided in his favour, whereat the odds went up to three to one against Buck.

There were no takers. Not a man believed him capable of the feat. Thornton had been hurried into the wager, heavy with doubt; and now that he looked at the sled itself, the concrete fact, with the regular team of ten Dogs curled up in the snow before it, the more impossible the task appeared. Matthewson waxed jubilant.

'Three to one!' he proclaimed. 'I'll lay you another thousand at that figure, Thornton. What d'ye say?'

Thornton's doubt was strong in his face, but his fighting spirit was aroused – the fighting spirit that soars above odds, fails to recognize the impossible, and is deaf to all save the clamour for battle. He called Hans and Pete to him. Their sacks were slim, and with his own the three partners could rake together only two hundred dollars. In the ebb of their fortunes, this sum was their total capital; yet they laid it unhesitatingly against Matthewson's six hundred.

The team of ten Dogs was unhitched; and Buck, with his own harness, was put into the sled. He had caught the contagion of the excitement, and he felt that in some way he must do a great thing for John Thornton. Murmurs of admiration at his splendid appearance went up. He was in perfect condition, without an ounce of superfluous flesh, and the one hundred and fifty pounds that he weighed were so many pounds of grit and virility. His furry coat shone with the sheen of silk. Down the neck and across the shoulders, his mane, in repose as it was, half bristled and seemed to lift with every movement, as though excess of vigour made each particular hair alive and active. The great breast and heavy forelegs were no more than in proportion with the rest of the body, where the muscles showed in tight rolls underneath the skin. Men felt these muscles and proclaimed them hard as iron, and the odds went down to two to one.

'Gad, sir! Gad, sir!' stuttered a member of the latest dynasty, a king of the Skookum Benches. 'I offer you eight hundred for him, sir, before the test, sir; eight hundred just as he stands.'

Thornton shook his head and stepped to Buck's side.

'You must stand off from him,' Matthewson protested. 'Free play and plenty of room.'

The crowd fell silent; only could be heard the voices of the gamblers vainly offering two to one. Everybody acknowledged Buck a magnificent animal, but twenty fifty-pound sacks of flour bulked too large in their eyes for them to loosen their pouch-strings.

Thornton knelt down by Buck's side. He took his head in his two hands and rested cheek on cheek. He did not playfully shake him, as was his wont, or murmur soft love curses; but he whispered in his ear. 'As you love me, Buck. As you love me,' was what he whispered. Buck whined with suppressed eagerness.

The crowd was watching curiously. The affair was growing mysterious. It seemed like a conjuration. As Thornton got to his feet, Buck seized his mittened hand between his jaws, pressing in with his teeth and releasing loosely, half-reluctantly. It was the answer, in terms, not of speech, but of love. Thornton stepped well back.

'Now, Buck,' he said.

Buck tightened the traces, then slacked them for a matter of several inches. It was the way he had learned.

'Gee!' Thornton's voice rang out, sharp in the tense silence.

Buck swung to the right, ending the movement in a plunge that took up the slack and with a sudden jerk arrested his one hundred and fifty pounds. The load quivered, and from under the runners arose a crisp crackling.

'Haw!' Thornton commanded.

Buck duplicated the manoeuvre, this time to the left. The crackling turned into a snapping, the sled pivoting and the runners slipping and grating several inches to the side. The sled was broken out. Men were holding their breaths, intensely unconscious of the fact.

'Now, MUSH!'

Thornton's command cracked out like a pistol shot. Buck threw himself forward, tightening the traces with a jarring lunge. His whole body was gathered compactly together in the trememdous effort, the muscles writhing and knotting like live things under the silky fur. His

great chest was low to the ground, his head forward and down, while his feet were flying like mad, the claws scarring the hard-packed snow in parallel grooves. The sled swayed and trembled, half-started forward. One of his feet slipped, and one man groaned aloud. Then the sled lurched ahead in what appeared a rapid succession of jerks, though it never really came to a dead stop again . . . half an inch . . . an inch . . . two inches. . . . The jerks perceptibly diminished; as the sled gained momentum, he caught them up, till it was moving steadily along.

Men gasped and began to breathe again, unaware that for a moment they had ceased to breathe. Thornton was running behind, encouraging Buck with short, cheery words. The distance had been measured off, and as he neared the pile of firewood which marked the end of the hundred yards, a cheer began to grow and grow, which burst into a roar as he passed the firewood and halted at command. Every man was tearing himself loose, even Matthewson. Hats and mittens were flying in the air. Men were shaking hands, it did not matter with whom, and bubbling over in a general incoherent babel.

But Thornton fell on his knees beside Buck. Head was against head, and he was shaking him back and forth. Those who hurried up heard him cursing Buck, and he cursed him long and fervently, and softly and lovingly.

'Gad, sir! Gad, sir!' spluttered the Skookum Bench king. 'I'll give you a thousand for him, sir, a thousand, sir – twelve hundred, sir.'

Thornton rose to his feet. His eyes were wet. The tears were streaming frankly down his cheeks. 'Sir,' he said to the Skookum Bench king, 'no, sir. You can go to hell, sir. It's the best I can do for you, sir.'

Buck seized Thornton's hand in his teeth. Thornton shook him back and forth. As though animated by a common impulse, the onlookers drew back to a respectful distance; nor were they again indiscreet enough to interrupt.

Black Beauty

ANNA SEWELL
Illustrated by Cecil Aldin

These extracts come from Black Beauty: The Autobiography of a Horse, *a novel which was first published in 1877.*

I

MY EARLY LIFE

The first place that I can well remember was a pleasant meadow with a pond of clear water in it. Some shady trees leaned over it, and rushes and water-lilies grew at the deep end. Over the hedge on one side we looked into a ploughed field, and on the other we looked over a gate at our master's house, which stood by the roadside; at the top of the meadow was a grove of fir-trees, and at the bottom a running brook, overhung by a steep bank.

While I was young I lived upon my mother's milk, as I could not eat grass. In the daytime I ran by her side, and at night I lay down close by her. When it was hot we used to stand by the pond in the shade of the trees, and when it was cold we had a warm shed near the grove.

As soon I was old enough to eat grass, my mother worked in the daytime, and came back in the evening.

There were six young colts in the meadow beside me; they were older than I was; some were nearly as large as grown-up Horses. I used to run with them and had great fun; we used to gallop all together round the field, as hard as we could go. Sometimes the play was rough, for they would frequently bite and kick, as well as gallop.

One day, when there was a good deal of kicking, my mother whinnied to me to come to her, and then she said: 'I wish you to pay

'The first place that I can well remember was a large pleasant
meadow with a pond of clear water in it'

attention to what I am going to say to you. The colts who live here are cart-horse colts, and, of course, they have not learned manners. You have been well-bred and well-born; your father has a great name in these parts, and your grandfather won the cup two years at the Newmarket races; your grandmother had the sweetest temper of any Horse I ever knew, and I think you have never seen me kick or bite. I hope you will grow up gentle and good, and never learn bad ways; do your work with a good will, lift your feet up well when you trot, and never bite or kick even in play.'

I have never forgotten my mother's advice; I knew she was a wise old Horse, and our master thought a great deal of her. Her name was Duchess, but he called her Pet.

Our master was a good, kind man. He gave us good food, good lodging and kind words. We all were fond of him, and my mother loved him very much. When she saw him at the gate she would neigh with joy, and trot up to him. He would pat and stroke her and say, 'Well, old Pet, and how is your little Darkie?' I was a dull black, so he called me Darkie; then he would give me a piece of bread, and sometimes he brought a carrot for my mother. All the Horses would come to him, but I think we were his favourites. My mother always took him to town on a market-day in a light gig.

We had a ploughboy, Dick, who sometimes came into our field to pluck blackberries from the hedge. When he had eaten all he wanted he would have what he called fun with the colts, throwing stones and sticks at them to make them gallop. We did not much mind him, for we could gallop off; but sometimes a stone would hit and hurt us. One day he was at this game, and did not know that the master was in the next field, but he was there, watching what was going on; over the hedge he jumped in a snap, and catching Dick by the arm, he gave him such a box on the ear that made him roar with the pain and surprise. As soon as we saw the master we trotted up nearer to see what went on.

'Bad boy!' he said, 'bad boy! to chase the colts. This is not the first time, nor the second, but it shall be the last. There – take your money and go home; I shall not want you on my farm again.' So we never saw

Dick any more. Old Daniel, the man who looked after the Horses, was just as gentle as our master; so we were well off.

★   ★   ★   ★

Before I was two years old a circumstance happened which I have never forgotten. It was early in the spring; there had been a little frost in the night, and a light mist still hung over the woods and meadows. We colts were feeding at the lower part of the field when we heard, quite in the distance, what sounded like the cry of Dogs. The oldest of the colts raised his head, pricked his ears and said, 'There are the Hounds!' and immediately cantered off, followed by the rest of us, to the upper part of the field, where we could look over the hedge and see several fields beyond. My mother and an old riding Horse of our master's were also standing near, and seemed to know all about it. 'They have found a Hare,' said my mother, 'and if they come this way we shall see the hunt.'

Soon the Dogs were all tearing down the field of young wheat next to ours. I never heard such a noise as they made. They did not bark, nor howl, nor whine, but kept on a 'yo! yo, o, o! yo! yo, o, o!' at the top of their voices. After them came a number of men on horseback, all galloping as fast as they could. The old Horses snorted and looked eagerly after them, and we young colts wanted to be galloping with them, but they were soon away into the fields lower down; here it seemed as if they had come to a stand; the Dogs left off barking and ran about every way with their noses to the ground. 'They have lost the scent,' said the old Horse; 'perhaps the Hare will get off.'

'What Hare?' I said.

'Oh, I don't know *what* Hare; likely enough it may be one of our own Hares out of the woods; any Hare they can find will do for the Dogs and men to run after'; and before long the Dogs began their 'yo! yo, o, o!' again, and back they came all together at full speed, making straight for our meadow at the part where the high bank and hedge overhang the brook.

On came the dogs, followed by the huntsmen

'Now we shall see the Hare,' said my mother; and just then a Hare, wild with fright, rushed by and made for the woods. On came the Dogs; they burst over the bank, leaped the stream and came dashing across the field, followed by the huntsmen. Six or eight men leaped their Horses clean over, close upon the Dogs. The Hare tried to get through the fence; it was too thick, and she turned sharp around to make for the road, but it was too late; the Dogs were upon her with their wild cries; we heard one shriek, and that was the end of her. One of the huntsmen rode up and whipped off the Dogs, who would soon have torn her to pieces. He held her up by the leg, torn and bleeding, and all the gentlemen seemed well pleased.

As for me, I was so astonished that I did not at first see what was going on by the brook; but when I did look, there was a sad sight; two fine Horses were down; one was struggling in the stream, and the other was groaning on the grass. One of the riders was getting out of the water covered with mud, the other lay quite still.

'His neck is broken,' said my mother.

'And serves him right, too,' said one of the colts.

I thought the same, but my mother did not join with us.

'Well, no,' she said, 'you must not say that; but though I am an old Horse, and have seen and heard a great deal, I never yet could make out why men are so fond of this sport; they often hurt themselves, often spoil good Horses, and tear up the fields, and all for a Hare, or a Fox, or a Stag, that they could get more easily some other way; but we are only Horses, and don't know.'

While my mother was saying this, we stood and looked on. Many of the riders had gone to the young man; but my master, who had been watching what was going on, was the first to raise him. His head fell back and his arms hung down, and every one looked very serious. There was no noise now; even the Dogs were quiet, and seemed to know that something was wrong. They carried him to our master's house. I heard afterwards that it was young George Gordon, the Squire's only son, a fine, tall young man, and the pride of his family.

They were now riding in all directions – to the doctor's, to the farrier's, and to Squire Gordon's, to let him know about his son. When the farrier looked at the black Horse that lay groaning on the grass, he felt him all over, and shook his head; one of his legs was broken. Then some one ran to our master's house and came back with a gun; presently there was a loud bang and a dreadful shriek, and then all was still; the black Horse moved no more.

My mother seemed much troubled; she said she had known that Horse for years, and that his name was 'Rob Roy'; he was a good Horse, and there was no vice in him. She never would go to that part of the field afterwards.

Not many days after, we heard the church-bell tolling for a long time, and looking over the gate, we saw a long strange coach covered with black cloth and drawn by black Horses; after them came another and another and another, and all were black, while the bell kept tolling, tolling. They were carrying young Gordon to the churchyard to bury him. He would never ride again. What they did with Rob Roy I never knew; but 'twas all for one little Hare.

★   ★   ★   ★

I was now beginning to grow handsome, my coat had grown fine and soft, and was bright black. I had one white foot and a pretty white star on my forehead. I was thought very handsome; my master would not sell me till I was four years old; he said lads ought not to work like men, and colts ought not to work like Horses till they were quite grown up.

When I was four years old, Squire Gordon came to look at me. He examined my eyes, my mouth, and my legs; he felt them all down, and then I had to walk and trot and gallop before him; he seemed to like me and said, 'When he has been well broken in he will do very well.' My master said he would break me in himself, as he should not like me to be frightened or hurt, and he lost no time about it, for the next day he began.

Every one may not know what breaking in is, therefore I will describe it. It means to teach a Horse to wear a saddle and bridle, and to carry on his back a man, woman or child; to go just the way they wish, and to go quietly. Besides this, he has to learn to wear a collar, a crupper, and a breeching, and to stand still while they are put on; then to have a cart or a chaise fixed behind, so that he cannot walk or trot without dragging it after him; and he must go fast or slow, just as his driver wishes. He must never start at what he sees, nor speak to other Horses, nor bite, nor kick, nor have any will of his own, but always do his master's will, even though he may be very tired or hungry; but the worst of all is, when his harness is once on, he may neither jump for joy nor lie down for weariness. So you see this breaking in is a great thing.

I had long been used to a halter and a head-stall, and to be led about in the fields and lanes quietly, but now I was to have a bit and bridle; my master gave me some oats as usual, and after a good deal of coaxing he got the bit into my mouth and the bridle fixed, but it was a nasty thing. Those who have never had a bit in their mouths cannot think how badly it feels; a great piece of cold hard steel as thick as a man's finger to be pushed into one's mouth, between one's teeth, and over one's tongue, with the ends coming out at the corners of your mouth, and held fast there by straps over your head, under your throat, round your nose, and under your chin; so that no way in the world can you get rid of the nasty hard thing; it is very bad! at least I thought so; but I knew my mother always wore one when she went out, and so what with the nice oats, and what with my master's pats, kind words, and gentle ways, I got to wear my bit and bridle.

Next came the saddle, but that was not half so bad; my master put it on my back very gently, while old Daniel held my head; he then made the girths fast under my body, patting and talking to me all the time; then I had a few oats, then a little leading about; and this he did every day till I began to look for the oats and the saddle. At length, one morning, my master got on my back and rode me around the meadow on the soft grass. It certainly did feel queer; but I must say I felt rather proud to carry my master, and as he continued to ride me a little every day, I soon became accustomed to it.

The next unpleasant business was putting on the iron shoes; that too was very hard at first. My master went with me to the smith's forge, to see that I was not hurt or got any fright. The blacksmith took my feet in his hand one after the other, and cut away some of the hoof. It did not pain me, so I stood still on three legs until he had done them all. Then he took a piece of iron the shape of my foot, and clapped it on, and drove some nails through the shoe quite into my hoof, so that the shoe was firmly on. My feet felt very stiff and heavy, but I got used to it.

And now having got so far, my master went on to break me to harness; there were more new things to wear. First, a stiff heavy collar just on my neck, and a bridle with great side-pieces against my eyes, called blinkers, and blinkers indeed they were, for I could not see on either side, but only straight in front of me; next there was a small saddle with a nasty stiff strap that went right under my tail; that was the crupper. I hated the crupper – to have my long tail doubled up and poked through that strap was almost as bad as the bit. I felt like kicking, but of course I could not kick such a good master, and so in time I got used to everything, and could do my work as well as my mother.

I must not forget to mention one part of my training, which I have always considered a very great advantage. My master sent me for a fortnight to a neighbouring farmer's, who had a meadow which was skirted on one side by the railway. Here were some Sheep and Cows, and I was turned in among them.

I shall never forget the first train that ran by. I was feeding quietly near the pales which separated the meadow from the railway, when I heard a strange sound at a distance, and before I knew whence it came – with a rush and a clatter, and a puffing of smoke – a long black train of something flew by, and was gone almost before I could draw my breath. I turned and galloped to the farther side of the meadow as fast as I could go, and there I stood snorting with astonishment and fear. In the course of the day many other trains went by, some more slowly; these drew up at the station close by, and sometimes made an awful shriek and groan before they stopped. I thought it very dreadful, but the Cows went on eating very quietly, and hardly raised their heads as the black, frightful thing came puffing and grinding past. For the first few days I could not feed in peace; but as I found that this terrible creature never came into the field, or did me any harm, I began to disregard it, and very soon I cared as little about the passing of a train as the Cows and Sheep did.

Since then I have seen many Horses much alarmed and restive at the sight or sound of a steam engine; but, thanks to my good master's care, I am as fearless at railway stations as in my own stable. Now if any one wants to break in a young Horse well, that is the way.

My master often drove me in double harness, with my mother, because she was steady and could teach me how to go better than a strange Horse. She told me the better I behaved the better I should be treated, and that it was wisest always to do my best to please my master. 'But,' said she, 'there are a great many kinds of men; there are good, thoughtful men, like our master, that any Horse may be proud to serve, and there are cruel men, who never ought to have a Horse or a Dog to call their own. Besides, there are a great many foolish men, ignorant and careless, who never trouble themselves to think; these spoil more Horses than all, just for want of sense; they don't mean it, but they do it for all that. I hope you will fall into good hands; but a Horse never knows who may buy him, or who may drive him, it is all a chance for us; but do your best wherever it is, and keep up your good name.'

* * * *

At this time I used to stand in the stable, and my coat was brushed every day till it shone like a rook's wing. It was early in May, when there came a man from Squire Gordon's, who took me away to the Hall. My master said, 'Good-bye, Darkie, be a good Horse and always do your best.' I could not say 'Good-bye,' so I put my nose into his hand; he patted me kindly, and I left my first home. As I lived some years with Squire Gordon I may as well tell something about the place.

Squire Gordon's park skirted the village of Birtwick. It was entered by a large iron gate, at which stood the first lodge, and then you trotted along on a smooth road between clumps of large old trees; then another lodge and another gate, which brought you to the house and the gardens. Beyond this lay the home paddock, the old orchard and the stables. There was accommodation for many Horses and carriages, but I need only describe the stable into which I was taken; this was very roomy, with four good stalls; a large swinging window opened into the yard, which made it pleasant and airy.

The first stall was a large square one, shut in behind with a wooden gate. The others were common stalls, not nearly so large. It had a low rack for hay and a low manger for corn; it was called a loose box, because the Horse that was put into it was not tied up, but left loose, to do as he liked. It is a great thing to have a loose box.

Inside this fine box the groom put me: it was clean, sweet and airy. I never was in a better box than that, and the sides were not so high but that I could see all that went on through the iron rails that were at the top.

He gave me some very nice oats, he patted me, spoke kindly, and then went away.

When I had eaten my oats I looked round. In the stall next to mine stood a little fat grey Pony, with a thick mane and tail, a very pretty head and a pert little nose.

I put my head to the iron rails at the top of my box and said, 'How do you do? What is your name?'

He turned round as far as his halter would allow, held up his head, and said, 'My name is Merrylegs. I am very handsome. I carry the young ladies on my back, and sometimes I take our mistress out in the low chaise. They think a great deal of me. Are you going to live next door to me in the box?' I said, 'Yes.'

'Well, then,' he said, 'I hope you are good-tempered; I do not like any one next door who bites.' Just then a Horse's head looked over from the stall beyond; the ears were laid back and the eyes looked rather ill-tempered. This was a tall chestnut mare, with a long, handsome neck; she looked across at me and said: 'So you have turned me out of my box; it is a very strange thing for a colt like you to come and turn a lady out of her own home.'

'I beg your pardon,' I said, 'I have turned no one out; the man put me here, and I had nothing to do with it; and as to my being a colt, I am turned four years old and am a grown-up Horse. I never had words yet with Horse or Mare, and it is my wish to live at peace.'

'Well,' she said, 'we shall see; I do not want to have words with a young thing like you.' I said no more.

In the afternoon, Merrylegs told me all about it. 'The thing is this,' said Merrylegs. 'Ginger has a habit of biting and snapping; that is why they call her Ginger, and when she was in the loose box she used to snap very much. One day she bit James in the arm and made it bleed, and so Miss Flora and Miss Jessie, who are very fond of me, were afraid to come into the stable. They used to bring me nice things to eat, an apple or a carrot or a piece of bread, but after Ginger stood in that box they dared not come, and I missed them very much. I hope they will now come again, if you do not bite or snap.'

I told him I never bit anything but grass, hay and corn, and could not think what pleasure Ginger found in it.

'Well, I don't think she does find pleasure,' said Merrylegs; 'it is just a bad habit; she says no one was ever kind to her, and why should she not bite? It is true she must have been very ill-used before she came here. John does all he can to please her, and James does all he can, and our master never uses a whip if a Horse acts right, so I think she might be good-tempered here; you see,' he said, with a wise look, 'I am twelve years old, I know a great deal, and I can tell you there is not a better place for a Horse all around the country than this. John is the best groom that ever was; he has been here fourteen years; and you never saw such a kind boy as James is; so that it is Ginger's own fault that she did not stay in that box.'

★ ★ ★ ★

The name of the coachman was John Manley; he had a wife and one little child, and they lived in the coachman's cottage very near the stables.

The next morning he took me into the yard and gave me a good grooming, and just as I was going into my box, with my coat soft and bright, the Squire came in to look at me, and seemed pleased. 'John,' he said, 'I meant to have tried the new Horse this morning, but I have other business. You may as well take him around after breakfast; go by the common and the Highwood, and back by the water-mill and the river; that will show his paces.'

'I will, sir,' said John. After breakfast he came and fitted me with a bridle. He was very particular in letting out and taking in the straps, to fit my head comfortably; then he brought a saddle, but it was not broad enough for my back; he saw it in a minute and went for another, which fitted nicely. He rode me first slowly, then a trot, then a canter, and when we were on the common he gave me a light touch with his whip, and we had a splendid gallop.

'Ho, ho! my boy,' he said, as he pulled me up, 'you would like to follow the Hounds, I think.'

We came back through the park and met the Squire and Mrs. Gordon walking; they stopped and John jumped off.

'Well, John, how does he go?'

'First-rate, sir,' answered John; 'he is as fleet as a Deer, and has a fine spirit too; but the slightest touch of the rein will guide him. At the end of the common we met one of those travelling carts hung all over with baskets, rugs and such like; you know, sir, many Horses won't pass those carts quietly; he just took a good look at it, and then went on as quiet and pleasant as could be. They were shooting Rabbits near the Highwood, and a gun went off close by; he pulled up a little and looked but didn't stir a step to right or left. I held the rein steady and didn't hurry him, and it's my opinion he has not been frightened or ill-used while he was young.'

'That's well,' said the Squire; 'I will try him myself to-morrow.'
The next day I was brought up for my master. I remembered my
mother's counsel and my good old master's, and I tried to do exactly
what he wanted me to do. I found he was a very good rider, and
thoughtful for his Horse, too. When he came home, the lady was at
the hall-door as he rode up. 'Well, my dear,' she said, 'how do you like
him?'

'He is exactly what John said,' he replied; 'a pleasanter creature I
never wish to mount. What shall we call him?'

And she said, 'Would you like "Ebony"? He is as black as ebony.'

'No, not Ebony.'

'Will you call him 'Blackbird,' like your uncle's old Horse?'

'No, he is far handsomer than old Blackbird ever was.'

'Yes,' she said, 'he is really quite a beauty, and he has such a sweet,
good-tempered face and such a fine, intelligent eye – what do you say
to calling him "Black Beauty?"'

'Black Beauty – why, yes, I think that is a very good name. If you
like, it shall be so,' and that is how I got my name.

II

MY LAST HOME

*Black Beauty's happy days at Birtwick Park are not destined to last. He is
sold, and falls on hard times.*

I shall never forget my next master; he had black eyes and a hooked
nose, his mouth was as full of teeth as a Bull-dog's, and his voice was
as harsh as the grinding of cart wheels over gravel stones. His name
was Nicholas Skinner, and I believe he was the same man that poor
Seedy Sam drove for.

I have heard men say that seeing is believing, but I should say that
feeling is believing; for much as I have seen before, I never knew until

now the utter misery of a Cab-horse's life. Skinner had a low set of cabs and a low set of drivers; he was hard on the men, and the men were hard on the Horses. In this place we had no Sunday rest, and it was in the heat of summer.

Sometimes on a Sunday morning a party of fast men would hire the cab for the day, four of them inside and another with the driver, and I had to take them ten or fifteen miles out into the country and back again; never would any of them get down to walk up a hill, let it be ever so steep, or the day ever so hot – unless, indeed, when the driver was afraid I should not manage it; and sometimes I was so fevered and worn that I could hardly touch my food. How I used to long for the nice bran mash with nitre in it that Jerry used to give us on Saturday nights in hot weather, that used to cool us down and make us so comfortable. Then we had two nights and a whole day for unbroken rest, and on Monday morning we were as fresh as young Horses again; but here there was no rest, and my driver was just as hard as his master. He had a cruel whip with something so sharp at the end that it sometimes drew blood, and he would even whip me under the belly, and flip the lash out at my head. Indignities like these took the heart out of me terribly, but still I did my best and never hung back, for, as poor Ginger said, it was no use; men are the strongest.

My life was now so wretched that I wished I might, like Ginger, drop down dead at my work, and be out of my misery, and one day my wish very nearly came to pass.

I went on the stand at eight in the morning, and had done a good share of work, when we had to take a fare to the railway. A long train was just expected in, so my driver pulled up at the back of some of the outside cabs, to take the chance of a return fare. It was a very heavy train, and as all the cabs were soon engaged, ours was called for. There was a party of four; a noisy, blustering man with a lady, a little boy, and a young girl, and a great deal of luggage. The lady and the boy got into the cab, and while the man ordered about the luggage, the young girl came and looked at me.

'Papa,' she said, 'I am sure this poor Horse cannot take us and all our luggage so far, he is so very weak and worn out; do look at him.'

'Oh! he's all right, miss,' said my driver, 'he's strong enough.' The porter, who was pulling about some heavy boxes, suggested to the gentleman, as there was so much luggage, that he had better take a second cab.

'Can your Horse do it, or can't he?' said the blustering man.

'Oh! he can do it all right, sir; send up the boxes, porter; he could take more than that,' and he helped to haul up a box so heavy that I could feel the springs go down.

'Papa, papa, do take a second cab,' said the young girl in a beseeching tone; 'I am sure it is very cruel.'

'Nonsense, Grace; don't make all this fuss; a pretty thing it would be if a man of business had to examine every Cab-horse before he hired it – the man knows his own business; get in and hold your tongue!'

My gentle friend had to obey; and box after box was lodged on the top of the cab, or settled by the side of the driver. At last all was ready, and with his usual jerk at the rein, and slash of the whip, he drove out of the station.

The load was very heavy, and I had had neither food nor rest since morning; but I did my best, as I always had done, in spite of cruelty and injustice.

I got along fairly till we came to Ludgate Hill, but there the heavy load and my own exhaustion were too much. I was struggling to keep on, goaded by constant chucks of the rein and use of the whip, when, in a single moment – I cannot tell how – my feet slipped from under me, and I fell heavily to the ground on my side; the suddenness and the force with which I fell seemed to beat all the breath out of my body. I lay perfectly still; indeed, I had no power to move, and I thought I heard that sweet, pitiful voice saying, 'Oh! that poor horse! it is all our fault.' Someone came and loosened the throat strap of my bridle, and undid the traces which kept the collar so tight upon me. Someone said, 'He's dead, he'll never get up again.' Then I could hear a policeman giving orders, but I did not even open my eyes; I could only draw a gasping breath now and then. Some cold water was thrown over my head, and some cordial was poured into my mouth, and something was covered over me. I cannot tell how long I lay there, but I found my life coming back, and a kind-voiced man was patting me and encouraging me to rise. After some more cordial had been given me, and after one or two attempts, I staggered to my feet, and was gently led to some stables which were close by. Here I was put into a well-littered stall, and some warm gruel was brought to me, which I drank thankfully.

In the evening I was sufficiently recovered to be led back to Skinner's stable, where I think they did the best for me they could. In the morning Skinner came with a farrier to look at me. He examined me very closely and said, 'This is a case of overwork more than disease, and if you could give him a run off for six months, he would be able to work again; but now there is not an ounce of strength in him.'

'Then he must just go to the Dogs,' said Skinner. 'I have no meadows to nurse sick Horses in – he might get well or he might not; that sort of thing don't suit my business; my plan is to work 'em as long as they'll go, and then sell 'em for what they'll fetch at the knacker's or elsewhere.'

'If he was broken-winded,' said the farrier, 'you had better have him killed out of hand, but he is not; there is a sale of Horses coming off in about ten days; if you rest him and feed him up, he may pick up, and you may get more than his skin is worth, at any rate.'

Upon this advice, Skinner, rather unwillingly, I think, gave orders that I should be well fed and cared for, and the stableman, happily for me, carried out the orders with a much better will than his master had in giving them. Ten days of perfect rest, hay, plenty of good oats, bran mashes, with boiled linseed mixed in them, did more to get up my condition than anything else could have done; those linseed mashes were delicious, and I began to think, after all, it might be better to live than to go to the Dogs. When the twelfth day after the accident came, I was taken to the sale, a few miles out of London. I felt that any change from my present place must be an improvement, so I held up my head, and hoped for the best.

★ ★ ★ ★

At this sale, of course, I found myself in company with the old broken-down Horses – some lame, some broken-winded, some old, and some that I am sure it would have been merciful to shoot.

The buyers, and sellers, too, many of them, looked not much better off than the poor beasts they were bargaining about. There were poor old men trying to get a Horse or Pony for a few pounds, that might drag about some little wood or coal cart. There were poor men trying to sell a worn-out beast for two or three pounds, rather than have the greater loss of killing him. Some of them looked as if poverty and hard times had hardened them all over; but there were others that I would have willingly used the last of my strength in serving; poor and shabby, but kind and humane, with voices that I could trust. There was one tottering old man that took a great fancy to me, and I to him, but I was not strong enough – it was an anxious time! Coming from the better part of the fair, I noticed a man who looked like a gentleman farmer, with a young boy by his side; he had a broad back and round shoulders, a kind, ruddy face, and he wore a broad-brimmed hat. When he came up to me and my companions he stood still and gave a pitiful look around upon us. I saw his eye rest on me; I had still a good mane and tail, which did something for my appearance. I pricked my ears and looked at him.

'There's a Horse,' said Willie, 'that has known better days.' And the boy said, 'Poor old fellow! do you think, grandpapa, he was ever a carriage Horse?'

'Oh, yes!' said the farmer, 'he might have been anything when he was young; look at his nostrils and his ears, the shape of his neck and shoulder; there's a deal of breeding about that Horse.' He put out his hand and gave me a kind pat on the neck. I put out my nose in answer to his kindness; the boy stroked my face.

'Poor old fellow! see, grandpapa, how well he understands kindness. Could not you buy him and make him young again as you did with Ladybird?'

'My dear boy, I can't make all old Horses young; besides, Ladybird was not so very old, as she was run down and badly used.'

'Well, grandpapa, I don't believe that this one is old; look at his mane and tail. I wish you would look into his mouth, and then you could tell; though he is very thin, his eyes are not sunk like some old Horses.'

The old gentleman laughed. 'Bless the boy! he is as horsey as his old grandfather.'

'But do look at his mouth, grandpapa, and ask the price; I am sure he would grow young in our meadows.'

The man who had brought me for sale now put in his word. 'The young gentleman's a real knowing one, sir. Now the fact is, this 'ere Horse is just pulled down with overwork in the cabs; he's not an old one, and I heard as how the veterinary should say that a six month's run off would set him right up, being as how his wind was not broken. I've had the tending of him these ten days past, and a gratefuller, pleasanter animal I never met with, and 'twould be worth a gentleman's while to give a five-pound note for him and let him have a chance. I'll be bound he'd be worth twenty pounds next spring.'

The old gentleman laughed, and the little boy looked up eagerly. 'Oh, grandpapa, did you not say the colt sold for five pounds more than you expected? You would not be poorer if you did buy this one.'

The farmer felt my legs, which were much swelled and strained; then he looked at my mouth. 'Thirteen or fourteen, I should say; just trot him out, will you?' I arched my poor thin neck, raised my tail a little, threw out my legs as well as I could, for they were very stiff.

'What is the lowest you will take for him?' said the farmer as I came back.

'Five pounds, sir, that was the lowest price my master set.'

' 'Tis a speculation,' said the old gentleman, shaking his head, but at the same time slowly drawing out his purse, 'quite a speculation! Have you any more business here?' he said, counting the sovereigns into his hands.

'No, sir, I can take him for you to the inn, if you please.'

'Do so; I am now going there.'

They walked forward, and I was led behind. The boy could hardly control his delight, and the old gentleman seemed to enjoy his pleasure. I had a good feed at the inn, and was then gently ridden home by a servant of my new master's, and turned into a large meadow with a shed in one corner of it.

Mr. Thoroughgood, for that was the name of my benefactor, gave orders that I should have hay and oats every night and morning, and the run of the meadow during the day; and, 'you, Willie,' said he, 'must take the oversight of him; I give him in charge of you.'

The boy was proud of his charge, and undertook it in all serious-ness. There was not a day when he did not pay me a visit; sometimes picking me out from among the other Horses and giving me a bit of carrot, or something good, or standing by while I ate my oats. He always came with kind words and caresses, and I grew very fond of him. He called me Old Crony; as I used to come to him in the field and follow him about. Sometimes he brought his grandfather, who always looked closely at my legs.

'This is our point, Willie,' he would say; 'but he is improving so steadily that I think we shall see a change for the better in the spring.'

The perfect rest, the good food, the soft turf and gentle exercise soon began to tell on my condition and my spirits. I had a good constitution from my mother and I was never strained when I was young, so that I had a better chance than many Horses who have been worked before they came to their full strength. During the winter my legs improved so much that I began to feel quite young again. The spring came around, and one day in March Mr. Thoroughgood determined that he would try me in the phaeton. I was well pleased, and he and Willie drove me a few miles. My legs were not stiff now, and I did the work with perfect ease.

'He's growing young, Willie; we must give him a little gentle work now, and by midsummer he will be as good as Ladybird. He has a beautiful mouth and good paces; they can't be better.'

'Oh, grandpapa, how glad I am you bought him!'

'So am I, my boy; but he has to thank you more than me; we must now be looking out for a quiet, genteel place for him, where he will be valued.'

★   ★   ★   ★

One day during this summer, the groom cleaned and dressed me with such extraordinary care that I thought some new change must be at hand; he trimmed my fetlocks and legs, passed the tar brush over my hoofs, and even parted my forelock. I think the harness had an extra polish. Willie seemed anxious, half merry, as he got into the chaise with his grandfather.

'If the ladies take to him,' said the old gentleman, 'they'll be suited and he'll be suited; we can but try.'

At the distance of a mile or two from the village we came to a pretty, low house, with a lawn and shrubbery at the front and a drive up to the door. Willie rang the bell and asked if Miss Blomefield or Miss Ellen was at home. Yes, they were. So, while Willie stayed with me, Mr. Thoroughgood went into the house. In about ten minutes he returned, followed by three ladies; one tall, pale lady, wrapped in a white shawl, leaned on a younger lady, with dark eyes and a merry face; the other, a very stately looking person, was Miss Blomefield. They all came and looked at me and asked questions. The young lady – that was Miss Ellen – took to me very much; she said she was sure she would like me, I had such a good face. The tall, pale lady said she should always be nervous in riding behind a Horse that had once been down, as I might come down again, and if I did she should never get over the fright.

'You see, ladies,' said Mr. Thoroughgood, 'many first-rate Horses have had their knees broken through the carelessness of their drivers, without any fault of their own, and from what I see of this Horse I should say that is his case; but, of course, I do not wish to influence you. If you incline, you can have him on trial, and then your coachman will see what he thinks of him.'

'You have always been a good adviser to us about our Horses,' said the stately lady, 'so that your recommendation would go a long way with me, and if my sister Lavinia sees no objection, we will accept your offer of a trial, with thanks.'

It was then arranged that I should be sent for the next day. In the morning a smart-looking young man came for me; at first he looked pleased, but when he saw my knees he said, in a disappointed voice; 'I didn't think, sir, you would have recommended my ladies a blemished Horse like that.'

'"Handsome is that handsome does,"' said my master. 'You are taking him only on trial, and I am sure you will do fairly by him, young man; if he is not as safe as any Horse you ever drove, send him back.'

I was led to my new home, placed in a comfortable stable, fed, and left to myself. The next day, when my groom was cleaning my face, he said, 'That is just like the star that "Black Beauty" had; he is much the same height, too; I wonder where he is now?'

A little further on he came to the place in my neck where I was bled, and where a little knot was left in the skin. He almost started, and began to look me over carefully, talking to himself.

'White star in the forehead, one white foot on the off side, this little knot just in that place'; then looking at the middle of my back – 'and as I am alive, there is that little patch of white hair that John used to call "Beauty's three-penny bit." It *must* be "Black Beauty." Why Beauty! Beauty! do you know me? little Joe Green, that almost killed you?' And he began patting and patting me as if he was quite overjoyed.

I could not say that I remembered him, for now he was a fine grown young fellow, with black whiskers and a man's voice, but I was sure he knew me, and that he was Joe Green, and I was very glad. I put my nose up to him and tried to say that we were friends. I never saw a man so pleased. 'Give you a fair trial! I should think so indeed! I wonder

I was driven every day for a week or so

who the rascal was that broke your knees, my old Beauty! You must have been badly served out somewhere. Well, well, it won't be my fault if you haven't good times of it now. I wish John Manley was here to see you.'

In the afternoon I was put into a low Park chair and brought to the door. Miss Ellen was going to try me, and Green went with her. I soon found that she was a good driver, and she seemed pleased with my paces. I heard Joe telling her about me, and that he was sure I was Squire Gordon's old 'Black Beauty.'

When we returned the other sisters came out to hear how I had behaved myself. She told them what she had just heard, and said, 'I shall certainly write to Mrs. Gordon and tell her that her favourite Horse has come to us. How pleased she will be.'

After this I was driven every day for a week or so, and as I appeared to be quite safe, Miss Lavinia at last ventured out in a small close carriage. After this it was quite decided to keep me and call me by my old name of 'Black Beauty.'

I have now lived in this happy place a whole year. Joe is the best and kindest of grooms. My work is easy and pleasant, and I feel my strength and spirits all coming back again. Mr. Thoroughgood said to Joe the other day:

'In your place he will last till he is twenty years old, – perhaps more.'

Willie always speaks to me when he can, and treats me as his special friend. My ladies have promised that I shall never be sold, and so I have nothing to fear; and here my story ends. My troubles are all over, and I am at home; and often before I am quite awake, I fancy I am still in the orchard at Birtwick, standing with my old friends under the apple trees.

School Stories

What Katy Did

SUSAN COOLIDGE
Illustrated by Gareth Floyd

The heroine of What Katy Did *(1872), from which this chapter comes, is a little American girl who always means well, but is forever getting herself into scrapes.*

Katy's name was Katy Carr. She lived in the town of Burnet, which wasn't a very big town, but was growing fast. The house she lived in stood on the edge of the town. It was a large square house, white, with green blinds, and had a porch in front, over which roses and clematis made a thick bower. Four tall locust trees shaded the gravel path which led to the front gate. On one side of the house was an orchard; on the other side were wood piles and barns, and an ice-house. Behind was a kitchen garden sloping to the south; and behind that a pasture with a brook in it, and butternut trees, and four cows – two red ones, a yellow one with sharp horns tipped with tin, and a dear little white one named Daisy.

There were six of the Carr children – four girls and two boys. Katy, the oldest, was twelve years old; little Phil, the youngest, was four, and the rest fitted in between.

Dr Carr, their papa, was a dear, kind, busy man, who was away from home all day, and sometimes all night too, taking care of sick people. The children hadn't any mamma. She had died when Phil was a baby, four years before my story began. Katy could remember her pretty well; to the rest she was but a sad, sweet name, spoken on Sunday, and at prayer times, or when Papa was specially gentle and solemn.

In place of this mamma, whom they recollected so dimly, there was Aunt Izzie, Papa's sister, who came to take care of them when

Mamma went away on that long journey, from which, for so many months, the little ones kept hoping she might return. Aunt Izzie was a small woman, sharp-faced and thin, rather old-looking, and very neat and particular about everything. She meant to be kind to the children, but they puzzled her much, because they were not a bit like herself when she was a child. Aunt Izzie had been a gentle, tidy little thing, who loved to sit as Curly Locks did, sewing long seams in the parlour, and to have her head patted by older people, and be told that she was a good girl; whereas Katy tore her dress every day, hated sewing, and didn't care a button about being called 'good', while Clover and Elsie shied off like restless ponies when anyone tried to pat their heads. It was very perplexing to Aunt Izzie, and she found it hard to quite forgive the children for being so 'strange', and so little like the good boys and girls in Sunday-school memoirs, who were the young people she liked best, and understood most about.

Then Dr Carr was another person who worried her. He wished to have the children hardy and bold, and encouraged climbing and rough plays, in spite of the bumps and ragged clothes which resulted. In fact, there was just one half-hour of the day when Aunt Izzie was really satisfied about her charges, and that was the half-hour before breakfast, when she had made a law that they were all to sit in their little chairs and learn the Bible verse for the day. At this time she looked at them with pleased eyes; they were all so spick and span, with such nicely brushed jackets and such neatly combed hair. But the moment the bell rang her comfort was over. From that time on, they were what she called 'not fit to be seen'. The neighbours pitied her very much. They used to count the sixty stiff white pantalette legs hung out to dry every Monday morning, and say to each other what a sight of washing those children made, and what a trouble it must be for poor Miss Carr to keep them so nice. But poor Miss Carr didn't think them at all nice – that was the worst of it.

'Clover, go upstairs and wash your hands! Dorry, pick your hat off the floor and hang it on the nail! Not that nail – the third nail from the corner!' These were the kind of things Aunt Izzie was saying all day long. The children minded her pretty well, but they didn't exactly love her, I fear. They called her 'Aunt Izzie' always, never 'Aunty'. Boys and girls will know what *that* meant.

I want to show you the little Carrs, and I don't know that I could ever have a better chance than one day when five out of the six were perched on top of the ice-house, like chickens on a roost. This ice-house was one of their favourite places. It was only a low roof set over a hole in the ground, and, as it stood in the middle of the side-yard, it always seemed to the children that the shortest road to every place was up one of its slopes and down the other. They also liked to mount to the ridge-pole, and then, still keeping the sitting position, to let go, and scrape slowly down over the warm shingles to the ground. It was bad for their shoes and trousers, of course, but what of that? Shoes and trousers, and clothes generally, were Aunt Izzie's affair; theirs was to slide and enjoy themselves.

Clover, next in age to Katy, sat in the middle. She was a fair, sweet dumpling of a girl, with thick pigtails of light brown hair, and short-sighted blue eyes, which seemed to hold tears, just ready to fall from under the blue. Really, Clover was the jolliest little thing in the world; but these eyes, and her soft cooing voice, always made people feel like petting her and taking her part. Once, when she was very small, she ran away with Katy's doll, and when Katy pursued, and tried to take it from her, Clover held fast and would not let go. Dr Carr, who wasn't attending particularly, heard nothing but the pathetic tone of Clover's voice, as she said, 'Me won't! Me want dolly!' and, without stopping to inquire, he called out sharply, 'For shame, Katy! give your sister *her* doll at once!', which Katy, much surprised, did; while Clover purred in triumph, like a satisfied kitten. Clover was sunny and sweet-tempered, a little indolent, and very modest about herself, though in fact she was particularly clever in all sorts of games, and extremely droll and funny in a quiet way. Everybody loved her, and she loved everybody, especially Katy, whom she looked up to as one of the wisest people in the world.

Pretty little Phil sat next on the roof to Clover, and she held him tight with her arm. Then came Elsie, a thin, brown child of eight, with beautiful dark eyes, and crisp, short curls covering the whole of her small head. Poor little Elsie was the 'odd one' among the Carrs. She didn't seem to belong exactly to either the older or the younger children. The great desire and ambition of her heart was to be allowed to go about with Katy and Clover and Cecy Hall, and to know their secrets, and be permitted to put notes into the little post offices they were for ever establishing in all sorts of hidden places. But they didn't want Elsie, and used to tell her to 'run away and play with the children', which hurt her feelings very much. When she wouldn't run away, I am sorry to say they ran away from her, which, as their legs were longest, it was easy to do. Poor Elsie, left behind, would cry bitter tears, and, as she was too proud to play much with Dorry and John, her principal comfort was tracking the older ones about and discovering their mysteries, especially the post offices, which were her greatest grievance. Her eyes were bright and quick as a bird's. She would peep and peer, and follow and watch, till at last, in some odd, unlikely place – the crotch of a tree, the middle of the asparagus bed, or perhaps on the very top step of the scuttle ladder – she spied the little paper box, with its load of notes, all ending with 'Be sure and not let Elsie know'. Then she would seize the box, and, marching up to wherever the others were, she would throw it down, saying, defiantly, 'There's your old post office!' but feeling all the time just like crying. Poor little Elsie! In almost every big family there is one of these unmated, left-out children. Katy, who had the finest plans in the world for being 'heroic', and of use, never saw, as she drifted on her heedless way, that here, in this lonely little sister, was the very chance she wanted for being a comfort to somebody who needed comfort very much. She never saw it, and Elsie's heavy heart went uncheered.

Dorry and Joanna sat on the two ends of the ridge-pole. Dorry was six years old: a pale, pudgy boy, with rather a solemn face, and smears of molasses on the sleeve of his jacket. Joanna, whom the children called 'John' and 'Johnnie', was a square, splendid child, a year younger than Dorry; she had big brave eyes and a wide rosy mouth,

The window opened and Katy's head appeared

which always looked ready to laugh. These two were great friends, though Dorry seemed like a girl who had got into boy's clothes by mistake, and Johnnie like a boy who, in a fit of fun, had borrowed his sister's frock. And now, as they all sat there chattering and giggling, the window above opened, a glad shriek was heard, and Katy's head appeared. In her hand she held a heap of stockings, which she waved triumphantly.

'Hurray!' she cried, 'all done, and Aunt Izzie says we may go. Are you tired out waiting? I couldn't help it, the holes were *so* big, and took so long. Hurry up, Clover, and get the things! Cecy and I will be down in a minute.'

The children jumped up gladly, and slid down the roof. Clover fetched a couple of baskets from the woodshed. Elsie ran for her kitten. Dorry and John loaded themselves with two great faggots of green boughs. Just as they were ready the side door banged, and Katy and Cecy Hall came into the yard.

I must tell you about Cecy. She was a great friend of the children's, and lived in a house next door. The yards of the houses were only separated by a green hedge, with no gate, so that Cecy spent two-thirds of her time at Dr Carr's, and was exactly like one of the family. She was a neat, dapper, pink-and-white girl, modest and prim in manner, with light shiny hair, which always kept smooth, and slim hands, which never looked dirty. How different from my poor Katy! Katy's hair was for ever untidy; her gowns were always catching on nails and 'tearing themselves'; and, in spite of her age and size, she was as heedless and innocent as a child of six. Katy was the *longest* girl that was ever seen. What she did to make herself grow so, nobody could tell; but there she was – up above Papa's ear, and half a head taller than poor Aunt Izzie. Whenever she stopped to think about her height she became very awkward, and felt as if she were all legs and elbows, and angles and joints. Happily, her head was so full of other things, of plans and schemes and fancies of all sorts, that she didn't often take time to remember how tall she was. She was a dear, loving child, for all her careless habits, and made bushels of good resolutions every week of her life, only unluckily she never kept any of them. She had fits of responsibility about the other children, and longed to set them a good example, but when the chance came she generally forgot to do so. Katy's days flew like the wind; for when she wasn't studying lessons, or sewing and darning with Aunt Izzie, which she hated extremely, there were always so many delightful schemes rioting in her brains, that all she wished for was ten pairs of hands to carry them out. These same active brains got her into perpetual scrapes. She was fond of building castles in the air, and dreaming of the time when something she had done would make her famous, so that everybody would hear of her, and want to know her. I don't think she had made up her mind what this wonderful thing was to be; but while thinking about it she often forgot to learn a lesson, or to lace her boots, and then she had a bad mark, or a scolding from Aunt Izzie. At such times she consoled herself with planning how, by and by, she would be beautiful and beloved, and amiable as an angel. A great deal was to happen to Katy before that time came. Her eyes, which were black, were to turn blue; her nose was to lengthen and straighten, and her mouth, quite too large at present to suit the part of a heroine, was to be made over into a sort of rosy button. Meantime, and until these charming changes should take place, Katy forgot her features as much as she could, though still, I think, the person on earth whom she most envied was that lady on the outside of the Tricopherous bottles with the wonderful hair which sweeps the ground.

* * * *

Mrs Knight's school, to which Katy and Clover and Cecy went, stood quite at the other end of the town from Dr Carr's. It was a low, one-storey building, and had a yard behind it, in which the girls played at recess. Unfortunately, next door to it was Miss Miller's school, equally large and popular, and with a yard behind it also. Only a high board fence separated the two playgrounds.

Mrs Knight was a stout, gentle woman, who moved slowly, and

463

had a face which made you think of an amiable and well-disposed cow. Miss Miller, on the contrary, had black eyes, with black cork-screw curls waving about them, and was generally brisk and snappy. A constant feud raged between the two schools as to the respective merits of the teachers and the instruction. The Knight girls, for some unknown reason, considered themselves genteel and the Miller girls vulgar, and took no pains to conceal this opinion; while the Miller girls, on the other hand, retaliated by being as aggravating as they knew how. They spent their recesses and intermissions mostly in making faces through the knot-holes in the fence, and over the top of it when they could get there, which wasn't an easy thing to do, as the fence was pretty high. The Knight girls could make faces too, for all their gentility. Their yard had one great advantage over the other: it possessed a woodshed, with a climbable roof, which commanded Miss Miller's premises, and upon this the girls used to sit in rows, turning up their noses at the next yard, and irritating the foe by jeering remarks. 'Knights' and 'Millerites', the two schools called each other; and the feud raged so high, that sometimes it was hardly safe for a Knight to meet a Millerite in the street; all of which, as may be imagined, was exceedingly improving both to the manners and morals of the young ladies concerned!

One morning, Katy was late. She could not find her things. Her algebra, as she expressed it, had 'gone and lost itself', her slate was missing, and the string was off her sun-bonnet. She ran about, searching for these articles and banging doors, till Aunt Izzie was out of patience.

'As for your algebra', she said, 'if it is that very dirty book with only one cover, and scribbled all over the leaves, you will find it under the kitchen table. Philly was playing before breakfast that it was a pig: no wonder, I'm sure, for it looks good for nothing else. How you do manage to spoil your school books in this manner, Katy, I cannot imagine. It is less than a month since your father got you a new algebra, and look at it now – not fit to be carried about. I do wish you would realize what books cost!

'About your slate,' she went on, 'I know nothing; but here is the bonnet-string'; taking it out of her pocket.

'Oh, thank you!' said Katy, hastily sticking it on with a pin.

'Katy Carr!' almost screamed Miss Izzie. 'What *are* you about? Pinning on your bonnet-string! Mercy on me, what shiftless thing will you do next? Now stand still, and don't fidget! You shan't stir till I have sewed it on properly.'

It wasn't easy to 'stand still and not fidget', with Aunt Izzie fussing away and lecturing, and now and then, in a moment of forgetfulness, sticking her needle into one's chin. Katy bore it as well as she could, only shifting perpetually from one foot to the other, and now and then uttering a little snort, like an impatient horse. The minute she was released she flew into the kitchen, seized the algebra, and rushed like a whirlwind to the gate, where good little Clover stood patiently waiting, though all ready herself, and terribly afraid she should be late.

'We shall have to run!' gasped Katy, quite out of breath. 'Aunt Izzie kept me! She has been so horrid!'

They did run as fast as they could, but time ran faster, and before they were half way to school the town clock struck nine, and all hope was over. This vexed Katy very much; for, though often late, she was always eager to be early.

'There,' she said, stopping short. 'I shall just tell Aunt Izzie that it was her fault. It is *too* bad.' And she marched into school in a very cross mood.

A day begun in this manner is pretty sure to end badly, as most of us know. All the morning through things seemed to go wrong. Katy missed twice in her grammar lesson, and lost her place in the class. Her hand shook so when she copied her composition, that the writing, not good at best, turned out almost illegible, so that Mrs Knight said it must all be done over again. This made Katy crosser than ever; and almost before she thought, she had whispered to Clover, 'How hateful!' And then, when just before recess all who had 'whispered' were requested to stand up, her conscience gave such a twinge that she was forced to get up with the rest, and see a black mark put against her

Out poured the Millerites, big and little

name on the list. The tears came into her eyes from vexation; and, for fear the other girls would notice them, she made a bolt for the yard as soon as the bell rang, and mounted up all alone to the wood-house roof, where she sat with her back to the school, fighting with her eyes, and trying to get her face in order before the rest should come.

Miss Miller's clock was about four minutes slower than Mrs Knight's, so the next playground was empty. It was a warm, breezy day, and as Katy sat there, suddenly a gust of wind came, and seizing her sun-bonnet, which was only half tied on, whirled it across the roof. She clutched after it as it flew, but too late. Once, twice, thrice it flapped, then it disappeared over the edge, and Katy, flying after, saw it lying a crumpled lilac heap in the very middle of the enemy's yard.

This was horrible! Not merely losing the bonnet, for Katy was comfortably indifferent as to what became of her clothes, but to lose it *so*. In another minute the Miller girls would be out. Already she seemed to see them dancing war-dances round the unfortunate bonnet, pinning it on a pole, using it as a football, waving it over the fence, and otherwise treating it as Indians treat a captive taken in war. Was it to be endured? Never! Better die first! And with very much the feeling of a person who faces destruction rather than forfeit honour, Katy set her teeth, and sliding rapidly down the roof, seized the fence, and with one bold leap vaulted into Miss Miller's yard.

Just then the recess bell tinkled; and a little Millerite who sat by the window, and who, for two seconds, had been dying to give the exciting information, squeaked out to the others: 'There's Katy Carr in our back-yard!'

Out poured the Millerites, big and little. Their wrath and indignation at this daring invasion cannot be described. With a howl of fury they precipitated themselves upon Katy, but she was quick as they, and, holding the rescued bonnet in her hand, was already half way up the fence.

There are moments when it is a fine thing to be tall. On this occasion Katy's long legs and arms served her an excellent turn. Nothing but a Daddy-long-legs ever climbed so fast or so wildly as she did now. In one second she had gained the top of the fence. Just as she went over a Millerite seized her by the last foot, and almost dragged her boot off.

Almost, not quite, thanks to the stout thread with which Aunt Izzie had sewed the buttons on. With a frantic kick Katy released herself, and had the satisfaction of seeing her assailant go head over heels backwards, while, with a shriek of triumph and fright, she herself plunged headlong into the midst of a group of Knights. They were listening with open mouths to the uproar, and now stood transfixed at the astonishing spectacle of one of their number absolutely returning alive from the camp of the enemy.

I cannot tell you what a commotion ensued. The Knights were beside themselves with pride and triumph. Katy was kissed and hugged, and made to tell her story over and over again, while rows of exulting girls sat on the wood-house roof to crow over the discomfited Millerites: and when, later, the foe rallied and began to retort over the fence, Clover, armed with a tack-hammer, was lifted up in the arms of one of the tall girls to rap the intruding knuckles as they appeared on the top. This she did with such goodwill that the Millerites were glad to drop down again, and mutter vengeance at a safe distance. Altogether it was a great day for the school, a day to be remembered. As time went on, Katy, what with the excitement of her adventure, and of being praised and petted by the big girls, grew perfectly reckless, and hardly knew what she said or did.

A good many of the scholars lived too far from school to go home at noon, and were in the habit of bringing their lunches in baskets, and staying all day. Katy and Clover were of this number. This noon, after the dinners were eaten, it was proposed that they should play something in the school-room, and Katy's unlucky star put it into her head to invent a new game, which she called the Game of Rivers.

It was played in the following manner: Each girl took the name of a river, and laid out for herself an appointed path through the room, winding among the desks and benches, and making a low, roaring sound, to imitate the noise of water. Cecy was the Platte; Marianne Brookes, a tall girl, the Mississippi; Alice Blair, the Ohio; Clover, the

Penobscot; and so on. They were instructed to run into each other once in a while, because, as Katy said, 'rivers do'.

As for Katy herself, she was 'Father Ocean' and, growling horribly, raged up and down the platform where Mrs Knight usually sat. Every now and then, when the others were at the far end of the room, she would suddenly cry out, 'Now for a meeting of the waters!' whereupon all the rivers, bouncing, bounding, scrambling, screaming, would turn and run toward Father Ocean, while he roared louder than all of them put together, and made short rushes up and down, to represent the movement of waves on a beach.

Such a noise as this beautiful game made was never heard in the town of Burnet before or since. It was like the bellowing of the bulls of Bashan, the squeaking of pigs, the cackle of turkey-cocks, and the laugh of wild hyenas all at once; and, in addition, there was a great banging of furniture and scraping of many feet on an uncarpeted floor. People going by stopped and stared, children cried, and an old lady asked why someone didn't run for a policeman; while the Miller girls listened with malicious pleasure, and told everybody that it was the noise that Mrs Knight's scholars 'usually made at recess'.

Mrs Knight coming back from dinner was much amazed to see a crowd of people collected in front of her school. As she drew near, the sounds reached her, and then she became really frightened, for she thought somebody was being murdered on her premises. Hurrying in, she threw open the door, and there, to her dismay, was the whole room in a frightful state of confusion and uproar: chairs flung down, desks upset, ink streaming on the floor; while in the midst of the ruin the frantic rivers raced and screamed, and Old Father Ocean, with a face as red as fire, capered like a lunatic on the platform.

'What *does* this mean?' gasped poor Mrs Knight, almost unable to speak for horror.

At the sound of her voice the Rivers stood still, Father Ocean brought his prances to an abrupt close, and slunk down from the platform. All of a sudden each girl seemed to realize what a condition the room was in, and what a horrible thing she had done. The timid ones cowered behind their desks, the bold ones tried to look unconscious and, to make matters worse, the scholars who had gone home to dinner began to return, staring at the scene of disaster, and asking, in whispers, what had been going on?

Mrs Knight rang the bell. When the school had come to order, she had the desks and chairs picked up, while she herself brought wet cloths to sop the ink from the floor. This was done in profound silence; and the expression of Mrs Knight's face was so direful and solemn, that a fresh damp fell upon the spirits of the guilty Rivers, and Father Ocean wished himself thousands of miles away.

When all was in order again, and the girls had taken their seats, Mrs Knight made a short speech. She said she never was so shocked in her life before; she had supposed that she could trust them to behave like ladies when her back was turned. The idea that they could act so disgracefully, make such an uproar, and alarm people going by, had never occurred to her, and she was deeply pained. It was setting a bad example to all the neighbourhood – by which Mrs Knight meant the rival school, Miss Miller having just sent over a little girl, with her compliments, to ask if anyone was hurt, and could *she* do anything? which was naturally aggravating! Mrs Knight hoped they were sorry; she thought they must be – sorry and ashamed. The exercises could now go on as usual. Of course some punishment would be inflicted for the offence, but she should have to reflect before deciding what it ought to be. Meantime she wanted them all to think it over seriously; and if anyone felt that she was more to blame than the others, now was the moment to rise and confess it.

Katy's heart gave a great thump, but she rose bravely: 'I made up the game, and I was Father Ocean,' she said to the astonished Mrs Knight, who glared at her for a minute, and then replied solemnly, 'Very well, Katy – sit down'; which Katy did, feeling more ashamed than ever, but somehow relieved in her mind. There is a saving grace in truth which helps truth-tellers through the worst of their troubles, and Katy found this out now.

The afternoon was long and hard. Mrs Knight did not smile once;

the lessons dragged; and Katy, after the heat and excitement of the forenoon, began to feel miserable. She had received more than one hard blow during the meetings of the waters, and had bruised herself almost without knowing it, against the desks and chairs. All these places now began to ache: her head throbbed so that she could hardly see, and a lump of something heavy seemed to be lying on her heart.

When school was over Mrs Knight rose and said: 'The young ladies who took part in the game this afternoon are requested to remain.' All the others went away, and shut the door behind them. It was a horrible moment: the girls never forgot it, or the hopeless sound of the door as the last departing scholar clapped it after her as she left.

I can't begin to tell you what it was that Mrs Knight said to them; it was very affecting, and before long most of the girls began to cry. The penalty for their offence was announced to be the loss of recess for three weeks; but that wasn't half so bad as seeing Mrs Knight so 'religious and afflicted', as Cecy told her mother afterwards. One by one the sobbing sinners departed from the school-room. When most of them were gone Mrs Knight called Katy up to the platform, and said a few words to her specially. She was not really severe, but Katy was too penitent and worn out to bear much, and before long was weeping like a waterspout, or like the ocean she had pretended to be.

At this, tender-hearted Mrs Knight was so much affected that she let her off at once, and even kissed her in token of forgiveness, which made poor Ocean sob harder than ever. All the way home she sobbed; faithful little Clover, running along by her side in great distress, begging her to stop crying, and trying in vain to hold up the fragments of her dress, which was torn in at least a dozen places. Katy could not stop crying, and it was fortunate that Aunt Izzie happened to be out, and that the only person who saw her in this piteous plight was Mary, the nurse, who doted on the children, and was always ready to help them out of their troubles.

On this occasion she petted and cosseted Katy exactly as if it had been Johnnie or little Phil. She took her on her lap, bathed the hot head, brushed the hair, put arnica on the bruises, and produced a clean frock, so that by tea time the poor child, except for her red eyes, looked like herself again, and Aunt Izzie didn't notice anything unusual.

For a wonder, Dr Carr was at home that evening. It was always a great treat to the children when this happened, and Katy thought herself happy when, after the little ones had gone to bed, she got Papa to herself, and told him the whole story.

'Papa,' she said, sitting on his knee, which, big girl as she was, she liked very much to do, 'what is the reason that makes some days so lucky and other days so unlucky? Now, today began all wrong, and everything that happened in it was wrong; and on other days I begin right, and all goes right, straight through. If Aunt Izzie hadn't kept me in the morning, I shouldn't have lost my mark, and then I shouldn't have been cross, and then *perhaps* I shouldn't have got in my other scrapes.'

'But what made Aunt Izzie keep you, Katy?'

'To sew on the string of my bonnet, Papa.'

'But how did it happen that the string was off?'

'Well,' said Katy reluctantly, 'I am afraid that was *my* fault, for it came off on Tuesday, and I didn't fasten it on.'

'So you see we must go back before Aunt Izzie for the beginning of this unlucky day of yours, Childie. Did you ever hear the old saying "For the want of a nail the shoe was lost"?'

'No, never – tell it to me!' cried Katy, who loved stories as well as when she was three years old.

So Dr Carr repeated:

> 'For the want of a nail the shoe was lost,
> For the want of a shoe the horse was lost,
> For the want of a horse the rider was lost,
> For the want of the rider the battle was lost,
> For the want of the battle the kingdom was lost,
>   And all for the want of a horse-shoe nail.'

'Oh, Papa!' exclaimed Katy, giving him a great hug as she got off his knee, 'I see what you mean! Who would have thought such a little speck of a thing as not sewing on my string could make a difference? But I don't believe I shall get into any more scrapes, for I shan't ever forget:

"For the want of a nail the shoe was lost".'

The Fight

THOMAS HUGHES
Illustrated by Arthur Hughes

Tom Brown's Schooldays (1857), from which this extract comes, was the most popular British school story of the nineteenth century. The school it depicts was Rugby and the Doctor of the novel was the famous Dr Arnold, its headmaster.

'Huzza, there's going to be a fight between Slogger Williams and Tom Brown!'

The news ran like wildfire about, and many boys who were on their way to tea at their several houses turned back, and sought the back of the chapel, where the fights come off.

'Just run and tell East to come and back me,' said Tom to a small School-house boy, who was off like a rocket to Harrowell's, just stopping for a moment to poke his head into the School-house hall, where the lower boys were already at tea, and sing out, 'Fight! Tom Brown and Slogger Williams.'

Up start half the boys at once, leaving bread, eggs, butter, sprats, and all the rest to take care of themselves. The greater part of the remainder follow in a minute, after swallowing their tea, carrying their food in their hands to consume as they go. Three or four only remain, who steal the butter of the more impetuous, and make to themselves an unctuous feast.

In another minute East and Martin tear through the quadrangle, carrying a sponge, and arrive at the scene of action just as the combatants are beginning to strip.

Tom felt he had got his work cut out for him, as he stripped off his jacket, waistcoat, and braces. East tied his handkerchief round his waist, and rolled up his shirt sleeves for him: 'Now, old boy, don't you open your mouth to say a word, or try to help yourself a bit, – we'll do all that; you keep all your breath and strength for the Slogger.' Martin meanwhile folded the clothes, and put them under the chapel rails; and now Tom, with East to handle him, and Martin to give him a knee, steps out on the turf, and is ready for all that may come: and here is the Slogger too, all stripped, and thirsting for the fray.

It doesn't look a fair match at first glance: Williams is nearly two inches taller, and probably a long year older than his opponent, and he is very strongly made about the arms and shoulders, – 'peels well,' as the little knot of big fifth-form boys, the amateurs, say; who stand outside the ring of little boys, looking complacently on, but taking no active part in the proceedings. But down below he is not so good by any means; no spring from the loins, and feeblish, not to say ship-wrecky about the knees. Tom, on the contrary, though not half so strong in the arms, is good all over, straight, hard, and springy, from neck to ankle, better perhaps in his legs than anywhere. Besides, you can see by the clear white of his eye, and fresh bright look of his skin, that he is in tip-top training, able to do all he knows; while the Slogger looks rather sodden, as if he didn't take much exercise and ate too much tuck. The time-keeper is chosen, a large ring made, and the two stand up opposite one another for a moment, giving us time just to make our little observations.

'If Tom'll only condescend to fight with his head and heels,' as East mutters to Martin, 'we shall do.'

But seemingly he won't, for there he goes in, making play with both hands. Hard all, is the word; the two stand to one another like men; rally follows rally in quick succession, each fighting as if he thought to finish the whole thing out of hand. 'Can't last at this rate,' say the knowing ones, while the partisans of each make the air ring with their shouts and counter-shouts, of encouragement, approval, and defiance.

'Take it easy, take it easy – keep away, let him come after you,' implores East, as he wipes Tom's face after the first round with a wet sponge, while he sits back on Martin's knee, sup-

ported by the Madman's long arms, which tremble a little from excitement.

'Time's up,' calls the time-keeper.

'There he goes again, hang it all!' growls East, as his man is at it again, as hard as ever. A very severe round follows, in which Tom gets out and out the worst of it, and is at last hit clean off his legs, and deposited on the grass by a right-hander from the Slogger.

Loud shouts rise from the boys of Slogger's house, and the School-house are silent and vicious, ready to pick quarrels anywhere.

'Two to one in half-crowns on the big 'un,' says Rattle, one of the amateurs, a tall fellow, in thunder-and-lightning waistcoat, and puffy good-natured face.

'Done !' says Groove, another amateur of quieter look, taking out his note-book to enter it, for our friend Rattle sometimes forgets these little things.

Meantime East is freshing up Tom with the sponges for next round, and has set two other boys to rub his hands.

'Tom, old boy,' whispers he, 'this may be fun for you, but it's death to me. He'll hit all the fight out of you in another five minutes, and then I shall go and drown myself in the island ditch. Feint him – use your legs! draw him about! he'll lose his wind then in no time, and you can go into him. Hit at his body too; we'll take care of his frontispiece by and by.'

Tom felt the wisdom of the counsel, and saw already that he couldn't go in and finish the Slogger off at mere hammer and tongs, so changed his tactics completely in the third round. He now fights cautiously, getting away from and parrying the Slogger's lunging hits, instead of trying to counter, and leading his enemy a dance all round the ring after him. 'He's funking; go in, Williams,' 'Catch him up,' 'Finish him off,' scream the small boys of the Slogger party.

'Just what we want,' thinks East, chuckling to himself, as he sees Williams, excited by these shouts, and thinking the game in his own hands, blowing himself in his exertions to get to close quarters again, while Tom is keeping away with perfect ease.

They quarter over the ground again and again, Tom always on the defensive.

The Slogger pulls up at last for a moment, fairly blown.

'Now then, Tom,' sings out East, dancing with delight. Tom goes in in a twinkling, and hits two heavy body blows, and gets away again before the Slogger can catch his wind, which when he does he rushes with blind fury at Tom, and being skilfully parried and avoided, over-reaches himself and falls on his face, amidst terrific cheers from the School-house boys.

'Double your two to one?' says Groove to Rattle, notebook in hand.

'Stop a bit,' says that hero, looking uncomfortably at Williams, who is puffing away on his second's knee, winded enough, but little the worse in any other way.

After another round the Slogger too seems to see that he can't go in and win right off, and has met his match or thereabouts. So he too begins to use his head, and tries to make Tom lose his patience, and come in before his time. And so the fight sways on, now one, and now the other getting a trifling pull.

Tom's face begins to look very one-sided – there are little queer bumps on his forehead, and his mouth is bleeding; but East keeps the wet sponge going so scientifically, that he comes up looking as fresh and bright as ever. Williams is only slightly marked in the face, but by the nervous movement of his elbows you can see that Tom's body blows are telling. In fact, half the vice of the Slogger's hitting is neutralized, for he daren't lunge out freely for fear of exposing his sides. It is too interesting by this time for much shouting, and the whole ring is very quiet.

'All right, Tommy,' whispers East; 'hold on's the horse that's to win. We've got the last. Keep your head, old boy.'

But where is Arthur all this time? Words cannot paint the poor little fellow's distress. He couldn't muster courage to come up to the ring, but wandered up and down from the great fives'-court to the corner of the chapel rails, now trying to make up his mind to throw himself between them, and try to stop them; then thinking of running in and telling his friend Mary, who he knew would instantly report to the Doctor. The stories he had heard of men being killed in prize-fights rose up horribly before him.

Once only, when the shouts of 'Well done, Brown!' 'Huzza for the School-house!' rose higher than ever, he ventured up to the ring, thinking the victory was won. Catching sight of Tom's face in the state I have described, all fear of consequences vanishing out of his mind, he rushed straight off to the matron's room, beseeching her to get the fight stopped, or he should die.

But it's time for us to get back to the close. What is this fierce tumult and confusion? The ring is broken, and high and angry words are being bandied about; 'It's all fair,' – 'It isn't' – 'No hugging!' the fight is stopped. The combatants, however, sit there quietly, tended by their seconds, while their adherents wrangle in the middle. East can't help shouting challenges to two or three of the other side, though he never leaves Tom for a moment, and plies the sponges as fast as ever.

The fact is, that at the end of the last round, Tom, seeing a good opening, had closed with his opponent, and after a moment's struggle, had thrown him heavily, by help of the fall he had learnt from his village rival in the vale of White Horse. Williams hadn't the ghost of a chance with Tom at wrestling; and the conviction broke at once on the Slogger faction, that if this were allowed their man must be licked. There was a strong feeling in the School against catching hold and throwing, though it was generally ruled all fair within limits; so the ring was broken and the fight stopped.

The School-house are over-ruled – the fight is on again, but there is to be no throwing; and East in high wrath threatens to take his man away after next round (which he don't mean to do, by the way), when suddenly young Brooke comes through the small gate at the end of the chapel. The School-house faction rush to him. 'Oh, hurra! now we shall get fair play.'

'Please, Brooke, come up, they won't let Tom Brown throw him.'

'Throw whom?' says Brooke, coming up to the ring. 'Oh! Williams, I see. Nonsense! of course he may throw him, if he catches him fairly above the waist.'

Now, young Brooke, you're in the sixth, you know, and you ought to stop all fights. He looks hard at both boys. 'Anything wrong?' says he to East, nodding at Tom.

'Not a bit.'

'Not beat at all?'

'Bless you, no! Heaps of fight in him. Ain't there, Tom?'

Tom looks at Brooke and grins.

'How's he?' nodding at Williams.

'So, so; rather done, I think, since his last fall. He won't stand above two more.'

'Time's up!' The boys rise again and face one another. Brooke can't find it in his heart to stop them just yet, so the round goes on, the Slogger waiting for Tom, and reserving all his strength to hit him out should he come in for the wrestling dodge again, for he feels that that must be stopped, or his sponge will soon go up in the air.

And now another new-comer appears on the field, to wit, the under-porter, with his long brush and great wooden receptacle for dust under his arm. He has been sweeping out the schools.

'You'd better stop, gentlemen,' he says; 'the Doctor knows that Brown's fighting – he'll be out in a minute.'

'You go to Bath, Bill,' is all that excellent servitor gets by his advice. And being a man of his hands, and a staunch upholder of the School-house, can't help stopping to look on for a bit, and see Tom Brown, their pet craftsman, fight a round.

It is grim earnest now, and no mistake. Both boys feel this, and summon every power of head, hand, and eye to their aid. A piece of luck on either side, a foot slipping, a blow getting well home, or another fall, may decide it. Tom works slowly round for an opening; he has all the legs, and can choose his own time; the Slogger waits for the attack, and hopes to finish it by some heavy right-handed blow. As they quarter slowly over the ground, the evening sun comes out from behind a cloud and falls full on Williams's face. Tom darts in; the heavy right-hand is delivered, but only grazes his head. A short rally at close quarters, and they close; in another moment the Slogger is thrown again heavily for the third time.

'I'll give you three or two on the little one in halfcrowns,' said Groove to Rattle.

'No, thank'ee,' answers the other, diving his hands further into his coat-tails.

Just at this stage of the proceedings, the door of the turret which leads to the Doctor's library suddenly opens, and he steps into the close, and makes straight for the ring, in which Brown and the Slogger are both seated on their seconds' knees for the last time.

'The Doctor! the Doctor!' shouts some small boy who catches sight

The Doctor steps into the close

481

of him, and the ring melts away in a few seconds, the small boys tearing off, Tom collaring his jacket and waistcoat, and slipping through the little gate by the chapel, and round the corner to Harrowell's with his backers, as lively as need be; Williams and his backers making off not quite so fast across the close; Groove, Rattle, and the other bigger fellows trying to combine dignity and prudence in a comical manner, and walking off fast enough, they hope, not to be recognized, and not fast enough to look like running away.

The Lucky Orphan

JEAN WEBSTER

Jerusha Abbott is the oldest girl in an orphanage. From it she is sent to college by an anonymous benefactor. In Daddy Long-Legs *(1912), from which this extract comes, she tells her benefactor in a series of letters about her life as a student. (In the end she marries him).*

The first Wednesday in every month was a Perfectly Awful Day – a day to be awaited with dread, endured with courage and forgotten with haste. Every floor must be spotless, every chair dustless, and every bed without a wrinkle. Ninety-seven squirming little orphans must be scrubbed and combed and buttoned into freshly starched ginghams; and all ninety-seven reminded of their manners, and told to say, 'Yes, sir', 'No, sir', whenever a Trustee spoke.

It was a distressing time; and poor Jerusha Abbott, being the oldest orphan, had to bear the brunt of it. But this particular first Wednesday, like its predecessors, finally dragged itself to a close. Jerusha escaped from the pantry where she had been making sandwiches for the asylum's guests, and turned upstairs to accomplish her regular work. Her special care was room F, where eleven little tots, from four to seven, occupied eleven little cots set in a row. Jerusha assembled her charges, straightened their rumpled frocks, wiped their noses, and started them in an orderly and willing line towards the dining-room to engage themselves for a blessed half-hour with bread and milk and prune pudding.

Then she dropped down on the window-seat and leaned throbbing temples against the cool glass. She had been on her feet since five that morning, doing everybody's bidding, scolded and hurried by a nervous matron. Mrs Lippett, behind the scenes, did not always maintain that calm and pompous dignity with which she faced an audience of Trustees and lady visitors. Jerusha gazed out across a broad stretch of frozen lawn, beyond the tall iron paling that marked the confines of the asylum, down undulating ridges sprinkled with country estates, to the spires of the village rising from the midst of bare trees.

The day was ended – quite successfully, so far as she knew. The Trustees and the visiting committee had made their rounds, and read their reports, and drunk their tea, and now were hurrying home to their own cheerful firesides, to forget their bothersome little charges for another month. Jerusha leaned forward watching with curiosity – and a touch of wistfulness – the stream of carriages and automobiles that rolled out of the asylum gates. In imagination she followed first one equipage, then another, to the big houses dotted along the hillside. She pictured herself in a fur coat and a velvet hat trimmed with feathers leaning back in the seat and nonchalantly murmuring 'Home' to the driver. But on the door-sill of her home the picture grew blurred.

Jerusha had an imagination – an imagination, Mrs Lippett told her, that would get her into trouble if she didn't take care – but keen as it was, it could not carry her beyond the front porch of the houses she would enter. Poor, eager, adventurous little Jerusha, in all her seventeen years, had never stepped inside an ordinary house; she could not picture the daily routine of those other human beings who carried on their lives undiscommoded by orphans.

> Je-ru-sha Ab-bott
> You are wan-ted
> In the of-fice,
> And I think you'd
> Better hurry up!

Tommy Dillon, who had joined the choir, came singing up the stairs and down the corridor, his chant growing louder as he approached room F. Jerusha wrenched herself from the window and refaced the troubles of life.

'Who wants me?' she cut into Tommy's chant with a note of sharp anxiety.

> Mrs Lippett in the office,
> And I think she's mad.
> Ah-a-men!

Tommy piously intoned, but his accent was not entirely malicious. Even the most hardened little orphan felt sympathy for an erring sister who was summoned to the office to face an annoyed matron; and Tommy liked Jerusha even if she did sometimes jerk him by the arm and nearly scrub his nose off.

Jerusha went without comment, but with two parallel lines on her brow. What could have gone wrong, she wondered. Were the sandwiches not thin enough? Were there shells in the nut cakes? Had a lady visitor seen the hole in Susie Hawthorn's stocking? Had – O horrors! – one of the cherubic little babes in her own room F 'sauced' a Trustee?

The long lower hall had not been lighted, and as she came downstairs, a last Trustee stood, on the point of departure, in the open door that led to the porte-cochère. Jerusha caught only a fleeting impression of the man – and the impression consisted entirely of tallness. He was waving his arm towards an automobile waiting in the curved drive. As it sprang into motion and approached, head-on for an instant, the glaring headlights threw his shadow sharply against the wall inside. The shadow pictured grotesquely elongated legs and arms that ran along the floor and up the wall of the corridor. It looked, for all the world, like a huge, wavering daddy-long-legs.

Jerusha's anxious frown gave place to quick laughter. She was by nature a sunny soul, and had always snatched the tiniest excuse to be amused. If one could derive any sort of entertainment out of the oppressive fact of a Trustee, it was something unexpected to the good. She advanced to the office quite cheered by the tiny episode, and presented a smiling face to Mrs Lippett. To her surprise the matron was also, if not exactly smiling, at least appreciably affable; she wore an expression almost as pleasant as the one she donned for visitors.

485

'Sit down, Jerusha. I have something to say to you.'

Jerusha dropped into the nearest chair and waited with a touch of breathlessness. An automobile flashed past the window; Mrs Lippett glanced after it.

'Did you notice the gentleman who has just gone?'

'I saw his back.'

'He is one of our most affluential Trustees, and has given large sums of money towards the asylum's support. I am not at liberty to mention his name; he expressly stipulated that he was to remain unknown.'

Jerusha's eyes widened slightly; she was not accustomed to being summoned to the office to discuss the eccentricities of Trustees with the matron.

'This gentleman has taken an interest in several of our boys. You remember Charles Benton and Henry Freize? They were both sent through college by Mr – er – this Trustee, and both have repaid with hard work and success the money that was so generously expended. Other payment the gentleman does not wish. Heretofore his philanthropies have been directed solely towards the boys; I have never been able to interest him in the slightest degree in any of the girls in the institution, no matter how deserving. He does not, I may tell you, care for girls.'

'No, ma'am,' Jerusha murmured, since some reply seemed to be expected at this point.

'Today, at the regular meeting, the question of your future was brought up.'

Mrs Lippett allowed a moment of silence to fall, then resumed in a slow, placid manner extremely trying to her hearer's suddenly tightened nerves.

'Usually, as you know, the children are not kept after they are sixteen, but an exception was made in your case. You had finished our school at fourteen, and having done so well in your studies – not always, I must say, in your conduct – it was determined to let you go on in the village high school. Now you are finishing that, and of

486

course the asylum cannot be responsible any longer for your support. As it is, you have had two years more than most.'

Mrs Lippett overlooked the fact that Jerusha had worked hard for her board during those two years; that the convenience of the asylum had come first and her education second; that on days like the present she was kept at home to scrub.

'As I say, the question of your future was brought up and your record was discussed – thoroughly discussed.'

Mrs Lippett brought accusing eyes to bear upon the prisoner in the dock, and the prisoner looked guilty because it seemed to be expected – not because she could remember any strikingly black pages in her record.

'Of course the usual disposition of one in your place would be to put you in a position where you could begin to work, but you have done well in school in certain branches; it seems that your work in English has even been brilliant. Miss Pritchard, who is on our visiting committee, is also on the school board; she has been talking with your rhetoric teacher, and made a speech in your favour. She also read aloud an essay that you had written entitled, 'Blue Wednesday'.

Jerusha's guilty expression this time was not assumed.

'It seemed to me that you showed little gratitude in holding up to ridicule the institution that has done so much for you. Had you not managed to be funny I doubt if you would have been forgiven. But fortunately for you, Mr – that is, the gentleman who has just gone – appears to have an immoderate sense of humour. On the strength of that impertinent paper, he has offered to send you to college.'

'To college?' Jerusha's eyes grew big.

Mrs Lippett nodded.

'He waited to discuss the terms with me. They are unusual. The gentleman, I may say, is erratic. He believes that you have originality, and he is planning to educate you to become a writer.'

'A writer?' Jerusha's mind was numbed. She could only repeat Mrs Lippett's words.

'That is his wish. Whether anything will come of it, the future will show. He is giving you a very liberal allowance, almost, for a girl who has never had any experience in taking care of money, too liberal. But he planned the matter in detail, and I did not feel free to make any suggestions. You are to remain here through the summer, and Miss Pritchard has kindly offered to superintend your outfit. Your board and tuition will be paid directly to the college, and you will receive in addition during the four years you are there, an allowance of thirty-five dollars a month. This will enable you to enter on the same standing as the other students. The money will be sent to you by the gentleman's private secretary once a month, and in return, you will write a letter of acknowledgment once a month. That is, you are not to thank him for the money; he doesn't care to have that mentioned, but you are to write a letter telling of the progress in your studies and the details of your daily life. Just such a letter as you would write to your parents if they were living.

'These letters will be addressed to Mr John Smith and will be sent in care of the secretary. The gentleman's name is not John Smith, but he prefers to remain unknown. To you he will never be anything but John Smith. His reason in requiring the letters is that he thinks nothing so fosters facility in literary expression as letter-writing. Since you have no family with whom to correspond, he desires you to write in this way; also, he wishes to keep track of your progress. He will never answer your letters, nor in the slightest particular take any notice of them. He detests letter-writing and does not wish you to become a burden. If any point should ever arise where an answer would seem to be imperative – such as in the event of your being expelled, which I trust will not occur – you may correspond with Mr Griggs, his secretary. These monthly letters are absolutely obligatory on your part; they are the only payment that Mr Smith requires, so you must be as punctilious in sending them as though it were a bill that you were paying. I hope that they will always be respectful in tone and will reflect credit on your training. You must remember that you are writing to a Trustee of the John Grier Home.'

Jerusha's eyes longingly sought the door. Her head was in a whirl of excitement, and she wished only to escape from Mrs Lippett's platitudes, and think. She rose and took a tentative step backwards. Mrs Lippett detained her with a gesture; it was an oratorical opportunity not to be slighted.

'I trust that you are properly grateful for this very rare good fortune that has befallen you? Not many girls in your position ever have such an opportunity to rise in the world. You must always remember—'

'I – yes, ma'am, thank you. I think, if that's all, I must go and sew a patch on Freddie Perkins's trousers.'

The door closed behind her, and Mrs Lippett watched it with dropped jaw, her peroration in mid air.

★　　★　　★　　★

215 FERGUSSEN HALL
September 24th.

Dear Kind-Trustee-Who-Sends-Orphans-to-College,

Here I am! I travelled yesterday for four hours in a train. It's a funny sensation, isn't it? I never rode in one before.

College is the biggest, most bewildering place – I get lost whenever I leave my room. I will write you a description later when I'm feeling less muddled; also I will tell you about my lessons. Classes don't begin until Monday morning, and this is Saturday night. But I wanted to write a letter first just to get acquainted.

It seems queer to be writing letters to somebody you don't know. It seems queer to me to be writing letters at all – I've never written more than three or four in my life, so please overlook it if these are not a model kind.

Before leaving yesterday morning, Mrs Lippett and I had a very serious talk. She told me how to behave all the rest of my life, and especially how to behave towards the kind gentleman who is doing so much for me. I must take care to be Very Respectful.

But how can one be very respectful to a person who wishes to be called John Smith? Why couldn't you have picked out a name with a little personality? I might as well write letters to Dear Hitching-Post or Dear Clothes-Prop.

I have been thinking about you a great deal this summer; having somebody take an interest in me after all these years makes me feel as though I had found a sort of family. It seems as though I belonged to somebody now, and it's a very comfortable sensation. I must say, however, that when I think about you, my imagination has very little to work upon. There are just three things that I know:

    I. You are tall.
    II. You are rich.
    III. You hate girls.

I suppose I might call you Dear Mr Girl-Hater. Only that's rather insulting to me. Or Dear Mr Rich-Man, but that's insulting to you, as though money were the only important thing about you. Besides, being rich is such a very external quality. Maybe you won't stay rich all your life; lots of very clever men get smashed up in Wall Street. But at least you will stay tall all your life! So I've decided to call you Dear Daddy-Long-Legs. I hope you won't mind. It's just a private pet name – we won't tell Mrs Lippett.

The ten o'clock bell is going to ring in two minutes. Our day is divided into sections by bells. We eat and sleep and study by bells. It's very enlivening; I feel like a fire-horse all of the time. There it goes! Lights out. Good night.

Observe with what precision I obey rules – due to my training in the John Grier Home.

Yours most respectfully,
JERUSHA ABBOTT

To Mr Daddy-Long-Legs Smith.

October 1st

Dear Daddy-Long-Legs,

I love college and I love you for sending me – I'm very, *very* happy, and so excited every moment of the time that I can scarcely sleep. You can't imagine how different it is from the John Grier Home. I never dreamed there was such a place in the world. I'm feeling sorry for everybody who isn't a girl and who can't come here; I am sure the college you attended when you were a boy couldn't have been so nice.

My room is up in a tower that used to be the contagious ward before they built the new infirmary. There are three other girls on the same floor of the tower – a Senior who wears spectacles and is always asking us please to be a little more quiet, and two Freshmen named Sallie McBride and Julia Rutledge Pendleton. Sallie has red hair and a turn-up nose and is quite friendly; Julia comes from one of the first families in New York and hasn't noticed me yet. They room together and the Senior and I have singles. Usually Freshmen can't get singles; they are very scarce, but I got one without even asking. I suppose the registrar didn't think it would be right to ask a properly brought-up girl to room with a foundling. You see there are advantages!

My room is on the north-west corner with two windows and a view. After you've lived in a ward for eighteen years with twenty room-mates, it is restful to be alone. This is the first chance I've ever had to get acquainted with Jerusha Abbott. I think I'm going to like her.

Do you think you are?

Tuesday.

They are organizing the Freshman basket-ball team and there's just a chance that I shall get in it. I'm little of course, but terribly quick and wiry and tough. While the others are hopping about in the air, I can dodge under their feet and grab the ball. It's loads of fun practising – out in the athletic field in the afternoon with the trees all red and yellow and the air full of the smell of burning leaves, and everybody laughing and shouting. These are the happiest girls I ever saw – and I am the happiest of all!

I meant to write a long letter and tell you all the things I'm learning (Mrs Lippett said you wanted to know), but 7th hour has just rung, and in ten minutes I'm due at the athletic field in gymnasium clothes. Don't you hope I'll get in the team?

Yours always,
JERUSHA ABBOTT.

PS. (9 o'clock.)

Sallie McBride just poked her head in at my door. This is what she said:

'I'm so homesick that I simply can't stand it. Do you feel that way?'

I smiled a little and said no, I thought I could pull through. At least homesickness is one disease that I've escaped! I never heard of anybody being asylum-sick, did you?

The Schoolboy's Story

CHARLES DICKENS
Illustrated by Fred Walker

Being rather young at present – I am getting on in years, but still I am rather young – I have no particular adventures of my own to fall back upon. It wouldn't much interest anybody here, I suppose, to know what a screw the Reverend is, or what a griffin *she* is, or how they do stick it into parents – particularly hair-cutting, and medical attendance. One of our fellows was charged in his half's account twelve and sixpence for two pills – tolerably profitable at six and threepence a-piece, I should think – and he never took them either, but put them up the sleeve of his jacket.

As to the beef, it's shameful. It's *not* beef. Regular beef isn't veins. You can chew regular beef. Besides which, there's gravy to regular beef, and you never see a drop to ours. Another of our fellows went home ill, and heard the family doctor tell his father that he couldn't account for his complaint unless it was the beer. Of course it was the beer, and well it might be!

However, beef and Old Cheeseman are two different things. So is beer. It was Old Cheeseman I meant to tell about; not the manner in which our fellows get their constitutions destroyed for the sake of profit.

Why, look at the pie-crust alone. There's no flakiness in it. It's solid – like damp lead. Then our fellows get nightmares, and are bolstered for calling out and waking other fellows. Who can wonder!

Old Cheeseman one night walked in his sleep, put his hat on over his nightcap, got hold of a fishing-rod and a cricket bat, and went down into the parlour, where they naturally thought from his appearance he was a Ghost. Why, he never would have done that if his meals had been wholesome. When we all begin to walk in our sleeps, I suppose they'll be sorry for it.

'*In the Midsummer holidays some of our fellows used to come back and climb the trees outside the playground wall to see Old Cheeseman*'

Old Cheeseman wasn't second Latin Master then; he was a fellow himself. He was first brought there, very small, in a post-chaise, by a woman who was always taking snuff and shaking him – and that was the most he remembered about it. He never went home for the holidays. His accounts (he never learnt any extras) were sent to a Bank, and the Bank paid them; and he had a brown suit twice a-year, and went into boots at twelve. They were always too big for him, too.

In the Midsummer holidays, some of our fellows who lived within walking distance, used to come back and climb the trees outside the playground wall, on purpose to look at Old Cheeseman reading there by himself. He was always as mild as the tea – and *that's* pretty mild, I should hope! – so when they whistled to him, he looked up and nodded; and when they said, 'Halloa, Old Cheeseman, what have you had for dinner?' he said, 'Boiled mutton;' and when they said, 'An't it solitary, Old Cheeseman?' he said, 'It is a little dull sometimes:' and then they said, 'Well, good-bye, Old Cheeseman!' and climbed down again. Of course it was imposing on Old Cheeseman to give him nothing but boiled mutton through a whole Vacation, but that was just like the system. When they didn't give him boiled mutton, they gave him rice pudding, pretending it was a treat. And saved the butcher.

So Old Cheeseman went on. The holidays brought him into other trouble besides the loneliness; because when the fellows began to come back, not wanting to, he was always glad to see them; which was aggravating when they were not at all glad to see him, and so he got his head knocked against walls, and that was the way his nose bled. But he was a favourite in general. Once a subscription was raised for him; and, to keep up his spirits, he was presented before the holidays with two white mice, a rabbit, a pigeon, and a beautiful puppy. Old Cheeseman cried about it – especially soon afterwards, when they all ate one another.

Of course Old Cheeseman used to be called by the names of all sorts of cheeses – Double Glo'sterman, Family Cheshireman, Dutchman, North Wiltshireman, and all that. But he never minded it. And I don't mean to say he was old in point of years – because he wasn't – only he was called from the first, Old Cheeseman.

At last, Old Cheeseman was made second Latin Master. He was brought in one morning at the beginning of a new half, and presented to the school in that capacity as 'Mr Cheeseman.' Then our fellows all agreed that Old Cheeseman was a spy, and a deserter, who had gone over to the enemy's camp, and sold himself for gold. It was no excuse for him that he had sold himself for very little gold – two pounds ten a quarter and his washing, as was reported. It was decided by a Parliament which sat about it, that Old Cheeseman's mercenary motives could alone be taken into account, and that he had 'coined our blood for Drachmas.' The Parliament took the expression out of the quarrel scene between Brutus and Cassius.

When it was settled in this strong way that Old Cheeseman was a tremendous traitor, who had wormed himself into our fellows' secrets on purpose to get himself into favour by giving up everything he knew, all courageous fellows were invited to come forward and enrol themselves in a Society for making a set against him. The President of the Society was First boy, named Bob Tarter. His father was in the West Indies, and he owned, himself, that his father was worth millions. He had great power among our fellows, and he wrote a parody, beginning –

> 'Who made believe to be so meek
> That we could hardly hear him speak,
> Yet turned out an Informing Sneak?
> Old Cheeseman.

– and on in that way through more than a dozen verses, which he used to go and sing, every morning, close by the new master's desk. He trained one of the low boys, too, a rosy-cheeked little Brass who didn't care what he did, to go up to him with his Latin Grammar one morning, and say it so: *Nominativus pronominum* – Old Cheeseman, *raro exprimitur* – was never suspected, *nisi distinctionis* – of being an informer, *aut emphasis gratia* – until he proved one. *Ut* – for instance,

Vos damnastis – when he sold the boys. *Quasi* – as though, *dicat* – he should say. *Praeterea nemo* – I'm a Judas! All this produced a great effect on Old Cheeseman. He had never had much hair; but what he had, began to get thinner and thinner every day. He grew paler and more worn; and sometimes of an evening he was seen sitting at his desk with a precious long snuff to his candle, and his hands before his face, crying. But no member of the Society could pity him, even if he felt inclined, because the President said it was Old Cheeseman's conscience.

So Old Cheeseman went on, and didn't he lead a miserable life! Of course the Reverend turned up his nose at him, and of course *she* did – because both of them always do that at all the masters – but he suffered from the fellows most, and he suffered from them constantly. He never told about it, that the Society could find out; but he got no credit for that, because the President said it was Old Cheeseman's cowardice.

He had only one friend in the world, and that one was almost as powerless as he was, for it was only Jane. Jane was a sort of wardrobe-woman to our fellows, and took care of the boxes. She had come at first, I believe, as a kind of apprentice – some of our fellows say from a Charity, but *I* don't know – and after her time was out, had stopped at so much a year. So little a year, perhaps I ought to say, for it is far more likely. However, she had put some pounds in the Savings' Bank, and she was a very nice young woman. She was not quite pretty; but she had a very frank, honest, bright face, and all our fellows were fond of her. She was uncommonly neat and cheerful, and uncommonly comfortable and kind. And if anything was the matter with a fellow's mother, he always went and showed the letter to Jane.

Jane was Old Cheeseman's friend. The more the Society went against him, the more Jane stood by him. She used to give him a good-humoured look out of her still-room window, sometimes, that seemed to set him up for the day. She used to pass out of the orchard and the kitchen garden (always kept locked, I believe you!) through the playground, when she might have gone the other way, only to give a turn of her head, as much as to say, 'Keep up your spirits!' to Old Cheeseman. His slip of a room was so fresh and orderly that it was well known who looked after it while he was at his desk; and when our fellows saw a smoking hot dumpling on his plate at dinner, they knew with indignation who had sent it up.

Under these circumstances, the Society resolved, after a quantity of meeting and debating, that Jane should be requested to cut Old Cheeseman dead; and that if she refused, she must be sent to Coventry herself. So a deputation, headed by the President, was appointed to wait on Jane, and inform her of the vote the Society had been under the painful necessity of passing. She was very much respected for all her good qualities, and there was a story about her having once waylaid the Reverend in his own study, and got a fellow off from severe punishment, of her own kind comfortable heart. So the deputation didn't much like the job. However, they went up, and the President told Jane all about it. Upon which Jane turned very red, burst into tears, informed the President and the deputation, in a way not at all like her usual way, that they were a parcel of malicious young savages, and turned the whole respected body out of the room. Consequently it was entered in the Society's book (kept in astronomical cypher for fear of detection), that all communication with Jane was interdicted: and the President addressed the members on this convincing instance of Old Cheeseman's undermining.

But Jane was as true to Old Cheeseman as Old Cheeseman was false to our fellows – in their opinion, at all events – and steadily continued to be his only friend. It was a great exasperation to the Society, because Jane was as much a loss to them as she was a gain to him; and being more inveterate against him than ever, they treated him worse than ever. At last, one morning, his desk stood empty, his room was peeped into, and found to be vacant, and a whisper went about among the pale faces of our fellows that Old Cheeseman, unable to bear it any longer, had got up early and drowned himself.

The mysterious looks of the other masters after breakfast, and the evident fact that Old Cheeseman was not expected, confirmed the

Society in this opinion. Some began to discuss whether the President was liable to hanging or only transportation for life, and the President's face showed a great anxiety to know which. However, he said that a jury of his country should find him game; and that in his address he should put it to them to lay their hands upon their hearts and say whether they as Britons approved of informers, and how they thought they would like it themselves. Some of the Society considered that he had better run away until he found a forest where he might change clothes with a wood-cutter, and stain his face with black-berries; but the majority believed that if he stood his ground, his father – belonging as he did to the West Indies, and being worth millions – could buy him off.

All our fellows' hearts beat fast when the Reverend came in, and made a sort of a Roman, or a Field-Marshal, of himself with the ruler; as he always did before delivering an address. But their fears were nothing to their astonishment when he came out with the story that Old Cheeseman, 'so long our respected friend and fellow-pilgrim in the pleasant plains of knowledge,' he called him – O yes! I dare say! Much of that! – was the orphan child of a disinherited young lady who had married against her father's wish, and whose young husband had died, and who had died of sorrow herself, and whose unfortunate baby (Old Cheeseman) had been brought up at the cost of a grand-father who would never consent to see it, baby, boy, or man: which grandfather was now dead, and serve him right – that's *my* putting in – and which grandfather's large property, there being no will, was now, and all of a sudden and for ever, Old Cheeseman's! Our so long respected friend and fellow-pilgrim in the pleasant plains of know-ledge, the Reverend wound up a lot of bothering quotations by saying, would 'come among us once more' that day fortnight, when he desired to take leave of us himself, in a more particular manner. With these words, he stared severely round at our fellows, and went solemnly out.

There was precious consternation among the members of the Society, now. Lots of them wanted to resign, and lots more began to try to make out that they had never belonged to it. However, the President stuck up, and said that they must stand or fall together, and that if a breach was made it should be over his body – which was meant to encourage the Society: but it didn't. The President further said, he would consider the position in which they stood, and would give them his best opinion and advice in a few days. This was eagerly looked for, as he knew a good deal of the world on account of his father's being in the West Indies.

After days and days of hard thinking, and drawing armies all over his slate, the President called our fellows together, and made the matter clear. He said it was plain that when Old Cheeseman came on the appointed day, his first revenge would be to impeach the Society, and have it flogged all round. After witnessing with joy the torture of his enemies, and gloating over the cries which agony would extort from them, the probability was that he would invite the Reverend, on pretence of conversation, into a private room – say the parlour into which Parents were shown, where the two great globes were which were never used – and would there reproach him with the various frauds and oppressions he had endured at his hands. At the close of his observations he would make a signal to a Prizefighter concealed in the passage, who would then appear and pitch into the Reverend, till he was left insensible. Old Cheeseman would then make Jane a present of from five to ten pounds, and would leave the establishment in fiendish triumph.

The President explained that against the parlour part, or the Jane part, of these arrangements he had nothing to say; but, on the part of the Society, he counselled deadly resistance. With this view he recommended that all available desks should be filled with stones, and that the first word of the complaint should be the signal to every fellow to let fly at Old Cheeseman. The bold advice put the Society in better spirits, and was unanimously taken. A post about Old Cheeseman's size was put up in the playground, and all our fellows practised at it till it was dinted all over.

When the day came, and Places were called, every fellow sat down in a tremble. There had been much discussing and disputing as to how Old Cheeseman would come; but it was the general opinion that he would appear in a sort of triumphal car drawn by four horses, with two livery servants in front, and the Prizefighter in disguise up behind. So, all our fellows sat listening for the sound of wheels. But no wheels were heard, for Old Cheeseman walked after all, and came into the school without any preparation. Pretty much as he used to be, only dressed in black.

'Gentlemen,' said the Reverend, presenting him, 'our so long respected friend and fellow-pilgrim in the pleasant plains of know-ledge, is desirous to offer a word or two. Attention, gentlemen, one and all!'

Every fellow stole his hand into his desk and looked at the President. The President was all ready, and taking aim at Old Cheeseman with his eyes.

What did Old Cheeseman then, but walk up to his old desk, look round him with a queer smile as if there was a tear in his eye, and begin in a quavering voice, 'My dear companions and old friends!'

Every fellow's hand came out of his desk, and the President suddenly began to cry.

'My dear companions and old friends,' said Old Cheeseman, 'you have heard of my good fortune. I have passed so many years under this roof – my entire life so far, I may say – that I hope you have been glad to hear of it for my sake. I could never enjoy it without exchanging congratulations with you. If we have ever misunderstood one another at all, pray, my dear boys, let us forgive and forget. I have a great tenderness for you, and I am sure you return it. I want in the fulness of a grateful heart to shake hands with you every one. I have come back to do it, if you please, my dear boys.'

Since the President had begun to cry, several other fellows had broken out here and there: but now, when Old Cheeseman began with him as first boy, laid his left hand affectionately on his shoulder and gave him his right; and when the President said 'Indeed, I don't deserve it, sir; upon my honour I don't;' there was sobbing and crying all over the school. Every other fellow said he didn't deserve it, much in the same way; but Old Cheeseman, not minding that a bit, went cheerfully round to every boy, and wound up with every master – finishing off the Reverend last.

Then a snivelling little chap in a corner, who was always under some punishment or other, set up a shrill cry of 'Success to Old Cheeseman! Hooray!' The Reverend glared upon him, and said, '*Mr* Cheeseman, Sir.' But, Old Cheeseman protesting that he liked his old name a great deal better than his new one, all our fellows took up the cry; and, for I don't know how many minutes, there was such a thundering of feet and hands, and such a roaring of Old Cheeseman, as never was heard.

After that, there was a spread in the dining-room of the most magnificent kind. Fowls, tongues, preserves, fruits, confectionaries, jellies, neguses, barley-sugar temples, trifles, crackers – eat all you can and pocket what you like – all at Old Cheeseman's expense. After that, speeches, whole holiday, double and treble sets of all manners of things for all manners of games, donkeys, pony-chaises and drive yourself, dinner for all the masters at the Seven Bells (twenty pounds a-head our fellows estimated it at), an annual holiday and feast fixed that day every year, and another on Old Cheeseman's birthday – Reverend bound down before the fellows to allow it, so that he could never back out – all at Old Cheeseman's expense.

And didn't our fellows go down in a body and cheer outside the Seven Bells? O no!

But there's something else besides. Don't look at the next story-teller, for there's more yet. Next day, it was resolved that the Society should make it up with Jane, and then be dissolved. What do you think of Jane being gone, though? 'What? Gone for ever?' said our fellows, with long faces. 'Yes, to be sure,' was all the answer they could get. None of the people about the house would say anything more. At length, the first boy took upon himself to ask the Reverend whether our old friend Jane was really gone? The Reverend (he has got a daughter at home – turn-up nose, and red) replied severely. 'Yes, Sir

Miss Pitt is gone.' The idea of calling Jane, Miss Pitt! Some said she had been sent away in disgrace for taking money from Old Cheeseman; others said she had gone into Old Cheeseman's service at a rise of ten pounds a year. All that our fellows knew, was, she was gone.

It was two or three months afterwards when, one afternoon, an open carriage stopped at the cricket field, just outside bounds, with a lady and gentleman in it, who looked at the game a long time and stood up to see it played. Nobody thought much about them, until the same little snivelling chap came in, against all rules, from the post where he was Scout, and said, 'It's Jane!' Both Elevens forgot the game directly, and ran crowding round the carriage. It *was* Jane! In such a bonnet! And if you'll believe me, Jane was married to Old Cheeseman.

It soon became quite a regular thing when our fellows were hard at it in the playground, to see a carriage at the low part of the wall where it joins the high part, and a lady and gentleman standing up in it, looking over. The gentleman was always Old Cheeseman, and the lady was always Jane.

The first time I ever saw them, I saw them in that way. There had been a good many changes among our fellows then, and it turned out that Bob Tarter's father wasn't worth Millions! He wasn't worth anything. Bob had gone for a soldier, and Old Cheeseman had purchased his discharge. But that's not the carriage. The carriage stopped, and all our fellows stopped as soon as it was seen.

'So you have never sent me to Coventry after all!' said the lady, laughing, as our fellows swarmed up the wall to shake hands with her. 'Are you never going to do it?'

'Never! never! never!' on all sides.

I didn't understand what she meant then, but of course I do now. I was very much pleased with her face though, and with her good way, and I couldn't help looking at her – and at him too – with all our fellows clustering so joyfully about them.

They soon took notice of me as a new boy, so I thought I might as well swarm up the wall myself, and shake hands with them as the rest did. I was quite as glad to see them as the rest were, and was quite as familiar with them in a moment.

'Only a fortnight now,' said Old Cheeseman, 'to the holidays. Who stops? Anybody?'

A good many fingers pointed at me, and a good many voices cried 'He does!' For it was the year when you were all away; and rather low I was about it, I can tell you.

'Oh!' said Old Cheeseman. 'But it's solitary here in the holiday time. He had better come to us.'

So I went to their delightful house, and was as happy as I could possibly be. They understand how to conduct themselves towards boys, *they* do. When they take a boy to the play, for instance, they *do* take him. They don't go in after it's begun, or come out before it's over. They know how to bring a boy up, too. Look at their own! Though he is very little as yet, what a capital boy he is! Why, my next favourite to Mrs Cheeseman and Old Cheeseman, is young Cheeseman.

So, now I have told you all I know about Old Cheeseman. And it's not much after all, I am afraid. Is it?

Anne of Green Gables

L. M. MONTGOMERY

Anne Shirley has been sent from an orphanage – by mistake for a boy – to work on a farm, Green Gables. This extract tells how she found life at school. Anne of Green Gables came out in 1908 and is based on the author's own early life as an orphan living with her grandparents on Prince Edward Island, Canada.

'What a splendid day!' said Anne, drawing a long breath. 'Isn't it good just to be alive on a day like this? I pity the people who aren't born yet for missing it. They may have good days, of course, but they can never have this one. And it's splendider still to have such a lovely way to go to school by, isn't it?'

'It's a lot nicer than going round by the road; that is so dusty and hot,' said Diana practically, peeping into her dinner basket and mentally calculating if the three juicy, toothsome, raspberry tarts reposing there were divided among ten girls how many bites each girl would have.

The little girls of Avonlea school always pooled their lunches, and to eat three raspberry tarts all alone or even to share them only with one's best chum would have for ever and ever branded as 'awful mean' the girl who did it. And yet, when the tarts were divided among ten girls you just got enough to tantalize you.

The way Anne and Diana went to school *was* a pretty one. Anne thought those walks to and from school with Diana couldn't be improved upon even by imagination. Going around by the main road would have been so unromantic; but to go by Lovers' Lane and Willowmere and Violet Vale and the Birch Path was romantic, if ever anything was.

Lovers' Lane opened out below the orchard at Green Gables and stretched far up into the woods to the end of the Cuthbert Farm. It was the way by which the cows were taken to the back pasture and the wood hauled home in winter. Anne had named it Lovers' Lane before she had been a month at 'Green Gables'.

'Not that lovers ever really walk there,' she explained to Marilla, 'but Diana and I are reading a perfectly magnificent book and there's a Lovers' Lane in it. So we want to have one, too. And it's a very pretty name, don't you think? So romantic! We can imagine the lovers into it, you know. I like that lane because you can think out loud there without people calling you crazy.'

Anne, starting out alone in the morning, went down Lovers' Lane as far as the brook. Here Diana met her, and the two little girls went on up the lane under the leafy arch of maples – 'maples are such sociable trees,' said Anne; 'they're always rustling and whispering to you,' – until they came to a rustic bridge. Then they left the lane and walked through Mr Barry's back field and past Willowmere. Beyond Willowmere came Violet Vale – a little green dimple in the shadow of Mr Andrew Bell's big woods. 'Of course there are no violets there now,' Anne told Marilla, 'but Diana says there are millions of them in spring. Oh, Marilla, can't you just imagine you see them? It actually takes away my breath. I named it Violet Vale. Diana says she never saw the beat of me for hitting on fancy names for places. It's nice to be clever at something, isn't it? But Diana named the Birch Path. She wanted to, so I let her; but I'm sure I could have found something more poetical than plain Birch Path. Anybody can think of a name like that. But the Birch Path is one of the prettiest places in the world, Marilla.'

It was. Other people besides Anne thought so when they stumbled on it. It was a little narrow, twisting path, winding down over a long hill straight through Mr Bell's woods, where the light came down sifted through so many emerald screens that it was as flawless as the heart of a diamond. It was fringed in all its length with slim young birches, white-stemmed and lissom-boughed; ferns and starflowers and wild lilies of the valley and scarlet tufts of pigeon berries grew thickly along it; and always there was a delightful spiciness in the air and music of bird calls and the murmur and laugh of wood winds in the trees overhead. Now and then you might see a rabbit skipping across the road if you were quiet – which, with Anne and Diana, happened about once in a blue moon. Down in the valley the path came out to the main road and then it was just up the spruce hill to the school.

The Avonlea school was a whitewashed building low in the eaves and wide in the windows, furnished inside with comfortable substantial old-fashioned desks that opened and shut, and were carved all over their lids with the initials and hieroglyphics of three generations of school-children. The schoolhouse was set back from the road and behind it was a dusky fir wood and a brook where all the children put their bottles of milk in the morning to keep cool and sweet until dinner hour.

Marilla had seen Anne start off to school on the first day of September with many secret misgivings. Anne was such an odd girl. How would she get on with the other children? And how on earth would she ever manage to hold her tongue during school hours?

Things went better than Marilla feared, however. Anne came home that evening in high spirits.

'I think I'm going to like school here,' she announced. 'I don't think much of the master, though. He's all the time curling his moustache and making eyes at Prissy Andrews. Prissy is grown-up, you know. She's sixteen and she's studying for the entrance examination into Queen's Academy at Charlottetown next year. Tillie Boulter says the master is *dead gone* on her. She's got a beautiful complexion and curly brown hair and she does it up so elegantly. She sits in the long seat at the back and he sits there, too, most of the time – to explain her lessons, he says. But Ruby Gillis says she saw him writing something on her slate and when Prissy read it she blushed as red as a beet and giggled; and Ruby Gillis says she doesn't believe it had anything to do with the lesson.'

'Anne Shirley, don't let me hear you talking about your teacher in that way again,' said Marilla sharply. 'You don't go to school to criticize the master. I guess he can teach *you* something and it's your business to learn. And I want you to understand right off that you are not to come home telling tales about him. That is something I won't encourage. I hope you were a good girl.'

'Indeed I was,' said Anne comfortably. 'It wasn't so hard as you might imagine, either. I sit with Diana. Our seat is right by the window and we can look down to the Lake of Shining Waters. There are a lot of nice girls in school and we had scrumptious fun playing at dinner-time. It's so nice to have a lot of little girls to play with. But of course I like Diana best and always will. I *adore* Diana. I'm dreadfully far behind the others. They're all in the fifth book and I'm only in the fourth. I feel that it's a kind of a disgrace. But there's not one of them has such an imagination as I have, and I soon found that out. We had reading and geography and Canadian History and dictation to-day. Mr Phillips said my spelling was disgraceful and he held up my slate so that everybody could see it, all marked over. I felt so mortified, Marilla; he might have been politer to a stranger, I think. Ruby Gillis gave me an apple and Sophia Sloane lent me a lovely pink card with "May I see you home?" on it. I'm to give it back to her to-morrow. And Tillie Boulter let me wear her bead ring all the afternoon. Can I have some of those pearl beads off the old pincushion in the garret to make myself a ring? And oh, Marilla, Jane Andrews told me that Minnie MacPherson told her that she heard Prissy Andrews tell Sara Gillis that I had a very pretty nose. Marilla, that is the first compliment I have ever had in my life and you can't imagine what a strange feeling it gave me. Marilla, have I really a pretty nose? I know you'll tell me the truth.'

'Your nose is well enough,' said Marilla shortly. Secretly she thought Anne's nose was a remarkably pretty one; but she had no intention of telling her so.

That was three weeks ago and all had gone smoothly so far. And now, this crisp September morning, Anne and Diana were tripping blithely down the Birch Path, two of the happiest little girls in Avonlea.

'I guess Gilbert Blythe will be in school to-day,' said Diana. 'He's been visiting his cousins over in New Brunswick all summer and he only came home Saturday night. He's *awf'ly* handsome, Anne. And he teases the girls something terrible. He just torments our lives out.'

Diana's voice indicated that she rather liked having her life tormented out than not.

'Gilbert Blythe?' said Anne. 'Isn't it his name that's written up on the porch wall with Julia Bell's and a big "Take Notice" over them?'

'Yes,' said Diana, tossing her head, 'but I'm sure he doesn't like Julia Bell so very much. I've heard him say he studied the multiplication table by her freckles.'

'Oh, don't speak about freckles to me,' implored Anne. 'It isn't delicate when I've got so many. But I do think that writing take-notices up on the wall about the boys and girls is the silliest ever. I should just like to see anybody dare to write my name up with a boy's. Not, of course,' she hastened to add, 'that anybody would.'

Anne sighed. She didn't want her name written up. But it was a little humiliating to know that there was no danger of it.

'Nonsense,' said Diana, whose black eyes and glossy tresses had played such havoc with the hearts of Avonlea schoolboys that her name figured on the porch walls in half a dozen take-notices. 'It's only meant as a joke. And don't you be too sure your name won't ever be written up. Charlie Sloane is *dead gone* on you. He told his mother – his *mother*, mind you – that you were the smartest girl in school. That's better than being good-looking.'

'No, it isn't,' said Anne, feminine to the core. 'I'd rather be pretty than clever. And I hate Charlie Sloane. I can't bear a boy with goggle eyes. If anyone wrote my name up with his I'd *never* get over it, Diana Berry. But it *is* nice to keep head of your class.'

'You'll have Gilbert in your class after this,' said Diana, 'and he's used to being head of his class, I can tell you. He's only in the fourth book although he's nearly fourteen. Four years ago his father was sick and he had to go out to Alberta for his health and Gilbert went with him. They were there three years and Gil didn't go to school hardly any until they came back. You won't find it so easy to keep head after this, Anne.'

'I'm glad,' said Anne quickly. 'I couldn't really feel proud of keeping head of little boys and girls of just nine or ten. I got up yesterday spelling "ebullition." Josie Pye was head and, mind you, she peeped in her book. Mr Phillips didn't see her – he was looking at Prissy Andrews – but I did. I just swept her a look of freezing scorn and she got as red as a beet and spelled it wrong after all.'

'Those Pye girls are cheats all round,' said Diana indignantly, as they climbed the fence of the main road. 'Gertie Pye actually went and put her milk bottle in my place in the brook yesterday. Did you ever? I don't speak to her now.'

When Mr Phillips was in the back of the room hearing Prissy Andrews' Latin, Diana whispered to Anne:

'That's Gilbert Blythe sitting right across the aisle from you, Anne. Just look at him and see if you don't think he's handsome.'

Anne looked accordingly. She had a good chance to do so, for the said Gilbert Blythe was absorbed in stealthily pinning the long yellow braid of Ruby Gillis, who sat in front of him, to the back of her seat. He was a tall boy, with curly brown hair, roguish hazel eyes and a mouth twisted into a teasing smile. Presently Ruby Gillis started up to take a sum to the master; she fell back into her seat with a little shriek, believing that her hair was pulled out by the roots. Everybody looked at her and Mr Phillips glared so sternly that Ruby began to cry. Gilbert had whisked the pin out of sight and was studying his history with the soberest face in the world; but when the commotion subsided he looked at Anne and winked with inexpressible drollery.

'I think your Gilbert Blythe *is* handsome,' confided Anne to Diana, 'but I think he's very bold. It isn't good manners to wink at a strange girl.'

But it was not until the afternoon that things really began to happen.

Mr Phillips was back in the corner explaining a problem in algebra to Prissy Andrews and the rest of the scholars were doing pretty much as they pleased, eating green apples, whispering, drawing pictures on their slates, and driving crickets, harnessed to strings, up and down the aisle. Gilbert Blythe was trying to make Anne Shirley look at him and failing utterly, because Anne was at that moment totally oblivious, not only of the very existence of Gilbert Blythe, but of every other scholar in Avonlea school and of Avonlea school itself. With her chin propped on her hands and her eyes fixed on the blue glimpse of the Lake of Shining Waters that the west window afforded, she was far away in a gorgeous dreamland, hearing and seeing nothing save her own wonderful visions.

Gilbert Blythe wasn't used to putting himself out to make a girl look at him and meeting with failure. She *should* look at him, that red-haired Shirley girl with the little pointed chin and big eyes that weren't like the eyes of any other girl in Avonlea school.

Gilbert reached across the aisle, picked up the end of Anne's long red braid, held it out at arm's length, and said in a piercing whisper:

'Carrots! Carrots!'

Then Anne looked at him with a vengeance!

She did more than look. She sprang to her feet, her bright fancies fallen into cureless ruin. She flashed one indignant glance at Gilbert from eyes whose angry sparkle was swiftly quenched in equally angry tears.

'You mean, hateful boy!' she exclaimed passionately. 'How dare you!'

And then – Thwack! Anne had brought her slate down on Gilbert's head and cracked it – slate, not head – clear across.

Avonlea school always enjoyed a scene. This was an especially enjoyable one. Everybody said, 'Oh,' in horrified delight. Diana gasped. Ruby Gillis, who was inclined to be hysterical, began to cry. Tommy Sloane let his team of crickets escape him altogether while he stared open-mouthed at the tableau.

Mr Phillips stalked down the aisle and laid his hand heavily on Anne's shoulder.

'Anne Shirley, what does this mean?' he said angrily.

Anne returned no answer. It was asking too much of flesh and blood to expect her to tell before the whole school that she had been called 'carrots.' Gilbert it was who spoke up stoutly.

'It was my fault, Mr Phillips. I teased her.'

Mr Phillips paid no heed to Gilbert.

'I am sorry to see a pupil of mine displaying such a temper and such a vindictive spirit,' he said in a solemn tone, as if the mere fact of being a pupil of his ought to root out all evil passions from the hearts of small imperfect mortals. 'Anne, go and stand on the platform in front of the blackboard for the rest of the afternoon.'

Anne would have infinitely preferred a whipping to this punishment, under which her sensitive spirit quivered as from a whiplash. With a white, set face she obeyed. Mr Phillips took a chalk crayon and wrote on the blackboard above her head:

'Ann Shirley has a very bad temper. Ann Shirley must learn to control her temper,' and then read it out loud, so that even the primer class, who couldn't read writing, should understand it.

Anne stood there the rest of the afternoon with that legend above her. She did not cry or hang her head. Anger was still too hot in her heart for that and it sustained her amid all her agony of humiliation. With resentful eyes and passion-red cheeks she confronted alike Diana's sympathetic gaze and Charlie Sloane's indignant nods and Josie Pye's malicious smiles. As for Gilbert Blythe, she would not even look at him. She would *never* look at him again! She would never speak to him!!

When school was dismissed Anne marched out with her red head held high. Gilbert Blythe tried to intercept her at the porch door.

'I'm awfully sorry I made fun of your hair, Anne,' he whispered contritely. 'Honest I am. Don't be mad for keeps, now.'

Anne swept by disdainfully, without look or sign of hearing. 'Oh, how could you, Anne?' breathed Diana as they went down the road, half reproachfully, half admiringly. Diana felt that *she* could never have resisted Gilbert's plea.

'I shall never forgive Gilbert Blythe,' said Anne firmly. 'And Mr

Phillips spelled my name without an *e*, too. The iron has entered into my soul, Diana.'

Diana hadn't the least idea what Anne meant, but she understood it was something terrible.

'You mustn't mind Gilbert making fun of your hair,' she said soothingly. 'Why, he makes fun of all the girls. He laughs at mine because it's so black. He's called me a crow a dozen times; and I never heard him apologize for anything before either.'

'There's a great deal of difference between being called a crow and being called carrots,' said Anne with dignity. 'Gilbert Blythe has hurt my feelings *excruciatingly*, Diana.'

It is possible the matter might have blown over without more excruciation if nothing else had happened. But when things begin to happen they are apt to keep on.

Avonlea scholars often spent noon hour picking gum in Mr Bell's spruce grove over the hill and across his big pasture field. From there they could keep an eye on Eben Wright's house, where the master boarded. When they saw Mr Phillips emerging therefrom they ran for the schoolhouse; but the distance being about three times longer than Mr Wright's lane they were very apt to arrive there, breathless and gasping, some three minutes too late.

On the following day Mr Phillips was seized with one of his spasmodic fits of reform and announced, before going to dinner, that he should expect to find all the scholars in their seats when he returned. Anyone who came in late would be punished.

All the boys and some of the girls went to Mr Bell's spruce grove as usual, fully intending to stay only long enough to 'pick a chew'. But spruce groves are seductive and yellow nuts of gum beguiling; they picked and loitered and strayed; and as usual the first thing that recalled them to a sense of the flight of time was Jimmy Glover shouting from the top of a patriarchal old spruce, 'Master's coming.'

The girls, who were on the ground, started first and managed to reach the schoolhouse in time, but without a second to spare. The boys, who had to wriggle hastily down from the trees, were later; and

Anne, who had not been picking gum at all but was wandering happily in the far end of the grove, waist deep among the bracken, singing softly to herself, with a wreath of rice lilies on her hair as if she were some wild divinity of the shadowy places, was latest of all. Anne could run like a deer, however; run she did with the impish result that she overtook the boys at the door and was swept into the schoolhouse among them just as Mr Phillips was in the act of hanging up his hat.

Mr Phillips' brief reforming energy was over; he didn't want the bother of punishing a dozen pupils; but it was necessary to do something to save his word, so he looked about for a scapegoat and found it in Anne, who had dropped into her seat, gasping for breath, with her forgotten lily wreath hanging askew over one ear and giving her a particularly rakish and dishevelled appearance.

'Anne Shirley, since you seem to be so fond of the boys' company we shall indulge your taste for it this afternoon,' he said sarcastically. 'Take those flowers out of your hair and sit with Gilbert Blythe.'

The other boys snickered. Diana, turning pale with pity, plucked the wreath from Anne's hair and squeezed her hand. Anne stared at the master as if turned to stone.

'Did you hear what I said, Anne?' queried Mr Phillips sternly.

'Yes, sir,' said Anne slowly, 'but I didn't suppose you really meant it.'

'I assure you I did' – still with the sarcastic inflection which all the children, and Anne especially, hated. It flicked on the raw. 'Obey me at once.'

For a moment Anne looked as if she meant to disobey. Then, realizing that there was no help for it, she rose haughtily, stepped across the aisle, sat down beside Gilbert Blythe, and buried her face in her arms on the desk. Ruby Gillis, who got a glimpse of it as it went down, told the others going home from school that she'd 'acksually never seen anything like it – it was so white, with awful little red spots on it.'

To Anne, this was as the end of all things. It was bad enough to be singled out for punishment from among a dozen equally guilty ones; it was worse still to be sent to sit with a boy; but that that boy should be Gilbert Blythe was heaping insult on injury to a degree utterly unbearable. Anne felt that she could not bear it and it would be of no use to try. Her whole being seethed with shame and anger and humiliation.

At first the other scholars looked and whispered and giggled and nudged. But as Anne never lifted her head and as Gilbert worked fractions as if his whole soul was absorbed in them and them only, they soon returned to their own tasks and Anne was forgotten. When Mr Phillips called the history class out Anne should have gone; but Anne did not move, and Mr Phillips, who had been writing some verses 'To Priscilla' before he called the class, was thinking about an obstinate rhyme still and never missed her. Once, when nobody was looking, Gilbert took from his desk a little pink candy heart with a gold motto on it, 'You are sweet,' and slipped it under the curve of Anne's arm. Whereupon Anne arose, took the pink heart gingerly between the tips of her fingers, dropped it on the floor, ground it to powder beneath her heel, and resumed her position without deigning to bestow a glance on Gilbert.

When school went out Anne marched to her desk, ostentatiously took out everything therein, books and writing tablet, pen and ink, testament and arithmetic, and piled them neatly on her cracked slate.

'What are you taking all those things home for, Anne?' Diana wanted to know, as soon as they were out on the road. She had not dared to ask the question before.

'I am not coming back to school any more,' said Anne.

Diana gasped and stared at Anne to see if she meant it.

'Will Marilla let you stay home?' she asked.

'She'll have to,' said Anne. 'I'll *never* go to school to that man again.'

'Oh, Anne!' Diana looked as if she were ready to cry. 'I do think you're mean. What shall I do? Mr Phillips will make me sit with that horrid Gertie Pye – I know he will, because she is sitting alone. Do come back, Anne.'

'I'd do almost anything in the world for you, Diana,' said Anne sadly. 'I'd let myself be torn limb from limb if it would do you any good. But I can't do this, so please don't ask it. You harrow up my very soul.'

'Just think of all the fun you will miss,' mourned Diana. 'We are going to build the loveliest new house down by the brook; and we'll be playing ball next week and you've never played ball, Anne. It's tremendously exciting. And we're going to learn a new song – Jane Andrews is practising it up now; and Alice Andrews is going to bring a new Pansy book next week and we're all going to read it out loud, chapter about, down by the brook. And you know you are so fond of reading out loud, Anne.'

Nothing moved Anne in the least. Her mind was made up. She would not go to school to Mr Phillips again; she told Marilla so when she got home.

'Nonsense,' said Marilla.

'It isn't nonsense at all,' said Anne, gazing at Marilla, with solemn, reproachful eyes. 'Don't you understand, Marilla? I've been insulted.'

'Insulted fiddlesticks! You'll go to school to-morrow as usual.'

'Oh, no.' Anne shook her head gently. 'I'm not going back, Marilla. I'll learn my lessons at home and I'll be as good as I can be and hold my tongue all the time if it's possible at all. But I will not go back to school I assure you.'

Marilla saw something remarkably like unyielding stubbornness looking out of Anne's small face. She understood that she would have trouble in overcoming it; but she resolved wisely to say nothing more just then.

'I'll run down and see Rachel about it this evening,' she thought. 'There's no use reasoning with Anne now. She's too worked up and I've an idea she can be awful stubborn if she takes the notion. Far as I can make out from her story, Mr Phillips has been carrying matters with a rather high hand. But it would never do to say so to her. I'll just talk it over with Rachel. She's sent ten children to school and she ought to know something about it. She'll have heard the whole story, too, by this time.'

Marilla found Mrs Lynde knitting quilts as industriously and cheerfully as usual.

'I suppose you know what I've come about,' she said, a little shamefacedly.

Mrs Rachel nodded.

'About Anne's fuss in school, I reckon,' she said. 'Tillie Boulter was in on her way home from school and told me about it.'

'I don't know what to do with her,' said Marilla. 'She declares she won't go back to school. I never saw a child so worked up. I've been expecting trouble ever since she started to school. I knew things were going too smooth to last. She's so high-strung. What would you advise, Rachel?'

'Well, since you've asked my advice, Marilla,' said Mrs Lynde amiably – Mrs Lynde dearly loved to be asked for advice – 'I'd just humour her a little at first, that's what I'd do. It's my belief that Mr Phillips was in the wrong. Of course, it doesn't do to say so to the children, you know. And of course he did right to punish her yesterday for giving way to temper. But to-day it was different. The others who were late should have been punished as well as Anne, that's what. And I don't believe in making the girls sit with the boys for punishment. It isn't modest. Tillie Boulter was real indignant. She took Anne's part right through and said all the scholars did, too. Anne seems real popular among them, somehow. I never thought she'd take with them so well.'

'Then you really think I'd better let her stay home,' said Marilla in amazement.

'Yes. That is, I wouldn't say school to her again until she said it herself. Depend upon it, Marilla, she'll cool off in a week or so and be ready enough to go back of her own accord, that's what, while, if you were to make her go back right off, dear knows what freak or tantrum she'd take next and make more trouble than ever. The less fuss made the better, in my opinion. She won't miss much by not going to school, as far as *that* goes. Mr Phillips isn't any good at all as a teacher. The order he keeps is scandalous, that's what, and he neglects the young fry and puts all his time on those big scholars he's getting ready for Queen's. He'd never have got the school for another year if his uncle hadn't been a trustee – the trustee, for he just leads the other two around by the nose, that's what. I declare, I don't know what education in this Island is coming to.'

Mrs Rachel shook her head, as much as to say if she were only at the head of the educational system of the Province things would be much better managed.

Marilla took Mrs Rachel's advice and not another word was said to Anne about going back to school. She learned her lessons at home, did her chores, and played with Diana in the chilly purple autumn twilights; but when she met Gilbert Blythe on the road or encountered him in Sunday school she passed him by with an icy contempt that was no whit thawed by his evident desire to appease her. Even Diana's efforts as a peacemaker were of no avail. Anne had evidently made up her mind to hate Gilbert Blythe to the end of life.

As much as she hated Gilbert, however, did she love Diana, with all the love of her passionate little heart, equally intense in its likes and dislikes. One evening Marilla, coming in from the orchard with a basket of apples, found Anne sitting alone by the east window in the twilight, crying bitterly.

'Whatever's the matter now, Anne?' she asked.

'It's about Diana,' sobbed Anne luxuriously. 'I love Diana so, Marilla. I cannot ever live without her. But I know very well when we grow up that Diana will get married and go away and leave me. And oh, what shall I do? I hate her husband – I just hate him furiously. I've been imagining it all out – the wedding and everything – Diana dressed in snowy garments, with a veil, and looking as beautiful and regal as a queen; and me the bridesmaid, with a lovely dress, too, and puffed sleeves, but with a breaking heart hid beneath my smiling face. And then bidding Diana good-bye-e-e—' Here Anne broke down entirely and wept with increasing bitterness.

Marilla turned quickly away to hide her twitching face; but it was no use; she collapsed on the nearest chair and burst into such a hearty and unusual peal of laughter that Matthew, crossing the yard outside, halted in amazement. When had he heard Marilla laugh like that before?

'Well, Anne Shirley,' said Marilla as soon as she could speak, 'if you must borrow trouble, for pity's sake borrow it handier home. I should think you had an imagination, sure enough.'

Voyages
and Shipwrecks

A Dangerous Fishing Trip

R. M. BALLANTYNE
Illustrated by A. Dudley

This is an extract from The Coral Island *(1858). Ralph, Jack and Peterkin have been shipwrecked on a South Sea island. At first it seems a peaceful, idyllic place. However, there are perils to be faced, as this chapter shows.*

For several days we did not wander far from our encampment, but gave ourselves up to forming plans for the future, and making our present abode comfortable.

There were various causes that induced this state of comparative inaction. In the first place, although everything around us was so delightful, and we could without difficulty obtain all that we required for our bodily comfort, we did not quite like the idea of settling down here for the rest of our lives, far away from our friends and our native land. To set energetically about preparations for a permanent residence seemed so like making up our minds to saying adieu to home and friends for ever, that we tacitly shrank from it, and put off our preparations, for one reason and another, as long as we could. Then there was a little uncertainty still as to there being natives on the island, and we entertained a kind of faint hope that a ship might come and take us off. But as day after day passed and neither savages nor ships appeared, we gave up all hope of an early deliverance, and set diligently to work at our homestead.

During this time, however, we had not been altogether idle. We made several experiments in cooking the coco-nut, most of which did not improve it. Then we removed our goods, and took up our abode in the cave, but found the change so bad that we returned gladly to the bower. Besides this, we bathed very frequently, and talked a great deal; at least Jack and Peterkin did – I listened. Among other useful things, Jack, who was ever the most active and diligent, converted about three inches of the hoop iron into an excellent knife. First he beat it quite flat with the axe. Then he made a rude handle, and tied the hoop iron to it with our piece of whip-cord, and ground it to an edge on a piece of sandstone. When it was finished he used it to shape a better handle, to which he fixed it with a strip of his cotton handkerchief – in which operation he had, as Peterkin pointed out, torn off one of Lord Nelson's noses. However, the whip-cord, thus set free, was used by Peterkin as a fishing-line. He merely tied a piece of oyster to the end of it. This the fish were allowed to swallow, and then they were pulled quickly ashore. But as the line was very short and we had no boat, the fish we caught were exceedingly small.

One day Peterkin came up from the beach, where he had been angling, and said in a very cross tone, 'I'll tell you what, Jack, I'm not going to be humbugged with catching such contemptible things any longer. I want you to swim out with me on your back, and let me fish in deep water.'

'Dear me, Peterkin!' replied Jack, 'I had no idea you were taking the thing so much to heart, else I would have got you out of that difficulty long ago. Let me see,' and Jack looked down at a piece of timber on which he had been labouring, with a peculiar gaze of abstraction, which he always assumed when trying to invent or discover anything.

'What say you to building a boat?' he inquired, looking up hastily.

'Take far too long,' was the reply; 'can't be bothered waiting. I want to begin at once!'

Again Jack considered. 'I have it!' he cried. 'We'll fell a large tree and launch the trunk of it in the water, so that when you want to fish you've nothing to do but to swim out to it.'

'Would not a small raft do better?' said I.

'Much better; but we have no ropes to bind it together with. Perhaps we may find something hereafter that will do as well, but in the meantime let us try the tree.'

This was agreed on, so we started off to a spot not far distant, where we knew of a tree that would suit us, which grew near the water's edge. As soon as we reached it Jack threw off his coat, and, wielding the axe with his sturdy arms, hacked and hewed at it for a quarter of an hour without stopping. Then he paused, and while he sat down to rest I continued the work. Then Peterkin made a vigorous attack on it, so that when Jack renewed his powerful blows, a few minutes' cutting brought it down with a terrible crash.

'Hurrah! now for it,' cried Jack; 'let us off with its head.'

So saying he began to cut through the stem again, at about six yards from the thick end. This done, he cut three strong, short poles or levers from the stout branches, with which to roll the log down the beach into the sea; for, as it was nearly two feet thick at the large end, we could not move it without such helps. With the levers, however, we rolled it slowly into the sea.

Having been thus successful in launching our vessel, we next shaped the levers into rude oars or paddles, and then attempted to embark. This was easy enough to do; but after seating ourselves astride the log, it was with the utmost difficulty we kept it from rolling round and plunging us into the water. Not that we minded that much; but we preferred, if possible, to fish in dry clothes. To be sure, our trousers were necessarily wet, as our legs were dangling in the water on each side of the log; but as they could be easily dried, we did not care. After half an hour's practice we became expert enough to keep our balance pretty steadily. Then Peterkin laid down his paddle, and having baited his line with a whole oyster, dropped it into deep water.

'Now then, Jack,' said he, 'be cautious; steer clear o' that seaweed. There! that's it; gently now, gently. I see a fellow at least a foot long down there coming to – ha! that's it! Oh bother! he's off.'

'Did he bite?' said Jack, urging the log onwards a little with his paddle.

'Bite? ay! He took it into his mouth, but the moment I began to haul he opened his jaws and let it out again.'

'Let him swallow it next time,' said Jack, laughing at the melancholy expression of Peterkin's visage.

'There he's again,' cried Peterkin, his eyes flashing with excitement.

'Look out! Now then! No! Yes! No! Why, the brute *won't* swallow it!'

'Try to haul him up by the mouth, then,' cried Jack. 'Do it gently.'

A heavy sigh and a look of blank despair showed that poor Peterkin had tried and failed again.

'Never mind, lad,' said Jack, in a voice of sympathy; 'we'll move on, and offer it to some other fish.' So saying, Jack plied his paddle; but scarcely had we moved from the spot, when a fish with an enormous head and a little body darted from under a rock and swallowed the bait at once.

'Got him this time – that's a fact!' cried Peterkin, hauling in the line. 'He's swallowed the bait right down to his tail, I declare. Oh, what a thumper!'

As the fish came struggling to the surface, we leaned forward to see it, and overbalanced the log. Peterkin threw his arms round the fish's neck, and in another instant we were all floundering in the water!

A shout of laughter burst from us as we rose to the surface like three drowned rats, and seized hold of the log. We soon recovered our position, and sat more warily, while Peterkin secured the fish, which had well-nigh escaped in the midst of our struggles. It was little worth having, however; but, as Peterkin remarked, it was better than the smouts he had been catching for the last two or three days; so we laid it on the log before us, and having re-baited the line, dropped it in again for another.

Now, while we were thus intent upon our sport, our attention was suddenly attracted by a ripple on the sea, just a few yards away from us. Peterkin shouted to us to paddle in that direction, as he thought it was a big fish, and we might have a chance of catching it. But Jack, instead of complying, said, in a deep, earnest tone of voice, which I never before heard him use, 'Haul up your line, Peterkin; seize your paddle; quick – it's a shark!'

The horror with which we heard this may well be imagined, for it must be remembered that our legs were hanging down in the water, and we could not venture to pull them up without upsetting the log.

Peterkin instantly hauled up the line, and grasping his paddle, exerted himself to the utmost, while we also did our best to make for shore. But we were a good way off, and the log being, as I have before said, very heavy, moved but slowly through the water. We now saw the shark quite distinctly swimming round and round us, its sharp fin every now and then protruding above the water. From its active and unsteady motions, Jack knew it was making up its mind to attack us, so he urged us vehemently to paddle for our lives, while he himself set us the example. Suddenly he shouted, 'Look out! there he comes!' and in a second we saw the monstrous fish dive close under us, and turn half over on his side. But we all made a great commotion with our paddles, which no doubt frightened it away for that time, as we saw it immediately after circling round us as before.

'Throw the fish to him,' cried Jack, in a quick, suppressed voice; 'we'll make the shore in time yet if we can keep him off for a few minutes.'

Peterkin stopped one instant to obey the command, and then plied his paddle again with all his might. No sooner had the fish fallen on the water than we observed the shark to sink. In another second we saw its white breast rising; for sharks always turn over on their sides when about to seize their prey, their mouths being not at the point of their heads like those of other fish, but, as it were, under their chins. In another moment his snout rose above the water; his wide jaws, armed with a terrific double row of teeth, appeared. The dead fish was engulfed, and the shark sank out of sight. But Jack was mistaken in supposing that it would be satisfied. In a few minutes it returned to us, and its quick motions led us to fear that it would attack us at once.

'Stop paddling,' cried Jack suddenly. 'I see it coming up behind us. Now, obey my orders *quickly*. Our lives may depend on it. Ralph, Peterkin, do your best to *balance the log*. Don't look out for the shark. Don't glance behind you. Do nothing but balance the log.'

Peterkin and I instantly did as we were ordered, being only too glad to do anything that afforded us a chance or a hope of escape, for we had implicit confidence in Jack's courage and wisdom. For a few seconds,

'In another moment the shark rose'

that seemed long minutes to my mind, we sat thus silently; but I could not resist glancing backward, despite the orders to the contrary. On doing so, I saw Jack sitting rigid like a statue, with his paddle raised, his lips compressed, and his eyebrows bent over his eyes, which glared savagely from beneath them down into the water. I also saw the shark, to my horror, quite close under the log, in the act of darting towards Jack's foot. I could scarce suppress a cry on beholding this. In another moment the shark rose. Jack drew his leg suddenly from the water, and threw it over the log. The monster's snout rubbed against the log as it passed, and revealed its hideous jaws, into which Jack instantly plunged the paddle, and thrust it down its throat. So violent was this act that Jack rose to his feet in performing it; the log was thereby rolled completely over, and we were once more plunged into the water. We all rose, sputtering and gasping, in a moment.

'Now, then, strike out for shore,' cried Jack. – 'Here, Peterkin, catch hold of my collar, and kick out with a will.'

Peterkin did as he was desired, and Jack struck out with such force that he cut through the water like a boat; while I, being free from all encumbrance, succeeded in keeping up with him. As we had by this time drawn pretty near to the shore, a few minutes more sufficed to carry us into shallow water; and, finally, we landed in safety, though very much exhausted, and not a little frightened by our terrible adventure.

Escaping on a Raft

MARK TWAIN
Illustrated by E. W. Kemble

First published in 1884, The Adventures of Huckleberry Finn *tells how Huck and a runaway slave, Jim, escape on a raft down the Mississippi. Huck, a happy-go-lucky urchin, tells the story in his own colourful way.*

It must a been close on to one o'clock when we got below the island at last, and the raft did seem to go mighty slow. If a boat was to come along, we was going to take to the canoe and break for the Illinois shore; and it was well a boat didn't come, for we hadn't ever thought to put the gun into the canoe, or a fishing-line or anything to eat. We was in ruther too much of a sweat to think of so many things. It warn't good judgment to put *everything* on the raft.

If the men* went to the island, I just expect they found the camp fire I built, and watched it all night for Jim to come. Anyways, they stayed away from us, and if my building the fire never fooled them it warn't no fault of mine. I played it as low-down on them as I could.

When the first streak of day begun to show, we tied up to a tow-head in a big bend on the Illinois side, and hacked off cotton-wood branches with the hatchet and covered up the raft with them so she looked like there had been a cave-in in the bank there. A tow-head is a sandbar that has cotton-woods on it as quick as harrow-teeth.

We had mountains on the Missouri shore and heavy timber on the Illinois side, and the channel was down the Missouri shore at that place, so we warn't afraid of anybody running across us. We laid there all day and watched the rafts and steamboats spin down the Missouri shore, and up-bound steamboats fight the big river in the middle. I

---

* These men are trying to recapture Jim.

told Jim all about the time I had jabbering with that woman; and Jim said she was a smart one, and if she was to start after us herself *she* wouldn't set down and watch a camp fire – no, sir, she'd fetch a dog. Well, then, I said, why couldn't she tell her husband to fetch a dog? Jim said he bet she did think of it by the time the men was ready to start, and he believed they must a gone up town to get a dog, and so they lost all that time, or else we wouldn't be here on a tow-head sixteen or seventeen mile below the village – no, indeedy, we would be in that same old town again. So I said I didn't care what was the reason they didn't get us, as long as they didn't.

When it was beginning to come on dark, we poked our heads out of the cottonwood thicket and looked up, and down, and across; nothing in sight; so Jim took up some of the top planks of the raft and built a snug wigwam to get under in blazing weather and rainy, and to keep the things dry. Jim made a floor for the wigwam, and raised it a foot or more above the level of the raft, so now the blankets and all the traps was out of the reach of steamboat waves. Right in the middle of the wigwam we made a layer of dirt about five or six inches deep with a frame around it for to hold it to its place; this was to build a fire on in sloppy weather or chilly; the wigwam would keep it from being seen. We made an extra steering oar, too, because one of the others might get broke, on a snag or something. We fixed up a short forked stick to hang the old lantern on; because we must always light the lantern whenever we see a steamboat coming down stream, to keep from getting run over; but we wouldn't have to light it for up-stream boats unless we see we was in what they call a 'crossing'; for the river was pretty high yet, very low banks being still a little under water; so up-bound boats didn't always run the channel, but hunted easy water.

This second night we run between seven and eight hours, with a current that was making over four mile an hour. We catched fish, and talked, and we took a swim now and then to keep off sleepiness. It was kind of solemn, drifting down the big still river, laying on our backs looking up at the stars, and we didn't ever feel like talking loud, and it warn't often that we laughed, only a little kind of a low chuckle. We had mighty good weather, as a general thing, and nothing ever happened to us at all, that night, nor the next, nor the next.

Every night we passed towns, some of them away up on black hillsides, nothing but just a shiny bed of lights, not a house could you see. The fifth night we passed St. Louis, and it was like the whole world lit up. In St. Petersburg they used to say there was twenty or thirty thousand people in St. Louis, but I never believed it till I see that wonderful spread of lights at two o'clock that still night. There warn't a sound there; everybody was asleep.

Every night, now, I used to slip ashore, towards ten o'clock, at some little village, and buy ten or fifteen cents' worth of meal or bacon or other stuff to eat; and sometimes I lifted a chicken that warn't roosting comfortable, and took him along. Pap always said, take a chicken when you get a chance, because if you don't want him yourself you can easy find somebody that does, and a good deed ain't ever forgot. I never see pap when he didn't want the chicken himself, but that is what he used to say anyway.

Mornings, before daylight, I slipped into corn-fields and borrowed a watermelon, or a mushmelon, or a punkin, or some new corn, or things of that kind. Pap always said it warn't no harm to borrow things, if you was meaning to pay them back, sometime; but the widow said it warn't anything but a soft name for stealing, and no decent body would do it. Jim said he reckoned the widow was partly right and pap was partly right; so the best way would be for us to pick out two or three things from the list and say we wouldn't borrow them any more – then he reckoned it wouldn't be no harm to borrow the others. So we talked it over all one night, drifting along down the river, trying to make up our minds whether to drop the watermelons, or the cantelopes, or the mushmelons, or what. But towards daylight we got it all settled satisfactory, and concluded to drop crabapples and p'simmons. We warn't feeling just right before that, but it was all comfortable now. I was glad the way it came out, too, because crabapples ain't ever good, and the p'simmons wouldn't be ripe for two or three months yet.

We shot a water-fowl now and then, that got up too early in the morning or didn't go to bed early enough in the evening. Take it all around, we lived pretty high.

The fifth night below St. Louis we had a big storm after midnight, with a power of thunder and lightning, and the rain poured down in a solid sheet. We stayed in the wigwam and let the raft take care of itself. When the lightning glared out we could see a big straight river ahead, and high rocky bluffs on both sides. By-and-by says I, 'Hel-*lo*, Jim, looky yonder!' It was a steamboat that had killed herself on a rock. We was drifting straight down for her. The lightning showed her very

The Wreck

distinct. She was leaning over, with part of her upper deck above water, and you could see every little chimbly-guy clean and clear, and a chair by the big bell, with an old slouch hat hanging on the back of it when the flashes come.

Well, it being away in the night, and stormy, and all so mysterious-like, I felt just the way any other boy would a felt when I see that wreck laying there so mournful and lonesome in the middle of the river. I wanted to get aboard of her and slink around a little, and see what there was there. So I says:

'Le's land on her, Jim.'

But Jim was dead against it, at first. He says:

'I doan' want to go fool'n 'long er no wrack. We's doin' blame' well, en we better let blame' well alone, as de good book says. Like as not dey's a watchman on dat wrack.'

'Watchman your grandmother!' I says; 'there ain't nothing to watch but the texas and the pilot-house; and do you reckon anybody's going to resk his life for a texas and a pilot-house such a night as this, when it's likely to break up and wash off down the river any minute?' Jim couldn't say nothing to that, so he didn't try. 'And besides,' I says, 'we might borrow something worth having, out of the captain's state-room. Seegars, *I* bet you – and cost five cents apiece, solid cash. Steamboat captains is always rich, and gets sixty dollars a month, and *they* don't care a cent what a thing costs, you know, long as they want it. Stick a candle in your pocket; I can't rest, Jim, till we give her a rummaging. Do you reckon Tom Sawyer would ever go by this thing? Not for pie, he wouldn't. He'd call it an adventure – that's what he'd call it; and he'd land on that wreck if it was his last act. And wouldn't he throw style into it? – wouldn't he spread himself, nor nothing? Why, you'd think it was Christopher C'lumbus discovering Kingdom-Come. I wish Tom Sawyer *was* here.'

Jim he grumbled a little, but give in. He said we mustn't take any more than we could help, and then talk mighty low. The lightning showed us the wreck again, just in time, and we fetched the stabboard derrick, and made fast there.

The deck was high out, here. We went sneaking down the slope of it to labboard, in the dark, towards the texas, feeling our way slow with our feet, and spreading our hands out to fend off the guys, for it was so dark we couldn't see no sign of them. Pretty soon we struck the forward end of the skylight, and clumb on to it; and the next step fetched us in front of the captain's door, which was open, and by Jimminy, away down through the texas hall we see a light! and all in the same second we seemed to hear low voices in yonder!

Jim whispered and said he was feeling powerful sick, and told me to come along. I says, all right; and was going to start for the raft; but just then I heard a voice wail out and say:

'Oh, please don't, boys: I swear I won't ever tell!'

Another voice said, pretty loud:

'It's a lie, Jim Turner. You've acted this way before. You always want more'n your share of the truck, and you've always got it, too, because you've swore 't if you didn't you'd tell. But this time you've said it jest one time too many. You're the meanest, treacherousest hound in this country.'

By this time Jim was gone for the raft. I was just a-biling with curiosity; and I says to myself, Tom Sawyer wouldn't back out now, and so I won't either; I'm agoing to see what's going on here. So I dropped on my hands and knees, in the little passage, and crept aft in the dark, till there warn't but about one stateroom betwixt me and the cross-hall of the texas. Then, in there I see a man stretched on the floor and tied hand and foot, and two men standing over him, and one of them had a dim lantern in his hand, and the other one had a pistol. This one kept pointing the pistol at the man's head on the floor and saying –

'I'd *like* to! And I orter, too, a mean skunk!'

The man on the floor would shrivel up, and say: 'Oh, please don't, Bill – I hain't ever goin' to tell.'

And every time he said that, the man with the lantern would laugh, and say:

''Deed you *ain't!* You never said no truer thing 'n that, you bet you.' And once he said: 'Hear him beg! and yit if we hadn't got the best of him and tied him, he'd a killed us both. And what *for?* Jist for noth'n. Jist because we stood on our *rights* – that's what for. But I lay you ain't agoin' to threaten nobody any more, Jim Turner. Put *up* that pistol, Bill.'

Bill says:

'I don't want to, Jake Packard. I'm for killin' him – and didn't he kill old Hatfield jist the same way – and don't he deserve it?'

'But I don't *want* him killed, and I've got my reasons for it.'

'Bless yo' heart for them words, Jake Packard! I'll never forgit you, long's I live!' says the man on the floor, sort of blubbering.

Packard didn't take no notice of that, but hung up his lantern on a nail, and started towards where I was, there in the dark, and motioned Bill to come. I craw-fished as fast as I could, about two yards, but the boat slanted so that I couldn't make very good time; so to keep from getting run over and catched I crawled into a stateroom on the upper side. The man come a-pawing along in the dark, and when Packard got to my stateroom, he says:

'Here – come in here.'

And in he came, and Bill after him. But before they got in, I was up in the upper berth, cornered, and sorry I come. Then they stood there, with their hands on the ledge of the berth, and talked. I couldn't see them, but I could tell where they was, by the whisky they'd been having. I was glad I didn't drink whisky; but it wouldn't made much difference, anyway, because most of the time they couldn't a treed me because I didn't breathe. I was too scared. And besides, a body *couldn't* breathe, and hear such talk. They talked low and earnest. Bill wanted to kill Turner. He says:

'He's said he'll tell, and he will. If we was to give both our shares to him *now*, it wouldn't make no difference after the row, and the way we've served him. Shore's you're born, he'll turn State's evidence; now you hear *me*. I'm for putting him out of his troubles.'

'So'm I,' says Packard, very quiet.

'Blame it, I'd sorter begun to think you wasn't. Well, then, that's all right. Le's go and do it.'

'Hold on a minute; I ain't had my say yit. You listen to me. Shooting's good, but there's quieter ways if the thing's *got* to be done. But what *I* say, is this; it ain't good sense to go court'n around after a halter, if you can git at what you're up to in some way that's jist as good and at the same time don't bring you into no resks. Ain't that so?'

'You bet it is. But how you goin' to manage it this time?'

'Well, my idea is this; we'll rustle around and gether up whatever pickins we've overlooked in the staterooms, and shove for shore and hide the truck. Then we'll wait. Now I say it ain't agoin' to be more'n two hours befo' this wrack breaks up and washes off down the river. See? He'll be drownded, and won't have nobody to blame for it but his own self. I reckon that a considerable sight bettern' killin' of him. I'm unfavourable to killin' a man as long as you can git around it; it ain't good sense, it ain't good morals. Ain't I right?'

'Yes – I reck'n you are. But s'pose she *don't* break up and wash off?'

'Well, we can wait the two hours, anyway, and see, can't we?'

'All right, then; come along.'

So they started, and I lit out, all in a cold sweat, and scrambled forward. It was dark as pitch there; but I said in a kind of coarse whisper, 'Jim!' and he answered up, right at my elbow, with a sort of moan, and I says:

'Quick, Jim, it ain't no time for fooling around and moaning; there's a gang of murderers in yonder, and if we don't hunt up their boat and set her drifting down the river so these fellows can't get away from the wreck, there's one of 'em going to be in a bad fix. But if we find their boat we can put *all* of 'em in a bad fix – for the Sheriff'll get 'em. Quick – hurry! I'll hunt the labboard side, you hunt the stabboard. You start at the raft, and –'

'Oh! my lordy, lordy! *Raf'*? Dey ain' no raf' no mo', she done broke loose en gone! – 'en here we is!'

★   ★   ★   ★

Well, I catched my breath and most fainted. Shut up on a wreck with such a gang as that! But it warn't no time to be sentimentering. We'd *got* to find that boat, now – had to have it for ourselves. So we went a-quaking and shaking down the stabboard side, and slow work it was, too – seemed a week before we got to the stern. No sign of a boat. Jim said he didn't believe he could go any further – so scared he hadn't hardly any strength left, he said. But I said come on, if we get left on

this wreck, we are in a fix, sure. So on we prowled, again. We struck
for the stern of the texas, and found it, and then scrabbled along
forwards on the skylight, hanging on from shutter to shutter, for the
edge of the skylight was in the water. When we got pretty close to the
cross-hall door, there was the skiff, sure enough! I could just barely see
her. I felt ever so thankful. In another second I would a been aboard of
her; but just then the door opened. One of the men stuck his head out,
only about a couple of foot from me, and I thought I was gone; but he
jerked it in again, and says:

'Heave that blame lantern out o'sight, Bill!'

He flung a bag of something into the boat, and then got in himself,
and set down. It was Packard. Then Bill *he* come out and got in.
Packard says, in a low voice:

'All ready – shove off!'

I couldn't hardly hang on to the shutters, I was so weak. But Bill
says:

'Hold on – 'd you go through him?'

'No. Didn't you?'

'No. So he's got his share o' the cash, yet.'

'Well, then, come along – no use to take truck and leave money.'

'Say – won't he suspicion what we're up to?'

'Maybe he won't. But we got to have it anyway. Come along.'

So they got out and went in.

The door slammed to, because it was in the careened side; and in half
a second I was in the boat, and Jim come a tumbling after me. I out
with my knife and cut the rope, and away we went!

We didn' touch an oar, and we didn' speak nor whisper, nor hardly
even breathe. We went gliding swift along, dead silent, past the tip of
the paddle-box, and past the stern; then in a second or two more we
was a hundred yards below the wreck, and the darkness soaked her up,
every last sign of her, and we was safe, and knowed it.

When we was three to four hundred yards down stream we see the
lantern show like a little spark at the texas door, for a second, and we
knowed by that the rascals had missed their boat, and was beginning

to understand that they was in just as much trouble now, as Jim Turner was.

Then Jim manned the oars, and we took out after our raft. Now was the first time that I begun to worry about the men – I reckon I hadn't had time to before. I begun to think how dreadful it was, even for murderers, to be in such a fix. I says to myself, there ain't no telling but I might come to be a murderer myself, yet, and then how would *I* like it? So says I to Jim:

'The first light we see, we'll land a hundred yards below it or above it, in a place where it's a good hiding-place for you and the skiff, and then I'll go and fix up some kind of a yarn, and get somebody to go for that gang and get them out of their scrape, so they can be hung when their time comes.'

But that idea was a failure; for pretty soon it begun to storm again, and this time worse than ever. The rain poured down, and never a light showed; everybody in bed, I reckon. We boomed along down the river, watching for lights and watching for our raft. After a long time the rain let up, but the clouds staid, and the lightning kept whimpering, and by-and-by a flash showed us a black thing ahead, floating, and we made for it.

It was the raft, and mighty glad was we to get aboard of it again. We seen a light, now, away down to the right, on shore. So I said I would go for it. The skiff was half full of plunder which that gang had stole, there on the wreck. We hustled it in to the raft in a pile, and I told Jim to float along down, and show a light when he judged he had gone about two mile, and keep it burning till I come; then I manned my oars and shoved for the light. As I got down towards it, three or four more showed – up on a hillside. It was a village. I closed in above the shore-light, and laid on my oars and floated. As I went by, I see it was a lantern hanging on the jackstaff of a double-hull ferry-boat. I skimmed around for the watchman, a-wondering whereabouts he slept; and by-and-by I found him roosting on the bitts, forward, with his head down between his knees. I give his shoulder two or three little shoves, and begun to cry.

He stirred up in a kind of startlish way; but when he see it was only me, took a good gap and stretch, and then he says:

'Hello, what's up? Don't cry, bub. What's the trouble?'

I says:

'Pap, and mam, and sis, and —'

Then I broke down. He says:

'Oh, dang it, now, *don't* take on so, we all has to have our troubles and this'n 'll come out all right. What's the matter with 'em?'

'They're – they're – are you the watchman of the boat?'

'Yes,' he says, kind of pretty-well-satisfied like. 'I'm the captain and the owner, and the mate, and the pilot, and watchman, and head deck-hand: and sometimes I'm the freight and passengers. I ain't as rich as old Jim Hornback, and I can't be so blame' generous and good to Tom, Dick, and Harry as what he is, and slam around the money the way he does; but I've told him a many a time 't I wouldn't trade places with him; for, says I, a sailor's life's the life for me, and I'm derned if *I'd* live two mile out o' town, where there ain't nothing ever goin' on, not for all his spondulicks and as much more on top of it. Says I —'

I broke in and says:

'They're in an awful peck of trouble, and —'

'*Who* is?'

'Why, pap, and mam, and sis, and Miss Hooker: and if you take your ferry-boat and go up there —'

'Up where? Where are they?

'On the wreck.'

'What wreck?'

'Why, there ain't but one.'

'What, you don't mean the *Walter Scott?*'

'Yes.'

'Good land! what are they doin' *there*, for gracious sakes?'

'Well, they didn't go there a-purpose.'

'I bet they didn't! Why, great goodness, there ain't no chance for 'em if they don't get off mighty quick! Why, how in the nation did they ever git into such a scrape?'

'Easy enough. Miss Hooker was a-visiting, up there to the town —'

'Yes, Booth's Landing – go on.'

'She was a-visiting, there at Booth's Landing, and just in the edge of the evening she started over with her serving woman in the horse-ferry, to stay all night at her friend's house, Miss What-you-may-call-her, I disremember her name, and they lost their steering-oar, and swung around and sent a-floating down, stern-first, about two mile, and saddle-baggsed on the wreck, and the ferry man and the serving woman and the horses was all lost but Miss Hooker she made a grab and got aboard the wreck. Well, about an hour after dark, we come along down in our trading-scow, and it was so dark we didn't notice the wreck till we was right on it; and so *we* saddle-baggsed; but all of us was saved but Bill Whipple – and oh, he *was* the best cretur! – I most wish't it had been me, I do.'

'My George! It's the beatenest thing I ever struck. And *then* what did you all do?'

'Well, we hollered and took on, but it's so wide there, we couldn't make nobody hear. So pap said somebody got to get ashore and get help somehow. I was the only one that could swim, so I made a dash for it, and Miss Hooker she said if I didn't strike help sooner, come here and hunt up her uncle, and he'd fix the thing. I made the land about a mile below, and been fooling along ever since, trying to get people to do something, but they said, "What, in such a night and such a current? there ain't no sense it; go for the steam-ferry." Now if you'll go, and —'

'By Jackson, I'd *like* to, and blame it I don't know but I will; but who in the 'dingnations agoin' to *pay* for it? Do you reckon your pap —'

'Why, *that's* all right. Miss Hooker she told me, *particular*, that her uncle Hornback —'

'Great guns! is *he* her uncle? Looky here, you break for that light over yonder-way, and turn out west when you git there, and about a quarter of a mile out you'll come to the tavern; tell 'em to dart you out to Jim Hornback's and he'll foot the bill. And don't you fool around any, because he'll want to know the news. Tell him I'll have his niece all safe before he can get to town. Hump yourself, now; I'm agoing up around the corner here, to roust out my engineer.'

I struck for the light, but as soon as he turned the corner I went back and got into my skiff and baled her out and then pulled up shore in the easy water about six hundred yards, and tucked myself in among some wood-boats; for I couldn't rest easy till I could see the ferry-boat start. But take it all around, I was feeling ruther comfortable on accounts of taking all this trouble for that gang, for not many would a done it. I wished the widow knowed about it. I judged she would be proud of me for helping these rapscallions, because rapscallions and dead beats is the kind the widow and good people takes the most interest in.

Well, before long, here comes the wreck, dim and dusky sliding along down! A kind of cold shiver went through me, and then I struck out for her. She was very deep, and I see in a minute there warn't much chance for anybody being alive in her. I pulled all around her and hollered a little, but there wasn't any answer; all dead still; I felt a little bit heavy-hearted about the gang, but not much, for I reckoned if they could stand it, I could.

Then here comes the ferry-boat; so I shoved for the middle of the river on a long down-stream slant; and when I judged I was out of eye-reach, I laid on my oars, and looked back and see her go and smell around the wreck for Miss Hooker's remainders, because the captain would know her uncle Hornback would want them; and then pretty soon the ferry-boat give it up and went for shore, and I laid into my work and went a-booming down the river.

It did seem a powerful long time before Jim's light showed up; and when it did show, it looked it was a thousand miles off. By the time I got there the sky was beginning to get a little gray in the east; so we struck for an island, and hid the raft, and sunk the skiff, and turned in and slept like dead people.

Shipwreck

R. L. STEVENSON
Illustrated by W. B. Hole

This is an extract from Kidnapped *(1886). David Balfour has been forced to board a ship bound for the East Indies, where he is to be sold as a slave. On the voyage he is befriended by Alan Breck, who forces Captain Hoseason to promise that he will set them both safely ashore in Scotland. But off the island of Mull the ship strikes a reef . . .*

I

THE REEF

It was already late at night, and as dark as it ever would be at that season of the year (and that is to say, it was still pretty bright), when Hoseason clapped his head into the round-house door.

'Here,' said he, 'come out and see if ye can pilot.'

'Is this one of your tricks?' asked Alan.

'Do I look like tricks?' cries the captain. 'I have other things to think of – my brig's in danger!'

By the concerned look of his face, and, above all, by the sharp tones in which he spoke of his brig, it was plain to both of us he was in deadly earnest; and so Alan and I, with no great fear of treachery, stepped on deck.

The sky was clear; it blew hard, and was bitter cold; a great deal of daylight lingered; and the moon, which was nearly full, shone brightly. The brig was close hauled, so as to round the south-west corner of the Island of Mull; the hills of which (and Ben More above them all, with a wisp of mist upon the top of it) lay full upon the larboard bow. Though it was no good point of sailing for the

Covenant, she tore through the seas at a great rate, pitching and straining, and pursued by the westerly swell.

Altogether it was no such ill night to keep the seas in; and I had begun to wonder what it was that sat so heavily upon the captain, when the brig rising suddenly on the top of a high swell, he pointed and cried to us to look. Away on the lee bow, a thing like a fountain rose out of the moonlit sea, and immediately after we heard a low sound of roaring.

'What do ye call that?' asked the captain, gloomily.

'The sea breaking on a reef,' said Alan. 'And now ye ken where it is; and what better would ye have?'

'Ay,' said Hoseason, 'if it was the only one.'

And sure enough just as he spoke there came a second fountain further to the south.

'There!' said Hoseason. 'Ye see for yourself. If I had kent* of these reefs, if I had had a chart, or if Shuan had been spared, it's not sixty guineas, no, nor six hundred, would have made me risk my brig in sic a stoneyard! But you, sir, that was to pilot us, have ye never a word?'

'I'm thinking,' said Alan, 'these'll be what they call the Torran Rocks.'

'Are there many of them?' says the captain.

'Truly, sir, I am nae pilot,' said Alan; 'but it sticks in my mind there are ten miles of them.'

Mr Riach and the captain looked at each other.

'There's a way through them, I suppose?' said the captain.

'Doubtless,' said Alan; 'but where? But it somehow runs in my mind once more, that it is clearer under the land.'

'So?' said Hoseason. 'We'll have to haul our wind then, Mr Riach; we'll have to come as near in about the end of Mull as we can take her, sir; and even then we'll have the land to keep the wind off us, and that stoneyard on our lee. Well, we're in for it now, and may as well crack on.'

*kent = known

With that he gave an order to the steersman, and sent Riach to the foretop. There were only five men on deck, counting the officers; these were all that were fit (or, at least, both fit and willing) for their work; and two of these were hurt. So, as I say, it fell to Mr Riach to go aloft, and he sat there looking out and hailing the deck with news of all he saw.

'The sea to the south is thick,' he cried; and then, after a while, 'It does seem clearer in by the land.'

'Well, sir,' said Hoseason to Alan, 'we'll try your way of it. But I think I might as well trust to a blind fiddler. Pray God you're right.'

'Pray God I am!' says Alan to me. 'But where did I hear it? Well, well, it will be as it must.'

As we got nearer to the turn of the land the reefs began to be sown here and there on our very path; and Mr Riach sometimes cried down to us to change the course. Sometimes, indeed, none too soon; for one reef was so close on the brig's weather board that when a sea burst upon it the lighter sprays fell upon her deck and wetted us like rain.

The brightness of the night showed us these perils as clearly as by day, which was, perhaps, the more alarming. It showed me, too, the face of the captain as he stood by the steersman, now on one foot, now on the other, and sometimes blowing in his hands, but still listening and looking and as steady as steel. Neither he nor Mr Riach had shown well in the fighting; but I saw they were brave in their own trade, and admired them all the more because I found Alan very white.

'Ochone, David,' says he, 'this is no the kind of death I fancy.'

'What, Alan!' I cried, 'you're not afraid?'

'No,' said he, wetting his lips, 'but you'll allow yourself, it's a cold ending.'

By this time, now and then sheering to one side or the other to avoid a reef, but still hugging the wind and the land, we had got round Iona and begun to come alongside Mull. The tide at the tail of the land ran very strong, and threw the brig about. Two hands were put to the helm, and Hoseason himself would sometimes lend a help; and it was strange to see three strong men throw their weight upon the tiller, and

*'Two hands were put to the helm, and Hoseason himself
sometimes helped'*

it (like a living thing) struggle against and drive them back. This
would have been the greater danger, had not the sea been for some
while free of obstacles. Mr Riach, besides, announced from the top
that he saw clear water ahead.

'Ye were right,' said Hoseason to Alan. 'Ye have saved the brig, sir;
I'll mind that when we come to clear accounts.' And I believe he not
only meant what he said, but would have done it; so high a place did
the *Covenant* hold in his affections.

But this is matter only for conjecture, things having gone otherwise than he forecast.

'Keep her away a point,' sings out Mr Riach. 'Reef to windward!'

And just at the same time the tide caught the brig, and threw the wind out of her sails. She came round into the wind like a top, and the next moment struck the reef with such a dunch as threw us all flat upon the deck, and came near to shake Mr Riach from his place upon the mast.

I was on my feet in a minute. The reef on which we had struck was close in under the south-west end of Mull, off a little isle they call Earraid, which lay low and black upon the larboard. Sometimes the swell broke clean over us; sometimes it only ground the poor brig upon the reef, so that we could hear her beat herself to pieces; and what with the great noise of the sails, and the singing of the wind, and the flying of the spray in the moonlight, and the sense of danger, I think my head must have been partly turned, for I could scarcely understand the things I saw.

Presently I observed Mr Riach and the seamen busy round the skiff; and still in the same blank, ran over to assist them; and as soon as I set my hand to work, my mind came clear again. It was no very easy task, for the skiff lay amidships and was full of hamper, and the breaking of the heavier seas continually forced us to give over and hold on; but we all wrought like horses while we could.

Meanwhile such of the wounded as could move came clambering out of the fore-scuttle and began to help; while the rest that lay helpless in their bunks harrowed me with screaming and begging to be saved.

The captain took no part. It seemed he was struck stupid. He stood holding by the shrouds, talking to himself and groaning out aloud whenever the ship hammered on the rock. His brig was like wife and child to him; he had looked on, day by day, at the mishandling of poor Ransome; but when it came to the brig, he seemed to suffer along with her.

All the time of our working at the boat, I remember only one other thing; that I asked Alan, looking across at the shore, what country it was; and he answered, it was the worst possible for him, for it was a land of the Campbells.

We had one of the wounded men told off to keep a watch upon the seas and cry us warning. Well, we had the boat about ready to be launched, when this man sang out pretty shrill: 'For God's sake, hold on!' We knew by his tone that it was something more than ordinary; and sure enough, there followed a sea so huge that it lifted the brig right up and canted her over on her beam. Whether the cry came too late or my hold was too weak, I know not; but at the sudden tilting of the ship I was cast clean over the bulwarks into the sea.

I went down, and drank my fill; and then came up, and got a blink of the moon; and then down again. They say a man sinks the third time for good. I cannot be made like other folk, then; for I would not like to write how often I went down or how often I came up again. All the while, I was being hurled along, and beaten upon and choked, and then swallowed whole; and the thing was so distracting to my wits, that I was neither sorry nor afraid.

Presently, I found I was holding to a spar, which helped me somewhat. And then all of a sudden I was in quiet water, and began to come to myself.

It was the spare yard I had got hold of, and I was amazed to see how far I had travelled from the brig. I hailed her, indeed; but it was plain she was already out of cry. She was still holding together; but whether or not they had yet launched the boat, I was too far off and too low down to see.

While I was hailing the brig, I spied a tract of water lying between us, where no great waves came, but which yet boiled white all over and bristled in the moon with rings and bubbles. Sometimes the whole tract swung to one side, like the tail of a live serpent; sometimes, for a glimpse, it all would disappear and then boil up again. What it was I had no guess, which for the time increased my fear of it; but I now know it must have been the roost or tide race, which had carried me away so fast and tumbled me about so cruelly, and at last, as if tired of that play, had flung out me and the spare yard upon its landward margin.

I now lay quite becalmed, and began to feel that a man can die of cold as well as of drowning. The shores of Earraid were close in; I could see in the moonlight the dots of heather and the sparkling of the mica in the rocks.

'Well,' thought I to myself, 'if I cannot get as far as that, it's strange!'

I had no skill of swimming, Essen water being small in our neighbourhood; but when I laid hold upon the yard with both arms, and kicked out with both feet, I soon begun to find that I was moving. Hard work it was, and mortally slow; but in about an hour of kicking and splashing, I had got well in between the points of a sandy bay surrounded by low hills.

The sea was here quite quiet; there was no sound of any surf; the moon shone clear; and I thought in my heart I had never seen a place so desert and desolate. But it was dry land; and when at last it grew so shallow that I could leave the yard and wade ashore upon my feet, I cannot tell if I was more tired or more grateful. Both at least, I was: tired as I never was before that night; and grateful to God as I trust I have been often, though never with more cause.

II
CAST ASHORE

With my stepping ashore I began the most unhappy part of my adventures. It was half-past twelve in the morning, and though the wind was broken by the land, it was a cold night. I dared not sit down (for I thought I should have frozen), but took off my shoes and walked to and fro upon the sand, barefoot, and beating my breast, with infinite weariness. There was no sound of man or cattle; not a cock crew, though it was about the hour of their first waking; only the surf broke outside in the distance, which put me in mind of my perils and those of my friend. To walk by the sea at that hour of the morning, and in a place so desert-like and lonesome, struck me with a kind of fear.

As soon as the day began to break I put on my shoes and climbed a hill – the ruggedest scramble I ever undertook – falling, the whole way, between big blocks of granite or leaping from one to another. When I got to the top the dawn was come. There was no sign of the brig, which must have lifted from the reef and sunk. The boat, too, was nowhere to be seen. There was never a sail upon the ocean; and in what I could see of the land, was neither house nor man.

I was afraid to think what had befallen my shipmates, and afraid to look longer at so empty a scene. What with my wet clothes and weariness, and my belly that now began to ache with hunger, I had enough to trouble me without that. So I set off eastward along the south coast, hoping to find a house where I might warm myself, and perhaps get news of those I had lost. And at the worst, I considered the sun would soon rise and dry my clothes.

After a little, my way was stopped by a creek or inlet of the sea, which seemed to run pretty deep into the land; and as I had no means to get across, I must needs change my direction to go about the end of it. It was still the roughest kind of walking; indeed the whole, not only of Earraid, but of the neighbouring part of Mull (which they call the Ross) is nothing but a jumble of granite rocks with heather in among. At first the creek kept narrowing as I had looked to see; but presently to my surprise it began to widen out again. At this I scratched my head, but had still no notion of the truth; until at last I came to a rising ground, and it burst upon me all in a moment that I was cast upon a little, barren isle, and cut off on every side by the salt seas.

Instead of the sun rising to dry me, it came on to rain, with a thick mist; so that my case was lamentable.

I stood in the rain, and shivered, and wondered what to do, till it occurred to me that perhaps the creek was fordable. Back I went to the narrowest point and waded in. But not three yards from shore, I plumped in head over ears; and if ever I was heard of more it was rather by God's grace than my own prudence. I was no wetter (for that could hardly be) but I was all the colder for this mishap; and having lost another hope, was the more unhappy.

And now, all at once, the yard came in my head. What had carried me through the roost, would surely serve me to cross that little quiet creek in safety. With that I set off, undaunted, across the top of the isle, to fetch and carry it back. It was a weary tramp in all ways, and if hope had not buoyed me up, I must have cast myself down and given up. Whether with the sea salt, or because I was growing fevered, I was distressed with thirst, and had to stop, as I went, and drink the peaty water out of the hags.

I came to the bay at last, more dead than alive; and at the first glance, I thought the yard was something further out than when I left it. In I went, for the third time, into the sea. The sand was smooth and firm and shelved gradually down; so that I could wade out till the water was almost to my neck and the little waves splashed into my face. But at that depth my feet began to leave me and I durst venture in no further. As for the yard, I saw it bobbing very quietly some twenty feet in front of me.

I had borne up well until this last disappointment; but at that I came ashore, and flung myself down upon the sands and wept.

The time I spent upon the island is still so horrible a thought to me, that I must pass it lightly over. In all the books I have read of people cast away, they had either their pockets full of tools, or a chest of things would be thrown upon the beach along with them, as if on purpose. My case was very different. I had nothing in my pockets but money and Alan's silver button; and being inland bred, I was as much short of knowledge as of means.

I knew indeed that shell-fish were counted good to eat; and among the rocks of the isle I found a great plenty of limpets, which at first I could scarcely strike from their places, not knowing quickness to be needful. There were, besides, some of the little shells that we call buckies; I think periwinkle is the English name. Of these two I made my whole diet, devouring them cold and raw as

I found them; and so hungry was I, that at first they seemed to me delicious.

Perhaps they were out of season, or perhaps there was something wrong in the sea about my island. But at least I had no sooner eaten my first meal than I was seized with giddiness and retching, and lay for a long time no better than dead. A second trial of the same food (indeed I had no other) did better with me and revived my strength. But as long as I was on the island, I never knew what to expect when I had eaten; sometimes all was well, and sometimes I was thrown into a miserable sickness; nor could I ever distinguish what particular fish it was that hurt me.

All day it streamed rain; the island ran like a sop; there was no dry spot to be found; and when I lay down that night, between two boulders that made a kind of roof, my feet were in a bog.

The second day I crossed the island to all sides. There was no one part of it better than another; it was all desolate and rocky; nothing living on it but game birds which I lacked the means to kill, and the gulls which haunted the outlying rocks in a prodigious number. But the creek, or straits, that cut off the isle from the main land of the Ross, opened out on the north into a bay, and the bay again opened into the sound of Iona; and it was the neighbourhood of this place that I chose to be my home; though if I had thought upon the very name of home in such a spot, I must have burst out weeping.

I had good reasons for my choice. There was in this part of the isle a little hut of a house like a pig's hut, where fishers used to sleep when they came there upon their business; but the turf roof of it had fallen entirely in; so that the hut was of no use to me, and gave me less shelter than my rocks. What was more important, the shell-fish on which I lived grew there in great plenty; when the tide was out I could gather a peck at a time: and this was doubtless a convenience. But the other reason went deeper. I had become in no way used to the horrid solitude of the isle, but still looked round me on all sides (like a man that was hunted) between fear and hope that I might see some human creature coming. Now, from a little up the hillside over the bay, I could catch a sight of the great, ancient church and the roofs of the people's houses in Iona. And on the other hand, over the low country of the Ross, I saw smoke go up, morning and evening, as if from a homestead in a hollow of the land.

I used to watch this smoke, when I was wet and cold, and had my head half turned with loneliness; and think of the fireside and the company, till my heart burned. It was the same with the roofs of Iona. Altogether, this sight I had of men's homes and comfortable lives, although it put a point on my own sufferings, yet it kept hope alive, and helped me to eat my raw shell-fish (which had soon grown to be a disgust) and saved me from the sense of horror I had whenever I was quite alone with dead rocks, and fowls, and the rain, and the cold sea.

I say it kept hope alive; and indeed it seemed impossible that I should be left to die on the shores of my own country, and within view of a church tower and the smoke of men's houses. But the second day passed; and though as long as the light lasted I kept a bright look-out for boats on the Sound or men passing on the Ross, no help came near me. It still rained; and I turned in to sleep, as wet as ever and with a cruel sore throat, but a little comforted, perhaps, by having said good night to my next neighbours, the people of Iona.

Charles the Second declared a man could stay outdoors more days in the year in the climate of England than in any other. This was very like a king with a palace at his back and changes of dry clothes. But he must have had better luck on his flight from Worcester than I had on that miserable isle. It was the height of the summer; yet it rained for more than twenty-four hours, and did not clear until the afternoon of the third day.

This was the day of incidents. In the morning I saw a red deer, a buck with a fine spread of antlers, standing in the rain on the top of the island; but he had scarce seen me rise from under my rock, before he trotted off upon the other side. I supposed he must have swum the straits; though what should bring any creature to Earraid, was more than I could fancy.

A little after, as I was jumping about after my limpets, I was startled by a guinea-piece, which fell upon a rock in front of me and glanced off into the sea. When the sailors gave me my money again, they kept back not only about a third of the whole sum, but my father's leather purse; so that from that day out, I carried my gold loose in a pocket with a button. I now saw there must be a hole, and clapped my hand to the place in a great hurry. But this was to lock the stable door after the steed was stolen. I had left the shore at Queensferry with near on fifty pounds; now I found no more than two guinea-pieces and a silver shilling.

It is true I picked up a third guinea a little after, where it lay shining on a piece of turf. That made a fortune of three pounds and four shillings, English money, for a lad, the rightful heir of an estate, and now starving on an isle at the extreme end of the wild Highlands.

This state of my affairs dashed me still further; and indeed my plight on that third morning was truly pitiful. My clothes were beginning to rot; my stockings in particular were quite worn through, so that my shanks went naked; my hands had grown quite soft with the continual soaking; my throat was very sore, my strength had much abated, and my heart so turned against the horrid stuff I was condemned to eat, that the very sight of it came near to sicken me.

And yet the worst was not yet come.

There is a pretty high rock on the north-west of Earraid, which (because it had a flat top and overlooked the Sound) I was much in the habit of frequenting; not that ever I stayed in one place, save when asleep, my misery giving me no rest. Indeed I wore myself down with continual and aimless goings and comings in the rain.

As soon, however, as the sun came out, I lay down on the top of that rock to dry myself. The comfort of the sunshine is a thing I cannot tell. It set me thinking hopefully of my deliverance, of which I had begun to despair; and I scanned the sea and the Ross with a fresh interest. On the south of my rock, a part of the island jutted out and hid the open ocean, so that a boat could thus come quite near me upon that side, and I be none the wiser.

Well, all of a sudden, a coble with a brown sail and a pair of fishers

I cried and waved to them

aboard of it, came flying round that corner of the isle, bound for Iona. I shouted out, and then fell on my knees on the rock and reached up my hands and prayed to them. They were near enough to hear – I could even see the colour of their hair; and there was no doubt but they observed me, for they cried out in the Gaelic tongue, and laughed. But the boat never turned aside, and flew on, right before my eyes, for Iona.

I could not believe such wickedness, and ran along the shore from rock to rock, crying on them piteously; even after they were out of reach of my voice, I still cried and waved to them; and when they were quite gone, I thought my heart would have burst. All the time of my troubles I wept only twice. Once, when I could not reach the yard; and now, the second time, when these fishers turned a deaf ear to my cries. But this time I wept and roared like a wicked child, tearing up the turf with my nails and grinding my face in the earth. If a wish would kill men, those two fishers would never have seen morning, and I should likely have died upon my island.

When I was a little over my anger, I must eat again, but with such loathing of the mess as I could now scarce control. Sure enough, I should have done as well to fast, for my fishes poisoned me again. I had all my first pains; my throat was so sore I could scarce swallow; I had a fit of strong shuddering, which clucked my teeth together; and there came on me that dreadful sense of illness, which we have no name for either in Scotch or English. I thought I should have died, and made my peace with God, forgiving all men, even my uncle and the fishers; and as soon as I had thus made up my mind to the worst, clearness came upon me: I observed the night was falling dry; my clothes were dried a good deal; truly, I was in a better case than ever before, since I had landed on the isle; and so I got to sleep at last, with a thought of gratitude.

The next day (which was the fourth of this horrible life of mine) I found my bodily strength run very low. But the sun shone, the air was sweet, and what I managed to eat of the shell-fish agreed well with me and revived my courage.

I was scarce back on my rock (where I went always the first thing after I had eaten) before I observed a boat coming down the Sound, and with her head, as I thought, in my direction.

I began at once to hope and fear exceedingly; for I thought these men might have thought better of their cruelty and be coming back to my assistance. But another disappointment, such as yesterday's, was more than I could bear. I turned my back, accordingly, upon the sea, and did not look again till I had counted many hundreds. The boat was still heading for the island. The next time I counted the full thousand, as slowly as I could, my heart beating so as to hurt me. And then it was out of all question. She was coming straight to Earraid!

I could no longer hold myself back, but ran to the sea side and out, from one rock to another, as far as I could go. It is a marvel I was not drowned; for when I was brought to a stand at last, my legs shook under me, and my mouth was so dry, I must wet it with the sea-water before I was able to shout.

All this time the boat was coming on; and now I was able to perceive it was the same two men as yesterday. This I knew by their hair, which the one had of a bright yellow and the other black. But now there was a third man along with them, who looked to be of a better class.

As soon as they were come within easy speech, they let down their sail and lay quiet. In spite of my supplications, they drew no nearer in, and what frightened me most of all, the new man tee-hee'd with laughter as he talked and looked at me.

Then he stood up in the boat and addressed me a long while, speaking fast and with many wavings of his hand. I told him I had no Gaelic; and at this he became very angry, and I began to suspect he thought he was talking English. Listening very close, I caught the word 'whateffer' several times; but all the rest was Gaelic, and might have been Greek and Hebrew for me.

'Whatever,' said I, to show him I had caught a word.

'Yes, yes – yes, yes,' says he, and then he looked at the other men, as much as to say, 'I told you I spoke English,' and began again as hard as ever in the Gaelic.

This time I picked out another word, 'tide'. Then I had a flash of hope. I remembered he was always waving his hand towards the mainland of the Ross.

'Do you mean when the tide is out—?' I cried, and could not finish.

'Yes, yes,' said he. 'Tide.'

At that I turned tail upon their boat (where my adviser had once more begun to tee-hee with laughter) leaped back the way I had come, from one stone to another, and set off running across the isle as I had never run before. In about half an hour I came out upon the shores of the creek; and, sure enough, it was shrunk into a little trickle of water, through which I dashed, not above my knees, and landed with a shout on the main island.

A sea-bred boy would not have stayed a day on Earraid; which is only what they call a tidal islet, and except in the bottom of the neaps, can be entered and left twice in every twenty-four hours, either dry-shod, or at the most by wading. Even I, who had the tide going out and in before me in the bay, and even watched for the ebbs, the better to get my shell-fish – even I (I say) if I had sat down to think, instead of raging at my fate, must have soon guessed the secret, and got free. It was no wonder the fishers had not understood me. The wonder was rather that they had ever guessed my pitiful illusion, and taken the trouble to come back. I had starved with cold and hunger on that island for close upon one hundred hours. But for the fishers, I might have left my bones there, in pure folly. And even as it was, I had paid for it pretty dear, not only in past sufferings, but in my present case; being clothed like a beggar-man, scarce able to walk, and in great pain of my sore throat.

I have seen wicked men and fools, a great many of both; and I believe they both get paid in the end; but the fools first.

A Voyage to Lilliput

JONATHAN SWIFT
Illustrated by T. Morten

Gulliver's Travels (1726) relates the four amazing voyages of Lemuel Gulliver: to Lilliput, to Brobdingnag (a land of giants), to Laputa (a flying island) and to a country inhabited by horses. The episodes reproduced here describe Gulliver's adventures in Lilliput.

These extracts have been kept just as Swift wrote them, except that some very old or hard phrases have been made a bit easier to understand.

I
SHIPWRECKED IN LILLIPUT

On the fifth of November, which was the beginning of summer in those parts, the weather being very hazy, the seamen spied a rock, within half a cable's length of the ship; but the wind was so strong, that we were driven directly upon it, and immediately split. Six of the crew, of whom I was one, having let down the boat into the sea, made a shift to get clear of the ship, and the rock. We rowed about three leagues, till we were able to work no longer. We therefore trusted ourselves to the mercy of the waves, and in about half an hour the boat was overset by a sudden flurry from the north. What became of my companions in the boat, as well as of those who escaped on the rock, or were left in the vessel, I cannot tell; but conclude they were all lost. For my own part, I swam as fortune directed me, and was pushed forward by wind and tide. I often let my legs drop, and could feel no bottom: but when I was almost gone, and able to struggle no longer, I found myself within my depth; and by this time the storm was much abated. I walked near a mile before I got to the shore, which I conjectured was about eight o'clock in the evening. I then advanced forward near half a mile, but could not discover any sign of houses or inhabitants; at least I was in so weak a condition, that I did not observe them. I was extremely tired, and with that, and the heat of the weather, and about half a pint of brandy that I drank as I left the ship, I found myself much inclined to sleep. I lay down on the grass, which was very short and soft, where I slept sounder than ever I remember to have done in my life, and, as I reckoned, above nine hours; for when I awaked, it was just day-light. I attempted to rise, but was not able to stir: for, as I happened to lie on my back, I found my arms and legs were strongly fastened on each side to the ground; and my hair, which was long and thick, tied down in the same manner. I likewise felt several slender ligatures across my body, from my arm-pits to my thighs. I could only look upwards; the sun began to grow hot, and the light offended my eyes. I heard a confused noise about me, but in the posture I lay, could see nothing except the sky. In a little time I felt something alive moving on my left leg, which advancing gently forward over my breast, came almost up to my chin; when bending my eyes downwards as much as I could, I perceived it to be a human creature not six inches high, with a bow and arrow in his hands, and a quiver at his back. In the mean time, I felt at least forty more of the same kind (as I conjectured) following the first. I was in the utmost astonishment, and roared so loud, that they all ran back in a fright; and some of them, as I was afterwards told, were hurt with the falls they got by leaping from my sides upon the ground. However, they soon returned, and one of them, who ventured so far as to get a full sight of my face, lifting up his hands and eyes by way of admiration, cried out in a shrill but distinct voice, *Hekinah degul*: the others repeated the same words several times, but I then knew not what they meant. I lay all this while, as the reader may believe, in great uneasiness: at length, struggling to get loose, I had the fortune to break the strings and wrench out the pegs that fastened my left arm to the ground; for, by lifting it up to my face, I discovered the methods they had taken to bind me. At the same time, with a violent pull, which gave me excessive pain, I a little loosened the strings that tied down my hair on the left side, so that I was just able to turn my head about two inches. But the creatures ran off a second time, before I could seize them; whereupon there was a great shout in a very shrill accent, and after it ceased, I heard one of them cry aloud, *Tolgo phonac*; when in an instant I felt above a hundred arrows discharged on my left hand, which pricked me like so many needles; and besides they shot another flight into the air, as we do bombs in Europe, whereof many, I suppose, fell on my body (though I felt them not) and some on my face, which I immediately covered with my left hand. When this shower of arrows was over, I fell a groaning with grief and pain. As I was striving again to get loose, they discharged another volley larger than the first, and some of them attempted with spears to stick me in the sides; but, by good luck, I had on me a buff jerkin, which they could not pierce. I thought it the most prudent method to lie still, and my design was to continue so till night, when, my left hand being already loose, I could easily free myself; and as for the inhabitants, I had reason to believe I might be a match for the greatest armies they could bring against me, if they were all of the same size with him that I saw. But fortune disposed otherwise of me. When the people observed I was quiet, they discharged no more arrows; but, by the noise I heard, I knew their numbers increased; and about four yards from me, over against my right ear, I heard a knocking for above an hour, like that of people at work; when turning my head that way, as well as the pegs and strings would permit me, I saw a stage erected, about a foot and a half from the ground, capable of holding four of the inhabitants, with two or three ladders to mount it: from whence one of them made me a long speech, of which I understood not one syllable. But I should have mentioned, that before the principal person began his oration, he cried out three times, *Langro dehul san* (these words and the former were afterwards repeated and explained to me). Immediately about fifty of the inhabitants came, and cut the strings that fastened the left side of my head, which gave me the liberty of turning it to the right, and of observing the person and gesture of him that was to speak. He

appeared to be of a middle age, and taller than any of the other three
who attended him. He acted every part of an orator, and I could
observe many periods of threatenings, and others of promises, pity,
and kindness. I answered in a few words, but in the most submissive
manner, lifting up my left hand and both my eyes to the sun, as calling
him for a witness; and being almost famished with hunger, having not
eaten a morsel for some hours before I left the ship, I found the
demands of nature so strong upon me, that I could not forbear
showing my impatience (perhaps against the strict rules of decency)
by putting my finger frequently on my mouth, to signify that I
wanted food. The *Hurgo* (for so they call a great lord, as I afterwards
learnt) understood me very well. He descended from the stage, and
commanded that several ladders should be applied to my sides, on
which above a hundred of the inhabitants mounted, and walked
towards my mouth, laden with baskets full of meat, which had been
provided by the King's orders, upon the first intelligence he received
of me. I observed there was the flesh of several animals, but could not
distinguish them by the taste. There were shoulders, legs, and loins,
shaped like those of mutton, and very well dressed, but smaller than
the wings of a lark. I ate them by two or three at a mouthful, and took
three loaves at a time, about the size of musket bullets. They supplied
me as they could, showing a thousand marks of wonder and astonishment at my bulk and appetite. I then made another sign that I wanted
drink. Being a most ingenious people, they slung up with great
dexterity one of their largest hogsheads, then rolled it towards my
hand, and beat out the top; I drank it off at a draught, which I might
well do, for it did not hold half a pint, and tasted like a wine of
Burgundy, but much more delicious. They brought me a second
hogshead, which I drank in the same manner, and made signs for
more, but they had none to give me. When I had performed these
wonders, they shouted for joy, and danced upon my breast, repeating
several times as they did at first, *Hekinah degul.* I confess I was often
tempted, while they were passing backwards and forwards on my
body, to seize forty or fifty of the first that came in my reach, and dash

them against the ground. But the remembrance of what I had felt, which probably might not be the worst they could do, and the promise of honour I made them, for so I interpreted my submissive behaviour, soon drove out these imaginations. Besides, I now considered myself as bound by the laws of hospitality to a people who had treated me with so much expense and magnificence. However, in my thoughts I could not sufficiently wonder at the bravery of these tiny mortals, who dared to mount and walk upon my body, while one of my hands was at liberty, without trembling at the very sight of so huge a creature as I must appear to them. After some time, when they observed that I made no more demands for meat, there appeared before me a person of high rank from his Imperial Majesty. His Excellency, having mounted on the small of my right leg, advanced forwards up to my face, with about a dozen of his retinue. And producing his credentials under the Signet Royal, which he applied close to my eyes, spoke about ten minutes, without any signs of anger, but with resolution; often pointing forwards, which, as I afterwards found, was towards the capital city, whither it was agreed by his Majesty in council that I must be conveyed. I answered in few words, but to no purpose, and made a sign with my hand that was loose, putting it to the other (but over his Excellency's head, for fear of hurting him or his train) and then to my own head and body, to signify that I desired my liberty. It appeared that he understood me well enough, for he shook his head, and held his hand in a posture to show that I must be carried as a prisoner. However, he made other signs to let me understand that I should have meat and drink enough, and very good treatment. I once more thought of attempting to break my bonds, but again, when I felt the smart of their arrows upon my face and hands, which were all in blisters, I gave tokens to let them know that they might do with me what they pleased. Upon this the *Hurgo* and his train withdrew with much civility and cheerful countenances. Soon after I heard a general shout, with frequent repetitions of the words, *Peplom selan*, and I felt great numbers of the people on my left side relaxing the cords to such a degree, that I was able to turn upon my right. But before this, they had daubed my face and both my hands with a sort of ointment very pleasant to the smell, which in a few minutes removed all the smart of their arrows. These circumstances, added to the refreshment I had received by their victuals and drink, which were very nourishing, disposed me to sleep. I slept about eight hours, as I was afterwards assured; and it was no wonder, for the physicians, by the Emperor's order, had mingled a sleepy potion in the hogsheads of wine.

II
GULLIVER MEETS THE EMPEROR

It seems that upon the first moment I was discovered sleeping on the ground after my landing, the Emperor had early notice of it by an express; and determined in council that I should be tied in the manner I have related (which was done in the night while I slept), that plenty of meat and drink should be sent me, and a machine prepared to carry me to the capital city.

Five hundred carpenters and engineers were immediately set to work to prepare a great frame of wood raised three inches above the ground, about seven foot long and four wide, moving upon twenty two wheels. Fifteen hundred of the Emperor's largest horses, each about four inches and a half high, were employed to draw me towards the metropolis.

About four hours after we began our journey, I was woken by a very ridiculous accident; for the carriage being stopped a while to adjust something that was out of order, two or three of the young natives had the curiosity to see how I looked when I was asleep. They climbed up into the engine, and advancing very softly to my face, one of them, an officer in the Guards, put the sharp end of his half-pike a good way up into my left nostril, which tickled my nose like a straw, and made me sneeze violently. They stole off unperceived, and it was three weeks before I knew the cause of my awaking so suddenly. We made a long march the remaining part of that day, and rested at night with five hundred guards on each side of me, half with torches, and half with bows and arrows, ready to shoot me if I should offer to stir. The next morning at sunrise we continued our march, and arrived within two hundred yards of the city gates about noon. The Emperor, and all his court, came out to meet us; but his great officers would by no means suffer his Majesty to endanger his person by mounting on my body.

At the place where the carriage stopped, there stood an ancient temple. In this edifice it was determined I should lodge. The great gate fronting to the north was about four foot high, and almost two foot wide, through which I could easily creep. On each side of the gate was a small window not above six inches from the ground; into that on the left side, the King's smiths conveyed fourscore and eleven chains, like those that hang to a lady's watch in Europe, and almost as large, which were locked to my left leg with six and thirty padlocks. Over against this temple, on t'other side of the great highway, at twenty foot distance, there was a tower at least five foot high. Here the Emperor ascended with many principal lords of his court, to have an opportunity of viewing me, as I was told, for I could not see them. It was reckoned that above a hundred thousand inhabitants came out of the town upon the same errand; and in spite of my guards, I believe there could not be fewer than ten thousand, at different times, who mounted upon my body by the help of ladders. But a proclamation was soon issued to forbid it upon pain of death. When the workmen found it was impossible for me to break loose, they cut all the strings that bound me; whereupon I rose up with as melancholy a disposition as ever I had in my life. But the noise and astonishment of the people at seeing me rise and walk, are not to be expressed. The chains that held my left leg were about two yards long, and gave me not only the liberty of walking backwards and forwards in a semicircle; but, being fixed within four inches of the gate, allowed me to creep in, and lie at my full length in the temple.

When I found myself on my feet, I looked about me, and must confess I never beheld a more entertaining prospect. The country round appeared like a continued garden, and the enclosed fields, which were generally forty foot square, resembled so many beds of flowers. These fields were intermingled with woods, and the tallest trees, as I could judge, appeared to be seven foot high. I viewed the town on my left hand, which looked like the painted scene of a city in a theatre.

The Emperor was already descended from the tower, and advancing on horseback towards me, which had like to have cost him dear; for the beast, though very well trained, yet wholly unused to such a sight, reared up on his hind feet: but that prince, who is an excellent horseman, kept his seat, till his attendants ran in, and held the bridle, while his master had time to dismount. When he alighted, he surveyed me round with great admiration, but kept outside the length of my chain. He ordered his cooks and butlers, who were already prepared, to give me food and drink, which they pushed forward in a sort of vehicle upon wheels till I could reach them. I took these vehicles, and soon emptied them all; twenty of them were filled with meat, and ten with liquor; each of the former afforded me two or three good mouthfuls, and I emptied the liquor of ten vessels, which was contained in earthen vials, into one vehicle, drinking it off at a draught; and so I did with the rest. The Empress, and young Princes of the blood, of both sexes, attended by many ladies, sat some distance in their chairs; but upon the accident that happened to the Emperor's horse, they alighted, and came near his person, which I am now going to describe. He is taller by almost the breadth of my nail than any of his court, which alone is enough to strike awe into the beholders. His features are strong and masculine, with an Austrian lip and arched nose, his complexion olive, his countenance erect, his body and limbs well proportioned, all his motions graceful, and his deportment majestic. He was then past his prime, being twenty-eight years and three quarters old. For the better convenience of beholding him, I lay on my side, so that my face was parallel to his, and he stood but three yards off: however, I have had him since many times in my hand, and therefore cannot be deceived in the description. His dress was very plain and simple, and the fashion of it between the Asiatic and the European; but he had on his head a light helmet of gold, adorned with jewels, and a plume on the crest. He held his sword drawn in his hand, to defend himself, if I should happen to break loose; it was almost three inches long, the hilt and scabbard were gold enriched with diamonds. His voice was shrill, but very clear and articulate, and I could distinctly hear it when I stood up. The ladies and courtiers were all most magnificently clad, so that the spot they stood upon seemed to resemble a petticoat spread on the ground, embroidered with figures of gold and silver. His Imperial Majesty spoke often to me, and I returned answers, but neither of us could understand a syllable. There were several of his priests and lawyers present (as I conjectured by their dress) who were commanded to address themselves to me, and I spoke to them in as many languages as I had the least smattering of, which were High and Low Dutch, Latin, French, Spanish, Italian, and Lingua Franca; but all to no purpose. After about two hours the court retired, and I was left with a strong guard, to prevent the impertinence, and probably the malice of the rabble, who were very impatient to crowd about me as near as they dared. Some of them had the impudence to shoot their arrows at me as I sat on the ground by the door of my house. The colonel ordered six of the ringleaders to be seized, and thought no punishment so proper as to deliver them bound into my hands, which some of his soldiers accordingly did, pushing them forwards with the butt-ends of their pikes into my reach. I took them all in my right hand, put five of them into my coat-pocket, and as to the sixth, I made a countenance as if I would eat him alive. The poor man squalled terribly, and the colonel and his officers were in much pain, especially when they saw me take out my penknife; but I soon put them out of fear; for, looking mildly, and immediately cutting the strings he was bound with, I set him gently on the ground, and away he ran. I treated the rest in the same manner, taking them one by one out of my pocket, and I observed both the soldiers and

people were highly obliged at this mark of my mercy, which was represented very much to my advantage at court.

Towards night I got with some difficulty into my house, where I lay on the ground, and continued to do so about a fortnight; during which time the Emperor gave orders to have a bed prepared for me. Six hundred beds of the common measure were brought in carriages, and worked up in my house; a hundred and fifty of their beds sewn together made up the breadth and length, and these were four thick, which however kept me but very indifferently from the hardness of the floor, which was of smooth stone. By the same computation they provided me with sheets, blankets, and coverlets, tolerable enough for one who had been so long accustomed to hardships as I.

As the news of my arrival spread through the kingdom, it brought great numbers of rich, idle, and curious people to see me; so that the villages were almost emptied, and great neglect of tillage and household affairs must have ensued. His Imperial Majesty directed that those who had already beheld me should return home, and not presume to come within fifty yards of my house without licence from court.

In the mean time, the Emperor held frequent councils to debate what course should be taken with me; and I was afterwards assured by a particular friend, a person of great quality, who was looked upon to be as much in the secret as any, that the court was under many difficulties concerning me. They feared my breaking loose, that my diet would be very expensive, and might cause a famine. Sometimes they determined to starve me, or at least to shoot me in the face and hands with poisoned arrows, which would soon despatch me: but again they considered, that the stench of so large a carcass might produce a plague in the metropolis, and probably spread through the whole kingdom. In the midst of these consultations, several officers of the army went to the door of the great council-chamber; and two of them being admitted, gave an account of my behaviour to the six criminals above-mentioned, which made so favourable an impression on his Majesty and the whole board, that an Imperial Commission was issued out, obliging all the villages nine hundred yards round the city, to deliver in every morning six beeves, forty sheep, and other food for my sustenance; together with a proportionable quantity of bread, and wine, and other liquors; for the due payment of which his Majesty gave assignments upon his treasury. An establishment was also made of six hundred persons to be my domestics, who had board-wages allowed for their maintenance, and tents built for them very conveniently on each side of my door. It was likewise ordered, that three hundred tailors should make me a suit of clothes after the fashion of the country: that six of his Majesty's greatest scholars should be employed to instruct me in their language: and, lastly, that the Emperor's horses, and those of the nobility, and troops of guards, should be frequently exercised in my sight, to accustom themselves to me. All these orders were duly put in execution, and in about three weeks I made a great progress in learning their language; during which time the Emperor frequently honoured me with his visits, and was pleased to assist my masters in teaching me.

III

LIFE IN LILLIPUT

My gentleness and good behaviour had gained so far on the Emperor and his court, and indeed upon the army and people in general, that I began to conceive hopes of getting my liberty in a short time. The natives came by degrees to be less apprehensive of any danger from me. I would sometimes lie down, and let five or six of them dance on my hand. And at last the boys and girls would venture to come and play at hide and seek in my hair. I had now made a good progress in understanding and speaking their language. The Emperor had a mind one day to entertain me with several of the country shows, wherein they exceed all nations I have known, both for dexterity and magnificence. I was diverted with none so much as that of the rope-dancers, performed upon a slender white thread, extended about two foot, and twelve inches from the ground.

The horses of the army, and those of the royal stables, having been daily led before me, were no longer shy, but would come up to my very feet without starting. The riders would leap them over my hand as I held it on the ground, and one of the Emperor's huntsmen, upon a large courser, took my foot, shoe and all; which was indeed a prodigious leap. I had the good fortune to divert the Emperor one day after a very extraordinary manner. I desired he would order several sticks of two foot high, and the thickness of an ordinary cane, to be brought me; whereupon his Majesty commanded the master of his woods to give directions accordingly; and the next morning six woodmen arrived with as many carriages, drawn by eight horses each. I took nine of these sticks, and fixing them firmly in the ground in a rectangle, two foot and a half square, I took four other sticks, and tied them parallel at each corner, about two foot from the ground; then I fastened my handkerchief to the nine sticks that stood erect, and extended it on all sides till it was as tight as the top of a drum; and the four parallel sticks rising about five inches higher than the handkerchief served as ledges on each side. When I had finished my work, I desired the Emperor to let a troop of his best horse, twenty-four in number, come and exercise upon this plain. His Majesty approved of the proposal, and I took them up one by one in my hands, ready mounted and armed, with the proper officers to exercise them. As soon as they got into order, they divided into two parties, performed mock skirmishes, discharged blunt arrows, drew their swords, fled and pursued, attacked and retired, and in short showed the best military discipline I ever saw. The parallel sticks secured them and their horses from falling over the stage; and the Emperor was so much delighted, that he ordered this entertainment to be repeated several days, and once was pleased to be lifted up and give the word of command; and, with great difficulty, persuaded even the Empress herself to let me hold her in her close chair within two yards of the stage, from whence she was able to take a full view of the whole performance. It was my good fortune that no ill accident happened in these entertainments, only once a fiery horse that belonged to one of the captains pawing with his hoof struck a hole in my handkerchief, and his foot slipping, he overthrew his rider and himself; but I immediately relieved them both, and covering the hole with one hand, I set down the troop with the other, in the same manner as I took them up. The horse that fell was strained in the left shoulder, but the rider got no hurt, and I repaired my handkerchief as well as I could: however, I would not trust to the strength of it any more in such dangerous enterprises.

About two or three days before I was set at liberty, as I was entertaining the court with these kind of feats, there arrived an express to inform his Majesty that some of his subjects riding near the place where I was first taken up, had seen a great black substance lying on the ground, very oddly shaped, extending its edges round as wide as his Majesty's bedchamber, and rising up in the middle as high as a man: that it was no living creature, as they at first thought, for it lay on the grass without motion, and some of them had walked round it several times. By mounting upon each other's shoulders, they had got to the top, which was flat and even, and stamping upon it they found it was hollow within. They humbly conceived it might be something belonging to the Man-Mountain, and if his Majesty pleased, they would undertake to bring it with only five horses. I presently knew what they meant, and was glad at heart to receive this news. It seems upon my first reaching the shore after our shipwreck, my hat, which I had fastened with a string to my head while I was rowing, and had stuck on all the time I was swimming, fell off after I came to land. I entreated his Imperial Majesty to give orders it might be brought to me as soon as possible, describing to him the use and the nature of it: and the next day the waggoners arrived with it, but not in a very good condition. They had bored two holes in the brim, within an inch and a half of the edge, and fastened two hooks in the holes; these hooks were tied by a long cord to the harness, and thus my hat was dragged along for above half an English mile: but the ground in that country being extremely smooth and level, it received less damage than I expected.

The first request I made after I had obtained my liberty, was, that I might have licence to see Mildendo, the metropolis; which the Emperor easily granted me, but with a special charge to do no hurt either to the inhabitants or their houses. The people had notice by proclamation of my design to visit the town. The wall which encompassed it is two foot and a half high, and at least eleven inches broad, so that a coach and horses may be driven very safely round it; and it is flanked with strong towers at ten foot distance. I stepped over the great Western Gate, and passed very gently, and sidled through the two principal streets, only in my short waistcoat, for fear of damaging the roofs and eaves of the houses with the skirts of my coat. I walked with the utmost circumspection, to avoid treading on any stragglers, that might remain in the streets, although the orders were very strict, that all people should keep in their houses at their own peril. The garret windows and tops of houses were so crowded with spectators, that I thought in all my travels I had not seen a more populous place. The city is an exact square, each side of the wall being five hundred foot long. The two great streets, which run cross and divide it into four quarters, are five foot wide. The lanes and alleys, which I could not enter, but only viewed them as I passed, are from twelve to eighteen inches. The town is capable of holding five hundred thousand souls. The houses are from three to five storeys. The shops and markets are well provided.

The Emperor's palace is in the centre of the city, where the two great streets meet. It is enclosed by a wall of two foot high, and twenty foot distant from the buildings. I had his Majesty's permission to step over this wall; and the space being so wide between that and the palace, I could easily view it on every side. The outward court is a square of forty foot, and includes two other courts: in the inmost are the royal apartments, which I was very keen to see, but found it extremely difficult; for the great gates, from one square into another, were but eighteen inches high and seven inches wide. Now the buildings of the outer court were at least five foot high, and it was impossible for me to stride over them without infinite damage to the pile, though the walls were strongly built of hewn stone, and four inches thick. At the same time the Emperor had a great desire that I should see the magnificence of his palace; but this I was not able to do till three days after, which I spent in cutting down with my knife some of the largest trees in the royal park, about a hundred yards distant from the city. Of these trees I made two stools, each about three foot high, and strong enough to bear my weight. The people having received notice a second time, I went again through the city to the palace, with my two stools in my hands. When I came to the side of the outer court, I stood upon one stool, and took the other in my hand; this I lifted over the roof, and gently set it down on the space between the first and second court, which was eight foot wide. I then stepped over the buildings very conveniently from one stool to the other, and drew up the first after me with a hooked stick. By this contrivance I got into the inmost court; and lying down upon my side, I applied my face to the windows of the middle storeys, which were left open on purpose, and saw the most splendid apartments that can be imagined. There I saw the Empress and the young Princes, in their several lodgings, with their chief attendants about them. Her Imperial Majesty was pleased to smile very graciously upon me, and gave me out of the window her hand to kiss.

IV

GULLIVER GOES TO WAR

After Gulliver has been in Lilliput for some time, he becomes involved in a war between Lilliput and the neighbouring island of Blefuscu.

The Empire of Blefuscu is an island situated to the north-north-east side of Lilliput, from whence it is parted only by a channel eight hundred yards wide. I had not yet seen it, and when I heard of an intended invasion, I avoided appearing on that side of the coast, for fear of being discovered by some of the enemy's ships, who had received no intelligence of me, all intercourse between the two empires having been strictly forbidden during the war, upon pain of death. I communicated to his Majesty a project I had formed of seizing the enemy's whole fleet: which, as our scouts assured us, lay at anchor in the harbour ready to sail with the first fair wind. I consulted the most experienced seamen, upon the depth of the channel. They told me that in the middle at high-water it was seventy *glumgluffs* deep, which is about six foot of European measure; and the rest of it fifty *glumgluffs* at the most. I walked towards the north-east coast over against Blefuscu; and lying down behind a hillock, took out my small pocket perspective-glass, and viewed the enemy's fleet at anchor, consisting of about fifty men of war, and a great number of transports. I then came back to my house, and gave order (for which I had a warrant) for a great quantity of the strongest cable and bars of iron. The cable was about as thick as packthread, and the bars of the length and size of a knitting-needle. I trebled the cable to make it stronger, and for the same reason I twisted three of the iron bars together, binding the extremities into a hook. Having thus fixed fifty hooks to as many cables, I went back to the north-east coast, and putting off my coat, shoes, and stockings, walked into the sea in my leathern jerkin, about half an hour before high water. I waded with what haste I could, and swam in the middle about thirty yards till I felt ground; I arrived at the fleet in less than half an hour. The enemy was so frightened when they saw me, that they leaped out of their ships, and swam to shore, where there could not be fewer than thirty thousand souls. I then took my tackling, and fastening a hook to the hole at the prow of each, I tied all the cords together at the end. While I was thus employed, the enemy discharged several thousand arrows, many of which stuck in my hands and face; and besides the excessive smart, gave me much disturbance in my work. My greatest apprehension was for my eyes, which I should have infallibly lost, if I had not suddenly thought of an expedient. I kept among other little necessaries a pair of spectacles in a private pocket, which, as I observed before, had escaped the Emperor's searchers. These I took out and fastened as strongly as I could upon my nose, and thus armed went on boldly with my work in spite of the enemy's arrows, many of which struck against the glasses of my spectacles, but without any other effect, further than a little to discompose them. I had now fastened all the hooks, and taking the knot in my hand, began to pull; but not a ship would stir, for they were all too fast held by their anchors, so that the boldest part of my enterprise remained. I therefore let go the cord, and leaving the hooks fixed to the ships, I resolutely cut with my knife the cables that fastened the anchors, receiving above two hundred shots in my face and hands; then I took up the knotted end of the cables to which my hooks were tied, and with great ease drew fifty of the enemy's largest men-of-war after me.

The Blefuscudians, who had not the least imagination of what I intended, were at first confounded with astonishment. They had seen me cut the cables, and thought my design was only to let the ships run a-drift, or fall foul on each other: but when they perceived the whole fleet moving in order, and saw me pulling at the end, they set up such a scream of grief and despair, that it is almost impossible to describe or conceive. When I had got out of danger, I stopped awhile to pick out the arrows that stuck in my hands and face, and rubbed on some of the same ointment that was given me at my first arrival, as I have formerly mentioned. I then took off my spectacles, and waiting about an hour, till the tide was a little fallen, I waded through the middle with my cargo, and arrived safe at the royal port of Lilliput.

The Emperor and his whole court stood on the shore expecting the issue of this great adventure. They saw the ships move forward in a large half-moon, but could not discern me, who was up to my breast in water. When I advanced to the middle of the channel, they were yet in more pain, because I was under water to my neck. The Emperor concluded me to be drowned, and that the enemy's fleet was approaching in a hostile manner: but he was soon eased of his fears, for

the channel growing shallower every step I made, I came in a short time within hearing, and holding up the end of the cable by which the fleet was fastened, I cried in a loud voice, *Long live the most puissant Emperor of Lilliput!* This great prince received me at my landing with all possible praise, and created me a *Nardac* upon the spot, which is the highest title of honour among them.

V

GULLIVER COMES HOME

After a quarrel with the Emperor Gulliver leaves Lilliput for Blefuscu.

Three days after my arrival in Blefuscu, walking out of curiosity to the north-east coast of the island, I observed, about half a league off, in the sea, something that looked like a boat overturned. I pulled off my shoes and stockings, and wading two or three hundred yards, I found the object to approach nearer by force of the tide; and then plainly saw it to be a real boat, which I supposed might, by some tempest, have been driven from a ship. I returned immediately towards the city, and desired his Imperial Majesty to lend me twenty of the tallest vessels he had left after the loss of his fleet, and three thousand seamen under the command of his Vice-Admiral. This fleet sailed round, while I went back the shortest way to the coast where I first discovered the boat; I found the tide had driven it still nearer. The seamen were all provided with cordage, which I had beforehand twisted to a sufficient strength. When the ships came up, I stripped myself, and waded till I came within a hundred yards of the boat, after which I was forced to swim till I got up to it. The seamen threw me the end of the cord, which I fastened to a hole in the fore-part of the boat, and the other end to a man of war; but I found all my labour to little purpose; for being out of my depth, I was not able to work. In this necessity, I was forced to swim behind, and push the boat forwards as often as I could, with one of my hands; and the tide favouring me, I advanced so far, that I could just hold up my chin and feel the ground. I rested two or three minutes, and then gave the boat another shove, and so on till the sea was no higher than my arm-pits; and now the most laborious part being over, I took out my other cables, which were stowed in one of the ships, and fastening them first to the boat, and then to nine of the vessels which attended me; the wind being favourable, the seamen towed, and I shoved till we arrived within forty yards of the shore; and waiting till the tide was out, I got dry to the boat, and by the assistance of two thousand men, with ropes and engines, I made a shift to turn it on its bottom, and found it was but little damaged.

I shall not trouble the reader with the difficulties I was under to get my boat to the royal port of Blefuscu, where a mighty concourse of people appeared upon my arrival, full of wonder at the sight of so huge a vessel. I told the Emperor of Blefuscu that my good fortune had thrown this boat in my way, to carry me to some place from whence I might return to my native country, and begged his Majesty's orders for getting materials to fit it up, together with his licence to depart; which, after some kind words, he was pleased to grant.

I did very much wonder, in all this time, not to have heard of any express relating to me from the Emperor of Lilliput. But I was afterwards given privately to understand, that his Imperial Majesty believed I would return to Lilliput in a few days. But he was at last in pain at my long absence; and after consulting with the Treasurer, and the rest of that cabal, a person of quality was dispatched with the copy of the articles against me. This envoy had instructions to represent to the monarch of Blefuscu the great mercy of his master, who was content to punish me no farther than with the loss of my eyes; that I had fled from justice, and if I did not return in two hours, I should be deprived of my title of *Nardac*, and declared a traitor. The envoy further added, that in order to maintain the peace and amity between both empires, his master expected, that his brother of Blefuscu would give orders to have me sent back to Lilliput, bound hand and foot, to be punished as a traitor.

The Emperor of Blefuscu having taken three days to consult, returned an answer consisting of many civilities and excuses. He said, that as for sending me bound, his brother knew it was impossible; that although I had deprived him of his fleet, yet he owed great obligations to me for many good offices I had done him in making the peace. That however both their Majesties would soon be made easy; for I had found a boat on the shore, able to carry me on the sea, which he had given order to fit up with my own assistance and direction; and he hoped in a few weeks both empires would be freed from so large an encumbrance.

With this answer the envoy returned to Lilliput, and the monarch of Blefuscu related to me all that had passed, offering me at the same time (but under the strictest confidence) his gracious protection, if I would continue in his service. Although I believed him sincere, yet I resolved never more to put any confidence in princes or ministers, where I could possibly avoid it; and therefore, with all due acknowledgements for his favourable intentions, I humbly begged to be excused. I told him that since fortune, whether good or evil, had thrown a vessel in my way, I was resolved to venture myself in the ocean, rather than be an occasion of difference between two such mighty monarchs. Neither did I find the Emperor at all displeased; and I discovered by a certain accident, that he was very glad of my resolution, and so were most of his ministers.

These considerations moved me to hasten my departure somewhat sooner than I intended; to which the court, impatient to have me gone, very readily contributed. Five hundred workmen were employed to make two sails to my boat, according to my directions, by quilting thirteen fold of their strongest linen together. I was at the pains of making ropes and cables, by twisting ten, twenty or thirty of the thickest and strongest of theirs. A great stone that I happened to find, after a long search, by the sea-shore, served me for an anchor. I had the tallow of three hundred cows for greasing my boat, and other uses. I was at incredible pains in cutting down some of the largest timber-trees for oars and masts, wherein I was, however, much assisted by his

Majesty's ship-carpenters, who helped me in smoothing them, after I had done the rough work.

In about a month, when all was prepared, I sent to receive his Majesty's commands, and to take my leave. The Emperor and Royal Family came out of the palace; I lay down on my face to kiss his hand, which he very graciously gave me: so did the Empress and young Princes of the blood. His Majesty presented me with fifty purses of two hundred *sprugs* a-piece, together with his picture at full length, which I put immediately into one of my gloves, to keep it from being hurt. The ceremonies at my departure were too many to trouble the reader with at this time.

I stored the boat with the carcases of a hundred oxen, and three hundred sheep, with bread and drink in proportion, and as much meat ready dressed as four hundred cooks could provide. I took with me six cows and two bulls alive, with as many ewes and rams, intending to carry them into my own country, and propagate the breed. And to feed them on board, I had a good bundle of hay, and a bag of corn. I would gladly have taken a dozen of the natives, but this was a thing the Emperor would by no means permit; and besides a diligent search into my pockets, his Majesty engaged my honour not to carry away any of his subjects, although with their own consent and desire.

Having thus prepared all things as well as I was able, I set sail on the twenty-fourth day of September 1701, at six in the morning; and when I had gone about four leagues to the northward, the wind being at south-east, at six in the evening I spotted a small island about half a league to the north-west. I advanced forward, and cast anchor on the lee-side of the island, which seemed to be uninhabited. I then took some refreshment, and went to my rest. I slept well. I ate my breakfast before the sun was up; and heaving anchor, the wind being favourable, I steered the same course that I had done the day before, wherein I was directed by my pocket-compass. My intention was to reach, if possible, one of those islands, which I had reason to believe lay to the north-east of Van Diemen's Land. I discovered nothing all that day; but upon the next, about three in the afternoon, when I had by my computation made twenty-four leagues from Blefuscu, I saw a sail steering to the south-east; my course was due east. I hailed her, but could get no answer; yet I found I gained upon her, for the wind slackened. I made all the sail I could, and in half an hour she noticed me, then hung out her ancient, and discharged a gun. It is not easy to express the joy I felt at the idea of once more seeing my beloved country, and the dear pledges I had left in it. The ship slackened her sails, and I came up with her between five and six in the evening, September 26; but my heart leaped within me to see her English colours. I put my cows and sheep into my coat-pockets, and got on board with all my little cargo of provisions. The vessel was an English merchantman, returning from Japan by the North and South Seas; the Captain, Mr John Biddle of Deptford, a very civil man, and an excellent sailor. We were now in the latitude of 30 degrees south; there were about fifty men in the ship; and here I met an old comrade of mine, one Peter Williams, who gave me a good character to the Captain. This gentleman treated me with kindness, and desired I would let him know what place I came from last, and where I was bound; which I did in few words, but he though I was raving, and that the dangers I underwent had disturbed my head. I took my black cattle and sheep out of my pocket, which, after great astonishment, clearly convinced him of my truthfulness. I then showed him the gold given me by the Emperor of Blefuscu, together with his Majesty's picture at full length, and some other rarities of that country. I gave him two purses of two hundred *sprugs* each, and promised, when we arrived in England, to make him a present of a cow and a sheep big with young.

I shall not trouble the reader with a particular account of this voyage, which was very prosperous for the most part. We arrived in the Downs on the 13th of April, 1702. I had only one misfortune, that the rats on board carried away one of my sheep; I found her bones in a hole, picked clean from the flesh. The rest of my cattle I got safe on shore and set them a grazing in a bowling-green at Greenwich, where the fineness of the grass made them feed very heartily.

Robinson Crusoe

DANIEL DEFOE
Illustrated by Thomas Stothard

Robinson Crusoe *(1719) was based on the adventures of Alexander Selkirk, who had been set ashore on a desert island fifteen years earlier and had remained there for five years. In Defoe's book, Crusoe is the only survivor of a shipwreck.*

I

THE WRECKED SHIP

The wave that came upon me again buried me at once twenty or thirty feet deep in its own body, and I could feel myself carried with a mighty force and swiftness towards the shore a very great way; but I held my breath and assisted myself to swim still forward with all my might. I was ready to burst with holding my breath, when, as I felt myself rising up, so to my immediate relief I found my head and hands shoot out above the surface of the water; and though it was not two seconds of time that I could keep myself so, yet it relieved me greatly, gave me breath and new courage. I was covered again with water a good while, but not so long but I held it out; and finding the water had spent itself and begun to return, I struck forward against the return of the waves, and felt ground again with my feet. I stood still a few moments to recover breath, and till the water went from me, and then took my heels and ran with what strength I had further towards the shore. But neither would this deliver me from the fury of the sea, which came pouring in after me again, and twice more I was lifted up by the waves and carried forward as before, the shore being very flat.

The last time of these two had well near been fatal to me, for the sea having hurried me along as before, landed me, or rather dashed me,

I resolved to hold fast by a piece of the rock

against a piece of a rock, and that with such force as it left me senseless and indeed helpless as to my own deliverance; for the blow taking my side and breast, beat the breath as it were quite out of my body, and had it returned again immediately, I must have been strangled in the water; but I recovered a little before the return of the waves, and seeing I should be covered again with the water, I resolved to hold fast by a piece of the rock, and so to hold my breath, if possible, till the wave went back. Now as the waves were not so high as at first, being near land, I held my hold till the wave abated, and then fetched another run, which brought me so near the shore that the next wave, though it went over me, yet did not so swallow me up as to carry me away; and the next run I took I got to the mainland, where, to my great comfort, I clambered up the cliffs of the shore and sat me down upon the grass, free from danger, and quite out of the reach of the water.

I was now landed, and safe on shore, and began to look up and thank God that my life was saved in a case wherein there was some minutes before scarce any room to hope.

I walked about on the shore lifting up my hands, and my whole being, as I may say, wrapped up in the contemplation of my deliverance, making a thousand gestures and motions which I cannot describe, reflecting upon all my comrades that were drowned, and that there should not be a soul saved but myself; for, as for them, I never saw them afterwards, or any sign of them, except three of their hats, one cap, and two shoes that were not fellows.

I cast my eyes to the stranded vessel, when the breach and froth of the sea being so big I could hardly see it, it lay so far off, and considered, 'Lord, how was it possible I could get on shore?'

After I had solaced my mind with the comfortable part of my condition, I began to look round me to see what kind of place I was in, and what was next to be done, and I soon found my comforts abate, and that in a word I had a dreadful deliverance, for I was wet, had no clothes to shift me, nor anything either to eat or drink to comfort me, neither did I see any prospect before me but that of perishing with hunger or being devoured by wild beasts. And that which was particularly afflicting to me was, that I had no weapon either to hunt and kill any creature for my sustenance, or to defend myself against any other creature that might desire to kill me for theirs – in a word, I had nothing about me but a knife, a tobacco-pipe, and a little tobacco in a box. This was all my provision, and this threw me into terrible agonies of mind, that for a while I ran about like a madman. Night coming upon me, I began with a heavy heart to consider what would be my lot if there were any ravenous beasts in that country, seeing at night they always come abroad for their prey.

All the remedy that offered to my thoughts at that time was to get up into a thick bushy tree like a fir, but thorny, which grew near me, and where I resolved to sit all night, and consider the next day what death I should die, for as yet I saw no prospect of life. I walked about a furlong from the shore to see if I could find any fresh water to drink, which I did, to my great joy; and having drunk, and put a little tobacco in my mouth to prevent hunger, I went to the tree, and getting up into it, endeavoured to place myself so as that if I should sleep I might not fall; and having cut me a short stick like a truncheon for my defence, I took up my lodging, and having been excessively fatigued, I fell fast asleep, and slept as comfortably as, I believe, few could have done in my condition, and found myself the most refreshed with it that I think I ever was on such an occasion.

*   *   *   *

When I waked it was broad day, the weather clear, and the storm abated, so that the sea did not rage and swell as before; but that which surprised me most was, that the ship was lifted off in the night from the sand where she lay by the swelling of the tide, and was driven up almost as far as the rock which I first mentioned, where I had been so bruised by the sea dashing me against it. This being within about a mile from the shore where I was, and the ship seeming to stand upright still, I wished myself on board, that at least I might have some necessary things for my use.

When I came down from my apartment in the tree, I looked about me again, and the first thing I found was the boat, which lay as the wind and the sea had tossed her up upon the land, about two miles on my right hand. I walked as far as I could upon the shore to have got to her, but found a neck or inlet of water between me and the boat which was about half a mile broad; so I came back for the present, being more intent upon getting at the ship, where I hoped to find something for my present subsistence.

A little after noon I found the sea very calm and the tide ebbed so far out that I could come within a quarter of a mile of the ship. And here I found a fresh renewing of my grief, for I saw evidently that if we had kept on board we had been all safe – that is to say, we had all got safe on shore, and I had not been so miserable as to be left entirely destitute of all comfort and company as I now was. This forced tears from my eyes again, but as there was little relief in that, I resolved, if possible, to get to the ship; so I pulled off my clothes, for the weather was hot to extremity, and took the water. But when I came to the ship, my difficulty was still greater to know how to get on board; for as she lay aground and high out of the water, there was nothing within my reach to lay hold of. I swam round her twice, and the second time I spied a small piece of a rope, which I wondered I did not see at first, hang down by the fore-chains so low as that with great difficulty I got hold of it, and by the help of that rope got up into the forecastle of the ship. Here I found that the ship was bulged, and had a great deal of water in her hold, but that she lay so on the side of a bank of hard sand, or rather earth, that her stern lay lifted up upon the bank, and her head low almost to the water. By this means all her quarter was free, and all that was in that part was dry; for you may be sure my first work was to search and to see what was spoiled and what was free. And first I found that all the ship's provisions were dry and untouched by the water, and being very well disposed to eat, I went to the bread-room and filled my pockets with biscuit, and ate it as I went about other things, for I had no time to lose. I also found some rum in the great cabin, of which I took a large dram, and which I had indeed need enough of to spirit me for what was before me. Now I wanted nothing but a boat to furnish myself with many things which I foresaw would be very necessary to me.

It was in vain to sit still and wish for what was not to be had, and this extremity roused my application. We had several spare yards, and two or three large spars of wood, and a spare topmast or two in the ship. I resolved to fall to work with these, and flung as many of them overboard as I could manage for their weight, tying every one with a rope that they might not drive away. When this was done I went down the ship's side, and pulling them to me, I tied four of them fast together at both ends as well as I could, in the form of a raft, and laying two or three short pieces of plank upon them crossways, I found I could walk upon it very well, but that it was not able to bear any great weight, the pieces being too light. So I went to work, and with the carpenter's saw I cut a spare topmast into three lengths, and added them to my raft, with a great deal of labour and pains; but hope of furnishing myself with necessaries encouraged me to go beyond what I should have been able to have done upon another occasion.

My raft was now strong enough to bear any reasonable weight. My next care was what to load it with, and how to preserve what I laid upon it from the surf of the sea. But I was not long considering this. I first laid all the planks or boards upon it that I could get, and having considered well what I most wanted, I first got three of the seamen's chests, which I had broken open and emptied, and lowered them down upon my raft. The first of these I filled with provisions – namely, bread, rice, three Dutch cheeses, five pieces of dried goat's flesh, which we lived much upon, and a little remainder of European corn, which had been laid by for some fowls which we brought to sea with us; but the fowls were killed. There had been some barley and wheat together, but to my great disappointment I found afterwards that the rats had eaten or spoiled it all. As for liquors, I found several cases of bottles belonging to our skipper, in which were some cordial waters, and in all about five or six gallons of rack. These I stowed by themselves, there being no need to put them into the chest, and no room for them. While I was doing this I found the tide began to flow, though very calm, and I had the mortification to see my coat, shirt, and waistcoat, which I had left on shore upon the sand, swim away; as for my breeches, which were only linen and open-kneed, I swam on board in them and my stockings. However, this put me on rummaging for clothes, of which I found enough, but took no more than I wanted for present use, for I had other things which my eye was more upon – as, first, tools to work with on shore; and it was after long searching that I found out the carpenter's chest, which was indeed a very useful prize to me, and much more valuable than a ship loading of gold would have been at that time. I got it down to my raft even whole as it was, without losing time to look into it, for I knew in general what it contained.

My next care was for some ammunition and arms. There were two very good fowling-pieces in the great cabin, and two pistols; these I secured first, with some powder-horns, and a small bag of shot, and two old rusty swords. I knew there were three barrels of powder in the ship, but knew not where our gunner had stowed them; but with much search I found them, two of them dry and good – the third had taken water. Those two I got to my raft with the arms; and now I thought myself pretty well freighted, and began to think how I should get to shore with them, having neither sail, oar, nor rudder, and the least capful of wind would have overset all my navigation.

I had three encouragements – first, a smooth calm sea; second, the tide rising and setting in to the shore; third, what little wind there was blew me towards the land. And thus, having found two or three broken oars belonging to the boat, and besides the tools which were in the chest, I found two saws, an axe, and a hammer, and with this cargo I put to sea. For a mile or thereabouts my raft went very well, only that I found it drive a little distant from the place where I had landed before; by which I perceived that there was some indraught of the water, and consequently I hoped to find some creek or river there, which I might make use of as a port to get to land with my cargo.

As I imagined, so it was. There appeared before me a little opening of the land, and I found a strong current of the tide set into it; so I guided my raft as well as I could to keep in the middle of the stream. But here I had like to have suffered a second shipwreck, which if I had, I think verily would have broken my heart; for, knowing nothing of the coast, my raft ran aground at one end of it upon a shoal, and not being aground at the other end, it wanted but a little that all my cargo had slipped off towards that end that was afloat, and so fallen into the water. I did my utmost, by setting my back against the chests, to keep them in their places, but could not thrust off the raft with all my strength, neither durst I stir from the posture I was in, but holding up the chests with all my might, stood in that manner near half an hour, in which time the rising of the water brought me a little more upon a level; and a little after, the water still rising, my raft floated again, and I thrust her off with the oar I had into the channel, and then driving up higher, I at length found myself in the mouth of a little river, with land on both sides, and a strong current or tide running up. I looked on both sides for a proper place to get to shore, for I was not willing to be driven too high up the river, hoping in time to see some ship at sea, and therefore resolved to place myself as near the coast as I could.

At length I spied a little cove on the right shore of the creek, to which with great pain and difficulty I guided my raft, and at last got so near as that, reaching ground with my oar, I could thrust her directly in. But here I had like to have dipped all my cargo in the sea again; for that shore lying pretty steep – that is to say, sloping – there was no place to land but where one end of my float, if it ran on shore, would lie so high, and the other sink lower as before, that it would endanger my cargo again. All that I could do was to wait till the tide was at the highest, keeping the raft with my oar like an anchor to hold the side of it fast to the shore, near a flat piece of ground, which I expected the water would flow over; and so it did. As soon as I found water enough – for my raft drew about a foot of water – I thrust her on upon that flat piece of ground, and there fastened or moored her by sticking my two broken oars into the ground, one on one side near one end, and one on the other side near the other end; and thus I lay till the water ebbed away, and left my raft and all my cargo safe on shore.

★　　★　　★　　★

My next work was to view the country, and seek a proper place for my habitation, and where to stow my goods to secure them from whatever might happen. Where I was I yet knew not, whether on the continent or on an island, whether inhabited or not inhabited, whether in danger of wild beasts or not. There was a hill not above a mile from me, which rose up very steep and high, and which seemed to overtop some other hills which lay as in a ridge from it northward. I took out one of the fowling-pieces and one of the pistols, and a horn of powder, and thus armed I travelled for discovery up to the top of that hill, where, after I had with great labour and difficulty got to the top, I saw that I was in an island, environed every way with the sea, no land to be seen, except some rocks which lay a great way off, and two small islands, less than this, which lay about three leagues to the west.

I found also that the island I was in was barren, and, as I saw good reason to believe, uninhabited, except by wild beasts, of which, however, I saw none; yet I saw abundance of fowls, but knew not their kinds, neither when I killed them could I tell what was fit for food and what not. At my coming back, I shot at a great bird which I saw sitting upon a tree on the side of a great wood. I believe it was the first gun that had been fired there since the creation of the world. I had no sooner fired, but from all the parts of the wood there arose an innumerable number of fowls of many sorts, making a confused screaming, and crying every one according to his usual note, but not one of them of any kind that I knew. As for the creature I killed, I took it to be a kind of a hawk, its colour and beak resembling it, but it had no talons or claws more than common; its flesh was carrion, and fit for nothing.

Contented with this discovery, I came back to my raft, and fell to work to bring my cargo on shore, which took me up the rest of that day. But what to do with myself at night I knew not, nor indeed where to rest; for I was afraid to lie down on the ground, not knowing but some wild beast might devour me, though as I afterwards found, there was really no need for those fears.

However, as well as I could, I barricaded myself round with the chests and boards that I had brought on shore, and made a kind of hut for that night's lodging. As for food, I yet saw not which way to supply myself, except that I had seen two or three creatures like hares run out of the wood where I shot the fowl.

I now began to consider that I might yet get a great many things out of the ship which would be useful to me, and particularly some of the rigging and sails, and such other things as might come to land; and I resolved to make another voyage on board the vessel, if possible; and as I knew that the first storm that blew must necessarily break her all in pieces, I resolved to set all other things apart until I got everything out of the ship that I could get. Then I called a council—that is to say, in my thoughts – whether I should take back the raft; but this appeared impracticable. So I resolved to go as before, when the tide was down; and I did so, only that I stripped before I went from my hut, having nothing on but a checkered shirt, and a pair of linen drawers, and a pair of pumps on my feet. I got on board the ship as before, and prepared a second raft; and having had experience of the first, I neither made this so unwieldy nor loaded it so hard, but yet I brought away several things very useful to me. As first, in the carpenter's stores, I found two or three bags full of nails and spikes, a great screw-jack, a dozen or two of hatchets, and, above all, that most useful thing called a grindstone. All these I secured together, with several things belonging to the gunner, particularly two or three iron crows, and two barrels of musket-bullets, seven muskets, and another fowling-piece, with some small quantity of powder more, a large bag full of small shot, and a great roll of sheet lead. But this last was so heavy I could not hoist it up to get it over the ship's side.

Besides these things I took all the men's clothes that I could find, and a spare fore-topsail, a hammock, and some bedding; and with this I loaded my second raft, and brought them all safe on shore, to my very great comfort.

I was under some apprehensions during my absence from the land that at least my provisions might be devoured on shore; but when I came back I found no sign of any visitor, only there sat a creature like a wild cat upon one of the chests, which, when I came towards it, ran away a little distance, and then stood still. She sat very composed and

Ferrying the raft

unconcerned, and looked full in my face, as if she had a mind to be acquainted with me. I presented my gun at her; but as she did not understand it, she was perfectly unconcerned at it, nor did she offer to stir away. Upon which I tossed her a bit of biscuit – though, by the way, I was not very free of it, for my store was not great. However, I spared her a bit, I say, and she went to it, smelled of it, and ate it, and looked, as pleased, for more; but I thanked her, and could spare no more. So she marched off.

Having got my second cargo on shore, though I was fain to open the barrels of powder, and bring them by parcels – for they were too heavy, being large casks – I went to work to make me a little tent with the sail and some poles which I cut for that purpose; and into this tent I brought everything that I knew would spoil either with rain or sun, and I piled all the empty chests and casks up in a circle round the tent, to fortify it from any sudden attempt either from man or beast.

When I had done this, I blocked up the door of the tent with some boards within, and an empty chest set up on end without, and spreading one of the beds upon the ground, laying my two pistols just at my head, and my gun at length by me, I went to bed for the first time, and slept very quietly all night, for I was very weary and heavy, for the night before I had slept little, and had laboured very hard all day, as well to fetch all those things from the ship as to get them on shore.

I had the biggest magazine of all kinds now that ever were laid up, I believe, for one man; but I was not satisfied still, for while the ship sat upright in that posture, I thought I ought to get everything out of her that I could; so every day at low water I went on board, and brought away something or other. But particularly the third time I went I brought away as much of the rigging as I could, as also all the small ropes and rope-twine I could get, with a piece of spare canvas, which was to mend the sails upon occasion, the barrel of wet gunpowder; in a word, I brought away all the sails first and last, only that I was fain to cut them in pieces, and bring as much at a time as I could, for they were no more useful to be sails, but as mere canvas only.

But that which comforted me still more was, that at last of all, after I had made five or six such voyages as these, and thought I had nothing more to expect from the ship that was worth my meddling with – I say, after all this, I found a great hogshead of bread, and three large runlets of rum or spirits, and a box of sugar, and a barrel of fine flour. This was surprising to me, because I had given over expecting any more provisions, excepting what was spoiled by the water. I soon emptied the hogshead of that bread, and wrapped it up parcel by parcel in pieces of the sails, which I cut out; and in a word, I got all this safe on shore also.

The next day I made another voyage; and now having plundered the ship of what was portable and fit to hand out, I began with the cables; and cutting the great cable into pieces such as I could move, I got two cables and a hawser on shore, with all the iron-work I could get; and having cut down the spritsail-yard, and the mizzenyard, and everything I could to make a large raft, I loaded it with all those heavy goods, and came away. But my good luck began now to leave me, for this raft was so unwieldy and so overloaden that after I was entered the little cove where I had landed the rest of my goods, not being able to guide it so handily as I did the other, it overset, and threw me and all my cargo into the water. As for myself, it was no great harm, for I was near the shore; but as to my cargo, it was great part of it lost, especially the iron, which I expected would have been of great use to me. However, when the tide was out, I got most of the pieces of cable ashore, and some of the iron, though with infinite labour, for I was fain to dip for it into the water, a work which fatigued me very much. After this I went every day on board, and brought away what I could get.

I had been now thirteen days on shore, and had been eleven times on board the ship, in which time I had brought away all that one pair of hands could well be supposed capable to bring; though I believe verily, had the calm weather held, I should have brought away the whole ship piece by piece. But preparing the twelfth time to go on board, I found the wind begin to rise. However, at low water, I went on board; and though I thought I had rummaged the cabin so effectually as that nothing more could be found, yet I discovered a locker with drawers in it, in one of which I found two or three razors and one pair of large scissors, with some ten or a dozen of good knives and forks; in another I found about thirty-six pounds value in money, some European coin, some Brazil, some pieces of eight, some gold, some silver.

I smiled to myself at the sight of this money. 'O drug!' said I aloud, 'what art thou good for? Thou art not worth to me, no not the taking off of the ground; one of these knives is worth all this heap. I have no manner of use for thee; even remain where thou art, and go to the bottom as a creature whose life is not worth saving.' However, upon second thoughts, I took it away, and wrapping all this in a piece of canvas, I began to think of making another raft; but while I was preparing this, I found the sky overcast, and the wind began to rise, and in a quarter of an hour it blew a fresh gale from the shore. It presently occurred to me that it was in vain to pretend to make a raft with the wind off shore, and that it was my business to be gone before the tide of flood began, otherwise I might not be able to reach the shore at all. Accordingly I let myself down into the water, and swam across the channel which lay between the ship and the sands, and even that with difficulty enough, partly with the weight of the things I had about me, and partly the roughness of the water, for the wind rose very hastily, and before it was quite high water it blew a storm.

But I was gotten home to my little tent, where I lay with all my wealth about me very secure. It blew very hard all that night; and in the morning when I looked out, behold, no more ship was to be seen! I was a little surprised, but recovered myself with this satisfactory reflection – namely, that I had lost no time, nor abated diligence to get everything out of her that could be useful to me, and that indeed there was little left in her that I was able to bring away, if I had had more time.

II

SETTING UP HOME ON THE ISLAND

I now gave over any more thoughts of the ship, or of anything out of her, except what might drive on shore from her wreck, as indeed divers pieces of her afterwards did; but those things were of small use to me.

My thoughts were now wholly employed about securing myself against either savages, if any should appear, or wild beasts, if any were in the island; and I had many thoughts of the method how to do this, and what kind of dwelling to make – whether I should make me a cave in the earth or a tent upon the earth. And, in short, I resolved upon both.

I soon found the place I was in was not for my settlement, particularly because it was upon a low moorish ground near the sea, and I believed would not be wholesome, and more particularly because there was no fresh water near it; so I resolved to find a more healthy and more convenient spot of ground.

I consulted several things in my situation which I found would be proper for me. First, health, and fresh water I just now mentioned. Secondly, shelter from the heat of the sun. Thirdly, security from ravenous creatures, whether men or beasts. Fourthly, a view to the sea, that if God sent any ship in sight I might not lose any advantage for my deliverance, of which I was not willing to banish all my expectation yet.

In search of a place proper for this, I found a little plain on the side of a rising hill, whose front towards this little plain was steep as a house-side, so that nothing could come down upon me from the top. On the side of this rock there was a hollow place worn a little way in like the entrance or door of a cave; but there was not really any cave or way into the rock at all.

On the flat of the green, just before this hollow place, I resolved to pitch my tent. This plain was not above a hundred yards broad, and about twice as long, and lay like a green before my door, and at the end of it descended irregularly every way down into the low grounds by the seaside. It was on the north-north-west side of the hill, so that I was sheltered from the heat every day till it came to a west and by south sun, or thereabouts, which in those countries is near the setting.

Before I set up my tent, I drew a half-circle before the hollow place, which took in about ten yards in its semi-diameter from the rock, and twenty yards in its diameter from its beginning and ending.

In this half-circle I pitched two rows of strong stakes, driving them into the ground till they stood very firm like piles, the biggest end being out of the ground about five feet and a half, and sharpened on the top. The two rows did not stand above six inches from one another.

Then I took the pieces of cable which I had cut in the ship, and laid them in rows one upon another within the circle, between these two rows of stakes, up to the top, placing other stakes in the inside, leaning against them, about two feet and a half high, like a spur to a post; and this fence was so strong that neither man nor beast could get into it or over it. This cost me a great deal of time and labour, especially to cut the piles in the wood, bring them to the place, and drive them into the earth.

The entrance into this place I made to be, not by a door, but by a short ladder to go over the top; which ladder, when I was in, I lifted over after me. And so I was completely fenced in and fortified, as I thought, from all the world, and consequently slept secure in the night, which otherwise I could not have done; though, as it appeared afterwards, there was no need of all this caution from the enemies that I apprehended danger from.

Into this fence or fortress, with infinite labour, I carried all my riches, all my provisions, ammunition, and stores, of which you have the account above. And I made me a large tent, which, to preserve me from the rains that in one part of the year are very violent there, I made double – namely, one smaller tent within, and one larger tent above it, and covered the uppermost with a large tarpaulin which I had saved among the sails.

And now I lay no more for a while in the bed which I had brought on shore, but in a hammock, which was indeed a very good one, and belonged to the mate of the ship.

Into this tent I brought all my provisions and everything that would spoil by the wet; and having thus enclosed all my goods, I made up the entrance, which till now I had left open, and so passed and repassed, as I said, by a short ladder.

When I had done this, I began to work my way into the rock, and bringing all the earth and stones that I dug down out through my tent, I laid them up within my fence in the nature of a terrace, that so it raised the ground within about a foot and a half; and thus I made me a cave just behind my tent, which served me like a cellar to my house.

It cost me much labour and many days before all these things were brought to perfection, and therefore I must go back to some other things which took up some of my thoughts. At the same time it happened after I had laid my scheme for the setting up my tent, and making the cave, that a storm of rain falling from a thick dark cloud, a sudden flash of lightning happened, and after that a great clap of thunder. I was not so much surprised with the lightning as I was with a thought which darted into my mind as swift as the lightning itself – Oh, my powder! My very heart sank within me when I thought that at one blast all my powder might be destroyed, on which not my defence only, but the providing me food, as I thought, entirely depended. I was nothing near so anxious about my own danger, though, had the powder taken fire, I had never known who had hurt me.

Such impression did this make upon me that after the storm was over I laid aside all my works, my building and fortifying, and applied myself to make bags and boxes to separate the powder and keep it a little and a little in a parcel, in hope that whatever might come it might not all take fire at once, and to keep it so apart that it should not be possible to make one part fire another. I finished this work in about a fortnight; and I think my powder, which in all was about two hundred and forty pounds weight, was divided in not less than a hundred parcels. As to the barrel that had been wet, I did not apprehend any danger from that; so I placed it in my new cave, which in my fancy I called my kitchen, and the rest I had up and down in holes among the rocks, so that no wet might come to it, marking very carefully where I laid it.

In the interval of time while this was doing, I went out once at least every day with my gun, as well to divert myself as to see if I could kill anything fit for food, and as near as I could to acquaint myself with what the island produced. The first time I went out I presently discovered that there were goats in the island, which was a great satisfaction to me; but then it was attended with this misfortune – namely, that they were so shy, so subtle, and so swift of foot that it was the difficultest thing in the world to come at them. But I was not discouraged at this, not doubting but I might now and then shoot one, as it soon happened; for after I had found their haunts a little, I laid wait in this manner for them: I observed if they saw me in the valleys, though they were upon the rocks, they would run away as in a terrible fright, but if they were feeding in the valleys, and I was upon the rocks, they took no notice of me; from whence I concluded that by the position of their optics their sight was so directed downward that they did not readily see objects that were above them. So afterwards I took this method. I always climbed the rocks first, to get above them, and then had frequently a fair mark. The first shot I made among these creatures I killed a she-goat which had a little kid by her which she gave suck to, which grieved me heartily. But when the old one fell the kid stood stock-still by her till I came and took her up; and not only so, but when I carried the old one with me upon my shoulders, the kid followed me quite to my enclosure: upon which I laid down the dam and took the kid in my arms, and carried it over my pale, in hopes to have bred it up tame; but it would not eat, so I was forced to kill it and eat it myself. These two supplied me with flesh a great while, for I ate sparingly, and saved my provisions (my bread especially) as much as possibly I could.

I had a dismal prospect of my condition; for as I was not cast away upon that island without being driven, as is said, by a violent storm quite out of the course of our intended voyage, and a great way – namely, some hundreds of leagues – out of the ordinary course of the trade of mankind, I had great reason to consider it as a determination of Heaven that in this desolate place and in this desolate manner I should end my life. The tears would run plentifully down my face when I made these reflections; and sometimes I would expostulate with myself why Providence should thus completely ruin its creatures and render them so absolutely miserable, so without help abandoned, so entirely depressed, that it could hardly be rational to be thankful for such a life.

But something always returned swift upon me to check these thoughts and to reprove me; and particularly one day, walking with my gun in my hand by the seaside, I was very pensive upon the subject of my present condition, when reason, as it were, expostulated with me the other way, thus: Well, you are in a desolate condition, it is true; but pray remember, where are the rest of you? Did not you come eleven of you into the boat? Where are the ten? Why were they not saved and you lost? Why were you singled out? Is it better to be here or there? And then I pointed to the sea. All evils are to be considered with the good that is in them, and with what worse attends them.

Then it occurred to me again how well I was furnished for my subsistence, and what would have been my case if it had not happened, which was a hundred thousand to one, that the ship floated from the place where she first struck, and was driven so near to the shore that I had time to get all those things out of her. What would have been my case if I had been to have lived in the condition in which I at first came on shore, without necessaries of life, or necessaries to supply and procure them? 'Particularly,' said I aloud (though to myself), 'what should I have done without a gun, without ammunition; without any tools to make anything, or to work with; without clothes, bedding, a tent, or any manner of covering?' And that now I had all these to a sufficient quantity, and was in a fair way to provide myself in such a manner as to live without my gun when my ammunition was spent; so that I had a tolerable view of subsisting without any want as long as I lived; for I considered from the beginning how I would provide for the accidents that might happen, and for the time that was to come, even not only after my ammunition should be spent, but even after my health or strength should decay.

I confess I had not entertained any notion of my ammunition being destroyed at one blast – I mean my powder being blown up by lightning – and this made the thoughts of it so surprising to me when it lightened and thundered, as I observed just now.

It was, by my account, the 30th of September when, in the manner as above said, I first set foot upon this horrid island, when the sun, being to us in its autumnal equinox, was almost just over my head; for I reckoned myself, by observation, to be in the latitude of 9° 22′ north of the line. After I had been there about ten or twelve days, it came into my thoughts that I should lose my reckoning of time for want of books and pen and ink, and should even forget the Sabbath days from the working days; but, to prevent this, I cut it with my knife upon a large post, in capital letters, and making it into a great cross, I set it up on the shore where I first landed – namely, 'I CAME ON SHORE HERE ON THE 30TH OF SEPTEMBER 1659.' Upon the sides of this square post I cut every day a notch with my knife, and every seventh notch was as long again as the rest, and every first day of the month as long again as that long one; and thus I kept my calendar, or weekly, monthly, and yearly reckoning of time.

Favourite Stories

The Land of Oz

FRANK BAUM
Illustrated by Kevin Maddison

The Wonderful Wizard of Oz (1900) was made into a famous film starring Judy Garland. This extract tells how Dorothy, the book's heroine, is magically transported by a cyclone from her Kansas farm to the Land of Oz, and how she sets off to find the Wizard of Oz – the only person who can tell her how to get home again.

I

THE CYCLONE

Dorothy lived in the midst of the great Kansas prairies, with Uncle Henry, who was a farmer, and Aunt Em, who was the farmer's wife. Their house was small, for the lumber to build it had to be carried by wagon many miles. There were four walls, a floor and a roof, which made one room; and this room contained a rusty looking cooking stove, a cupboard for the dishes, a table, three or four chairs, and the beds. Uncle Henry and Aunt Em had a big bed in one corner and Dorothy a little bed in another corner. There was no garret at all, and no cellar – except a small hole, dug in the ground, called a cyclone cellar, where the family could go in case one of those great whirlwinds arose, mighty enough to crush any building in its path. It was reached by a trap-door in the middle of the floor, from which a ladder led down into the small, dark hole.

When Dorothy stood in the doorway and looked around, she could see nothing but the great grey prairie on every side. Not a tree nor a house broke the broad sweep of flat country that reached the edge of the sky in all directions. The sun had baked the ploughed land into a grey mass, with little cracks running through it. Even the grass was not green, for the sun had burned the tops of the long blades until they were the same grey colour to be seen everywhere. Once the house had been painted, but the sun blistered the paint and the rains washed it away, and now the house was as dull and grey as everything else.

When Aunt Em came there to live she was a young pretty wife. The sun and wind had changed her, too. They had taken the sparkle from her eyes and left them a sober grey; they had taken the red from her cheeks and lips, and they were grey also. She was thin and gaunt, and never smiled, now. When Dorothy, who was an orphan, first came to her, Aunt Em had been so startled by the child's laughter that she would scream and press her hand upon her heart whenever Dorothy's merry voice reached her ears; and she still looked at the little girl with wonder that she could find anything to laugh at.

Uncle Henry never laughed. He worked hard from morning till night and did not know what joy was. He was grey also, from his long beard to his rough boots, and he looked stern and solemn, and rarely spoke.

It was Toto that made Dorothy laugh, and saved her from growing as grey as her other surroundings. Toto was not grey; he was a little black dog, with long silky hair and small black eyes that twinkled merrily on either side of his funny, wee nose. Toto played all day long, and Dorothy played with him, and loved him dearly.

Today, however, they were not playing. Uncle Henry sat upon the door-step and looked anxiously at the sky, which was even greyer than usual. Dorothy stood in the door with Toto in her arms, and looked at the sky too. Aunt Em was washing the dishes.

From the far north they heard a low wail of the wind, and Uncle Henry and Dorothy could see where the long grass bowed in waves before the coming storm. There now came a sharp whistling in the air from the south, and as they turned their eyes that way they saw ripples in the grass coming from that direction also.

Suddenly Uncle Henry stood up.

'There's a cyclone coming, Em,' he called to his wife: 'I'll go look

There came a great shriek from the wind

after the stock.' Then he ran towards the sheds where the cows and horses were kept.

Aunt Em dropped her work and came to the door. One glance told her of the danger close at hand.

'Quick, Dorothy!' she screamed; 'run for the cellar!'

Toto jumped out of Dorothy's arms and hid under the bed, and the girl started to get him. Aunt Em, badly frightened, threw open the trap-door in the floor and climbed down the ladder into the small, dark hole. Dorothy caught Toto at last, and started to follow her aunt. When she was half way across the room there came a great shriek from the wind, and the house shook so hard that she lost her footing and sat down suddenly upon the floor.

A strange thing then happened.

The house whirled around two or three times and rose slowly through the air. Dorothy felt as if she were going up in a balloon.

The north and south winds met where the house stood, and made it the exact centre of the cyclone. In the middle of a cyclone the air is generally still, but the great pressure of the wind on every side of the house raised it up higher and higher, until it was at the very top of the cyclone; and there it remained and was carried miles and miles away as easily as you could carry a feather.

It was very dark, and the wind howled horribly around her, but Dorothy found she was riding quite easily. After the first few whirls around, and one other time when the house tipped badly, she felt as if she were being rocked gently, like a baby in a cradle.

Toto did not like it. He ran about the room, now here, now there, barking loudly; but Dorothy sat quite still on the floor and waited to see what would happen.

Once Toto got too near the open trap-door, and fell in; and at first the little girl thought she had lost him. But soon she saw one of his ears sticking up through the hole, for the strong pressure of the air was keeping him up so that he could not fall. She crept to the hole, caught Toto by the ear, and dragged him into the room again; afterwards closing the trap-door so that no more accidents could happen.

Hour after hour passed away, and slowly Dorothy got over her fright; but she felt quite lonely, and the wind shrieked so loudly all about her that she nearly became deaf. At first she had wondered if she would be dashed to pieces when the house fell again; but as the hours passed and nothing terrible happened, she stopped worrying and resolved to wait calmly and see what the future would bring. At last she crawled over the swaying floor to her bed, and lay down upon it; and Toto followed and lay down beside her.

In spite of the swaying of the house and the wailing of the wind, Dorothy soon closed her eyes and fell fast asleep.

II

THE COUNCIL WITH THE MUNCHKINS

She was awakened by a shock, so sudden and severe that if Dorothy had not been lying on the soft bed she might have been hurt. As it was, the jar made her catch her breath and wonder what had happened; and Toto put his cold little nose into her face and whined dismally. Dorothy sat up and noticed that the house was not moving; nor was it dark, for the bright sunshine came in at the window, flooding the little room. She sprang from her bed and with Toto at her heels ran and opened the door.

The little girl gave a cry of amazement and looked about her, her eyes growing bigger and bigger at the wonderful sights she saw.

The cyclone had set the house down, very gently – for a cyclone – in the midst of a country of marvellous beauty. There were lovely patches of green sward all about, with stately trees bearing rich and luscious fruits. Banks of gorgeous flowers were on every hand, and birds with rare and brilliant plumage sang and fluttered in the trees and bushes. A little way off was a small brook, rushing and sparkling along between green banks, and murmuring in a voice very grateful to a little girl who had lived so long on the dry, grey prairies.

While she stood looking eagerly at the strange and beautiful sights, she noticed coming towards her a group of the queerest people she had ever seen. They were not as big as the grown folk she had always been used to; but neither were they very small. In fact, they seemed about as tall as Dorothy, who was a well-grown child for her age, although they were, so far as looks go, many years older.

Three were men and one a woman, and all were oddly dressed. They wore round hats that rose to a small point a foot above their heads, with little bells around the brims that tinkled sweetly as they moved. The hats of the men were blue; the little woman's hat was white, and she wore a white gown that hung in pleats from her shoulders; over it were sprinkled little stars that glistened in the sun like diamonds. The men were dressed in blue, of the same shade as their hats, and wore well polished boots with a deep roll of blue at the tops. The men, Dorothy thought, were about as old as Uncle Henry, for two of them had beards. But the little woman was doubtless much older: her face was covered with wrinkles, her hair was nearly white, and she walked rather stiffly.

When these people drew near the house where Dorothy was standing in the doorway, they paused and whispered among themselves, as if afraid to come farther. But the little old woman walked up to Dorothy, made a low bow and said, in a sweet voice,

'You are welcome, most noble Sorceress, to the land of the Munchkins. We are so grateful to you for having killed the Wicked Witch of the East, and for setting our people free from bondage.'

Dorothy listened to this speech with wonder. What could the little woman possibly mean by calling her a sorceress, and saying she had killed the wicked Witch of the East? Dorothy was an innocent, harmless little girl, who had been carried by a cyclone many miles from home; and she had never killed anything in all her life.

But the little woman evidently expected her to answer; so Dorothy said, with hesitation,

'You are very kind; but there must be some mistake. I have not killed anything.'

'Your house did, anyway,' replied the little old woman, with a laugh; 'and that is the same thing. See!' she continued, pointing to the corner of the house; 'there are her two toes, still sticking out from under a block of wood.'

Dorothy looked, and gave a little cry of fright. There, indeed, just under the corner of the great beam the house rested on, two feet were sticking out, shod in silver shoes with pointed toes.

'Oh, dear! oh, dear!' cried Dorothy, clasping her hands together in dismay; 'the house must have fallen on her. What ever shall we do?'

'There is nothing to be done,' said the little woman, calmly.

'But who was she?' asked Dorothy.

'She was the Wicked Witch of the East, as I said,' answered the little woman. 'She has held all the Munchkins in bondage for many years, making them slave for her night and day. Now they are all set free, and are grateful to you for the favour.'

'Who are the Munchkins?' enquired Dorothy.

'They are the people who live in this land of the East, where the wicked Witch ruled.'

'Are you a Munchkin?' asked Dorothy.

'No; but I am their friend, although I live in the land of the North. When they saw the Witch of the East was dead the Munchkins sent a swift messenger to me, and I came at once. I am the Witch of the North.'

'Oh, gracious!' cried Dorothy; 'are you a real witch?'

'Yes, indeed,' answered the little woman. 'But I am a good witch, and the people love me. I am not as powerful as the Wicked Witch was who ruled here, or I should have set the people free myself.'

'But I thought all witches were wicked,' said the girl, who was half frightened at facing a real witch.

'Oh, no; that is a great mistake. There were only four witches in all the Land of Oz, and two of them, those who live in the North and the South, are good witches. I know this is true, for I am one of them myself, and cannot be mistaken. Those who dwelt in the East and the West were, indeed, wicked witches; but now that you have killed one of them, there is but one wicked Witch in all the Land of Oz – the one who lives in the West.'

'But,' said Dorothy, after a moment's thought, 'Aunt Em has told me that the witches were all dead – years and years ago.'

'Who is Aunt Em?' enquired the little old woman.

'She is my aunt who lives in Kansas, where I came from.'

The Witch of the North seemed to think for a time, with her head bowed and her eyes upon the ground. Then she looked up and said,

'I do not know where Kansas is, for I have never heard that country mentioned before. But tell me, is it a civilized country?'

'Oh, yes;' replied Dorothy.

'Then that accounts for it. In the civilized countries I believe there are no witches left; nor wizards, nor sorceresses, nor magicians. But, you see, the Land of Oz has never been civilized, for we are cut off from all the rest of the world. Therefore we still have witches and wizards amongst us.'

'Who are the Wizards?' asked Dorothy.

'Oz himself is the Great Wizard,' answered the Witch, sinking her voice to a whisper. 'He is more powerful than all the rest of us together. He lives in the City of Emeralds.'

Dorothy was going to ask another question, but just then the Munchkins, who had been standing silently by, gave a loud shout and pointed to the corner of the house where the Wicked Witch had been lying.

'What is it?' asked the little old woman; and looked, and began to laugh. The feet of the dead Witch had disappeared entirely and nothing was left but the silver shoes.

'She was so old,' explained the Witch of the North, 'that she dried up quickly in the sun. That is the end of her. But the silver shoes are yours, and you shall have them to wear.' She reached down and picked up the shoes, and after shaking the dust out of them handed them to Dorothy.

'The Witch of the East was proud of those silver shoes,' said one of

'But the silver shoes are yours and you shall have them to wear'

the Munchkins; 'and there is some charm connected with them; but what it is we never knew.'

Dorothy carried the shoes into the house and placed them on the table. Then she came out again to the Munchkins and said,

'I am anxious to get back to my Aunt and Uncle, for I am sure they will worry about me. Can you help me find my way?'

The Munchkins and the Witch first looked at one another, and then at Dorothy, and then shook their heads.

'At the East, not far from here,' said one, 'there is a great desert, and none could live to cross it.'

'It is the same at the South,' said another, 'for I have been there and seen it. The South is the country of the Quadlings.'

'I am told,' said the third man, 'that it is the same at the West. And that country, where the Winkies live, is ruled by the Wicked Witch of the West, who would make you her slave if you passed her way.'

'The North is my home,' said the old lady, 'and at its edge is the same great desert that surrounds this land of Oz. I'm afraid, my dear, you will have to live with us.'

Dorothy began to sob at this, for she felt lonely among all these strange people. Her tears seemed to grieve the kind-hearted Munchkins, for they immediately took out their handkerchiefs and began to weep also. As for the little old woman, she took off her cap and balanced the point on the end of her nose, while she counted 'one, two, three' in a solemn voice. At once the cap changed to a slate, on which was written in big, white chalk marks:

LET DOROTHY GO TO THE CITY OF EMERALDS

The little old woman took the slate from her nose, and having read the words on it, asked,

'Is your name Dorothy, my dear?'

'Yes,' answered the child, looking up and drying her tears.

'Then you must go to the City of Emeralds. Perhaps Oz will help you.'

'Where is this City?' asked Dorothy.

'It is exactly in the centre of the country, and is ruled by Oz, the Great Wizard I told you of.'

'Is he a good man?' enquired the girl, anxiously.

'He is a good Wizard. Whether he is a man or not I cannot tell, for I have never seen him.'

'How can I get there?' asked Dorothy.

'You must walk. It is a long journey, through a country that is sometimes pleasant and sometimes dark and terrible. However, I will use all the magic arts I know of to keep you from harm.'

'Won't you go with me?' pleaded the girl, who had begun to look upon the little old woman as her only friend.

'No, I cannot do that,' she replied; 'but I will give you my kiss, and no one will dare injure a person who has been kissed by the Witch of the North.'

She came close to Dorothy and kissed her gently on the forehead. Where her lips touched the girl they left a round, shining mark, as Dorothy found out soon after.

'The road to the City of Emeralds is paved with yellow brick,' said the Witch; 'so you cannot miss it. When you get to Oz do not be afraid of him, but tell your story and ask him to help you. Goodbye, my dear.'

The three Munchkins bowed low to her and wished her a pleasant journey, after which they walked away through the trees. The Witch gave Dorothy a friendly little nod, whirled around on her left heel three times, and straightway disappeared, much to the surprise of little Toto, who barked after her loudly enough when she had gone, because he had been afraid even to growl while she stood by.

But Dorothy, knowing her to be a witch, had expected her to disappear in just that way, and was not surprised in the least.

III

HOW DOROTHY SAVED THE SCARECROW

When Dorothy was left alone she began to feel hungry. So she went to the cupboard and cut herself some bread, which she spread with butter. She gave some to Toto, and taking a pail from the shelf she carried it down to the little brook and filled it with clear, sparkling water. Toto ran over to the trees and began to bark at the birds sitting there. Dorothy went to get him, and saw such delicious fruit hanging from the branches that she gathered some of it, finding it just what she wanted to help out her breakfast.

Then she went back to the house, and having helped herself and Toto to a good drink of the cool, clear water, she set about making ready for the journey to the City of Emeralds.

Dorothy had only one other dress, but that happened to be clean and was hanging on a peg beside her bed. It was gingham, with checks of white and blue; and although the blue was somewhat faded with many washings, it was still a pretty frock. The girl washed herself carefully, dressed herself in the clean gingham, and tied her pink sunbonnet on her head. She took a little basket and filled it with bread from the cupboard, laying a white cloth over the top. Then she looked down at her feet and noticed how old and worn her shoes were.

'They surely will never do for a long journey, Toto,' she said. And Toto looked up into her face with his little black eyes and wagging his tail to show he knew what she meant.

At that moment Dorothy saw lying on the table the silver shoes that had belonged to the Witch of the East.

'I wonder if they will fit me,' she said to Toto. 'They would be just the thing to take a long walk in, for they could not wear out.'

She took off her old leather shoes and tried on the silver ones, which fitted her as well as if they had been made for her.

Finally she picked up her basket.

'Come along, Toto,' she said, 'we will go to the Emerald City and ask the great Oz how to get back to Kansas again.'

She closed the door, locked it, and put the key carefully in the pocket of her dress. And so, with Toto trotting along soberly behind her, she started on her journey.

There were several roads nearby, but it did not take her long to find the one paved with yellow brick. Within a short time she was walking briskly towards the Emerald City, her silver shoes tinkling merrily on the hard, yellow roadbed. The sun shone bright and the birds sang sweetly and Dorothy did not feel nearly so bad as you might think a little girl would who had been suddenly whisked away from her own country and set down in the midst of a strange land.

She was surprised, as she walked along, to see how pretty the country was about her. There were neat fences at the sides of the road, painted a dainty blue colour, and beyond them were fields of grain and vegetables in abundance. Evidently the Munchkins were good farmers and able to raise large crops. Once in a while she would pass a house, and the people came out to look at her and bow low as she went by; for everyone knew she had been the means of destroying the wicked witch and setting them free from bondage. The houses of the Munchkins were odd looking dwellings, for each was round, with a big dome for a roof. All were painted blue, for in this country of the East blue was the favourite colour.

Towards evening, when Dorothy was tired with her long walk and began to wonder where she should pass the night, she came to a house rather larger than the rest. On the green lawn before it many men and women were dancing. Five little fiddlers played as loudly as possible and the people were laughing and singing, while a big table near by was loaded with delicious fruits and nuts, pies and cakes, and many other good things to eat.

The people greeted Dorothy kindly, and invited her to supper and to pass the night with them; for this was the home of one of the richest Munchkins in the land, and his friends were gathered with him to celebrate their freedom from the bondage of the wicked witch.

Dorothy ate a hearty supper and was waited upon by the rich Munchkin himself, whose name was Boq. Then she sat down upon a settee and watched the people dance.

When Boq saw her silver shoes he said,

'You must be a great sorceress.'

'Why?' asked the girl.

'Because you wear silver shoes and have killed the Wicked Witch.

Besides, you have white in your frock, and only witches and sorceresses wear white.'

'My dress is blue and white checked,' said Dorothy, smoothing out the wrinkles in it.

'It is kind of you to wear that,' said Boq. 'Blue is the colour of the Munchkins, and white is the witch colour, so we know you are a friendly witch.'

Dorothy did not know what to say to this, for all the people seemed to think her a witch, and she knew very well she was only an ordinary little girl who had come by the chance of a cyclone into a strange land.

When she had tired watching the dancing, Boq led her into the house, where he gave her a room with a pretty bed in it. The sheets were made of blue cloth, and Dorothy slept soundly in them till morning, with Toto curled up on the blue rug beside her.

She ate a hearty breakfast, and watched a wee Munchkin baby, who played with Toto and pulled his tail and crowed and laughed in a way that greatly amused Dorothy. Toto was a fine curiosity to all the people, for they had never seen a dog before.

'How far is it to the Emerald City?' the girl asked.

'I do not know,' answered Boq, gravely, 'for I have never been there. It is better for people to keep away from Oz, unless they have business with him. But it is a long way to the Emerald City, and it will take you many days. The country here is rich and pleasant, but you must pass through rough and dangerous places before you reach the end of your journey.'

This worried Dorothy a little, but she knew that only the great Oz could help her get to Kansas again, so she bravely resolved not to turn back.

She bade her friends goodbye, and again started along the road of yellow brick. When she had gone several miles she thought she would stop to rest, and so climbed to the top of the fence beside the road and sat down. There was a great cornfield beyond the fence, and not far away she saw a Scarecrow, placed high on a pole to keep the birds from the ripe corn.

*Dorothy leaned her chin upon her hand and gazed thoughtfully
at the Scarecrow*

Dorothy leaned her chin upon her hand and gazed thoughtfully at the Scarecrow. Its head was a small sack stuffed with straw, with eyes, nose and mouth painted on it to represent a face. An old, pointed blue hat, that had belonged to some Munchkin, was perched on this head, and the rest of the figure was a blue suit of clothes, worn and faded, which had also been stuffed with straw. On the feet were some old boots with blue tops, such as every man wore in this country, and the figure was raised above the stalks of corn by means of the pole stuck up its back.

While Dorothy was looking earnestly into the queer, painted face of the Scarecrow, she was surprised to see one of the eyes slowly wink at her. She thought she must have been mistaken, at first, for none of the scarecrows in Kansas ever wink; but presently the figure nodded its head to her in a friendly way. Then she climbed down from the fence and walked up to it, while Toto ran around the pole and barked.

'Good day,' said the Scarecrow, in a rather husky voice.

'Did you speak?' asked the girl, in wonder.

'Certainly,' answered the Scarecrow; 'how do you do?'

'I'm pretty well, thank you,' replied Dorothy, politely; 'how do you do?'

'I'm not feeling well,' said the Scarecrow, with a smile, 'for it is very tedious being perched up here night and day to scare away crows.'

'Can't you get down?' asked Dorothy.

'No, for this pole is stuck up my back. If you will please take away the pole I shall be greatly obliged to you.'

Dorothy reached up both arms and lifted the figure off the pole; for, being stuffed with straw, it was quite light.

'Thank you very much,' said the Scarecrow, when he had been set down on the ground. 'I feel like a new man.'

Dorothy was puzzled at this, for it sounded queer to hear a stuffed man speak, and to see him bow and walk along beside her.

'Who are you?' asked the Scarecrow when he had stretched himself and yawned, 'and where are you going?'

'My name is Dorothy,' said the girl, 'and I am going to the Emerald City, to ask the great Oz to send me back to Kansas.'

'Where is the Emerald City?' he enquired; 'and who is Oz?'

'Why, don't you know?' she returned, in surprise.

'No, indeed; I don't know anything. You see, I am stuffed, so I have no brains at all,' he answered sadly.

'Oh,' said Dorothy; 'I'm awfully sorry for you.'

'Do you think,' he asked, 'if I go to the Emerald City with you, that Oz would give me some brains?'

'I cannot tell,' she returned; 'but you may come with me, if you like. If Oz will not give you any brains you will be no worse off than you are now.'

'That is true,' said the Scarecrow. 'You see,' he continued, confidentially, 'I don't mind my legs and arms and body being stuffed, because I cannot get hurt. If anyone treads on my toes or sticks a pin into me, it doesn't matter, for I can't feel it. But I do not want people to call me a fool, and if my head stays stuffed with straw instead of with brains, as yours is, how am I ever to know anything?'

'I understand how you feel,' said the little girl, who was truly sorry for him. 'If you will come with me I'll ask Oz to do all he can for you.'

'Thank you,' he answered, gratefully.

They walked back to the road, Dorothy helped him over the fence, and they started along the path of yellow brick for the Emerald City.

Toto did not like this addition to the party, at first. He smelled around the stuffed man as if he suspected there might be a nest of rats in the straw, and he often growled in an unfriendly way at the Scarecrow.

'Don't mind Toto,' said Dorothy, to her new friend; 'he never bites.'

'Oh, I'm not afraid,' replied the Scarecrow, 'he can't hurt the straw. Do let me carry that basket for you. I shall not mind it, for I can't get tired. I'll tell you a secret,' he continued, as he walked along; 'there is only one thing in the world I am afraid of.'

'What is that?' asked Dorothy; 'the Munchkin farmer who made you?'

'No,' answered the Scarecrow; 'it's a lighted match!'

The Treasure Seekers

E. NESBIT

This is the opening section of The Treasure Seekers *(1899), in which E. Nesbit describes how the Bastable children hunted for hidden treasure.*

When we had agreed to dig for treasure we all went down into the cellar and lighted the gas. Oswald would have liked to dig there, but it is stone flags. We looked among the old boxes and broken chairs and fenders and empty bottles and things, and at last we found the spades we had to dig in the sand with when we went to the seaside three years ago. They are not silly, babyish, wooden spades, that split if you look at them, but good iron, with a blue mark across the top of the iron part, and yellow wooden handles. We wasted a little time getting them dusted, because the girls wouldn't dig with spades that had cobwebs on them. Girls would never do for African explorers or anything like that, they are too beastly particular.

It was no use doing the thing by halves. We marked out a sort of square in the mouldy part of the garden, about three yards across, and began to dig. But we found nothing except worms and stones – and the ground was very hard.

So we thought we'd try another part of the garden, and we found a place in the big round flower bed, where the ground was much softer. We thought we'd make a smaller hole to begin with, and it was much better. We dug and dug and dug, and it was jolly hard work! We got very hot digging, but we found nothing.

Presently Albert-next-door looked over the wall. We do not like him very much, but we let him play with us sometimes, because his father is dead, and you must not be unkind to orphans, even if their mothers are alive. Albert is always very tidy. He wears frilly collars and velvet knickerbockers. I can't think how he can bear to.

So we said, 'Hullo!'

And he said, 'What are you up to?'

'We're digging for treasure,' said Alice; 'an ancient parchment revealed to us the place of concealment. Come over and help us. When we have dug deep enough we shall find a great pot of red clay, full of gold and precious jewels.'

Albert-next-door only sniggered and said, 'What silly nonsense!' He cannot play properly at all. It is very strange, because he has a very nice uncle. You see, Albert-next-door doesn't care for reading, and he has not read nearly so many books as we have, so he is very foolish and ignorant, but it cannot be helped, and you just have to put up with it when you want him to do anything. Besides, it is wrong to be angry with people for not being so clever as you are yourself. It is not always their faults.

So Oswald said, 'Come and dig! Then you shall share the treasure when we've found it.'

But he said, 'I shan't – I don't like digging – and I'm just going in to my tea.'

'Come along and dig, there's a good boy,' Alice said. 'You can use my spade. It's much the best —'

So he came along and dug, and when once he was over the wall we kept him at it, and we worked as well, of course, and the hole got deep. Pincher worked too – he is our dog and he is very good at digging. He digs for rats in the dustbin sometimes, and gets very dirty. But we love our dog, even when his face wants washing.

'I expect we shall have to make a tunnel,' Oswald said, 'to reach the rich treasure.' So he jumped into the hole and began to dig at one side. After that we took it in turns to dig at the tunnel, and Pincher was most useful in scraping the earth out of the tunnel – he does it with his back feet when you say 'Rats!' and he digs with his front ones, and burrows with his nose as well.

At last the tunnel was nearly a yard long, and big enough to creep along to find the treasure, if only it had been a bit longer. Now it was Albert's turn to go in and dig, but he funked it.

'Take your turn like a man,' said Oswald – nobody can say that Oswald doesn't take his turn like a man. But Albert wouldn't. So we had to make him, because it was only fair.

'It's quite easy,' Alice said. 'You just crawl in and dig with your hands. Then when you come out we can scrape out what you've done, with the spades. Come – be a man. You won't notice it being dark in the tunnel if you shut your eyes tight. We've all been in except Dora – and she doesn't like worms.'

'I don't like worms neither.' Albert-next-door said this; but we remembered how he had picked a fat red and black worm up in his fingers and thrown it at Dora only the day before.

So we put him in.

But he would not go in head first, the proper way, and dig with his hands as we had done, and though Oswald was angry at the time, for he hates snivellers, yet afterwards he owned that perhaps it was just as well. You should never be afraid to own that perhaps you were mistaken – but it is cowardly to do it unless you are quite sure you are in the wrong.

'Let me go in feet first,' said Albert-next-door. 'I'll dig with my boots – I will truly, honour bright.'

So we let him get in feet first – and he did it very slowly and at last he was in, and only his head sticking out into the hole; and all the rest of him in the tunnel.

'Now dig with your boots,' said Oswald; 'and Alice, do catch hold of Pincher, he'll be digging again in another minute, and perhaps it would be uncomfortable for Albert if Pincher threw the mould into his eyes.'

You should always try to think of these little things. Thinking of other people's comfort makes them like you. Alice held Pincher, and we all shouted, 'Kick! dig with your feet, for all you're worth!'

So Albert-next-door began to dig with his feet, and we stood on the ground over him, waiting – and all in a minute the ground gave way, and we tumbled together in a heap: and when we got up there was a little shallow hollow where we had been standing, and Albert-next-door was underneath, stuck quite fast, because the roof of the tunnel had tumbled in on him. He is a horribly unlucky boy to have anything to do with.

It was dreadful the way he cried and screamed, though he had to own it didn't hurt, only it was rather heavy and he couldn't move his legs. We would have dug him out all right enough, in time, but he screamed so we were afraid the police would come, so Dicky climbed over the wall, to tell the cook there to tell Albert-next-door's uncle he had been buried by mistake, and to come and help dig him out.

Dicky was a long time gone. We wondered what had become of him, and all the while the screaming went on and on, for we had taken the loose earth off Albert's face so that he could scream quite easily and comfortably.

Presently Dicky came back and Albert-next-door's uncle came with him. He has very long legs, and his hair is light and his face is brown. He has been to sea, but now he writes books. I like him.

He told his nephew to stow it, so Albert did, and then he asked him if he was hurt – and Albert had to say he wasn't, for though he is a coward and very unlucky, he is not a liar like some boys are.

'This promises to be a protracted if agreeable task,' said Albert-next-door's uncle, rubbing his hands and looking at the hole with Albert's head in it. 'I will get another spade,' so he fetched the big spade out of the next door garden tool-shed, and began to dig his nephew out.

'Mind you keep very still,' he said, 'or I might chunk a bit out of you with the spade.' Then after a while he said –

'I confess that I am not absolutely insensible to the dramatic interest of the situation. My curiosity is excited. I own that I should like to know how my nephew happened to be buried. But don't tell me if you'd rather not. I suppose no force was used?'

'Only moral force,' said Alice. They used to talk a lot about moral force at the High School where she went, and in case you don't know what it means I'll tell you that it is making people do what they don't want to, just by slanging them, or laughing at them, or promising them things if they're good.

'Only moral force, eh?' said Albert-next-door's uncle. 'Well?'

'Well,' Dora said, 'I'm very sorry it happened to Albert – I'd rather it had been one of us. It would have been my turn to go into the tunnel, only I don't like worms, so they let me off. You see we were digging for treasure.'

'Yes,' said Alice, 'and I think we were just coming to the underground passage that leads to the secret hoard, when the tunnel fell in on Albert. He *is* so unlucky,' and she sighed.

Then Albert-next-door began to scream again, and his uncle wiped his face – his own face, not Albert's – with his silk handkerchief, and then he put it in his trousers pocket. It seems a strange place to put a handkerchief, but he had his coat and waistcoat off and I suppose he wanted the handkerchief handy. Digging was warm work.

He told Albert-next-door to drop it, or he wouldn't proceed further in the matter, so Albert stopped screaming, and presently his uncle finished digging him out. Albert did look so funny, with his hair all dusty and his velvet suit covered with mould and his face muddy with earth and crying.

We all said how sorry we were, but he wouldn't say a word back to us. He was most awfully sick to think he'd been the one buried, when it might just as well have been one of us. I felt myself that it was hard lines.

'So you were digging for treasure,' said Albert-next-door's uncle, wiping his face again with his handkerchief. 'Well, I fear that your chances of success are small. I have made a careful study of the whole subject. What I don't know about buried treasure is not worth knowing. And I never knew more than one coin buried in any one garden – and that is generally – Hullo – what's that?'

He pointed to something shining in the hole he had just dragged Albert out of. Oswald picked it up. It was a half-crown. We looked at each other, speechless with surprise and delight, like in books.

'Well, that's lucky, at all events,' said Albert-next-door's uncle. 'Let's see, that's fivepence each for you.'

'It's fourpence-something; I can't do fractions,' said Dicky; 'there are seven of us, you see.'

'Oh, you count Albert as one of yourselves on this occasion, eh?'

'Of course,' said Alice; 'and I say, he was buried after all. Why shouldn't we let him have the odd somethings, and we'll have fourpence each.'

We all agreed to this, and told Albert-next-door we would bring his share as soon as we could get the half-crown changed. He cheered up a little at that, and his uncle wiped his face again – he did look hot – and began to put on his coat and waistcoat.

When he had done it he stooped and picked up something. He held it up, and you will hardly believe it, but it is quite true – it was another half-crown!

'To think that there should be two!' he said; 'in all my experience of buried treasure I never heard of such a thing!'

I wish Albert-next-door's uncle would come treasure-seeking with us regularly; he must have very sharp eyes: for Dora says she was looking just the minute before at the very place where the second half-crown was picked up from, and *she* never saw it.

The Robin who Showed the Way

FRANCES HODGSON BURNETT
Illustrated by Angela Barratt

This extract comes from The Secret Garden *(1911). Mary Lennox, the orphaned daughter of a British official in India, has been sent back to live with her uncle at Misselthwaite Manor in Yorkshire. She discovers that the Manor has a secret, walled garden which is always locked up. One day she finds a key . . .*

She looked at the key quite a long time. She turned it over and over, and thought about it. As I have said before, she was not a child who had been trained to ask permission or consult her elders about things. All she thought about the key was that if it was the key to the closed garden, and she could find out where the door was, she could perhaps open it and see what was inside the walls, and what had happened to the old rose-trees. It was because it had been shut up so long that she wanted to see it. It seemed as if it must be different from other places and that something strange must have happened to it during ten years. Besides that, if she liked it she could go into it every day and shut the door behind her, and she could make up some play of her own and play it quite alone, because nobody would ever know where she was, but would think the door was still locked and the key buried in the earth. The thought of that pleased her very much.

Living, as it were, all by herself in a house with a hundred mysteriously closed rooms and having nothing whatever to do to amuse herself, had set her inactive brain to work and was actually awakening her imagination. There is no doubt that the fresh, strong, pure air from the moor had a great deal to do with it. Just as it had given her an appetite, and fighting with the wind had stirred her blood, so the same things had stirred her mind. In India she had always been too hot and languid and weak to care much about anything, but in this place she was beginning to care and to want to do new things. Already she felt less 'contrary', though she did not know why.

She put the key in her pocket and walked up and down her walk. No one but herself ever seemed to come there, so she could walk slowly and look at the wall, or, rather, at the ivy growing on it. The ivy was the baffling thing. Howsoever carefully she looked, she could see nothing but thickly growing, glossy, dark green leaves. She was very much disappointed. Something of her contrariness came back to her as she paced the wall and looked over it at the tree-tops inside. It seemed so silly, she said to herself, to be near it and not be able to get in. She took the key in her pocket when she went back to the house, and she made up her mind that she would always carry it with her when she went out, so that if she ever should find the hidden door she would be ready.

Mrs Medlock had allowed Martha to sleep all night at the cottage, but she was back at her work in the morning with cheeks redder than ever and in the best of spirits.

'I got up at four o'clock,' she said. 'Eh! it was pretty on th' moor with th' birds gettin' up an' th' rabbits scamperin' about an' th' sun risin'. I didn't walk all th' way. A man gave me a ride in his cart an' I can tell you I did enjoy myself.'

She was full of stories of the delights of her day out. Her mother had been glad to see her, and they had got the baking and washing all out of the way. She had even made each of the children a dough-cake with a bit of brown sugar in it.

'I had 'em all pipin' hot when they came in from playin' on th' moor. An' th' cottage all smelt o' nice, clean, hot bakin' an' there was a good fire, an' they just shouted for joy. Our Dickon, he said our cottage was good enough for a king to live in.'

In the evening they had all sat round the fire, and Martha and her mother had sewed patches on torn clothes and mended stockings, and Martha had told them about the little girl who had come from India and who had been waited on all her life by what

Martha called 'blacks' until she didn't know how to put on her own stockings.

'Eh! they did like to hear about you,' said Martha. 'They wanted to know all about th' blacks an' about th' ship you came in. I couldn't tell 'em enough.'

Mary reflected a little.

'I'll tell you a great deal more before your next day out,' she said, 'so that you will have more to talk about. I dare say they would like to hear about riding on elephants and camels, and about the officers going to hunt tigers.'

'My word!' cried delighted Martha. 'It would set 'em clean off their heads. Would tha' really do that, Miss? It would be the same as a wild beast show like we heard they had in York once.'

'India is quite different from Yorkshire,' Mary said slowly, as she thought the matter over. 'I never thought of that. Did Dickon and your mother like to hear you talk about me?'

'Why, our Dickon's eyes nearly started out o' his head, they got that round,' answered Martha. 'But Mother, she was put out about your seemin' to be all by yourself like. She said: "Hasn't Mr Craven got no governess for her, nor no nurse?" and I said: "No, he hasn't, though Mrs Medlock says he will when he thinks of it, but she says he mayn't think of it for two or three years."'

'I don't want a governess,' said Mary sharply.

'But Mother says you ought to be learnin' your book by this time an' you ought to have a woman to look after you, an' she says: "Now, Martha, you just think how you'd feel yourself, in a big place like that, wanderin' about alone, an' no mother. You do your best to cheer her up," she says, an' I said I would.'

Mary gave her a long, steady look.

'You do cheer me up,' she said. 'I like to hear you talk.'

Presently Martha went out of the room and came back with something held in her hands under her apron.

'What does tha' think,' she said, with a cheerful grin. 'I've brought thee a present.'

'A present!' exclaimed Mistress Mary. How could a cottage full of fourteen hungry people give anyone a present!

'A man was drivin' across the moor peddlin',' Martha explained. 'An' he stopped his cart at our door. He had pots an' pans an' odds an' ends, but Mother had no money to buy anythin'. Just as he was goin' away our 'Lizbeth Ellen called out: "Mother, he's got skippin'-ropes with red an' blue handles." An' Mother, she calls out quite sudden: "Here, stop, mister! How much are they?" An' he says "Tuppence," an' Mother she began fumblin' in her pocket, an' she says to me: "Martha, tha's brought me thy wages like a good lass, an' I've got four places to put every penny, but I'm just goin' to take tuppence out of it to buy that child a skippin'-rope," an' she bought one, an' here it is.'

She brought it out from under her apron and exhibited it quite proudly. It was a strong, slender rope with a striped red and blue handle at each end, but Mary Lennox had never seen a skipping-rope before. She gazed at it with a mystified expression.

'What is it for?' she asked curiously.

'For!' cried out Martha. 'Does tha' mean that they've not got skippin'-ropes in India, for all they've got elephants and tigers and camels? No wonder most of 'em's black. This is what it's for; just watch me.'

And she ran into the middle of the room and, taking a handle in each hand, began to skip, and skip, and skip, while Mary turned in her chair to stare at her, and the queer faces in the old portraits seemed to stare at her, too, and wonder what on earth this common little cottager had the impudence to be doing under their very noses. But Martha did not even see them. The interest and curiosity in Mistress Mary's face delighted her, and she went on skipping and counted as she skipped until she had reached a hundred.

'I could skip longer than that,' she said when she stopped. 'I've skipped as much as five hundred when I was twelve, but I wasn't as fat then as I am now, an' I was in practice.'

Mary got up from her chair beginning to feel excited herself.

'It looks nice,' she said. 'Your mother is a kind woman. Do you think I could ever skip like that?'

'You just try it,' urged Martha, handing her the skipping-rope. 'You can't skip a hundred at first, but if you practise you'll mount up. That's what Mother said. She says: "Nothin' will do her more good than skippin'-rope. It's th' sensiblest toy a child can have. Let her play out in th' fresh air skippin' an' it'll stretch her legs an' arms an' give her some strength in 'em."'

It was plain that there was not a great deal of strength in Mistress Mary's arms and legs when she first began to skip. She was not very clever at it, but she liked it so much that she did not want to stop.

'Put on tha' things and run an' skip out o' doors,' said Martha. 'Mother said I must tell you to keep out o' doors as much as you could, even when it rains a bit, so as tha' wrap up warm.'

Mary put on her coat and hat and took her skipping-rope over her arm. She opened the door to go out, and then suddenly thought of something and turned back rather slowly.

'Martha,' she said, 'they were your wages. It was your twopence really. Thank you.' She said it stiffly because she was not used to thanking people or noticing that they did things for her. 'Thank you,' she said, and held out her hand because she did not know what else to do.

Martha gave her hand a clumsy little shake, as if she was not accustomed to this sort of thing either. Then she laughed.

'Eh! tha' art a queer, old-womanish thing,' she said. 'If tha'd been our 'Lizabeth Ellen tha'd have given me a kiss.'

Mary looked stiffer than ever.

'Do you want me to kiss you?'

Martha laughed again.

'Nay, not me,' she answered. 'If tha' was different, p'raps tha'd want to thysel'. But tha' isn't. Run off outside an' play with thy rope.'

Mistress Mary felt a little awkward as she went out of the room. Yorkshire people seemed strange, and Martha was always rather a puzzle to her. At first she had disliked her very much, but now she did not.

The robin was hopping about him

The skipping-rope was a wonderful thing. She counted and skipped, and skipped and counted, until her cheeks were quite red, and she was more interested than she had even been since she was born. The sun was shining and a little wind was blowing – not a rough wind, but one which came in delightful little gusts and brought a fresh scent of newly turned earth with it. She skipped round the fountain garden, and up one walk and down another. She skipped at last into the kitchen-garden and saw Ben Weatherstaff digging and talking to his robin, which was hopping about him. She skipped down the walk towards him and he lifted his head and looked at her with a curious expression. She had wondered if he would notice her. She really wanted him to see her skip.

'Well!' he exclaimed. 'Upon my word! P'raps tha' art a young 'un, after all, an' p'raps tha's got child's blood in thy veins instead of sour buttermilk. Tha's skipped red into thy cheeks as sure as my name's Ben Weatherstaff. I wouldn't have believed tha' could do it.'

'I never skipped before,' Mary said. 'I'm just beginning. I can only go up to twenty.'

'Tha' keep on,' said Ben. 'Tha' shapes well enough at it for a young 'un that's lived with heathen. Just see how he's watchin' thee,' jerking his head towards the robin. 'He followed after thee yesterday. He'll be at it again today. He'll be bound to find out what th' skippin'-rope is. He's never seen one. Eh!' shaking his head at the bird, 'tha' curiosity will be th' death of thee some time if tha' doesn't look sharp.'

Mary skipped round all the gardens and round the orchard, resting every few minutes. At length she went to her own special walk and made up her mind to try if she could skip the whole length of it. It was a good long skip, and she began slowly, but before she had gone half-way down the path she was so hot and breathless that she was obliged to stop. She did not mind much, because she had already counted up to thirty. She stopped with a little laugh of pleasure, and there, lo and behold, was the robin swaying on a long branch of ivy. He had followed her, and he greeted her with a chirp. As Mary had skipped towards him she felt something heavy in her pocket strike against her at each jump, and when she saw the robin she laughed again.

'You showed me where the key was yesterday,' she said. 'You ought to show me the door today; but I don't believe you know!'

The robin flew from his swinging spray of ivy on to the top of the wall and he opened his beak and sang a loud, lovely trill, merely to show off. Nothing in the world is quite as adorably lovely as a robin when he shows off – and they are nearly always doing it.

Mary Lennox had heard a great deal about Magic in her Ayah's stories, and she always said what happened almost at that moment was Magic.

One of the nice little gusts of wind rushed down the walk, and it was a stronger one than the rest. It was strong enough to wave the branches of the trees, and it was more than strong enough to sway the trailing sprays of untrimmed ivy hanging from the wall. Mary had stepped close to the robin, and suddenly the gust of wind swung aside some loose ivy trails, and more suddenly still she jumped towards it and caught it in her hand. This she did because she had seen something under it – a round knob which had been covered by the leaves hanging over it. It was the knob of a door.

She put her hands under the leaves and began to pull and push them aside. Thick as the ivy hung, it nearly all was a loose and swinging curtain, though some had crept over wood and iron. Mary's heart began to thump and her hands to shake a little in her delight and excitement. The robin kept singing and twittering away and tilting his head on one side, as if he were as excited as she was. What was this under her hands which was square and made of iron and which her fingers found a hole in?

It was the lock of the door which had been closed ten years, and she put her hand in her pocket, drew out the key, and found it fitted the keyhole. She put the key in and turned it. It took two hands to do it, but it did turn.

And then she took a long breath and looked behind her up the long walk to see if anyone was coming. No one was coming. No one ever did come, it seemed, and she took another long breath, because she could not help it, and she held back the swinging curtain of ivy and pushed back the door which opened slowly – slowly.

Then she slipped through it, and shut it behind her, and stood with her back against it, looking about her and breathing quite fast with excitement, and wonder, and delight.

She was standing *inside* the secret garden.

Pirate's Gold

ROBERT LOUIS STEVENSON
Illustrated by Walter Paget

This extract is from Treasure Island *(1882). Jim Hawkins is cabin-boy aboard the* Hispaniola *on a treasure-hunting expedition. When the ship reaches Treasure Island the villainous one-legged Long John Silver leads some of the crew in a mutiny. The officers and loyal seamen take refuge in a stockade on the island, but Jim is captured by the mutineers and held as a hostage while they hunt for the buried gold.*

We made a curious figure, had anyone been there to see us; all in soiled sailor clothes, and all but me armed to the teeth. Silver had two guns slung about him – one before and one behind – besides the great cutlass at his waist, and a pistol in each pocket of his square-tailed coat. To complete his strange appearance, Captain Flint* sat perched upon his shoulder and gabbling odds and ends of purposeless sea-talk. I had a line about my waist, and followed obediently after the sea-cook, who held the loose end of the rope, now in his free hand, now between his powerful teeth. For all the world, I was led like a dancing bear.

The other men were variously burthened; some carrying picks and shovels – for that had been the very first necessary they brought ashore from the *Hispaniola* – others laden with pork, bread, and brandy for the midday meal.

Well, thus equipped, we all set out – even the fellow with the broken head, who should certainly have kept in shadow – and straggled, one after another, to the beach, where the two gigs awaited us. Even these

---

* Captain Flint is Long John Silver's parrot. The bird is named after the pirate whose gold is buried on Treasure Island.

bore trace of the drunken folly of the pirates, one in a broken thwart, and both in their muddied and unbaled condition. Both were to be carried along with us, for the sake of safety; and so, with our numbers divided between them, we set forth upon the bosom of the anchorage.

As we pulled over, there was some discussion on the chart. The red cross was, of course, far too large to be a guide; and the terms of the note on the back, as you will hear, admitted of some ambiguity. They ran, the reader may remember, thus:

> Tall tree, Spy-glass Shoulder, bearing a point to the N. of N.N.E.
> Skeleton Island E.S.E. and by E.
> Ten feet.

A tall tree was thus the principal mark. Now, right before us, the anchorage was bounded by a plateau from two to three hundred feet high, adjoining on the north the sloping shoulder of the Spy-glass, and rising again towards the south into the rough cliffy eminence called the Mizzen-mast Hill. The top of the plateau was dotted thickly with pine trees of varying heights. Every here and there, one of a different species rose forty or fifty feet clear above its neighbours, and which of these was the particular 'tall tree' of Captain Flint could only be decided on the spot, and by the readings of the compass.

Yet, although that was the case, every man on board the boats had picked a favourite of his own ere we were half-way over, Long John alone shrugging his shoulders and bidding them wait till they were there.

We pulled easily, by Silver's directions, not to weary the hands prematurely; and, after quite a long passage, landed at the mouth of the second river – that which runs down a woody cleft of the Spy-glass. Thence, bending to our left, we began to ascend the slope towards the plateau.

At the first outset, heavy, miry ground and a matted, marish vegetation greatly delayed our progress; but by little and little the hill began to steepen and become stony under foot, and the wood to change its character and to grow in a more open order. It was, indeed, a most pleasant portion of the island that we were now approaching. A heavy-scented broom and many flowering shrubs had almost taken the place of grass. Thickets of green nutmeg trees were dotted here and there with the red columns and the broad shadow of the pines; and the first mingled their spice with the aroma of the others. The air, besides, was fresh and stirring, and this, under the sheer sunbeams, was a wonderful refreshment to our senses.

The party spread itself abroad, in a fan shape, shouting and leaping to and fro. About the centre, and a good way behind the rest, Silver and I followed – I tethered by my rope, he ploughing, with deep pants, among the sliding gravel. From time to time, indeed, I had to lend him a hand, or he must have missed his footing and fallen backward down the hill.

We had thus proceeded for about half a mile, and were approaching the brow of the plateau, when the man upon the farthest left began to cry aloud, as if in terror. Shout after shout came from him, and the others began to run in his direction.

'He can't 'a' found the treasure,' said old Morgan, hurrying past us from the right, 'for that's clean a-top.'

Indeed, as we found when we also reached the spot, it was something very different. At the foot of a pretty big pine, and involved in a green creeper, which had even partly lifted some of the smaller bones, a human skeleton lay, with a few shreds of clothing, on the ground. I believe a chill struck for a moment to every heart.

'He was a seaman,' said George Merry, who, bolder than the rest, had gone up close, and was examining the rags of clothing. 'Leastways, this is good sea-cloth.'

'Ay, ay,' said Silver, 'like enough; you wouldn't look to find a bishop here, I reckon. But what sort of a way is that for bones to lie? 'Tain't in natur'.'

Indeed, on a second glance, it seemed impossible to fancy that the body was in a natural position. But for some disarray (the work, perhaps, of the birds that had fed upon him, or of the slow-growing creeper that had gradually enveloped his remains) the man lay perfectly

'There ain't a thing left here,' said Merry

straight – his feet pointing in one direction, his hands, raised above his head like a diver's, pointing directly in the opposite.

'I've taken a notion into my old numskull,' observed Silver. 'Here's the compass; there's the tip-top p'int o' Skeleton Island, stickin' out like a tooth. Just take a bearing, will you, along the line of them bones.'

It was done. The body pointed straight in the direction of the island, and the compass read duly E.S.E. and by E.

'I thought so,' cried the cook; 'this here is a p'inter. Right up there is our line for the Pole Star and the jolly dollars. But, by thunder! if it don't make me cold inside to think of Flint. This is one of *his* jokes, and no mistake. Him and these six was alone here; he killed 'em, every man; and this one he hauled here and laid down by compass, shiver my timbers! They're long bones, and the hair's been yellow. Ay, that would be Allardyce. You mind Allardyce, Tom Morgan?'

'Ay, ay,' returned Morgan, 'I mind him; he owed me money, he did, and took my knife ashore with him.'

'Speaking of knives,' said another, 'why don't we find his'n lying round? Flint warn't the man to pick a seaman's pocket; and the birds, I guess, would leave it be.'

'By the powers, and that's true!' cried Silver.

'There ain't a thing left here,' said Merry, still feeling round among the bones, 'not a copper doit nor a baccy-box. It don't look nat'ral to me.'

'No, by gum, it don't,' agreed Silver; 'not nat'ral, nor not nice, says you. Great guns! messmates, but if Flint was living, this would be a hot spot for you and me. Six they were, and six we are; and bones is what they are now.'

'I saw him dead with these here deadlights,' said Morgan. 'Billy took me in. There he laid, with penny-pieces on his eyes.'

'Dead – ay, sure enough he's dead and gone below,' said the fellow with the bandage; 'but if ever sperrit walked, it would be Flint's. Dear heart, but he died bad, did Flint!'

'Ay, that he did,' observed another; 'now he raged, and now he hollered for the rum, and now he sang. *Fifteen Men* were his only song, mates; and I tell you true, I never rightly liked to hear it since. It was main hot, and the windy was open, and I hear that old song comin' out as clear as clear – and the death-haul on the man already.'

'Come, come,' said Silver, 'stow this talk. He's dead, and he don't walk, that I know; leastways, he won't walk by day, and you may lay to that. Care killed a cat. Fetch ahead for the doubloons.'

We started, certainly; but in spite of the hot sun and the staring daylight, the pirates no longer ran separate and shouting through the wood, but kept side by side and spoke with bated breath. The terror of the dead buccaneer had fallen on their spirits.

*   *   *   *

Partly from the damping influence of this alarm, partly to rest Silver and the sick folk, the whole party sat down as soon as they had gained the brow of the ascent.

The plateau being somewhat tilted towards the west, this spot on which we had paused commanded a wide prospect on either hand. Before us, over the tree-tops, we beheld the Cape of the Woods fringed with surf; behind, we not only looked down upon the anchorage and Skeleton Island, but saw – clear across the spit and the eastern lowlands – a great field of open sea upon the east. Sheer above us rose the Spy-glass, here dotted with single pines, there black with precipices. There was no sound but that of the distant breakers, mounting from all round, and the chirp of countless insects in the brush. Not a man, not a sail upon the sea; the very largeness of the view increased the sense of solitude.

Silver, as he sat, took certain bearings with his compass.

'There are three "tall trees",' said he, 'about in the right line from Skeleton Island. "Spy-glass Shoulder," I take it, means that lower p'int there. It's child's play to find the stuff now. I've half a mind to dine first.'

'I don't feel sharp,' growled Morgan. 'Thinkin' o' Flint – I think it were – has done me.'

'Ah, well, my son, you praise your stars he's dead,' said Silver.

'He were an ugly devil,' cried a third pirate, with a shudder; 'that blue in the face, too!'

'That was how the rum took him,' added Merry. 'Blue! well, I reckon he was blue. That's a true word.'

Ever since they had found the skeleton and got upon this train of thought, they had spoken lower and lower, and they had almost got to whispering by now, so that the sound of their talk hardly interrupted the silence of the wood. All of a sudden, out of the middle of the trees in front of us, a thin, high, trembling voice struck up the well-known air and words:

'Fifteen men on the dead man's chest —
Yo-ho-ho, and a bottle of rum!'

I never have seen men more dreadfully affected than the pirates. The colour went from their six faces like enchantment; some leaped to their feet, some clawed hold of others; Morgan grovelled on the ground.

'It's Flint, by —!' cried Merry.

The song had stopped as suddenly as it began – broken off, you would have said, in the middle of a note, as though someone had laid his hand upon the singer's mouth. Coming so far through the clear, sunny atmosphere among the green tree-tops, I thought it had sounded airily and sweetly; and the effect on my companions was the stranger.

'Come,' said Silver, struggling with his ashen lips to get the word out, 'this won't do. Stand by to go about. This is a rum start, and I can't name the voice, but it's someone skylarking – someone that's flesh and blood, and you may lay to that.'

His courage had come back as he spoke, and some of the colour to his face along with it. Already the others had begun to lend an ear to this encouragement, and were coming a little to themselves, when the same voice broke out again – not this time singing, but in a faint distant hail, that echoed yet fainter among the clefts of the Spy-glass.

'Darby M'Graw,' it wailed – for that is the word that best described the sound – 'Darby M'Graw! Darby M'Graw!' again and again and again; and then rising a little higher, and with an oath that I leave out: 'Fetch aft the rum, Darby!'

The buccaneers remained rooted to the ground, their eyes starting from their heads. Long after the voice had died away, they still stared in silence, dreadfully, before them.

'That fixes it!' gasped one. 'Let's go.'

'They was his last words,' moaned Morgan, 'his last words above board.'

Dick had his Bible out, and was praying volubly. He had been well brought up, had Dick, before he came to sea and fell among bad companions.

Still, Silver was unconquered. I could hear his teeth rattle in his head, but he had not yet surrendered.

'Nobody in this here island ever heard of Darby,' he muttered, 'not one but us that's here.' And then, making a great effort, 'Shipmates,' he cried, 'I'm here to get that stuff, and I'll not be beat by man nor devil. I never was feared of Flint in his life, and, by the powers, I'll face him dead. There's seven hundred thousand pound not a quarter of a mile from here. When did ever a gentleman o' fortune show his stern to that much dollars, for a boozy old seaman with a blue mug – and him dead, too?'

But there was no sign of reawakening courage in his followers; rather, indeed, of growing terror at the irreverence of his words.

'Belay there, John!' said Merry. 'Don't you cross a sperrit.'

And the rest were all too terrified to reply. They would have run away severally had they dared; but fear kept them together, and kept them close by John, as if his daring helped them. He, on his part, had pretty well fought his weakness down.

'Sperrit? Well, maybe,' he said, 'But there's one thing not clear to me. There was an echo. Now, no man ever seen a sperrit with a shadow; well, then, what's he doing with an echo to him, I should like to know? That ain't in natur', surely?'

This argument seemed weak enough to me. But you can never tell what will affect the superstitious, and, to my wonder, George Merry was greatly relieved.

'Well, that's so,' he said, 'You've a head upon your shoulders, John, and no mistake. 'Bout ship, mates! this here crew is on a wrong tack, I do believe. And come to think on it, it was like Flint's voice, I grant you, but not just so clear-away like it, after all. It was liker somebody else's voice, now – it was liker —'

'By the powers, Ben Gunn!' roared Silver.

'Ay, and so it were,' cried Morgan, springing on his knees. 'Ben Gunn it were!'

'It don't make much odds, do it, now?' asked Dick. 'Ben Gunn's not here in the body, any more'n Flint.'

But the older hands greeted this remark with scorn.

'Why, nobody minds Ben Gunn,' cried Merry; 'dead or alive, nobody minds him.'

It was extraordinary how their spirits had returned, and how the natural colour had revived in their faces. Soon they were chatting together, with intervals of listening; and not long after, hearing no further sound, they shouldered the tools and set forth again, Merry walking first with Silver's compass to keep them on the right line with Skeleton Island. He had said the truth: dead or alive, nobody minded Ben Gunn.

Dick alone still held his Bible, and looked around him as he went, with fearful glances; but he found no sympathy, and Silver even joked him on his precautions.

'I told you,' said he – 'I told you, you had sp'iled your Bible. If it ain't no good to swear by, what do you suppose a sperrit would give for it? Not that!' and he snapped his big fingers, halting a moment on his crutch.

But Dick was not to be comforted; indeed, it was soon plain to me that the lad was falling sick; hastened by heat, exhaustion, and the shock of his alarm, the fever, predicted by Dr. Livesey, was evidently growing swiftly higher.

It was fine open walking here, upon the summit; our way lay a little downhill, for, as I have said, the plateau tilted towards the west. The pines, great and small, grew wide apart: and even between the clumps of nutmeg and azalea, wide open spaces baked in the hot sunshine. Striking, as we did, pretty near north-west across the island, we drew, on the one hand, ever nearer under the shoulders of the Spy-glass, and on the other, looked ever wider over that western bay where I had once tossed and trembled in the coracle.

The first of the tall trees was reached, and, by the bearing, proved the wrong one. So with the second. The third rose nearly two hundred feet into the air above a clump of underwood; a giant of a vegetable, with a red column as big as a cottage, and a wide shadow around in which a company could have manoeuvred. It was conspicuous far to sea both on the east and west, and might have been entered as a sailing mark upon the chart.

But it was not its size that now impressed my companions; it was the knowledge that seven hundred thousand pounds in gold lay somewhere buried below its spreading shadow. The thought of the money, as they drew nearer, swallowed up their previous terrors. Their eyes burned in their heads; their feet grew speedier and lighter; their whole soul was bound up in that fortune, that whole lifetime of extravagance and pleasure, that lay waiting there for each of them.

Silver hobbled, grunting, on his crutch; his nostrils stood out and quivered; he cursed like a madman when the flies settled on his hot and shiny countenance; he plucked furiously at the line that held me to him, and, from time to time, turned his eyes upon me with a deadly look. Certainly he took no pains to hide his thoughts; and certainly I read them like print. In the immediate nearness of the gold, all else had been forgotten; his promise and the doctor's warning were both things of the past; and I could not doubt that he hoped to seize upon the treasure, find and board the *Hispaniola* under cover of night, cut every honest throat about that island, and sail away as he had at first intended, laden with crimes and riches.

Shaken as I was with these alarms, it was hard for me to keep up with the rapid pace of the treasure-hunters. Now and again I stumbled; and it was then that Silver plucked so roughly at the rope and launched at me his murderous glances. Dick, who had dropped behind us, and now brought up the rear, was babbling to himself both prayers and curses, as his fever kept rising. This also added to my wretchedness, and, to crown all, I was haunted by the thought of the tragedy that had once been acted on that plateau, when that ungodly buccaneer with the blue face – he who died at Savannah, singing and shouting for drink – had there, with his own hand, cut down his six accomplices. This grove, that was now so peaceful, must then have rung with cries, I thought; and even with the thought I could believe I heard it ringing still.

We were now at the margin of the thicket.

'Huzza, mates, all together!' shouted Merry; and the foremost broke into a run.

And suddenly, not ten yards further we beheld them stop. A low cry arose. Silver doubled his pace, digging away with the foot of his crutch like one possessed; and next moment he and I had come also to a dead halt.

Before us was a great excavation, not very recent, for the sides had fallen in and grass had sprouted on the bottom. In this were the shaft of a pick broken in two and the boards of several packing-cases strewn around. On one of these boards I saw, branded with a hot iron, the name *Walrus* – the name of Flint's ship.

All was clear to probation. The cache had been found and rifled; the seven hundred thousand pounds were gone!

Heidi's Grandfather

JOHANNA SPYRI

Illustrated by Jeremy Blezzard

This extract from Heidi *(1881) introduces the little orphan after whom the book is named.*

The village of Maienfeld nestles in the hollow of a pleasant valley. The village's only street turns into a road wide enough for the carts which make their way among the fields. Then this road narrows and becomes a steep path which climbs up towards the alpine pastures.

Along this path two people were briskly walking. One was a well-built young woman, the other a child scarcely five years old who found it difficult to trot along the stony surface. The hot June sun brought out the scent of the plants and the flowers; all the same, the little girl was wearing a woollen dress and over it a shawl, just as though it was winter.

'Are you tired, Heidi?' asked the woman.

'No, Aunt Dete, but I'm hot.'

'One more effort. If you stretch your little legs we shall be up there in less than an hour.'

Half-way up the slope they could see the little village of Dörfli. Dete had grown up there; she knew everyone and several of her friends asked her to stop for a moment for a chat. But Dete said she was sorry; she had to hurry.

'It's such a nice day,' said a plump and cheerful young woman who lived in the last house in the village. 'I'll come part of the way with you. I'd like to go up there too.'

'Come along then, Barbel, but don't delay us.'

The two friends set off at a good pace, with Heidi trailing along behind them. Their tongues wagged as fast as their legs were moving!

They had such a lot of things to talk over: everything that had happened during the two months since they had last seen one another.

'But who is this pretty little creature, Dete? Isn't she the little orphan you look after?'

'That's right, Barbel. This is Heidi. My poor sister left her to us when she died. I have brought her up until now; but the time has come when I can do so no longer.'

'I see. But why not, Dete?'

'Let me explain. Last year, as you know, when Mother died, I went down to Ragaz to work as a chambermaid in a hotel. On my floor some very nice people from Frankfurt were staying. They have returned this year and they have suggested that I should go back with them and work for them full time. Isn't it wonderful?'

'Yes, indeed. But what are you going to do with the little one?'

'Last year at Ragaz Heidi and I boarded with Ursula Pfäffer; but now that I'm leaving for Frankfurt this arrangement is no longer possible. So I'm taking her to my Uncle. She will stay with him.'

'Dete, you're crazy. One thing I'm sure of, the old man will send you packing, you and your schemes.'

'He really must look after her. I have done everything I could for the little girl because I promised Mother I would. But now it's for the old man to take over. After all, he is the nearest thing to a parent Heidi has.'

'I would rather not be in the little girl's shoes! The old man will treat her badly. Anyone would suppose you don't know him – this dreadful "Uncle of the Alps". How was it that he came to get such a nickname, anyway?'

'Don't ask me everything at once; let me sort out my ideas. I know a good many things about the Uncle that I would not like everyone in the valley to know.'

'Don't you believe I can keep a secret?' Barbel asked, frowning.

The two young women drew closer together and Barbel linked her arm with her friend's. They wanted to be able to talk privately together. Heidi left them without a sound and allowed them to go on ahead.

'I say, look at your little girl. She has met Peter the little goatherd. That's best, after all; he will look after her better than we can . . . Dete, dear, tell me about the Uncle. Has he always been such a beast?'

'To tell you the truth, I know nothing about it. I am only twenty-six, and he is at least seventy. But my Mother, who was born like him at Domleschg, has often spoken to me about him, and not too favourably either, believe you me.'

'Is he rich?'

'He inherited the big estate of Domleschg. But instead of working, he preferred to play at being a gentleman and to visit the gambling casinos. That killed his parents.'

'Is he an only son, then?'

'No, he did have a younger brother who was more serious and sensible than he was. This brother disappeared after the bankruptcy and the Uncle too left the country. He was not seen again until, fifteen years later, he returned to Domleschg together with a young boy called Tobias. He wanted to present him to his family, but all doors were shut against him.'

'Why was that?'

'People distrusted him. It was known that he had served as a soldier at Naples and that his wife, who was from the Grisons district of Switzerland, had died soon after Tobias was born. It was also said that he had killed a man in Naples, not in a war but in a brawl, and that he had deserted from the army.'

'Do you know why he is called "Uncle"?'

'That's easily answered. Here in the valley we are all more or less related to one another. That's how he came to be called the Uncle of the Alp, because he lives up there.'

'But what happened to Tobias?'

'He apprenticed the boy to a carpenter. And, furious at the reception he had met with, he determined never to set foot in Dörfli again.'

'And Tobias?'

'Give me time to breathe, Barbel! Tobias was a fine boy, gentle and a good worker. My sister had loved him for a long time and he loved her. They were happy together, specially when their baby was born. But alas, hardly two months later Tobias was killed by the fall of a balk of timber in his carpenter's yard! Poor Adelaïde never recovered. She too was buried a few weeks after Tobias. It was a tragedy and the people of Dörfli said it came about as a punishment for the old man's godlessness. The village priest reproached him, but Uncle would not listen. He became still more unsociable. He settled down in the Alp and never wanted to leave it.'

'Dete, surely you aren't going to leave Heidi with the Uncle?'

'What else is there to do? I can't take a little girl of five with me to Frankfurt!'

The two friends were now half way up to the Alp.

'I stop here,' Barbel said. 'I must talk to Peter's mother, who lives there, in that chalet. In the winter she does knitting for me. Good-bye, Dete, and good luck.'

The young woman sat down at the side of the path to wait until the two children caught up with her. After ten minutes she began to grow uneasy, when they were still not to be seen. At last she saw them pass the chalet on their way to rejoin her.

'Where have you been? And Heidi, whatever have you done with your Sunday dress? Where are your new shoes, and the stockings I knitted for you?'

'It was so hot, Aunt Dete; I took them off.'

And the little girl pointed her finger at a coloured heap of clothes, clearly visible in contrast to the deep green of the meadow.

'Will you tell my why you took your things off?'

'I didn't need them any more. Oh, Aunt Dete, we had such a good time together, Peter and I. Every day he looks after the goats and his mother calls him the goatherd. He has a grandmother too, and he knows all the mountain paths.'

'You had better be quiet, you little chatterbox. And you, you rascal, don't stand there like an idiot, but run as fast as you can to look for the clothes.'

'I'm late already,' the little goatherd replied, his two fists stuck into the pockets of his trousers.

'Don't go on staring at me with those round eyes. If you run fast I'll give you this lovely new penny.'

The young scamp, who had never possessed such a treasure, dashed off down the hill and was soon back with the bundle under his arm. Dete congratulated him.

'And now you might as well come up with us to Uncle. Carry this parcel; that will help us.'

And the little party set off for Uncle's chalet. Peter cracked his whip while the goats and Heidi danced happily round him.

The chalet stood on a spur of the hills, exposed to the sun and to every wind that blew. From there the whole valley could be seen. At its back, a small plantation of firs gave a little shade, then the meadow sloped up again until it reached a wall of bare rock. On a bench sat the old man, smoking his pipe and watching the arrival of his visitors.

A few yards from the chalet Heidi began to run so as to be the first to reach him.

'Good evening, Grandfather.'

The old man stared at her from under his thick, grey eyebrows. He muttered to himself as he turned to watch her cheeky approach.

'What's that you're saying?'

The little girl wasn't to be put off by the old man's unkempt beard, his surly air and his mistrustful look. Meanwhile Dete had arrived. Peter stood apart, watching to see what was going to happen.

'Good-day, Uncle,' said Dete. 'I've brought you Heidi. She is Tobias and Adelaïde's daughter. I'm sure that you won't recognise her after all this time . . .'

'Oh, and why do you bring her to me?'

('What are you doing there,' he said to the boy. 'You're late already with the goats. Take mine too whilst you are about it.')

The little goatherd made off at once without even asking for a rest. He could tell from his look that the old man wasn't in a joking mood.

'I have had her for four years,' continued Dete. 'It's your turn now.'

'I see. And what if the little girl doesn't like me and starts to cry . . .'

'That's your business, not mine. Did anyone help me when she was a babe in arms, hardly a year old, and when I had my mother to look after too? Now I can't do any more. You are the nearest there is to a parent for her; if she is badly cared for it will be your fault – and that won't be the only thing you will have to reproach yourself with!'

After saying these terrible words, Dete felt rather uneasy. She had said more than she meant to. But she could not unsay the words as the old man looked at her angrily. Startled, she retreated a pace or two.

'Off you go! Go back to where you came from, but don't ever come back here again!'

Dete did not give him time to repeat what he had said. She turned on her heels and fled.

'Good-bye, Uncle, Good-bye, Heidi,' she cried.

She ran right through the village of Dörfli without replying to the questions people were asking her.

'What have you done with the little girl?'

'Have you left her with the Uncle, up there?'

Dete continued on her way, worried by the thoughts that kept repeating themselves in her head.

'Poor little thing, with no one to help her at the Uncle's. It's a bad business.'

Dete ran faster to stifle the voice of conscience. After all, she had promised her mother that she would never abandon Heidi.

'I'll look after her later when I've earned some money,' she said to herself.

But in reality Dete's only thought was to escape as fast as she could from the valley where everyone knew about everything she did, and to get to the big city. There she would at least be left in peace.

After Dete had gone, the Grandfather returned to his seat on the bench and, silently, puffed big clouds of white smoke from his pipe.

Heidi walked right round the chalet and up to the old fir trees. But as the wind blew so strongly and made such a noise in the branches, she returned to the old man.

'I'd like to see your house, Grandfather.'

'Off you go then. But take your bundle of clothes with you.'

'I don't need them now.'

'How is that?'

'I'd rather walk bare-legged like the goats.'

'You're quite right. But take your clothes just the same. We must put them away.'

The chalet was poorly furnished. In one corner was Grandfather's bed and opposite it was the fire-place with its big cooking-pot. There were also a table, a chair and a cupboard. Grandfather opened the door of the cupboard. His socks and shirts didn't take up much space; there was still plenty of room on the shelves for Heidi's clothes.

'Where do you sleep, Grandfather?'

'There, in that bed.'

'And me?'

'Where you like.'

This answer suited the little girl very well. She had noticed a ladder leading to the hay-loft and, laughing, she climbed its rungs.

'I'm going to sleep here, Grandfather. And when I wake up I shall see the sun in the valley.'

'Fine, that's agreed then. But I'm going to lay this sack on the hay to keep the straw from tickling your nose.'

Suddenly Heidi remembered that she had had nothing to eat since morning: only a little coffee and a slice of bread and butter.

'I'm hungry, Grandfather.'

The old man lit a fire of sticks under the pot. Heidi watched him for a moment or two, then she decided to help. She laid the table with two plates and forks; but as there was only one glass, she took a cup for herself from the hanging shelves.

The old man watched her at work out of the corner of his eye. He was pleased to see that his little girl was so wide-awake.

Peter the goatherd appeared with his flock

'I've no chair to sit on, Grandfather.'

'To-day you must eat standing up, but after we have eaten I shall make you a stool.'

The old man found a little plank of wood of about the right thickness in his wood-shed. In it he bored three holes into which he inserted the stool's legs. The little girl was amazed at how skilful the old man was.

Already evening was coming on ... When it was dusk, Peter the goatherd appeared with his flock. Heidi was happy to see him and ran to meet him. A beautiful white goat, and another one that was black and smaller, separated themselves from the flock and trotted towards Uncle, who waited for them, a fistful of salt in the palm of his rough hand.

The two goats greedily licked up the salt.

'Aren't they pretty? The dark one there is called Blackie, and the name of the other one is Snowflake.'

In another moment or two, Grandfather had milked the two goats and Heidi was drinking from a big bowl of fresh milk which gave her a white moustache. Never had she tasted anything so good.

The little girl said to herself that her terrifying Grandfather was really very nice and that she would be happy with him and the goats up there on the Alp.

Uncle got supper ready and Heidi laid the table again as she had done at mid-day. But now she did not have to eat standing up. Perched on her new stool, she sat opposite her Grandfather and smiled at him.

'That's delicious. I was really hungry.'

'It's the effect of good mountain air. But tell me: aren't you afraid to sleep all alone in the hay-loft, with the noisy wind we have this evening?'

'Not me. Quick, let's finish the meal and I'll go upstairs to bed.'

In the middle of the night Uncle woke up.

'This wind will stop her from sleeping,' he said to himself.

Silently, he climbed the rungs of the ladder and slipped his head through the trap-door. It was a clear night and he could see Heidi, who was sleeping like an angel. A moonbeam shone down on her and she was smiling, as if she was having beautiful dreams.

The old man lay down on his bed once more and fell asleep again, moved by what he had seen. The coming of this sweet little girl had completely changed his life. In future the chalet was to resound with laughter and song.

Oliver Twist

CHARLES DICKENS

Illustrated by George Cruikshank

Oliver, an orphan, is apprenticed to an undertaker who treats him so badly that he runs away to London. There he is taken in by an old man, Fagin, and two boys called Charley Bates and Jack Dawkins (the Artful Dodger). They promise to teach Oliver how to earn his living. Oliver does not realise that they are pickpockets, and the business they intend to teach him is stealing . . .

The three boys sallied out; the Dodger with his coat-sleeves tucked up, and his hat cocked, as usual; Master Bates sauntering along with his hands in his pockets; and Oliver between them, wondering where they were going, and what branch of manufacture he would be instructed in, first.

The pace at which they went, was such a very lazy, ill-looking saunter, that Oliver soon began to think his companions were going to deceive the old gentleman, by not going to work at all. The Dodger had a vicious propensity, too, of pulling the caps from the heads of small boys and tossing them down areas, while Charley Bates exhibited some very loose notions concerning the rights of property, by pilfering divers apples and onions from the stalls at the kennel sides, and thrusting them into pockets which were so surprisingly capacious, that they seemed to undermine his whole suit of clothes in every direction. These things looked so bad, that Oliver was on the point of declaring his intention of seeking his way back, in the best way he could, when his thoughts were suddenly directed into another channel, by a very mysterious change of behaviour on the part of the Dodger.

They were just emerging from a narrow court not far from the open square in Clerkenwell, which is yet called, by some strange perversion of terms, 'The Green', when the Dodger made a sudden stop; and, laying his finger on his lip, drew his companions back again, with the greatest caution and circumspection.

'What's the matter?' demanded Oliver.

'Hush!' replied the Dodger. 'Do you see the old cove at the bookstall?'

'The old gentleman over the way?' said Oliver. 'Yes, I see him.'

'He'll do,' said the Dodger.

'A prime plant,' observed Master Charley Bates.

Oliver looked from one to the other, with the greatest surprise; but he was not permitted to make any inquiries; for the two boys walked stealthily across the road, and slunk close behind the old gentleman towards whom his attention had been directed. Oliver walked a few paces after them; and, not knowing whether to advance, or retire, stood looking on in silent amazement.

The old gentleman was a very respectable-looking personage, with a powdered head and gold spectacles. He was dressed in a bottle-green coat with a black velvet collar; wore white trousers; and carried a smart bamboo cane under his arm. He had taken up a book from the stall, and there he stood, reading away, as hard as if he were in his elbow-chair, in his own study. It is very possible that he fancied himself there, indeed; for it was plain, from his abstraction, that he saw not the bookstall, nor the street, nor the boys, nor, in short, anything but the book itself: which he was reading straight through: turning over the leaf when he got to the bottom of a page, beginning at the top line of the next one, and going regularly on, with the greatest interest and eagerness.

What was Oliver's horror and alarm as he stood a few paces off, looking on with his eyelids as wide open as they would possibly go, to see the Dodger plunge his hand into the old gentleman's pocket, and draw from thence a handkerchief! To see him hand the same to Charley Bates; and finally to behold them, both, running away round the corner at full speed.

In an instant the whole mystery of the handkerchiefs, and the watches, and the jewels, and the Jew, rushed upon the boy's mind. He

The Dodger plunged his hand into the old gentleman's pocket.

stood, for a moment, with the blood so tingling through all his veins from terror, that he felt as if he were in a burning fire; then, confused and frightened, he took to his heels; and, not knowing what he did, made off as fast as he could lay his feet to the ground.

This was all done in a minute's space, and the very instant that Oliver began to run, the old gentleman, putting his hand to his pocket, and missing his handkerchief, turned sharp round. Seeing the boy scudding away at such a rapid pace, he very naturally concluded him to be the depredator; and, shouting 'Stop thief!' with all his might, made off after him, book in hand.

But the old gentleman was not the only person who raised the hue-and-cry. The Dodger and Master Bates, unwilling to attract public attention by running down the open street, had merely retired into the very first doorway round the corner. They no sooner heard the cry, and saw Oliver running, than, guessing exactly how the matter stood, they issued forth with great promptitude; and, shouting 'Stop thief!' too, joined in the pursuit like good citizens.

Although Oliver had been brought up by philosophers, he was not theoretically acquainted with the beautiful axiom that self-preservation is the first law of nature. If he had been, perhaps he would have been prepared for this. Not being prepared, however, it alarmed him the more; so away he went like the wind, with the old gentleman and the two boys roaring and shouting behind him.

'Stop thief! Stop thief!' There is a magic in the sound. The trades-man leaves his counter, and the carman his waggon; the butcher throws down his tray, the baker his basket, the milkman his pail, the errand-boy his parcels, the school-boy his marbles, the paviour his pick-axe, the child his battledore. Away they run, pell-mell, helter-skelter, slap-dash: tearing, yelling, screaming, knocking down the passengers as they turn the corners, rousing up the dogs, and astonish-ing the fowls: and streets, squares, and courts re-echo with the sound.

'Stop thief! Stop thief!' The cry is taken up by a hundred voices, and the crowd accumulate at every turning. Away they fly, splashing through the mud, and rattling along the pavements; up go the windows, out run the people, onward bear the mob; a whole audience desert Punch in the very thickest of the plot, and, joining the rushing throng, swell the shout, and lend fresh vigour to the cry, 'Stop thief! Stop thief!'

'Stop thief! Stop thief!' There is a passion *for hunting something* deeply implanted in the human breast. One wretched breathless child, pant-ing with exhaustion; terror in his looks; agony in his eyes; large drops of perspiration streaming down his face, strains every nerve to make head upon his pursuers; and as they follow on his track, and gain upon him every instant, they hail his decreasing strength with still louder shouts, and whoop and scream with joy. 'Stop thief!' Ay, stop him for God's sake, were it only in mercy!

Stopped at last! A clever blow. He is down upon the pavement; and the crowd eagerly gather round him: each new-comer jostling and struggling with the others to catch a glimpse. 'Stand aside!' – 'Give him a little air!' – 'Nonsense! he don't deserve it.' – 'Where's the gentleman?' – 'Here he is, coming down the street.' – 'Make room there for the gentleman!' – 'Is this the boy, sir!' – 'Yes'.

Oliver lay, covered with mud and dust, and bleeding from the mouth, looking wildly round upon the heap of faces that surrounded him, when the old gentleman was officiously dragged and pushed into the circle by the foremost of the pursuers.

'Yes,' said the gentleman, 'I am afraid it is the boy.'

'Afraid!' murmured the crowd. 'That's a good 'un!'

'Poor fellow!' said the gentleman, 'he has hurt himself.'

'*I* did that, sir,' said a great lubberly fellow, stepping forward; 'and preciously I cut my knuckles agin' his mouth. *I* stopped him, sir.'

The fellow touched his hat with a grin, expecting something for his pains; but, the old gentleman, eyeing him with an expression of dislike, looked anxiously round, as if he contemplated running away himself: which it is very possible he might have attempted to do, and thus have afforded another chase, had not a police officer (who is generally the last person to arrive in such cases) at that moment made his way through the crowd, and seized Oliver by the collar.

'Come, get up,' said the man, roughly.

'It wasn't me indeed, sir. Indeed, indeed, it was two other boys,' said Oliver, clasping his hands passionately, and looking round. 'They are here somewhere.'

'Oh no, they ain't' said the officer. He meant this to be ironical, but it was true besides; for the Dodger and Charley Bates had filed off down the first convenient court they came to. 'Come, get up!'

'Don't hurt him,' said the old gentleman, compassionately.

'Oh no, I won't hurt him,' replied the officer, tearing his jacket half off his back, in proof thereof. 'Come, I know you; it won't do. Will you stand upon your legs, you young devil?'

Oliver, who could hardly stand, made a shift to raise himself on his feet, and was at once lugged along the streets by the jacket-collar, at a rapid pace. The gentleman walked on with them by the officer's side; and as many of the crowd as could achieve the feat, got a little a-head, and stared back at Oliver from time to time. The boys shouted in triumph; and on they went.

★   ★   ★   ★

The offence had been committed within the district, and indeed in the immediate neighbourhood of, a very notorious metropolitan police office. The crowd had only the satisfaction of accompanying Oliver through two or three streets, and down a place called Mutton Hill, when he was led beneath a low archway, and up a dirty court, into this dispensary of summary justice, by the back way. It was a small paved yard into which they turned; and here they encountered a stout man with a bunch of whiskers on his face, and a bunch of keys in his hand.

'What's the matter now?' said the man carelessly.

'A young fogle-hunter,' replied the man who had Oliver in charge.

'Are you the party that's been robbed, sir?' inquired the man with the keys.

'Yes, I am,' replied the old gentleman; 'but I am not sure that this boy actually took the handkerchief. I – I would rather not press the case.'

'Must go before the magistrate now, sir,' replied the man. 'His worship will be disengaged in half a minute. Now, young gallows!'

This was an invitation for Oliver to enter through a door which he unlocked as he spoke, and which led into a stone cell. Here he was searched; and nothing being found upon him, locked up.

This cell was in shape and size something like an area cellar, only not so light. It was most intolerably dirty; for it was Monday morning, and it had been tenanted by six drunken people, who had been locked up, elsewhere, since Saturday night. But this is little. In our station-houses, men and women are every night confined on the most trivial *charges* – the word is worth noting – in dungeons, compared with which, those in Newgate, occupied by the most atrocious felons, tried, found guilty, and under sentence of death, are palaces. Let anyone who doubts this, compare the two.

The old gentleman looked almost as rueful as Oliver when the key grated in the lock. He turned with a sigh to the book, which had been the innocent cause of all this disturbance.

'There is something in that boy's face,' said the old gentleman to himself as he walked slowly away, tapping his chin with the cover of the book, in a thoughtful manner; 'something that touches and interests me. Can he be innocent? He looked like. – By the bye,' exclaimed the old gentleman, halting very abruptly, and staring up into the sky, 'God bless my soul! Where have I seen something like that look before?'

After musing for some minutes, the old gentleman walked, with the same meditative face, into a back ante-room opening from the yard; and there, retiring into a corner, called up before his mind's eye a vast amphitheatre of faces over which a dusky curtain had hung for many years. 'No,' said the old gentleman, shaking his head; 'it must be imagination.'

He wandered over them again. He had called them into view, and it was not easy to replace the shroud that had so long concealed them. There were the faces of friends, and foes, and of many that had been almost strangers peering intrusively from the crowd; there were the faces of young and blooming girls that were now old women; there were others that the grave had changed to ghastly trophies of death, but which the mind, superior to its power, still dressed in their old freshness and beauty, calling back the lustre of the eyes, the brightness of the smile, the beaming of the soul through its mask of clay, and whispering of beauty beyond the tomb, changed but to be heightened, and taken from earth only to be set up as a light, to shed a soft and gentle glow upon the path to Heaven.

But the old gentleman could recall no one countenance of which Oliver's features bore a trace. So, he heaved a sigh over the recollections he had awakened; and being, happily for himself, an absent old gentleman, buried them again in the pages of the musty book.

He was roused by a touch on the shoulder, and a request from the man with the keys to follow him into the office. He closed his book hastily; and was at once ushered into the imposing presence of the renowned Mr Fang.

The office was a front parlour, with a panelled wall. Mr Fang sat behind a bar, at the upper end; and on one side the door was a sort of wooden pen in which poor little Oliver was already deposited, trembling very much at the awfulness of the scene.

Mr Fang was a lean, long-backed, stiff-necked, middle-sized man, with no great quantity of hair, and what he had, growing on the back and sides of his head. His face was stern, and much flushed. If he were really not in the habit of drinking rather more than was exactly good for him, he might have brought an action against his countenance for libel, and have recovered heavy damages.

The old gentleman bowed respectfully; and advancing to the magistrate's desk, said, suiting the action to the word, 'That is my name and address, sir.' He then withdrew a pace or two; and, with another polite and gentlemanly inclination of the head, waited to be questioned.

Now, it so happened that Mr Fang was at that moment perusing a leading article in a newspaper of the morning, adverting to some recent decision of his, and commending him, for the three hundred and fiftieth time, to the special and particular notice of the Secretary of State for the Home Department. He was out of temper; and he looked up with an angry scowl.

'Who are you?' said Mr Fang.

The old gentleman pointed, with some surprise, to his card.

'Officer!' said Mr Fang, tossing the card contemptuously away with the newspaper. 'Who is this fellow?'

'My name, sir,' said the old gentleman, speaking *like* a gentleman, 'my name, sir, is Brownlow. Permit me to inquire the name of the magistrate who offers a gratuitous and unprovoked insult to a respectable person, under the protection of the bench.' Saying this, Mr Brownlow looked round the office as if in search of some person who would afford him the required information.

'Officer!' said Mr Fang, throwing the paper on one side, 'what's this fellow charged with?'

'He's not charged at all, your worship,' replied the officer. 'He appears against the boy, your worship.'

His worship knew this perfectly well; but it was a good annoyance, and a safe one.

'Appears against the boy, does he?' said Fang, surveying Mr Brownlow contemptuously from head to foot. 'Swear him!'

'Before I am sworn, I must beg to say one word,' said Mr Brownlow: 'and that is, that I really never, without actual experience, could have believed–'

'Hold your tongue, sir!' said Mr Fang, peremptorily.

'I will not, sir!' replied the old gentleman.

'Hold your tongue this instant, or I'll have you turned out of the office!' said Mr Fang. 'You're an insolent, impertinent fellow. How dare you bully a magistrate!'

'What!' exclaimed the old gentleman, reddening.

'Swear this person!' said Fang to the clerk. 'I'll not hear another word. Swear him.'

Mr Brownlow's indignation was greatly roused; but reflecting perhaps, that he might only injure the boy by giving vent to it, he suppressed his feelings and submitted to be sworn at once.

'Now,' said Fang. 'What's the charge against this boy? What have you got to say, sir?'

'I was standing at a bookstall –' Mr Brownlow began.

'Hold your tongue, sir,' said Mr Fang. 'Policeman! Where's the policeman? Here, swear this policeman. Now, policeman, what is this?'

The policeman, with becoming humility, related how he had taken the charge; how he had searched Oliver, and found nothing on his person; and how that was all he knew about it.

'Are there any witnesses?' inquired Mr Fang.

'None, your worship,' replied the policeman.

Mr Fang sat silent for some minutes, and then, turning round to the prosecutor, said in a towering passion,

'Do you mean to state what your complaint against this boy is, man, or do you not? You have been sworn. Now, if you stand there, refusing to give evidence, I'll punish you for disrespect to the bench; I will, by—'

By what, or by whom, nobody knows, for the clerk and jailor coughed very loud, just at the right moment; and the former dropped a heavy book upon the floor, thus preventing the word from being heard – accidentally, of course.

With many interruptions, and repeated insults, Mr Brownlow contrived to state his case; observing that, in the surprise of the moment, he had run after the boy because he saw him running away; and expressing his hope that, if the magistrate should believe him, although not actually the thief, to be connected with thieves, he would deal as leniently with him as justice would allow.

'He has been hurt already,' said the old gentleman in conclusion. 'And I fear,' he added, with great energy, looking towards the bar, 'I really fear that he is very ill.'

'Oh! yes, I dare say!' said Mr Fang, with a sneer. 'Come, none of your tricks here, you young vagabond; they won't do. What's your name?'

Oliver tried to reply, but his tongue failed him. He was deadly pale; and the whole place seemed turning round and round.

'What's your name, you hardened scoundrel?' thundered Mr Fang. 'Officer, what's his name?'

This was addressed to a bluff old fellow, in a striped waistcoat, who was standing by the bar. He bent over Oliver, and repeated the inquiry; but finding him really incapable of understanding the question; and knowing that his not replying would only infuriate the magistrate the more, and add to the severity of his sentence; he hazarded a guess.

'He says his name's Tom White, your worship,' said this kind-hearted thief-taker.

'Oh, he won't speak out, won't he?' said Fang. 'Very well, very well. Where does he live?'

'Where he can, your worship,' replied the officer: again pretending to receive Oliver's answer.

'Has he any parents?' inquired Mr Fang.

'He says they died in his infancy, your worship,' replied the officer, hazarding the usual reply.

At this point of the inquiry, Oliver raised his head; and, looking round with imploring eyes, murmured a feeble prayer for a draught of water.

'Stuff and nonsense!' said Mr Fang: 'don't try to make a fool of me.'

'I think he really is ill, your worship,' remonstrated the officer.

'I know better,' said Mr Fang.

'Take care of him, officer,' said the old gentleman, raising his hands instinctively; 'he'll fall down.'

'Stand away, officer,' cried Fang savagely; 'let him, if he likes.'

Oliver availed himself of the kind permission, and fell to the floor in a fainting fit. The men in the office looked at each other, but no one dared to stir.

'I knew he was shamming,' said Fang, as if this were incontestable proof of the fact. 'Let him lie there; he'll soon be tired of that.'

'How do you propose to deal with the case, sir?' inquired the clerk in a low voice.

'Summarily,' replied Mr Fang. 'He stands committed for three months – hard labour of course. Clear the office.'

The door was open for this purpose, and a couple of men were preparing to carry the insensible boy to his cell; when an elderly man of decent but poor appearance, clad in an old suit of black, rushed hastily into the office, and advanced towards the bench.

'Stop, stop! Don't take him away! For Heaven's sake stop a moment!' cried the new-comer, breathless with haste.

Although the presiding Genii in such an office as this, exercise a summary and arbitrary power over the liberties, the good name, the character, almost the lives, of Her Majesty's subjects, especially of the poorer class; and although, within such walls, enough fantastic tricks are daily played to make the angels blind with weeping; they are closed to the public, save through the medium of the daily press. Mr Fang was consequently not a little indignant to see an unbidden guest enter in such irreverent disorder.

'What is this? Who is this? Turn this man out. Clear the office!' cried Mr Fang.

'I *will* speak,' cried the man; 'I will not be turned out. I saw it all. I keep the bookstall. I demand to be sworn. I will not be put down. Mr Fang, you must hear me. You must not refuse, sir.'

The man was right. His manner was determined; and the matter was growing rather too serious to be hushed up.

'Swear the man,' growled Mr Fang, with a very ill grace. 'Now, man, what have you got to say?'

'This,' said the man: 'I saw three boys – two others and the prisoner here – loitering on the opposite side of the way, when this gentleman was reading. The robbery was committed by another boy. I saw it done; and I saw that this boy was perfectly amazed and stupefied by it.' Having by this time recovered a little breath, the worthy bookstall keeper proceeded to relate, in a more coherent manner, the exact circumstances of the robbery.

'Why didn't you come here before?' said Fang, after a pause.

'I hadn't a soul to mind the shop,' replied the man. 'Everybody who could have helped me, had joined in the pursuit. I could get nobody till five minutes ago; and I've run here all the way.'

'The prosecutor was reading, was he?' inquired Fang, after another pause.

'Yes,' replied the man. 'The very book he has in his hand.'

'Oh, that book, eh?' said Fang. 'Is it paid for?'

'No, it is not,' replied the man, with a smile.

'Dear me, I forgot all about it!' exclaimed the absent old gentleman, innocently.

'A nice person to prefer a charge against a poor boy!' said Fang, with a comical effort to look humane. 'I consider, sir, that you have obtained possession of that book, under very suspicious and disreputable circumstances; and you may think yourself very fortunate that the owner of the property declines to prosecute. Let this be a lesson to you, my man, or the law will overtake you yet. The boy is discharged. Clear the office.'

'D–n me!' cried the old gentleman, bursting out with the rage he had kept down so long, 'd–n me! I'll–'

'Clear the office!' said the magistrate. 'Officers, do you hear? Clear the office!'

The mandate was obeyed; and the indignant Mr Brownlow was conveyed out, with the book in one hand, and the bamboo cane in the other: in a perfect frenzy of rage and defiance.

He reached the yard; and his passion vanished in a moment. Little Oliver Twist lay on his back on the pavement, with his shirt unbuttoned, and his temples bathed with water; his face a deadly white; and a cold tremble convulsing his whole frame.

'Poor boy, poor boy!' said Mr Brownlow, bending over him. 'Call a coach, somebody, pray. Directly!'

A coach was obtained, and Oliver, having been carefully laid on one seat, the old gentleman got in and sat himself on the other.

'May I accompany you?' said the bookstall keeper, looking in.

'Bless me, yes, my dear sir,' said Mr Brownlow quickly. 'I forgot you. Dear, dear! I have this unhappy book still! Jump in. Poor fellow! There's no time to lose.'

The bookstall keeper got into the coach; and away they drove.

The coach rattled away, over nearly the same ground as that which Oliver had traversed when he first entered London in company with the Dodger; and, turning a different way when it reached the Angel at Islington, stopped at length before a neat house, in a quiet shady street near Pentonville. Here, a bed was prepared, without loss of time, in which Mr Brownlow saw his young charge carefully and comfortably deposited; and here, he was tended with a kindness and solicitude that knew no bounds.

The Laurence Boy

LOUISA M. ALCOTT

Illustrated by David Hopkins

This extract comes from Little Women *(1868). The 'Little Women' are Meg, Jo, Beth and Amy. Their father is away fighting in the American Civil War, and they are far from rich. They are happy nonetheless, as this chapter shows.*

'Jo! Jo! where are you?' cried Meg, at the foot of the garret stairs.

'Here!' answered a husky voice from above; and running up, Meg found her sister eating apples and crying over the 'Heir of Redcliffe', wrapped up in a comforter on an old three-legged sofa by the sunny window. This was Jo's favourite refuge; and here she loved to retire with half-a-dozen russets and a nice book, to enjoy the quiet and the society of a pet rat who lived near by, and didn't mind her a particle. As Meg appeared, Scrabble whisked into his hole. Jo shook the tears off her cheeks, and waited to hear the news.

'Such fun! only see! a regular note of invitation from Mrs. Gardiner for to-morrow night!' cried Meg, waving the precious paper, and then proceeding to read it, with girlish delight.

'"Mrs. Gardiner would be happy to see Miss March and Miss Josephine at a little dance on New Year's Eve." Marmee is willing we should go; now what *shall* we wear?'

'What's the use of asking that, when you know we shall wear our poplins, because we haven't got anything else,' answered Jo, with her mouth full.

'If I only had a silk!' sighed Meg. 'Mother says I may when I'm eighteen, perhaps; but two years is an everlasting time to wait.'

'I'm sure our pops look like silk, and they are nice enough for us. Yours is as good as new, but I forgot the burn and the tear in mine. Whatever shall I do? the burn shows badly, and I can't take any out.'

'You must sit still all you can, and keep your back out of sight; the front is all right. I shall have a new ribbon for my hair, and Marmee will lend me her little pearl pin, and my new slippers are lovely, and my gloves will do, though they aren't as nice as I'd like.'

'Mine are spoilt with lemonade, and I can't get any new ones, so I shall have to go without,' said Jo, who never troubled herself much about dress.

'You *must* have gloves, or I won't go,' cried Meg decidedly. 'Gloves are more important than anything else; you can't dance without them, and if you don't I should be *so* mortified.'

'Then I'll stay still. I don't care much for company dancing; it's no fun to go sailing round; I like to fly about and cut capers.'

'You can't ask mother for new ones, they are so expensive, and you are so careless. She said, when you spoilt the others, that she shouldn't get you any more this winter. Can't you make them do?' asked Meg anxiously.

'I can hold them crumpled up in my hand, so no one will know how stained they are; that's all I can do. No! I'll tell you how we can manage – each wear one good one and carry a bad one; don't you see?'

'Your hands are bigger than mine, and you will stretch my glove dreadfully,' began Meg, whose gloves were a tender point with her.

'Then I'll go without. I don't care what people say!' cried Jo, taking up her book.

'You may have it, you may! only don't stain it, and do behave nicely. Don't put your hands behind you, or stare, or say "Christopher Colombus!" will you?'

'Don't worry about me; I'll be as prim as I can, and not get into any scrapes, if I can help it. Now go and answer your note, and let me finish this splendid story.'

So Meg went away to 'accept with thanks', look over her dress, and sing blithely as she did up her one real lace frill; while Jo finished her story, her four apples, and had a game of romps with Scrabble.

Getting ready for the party

On New Year's Eve the parlour was deserted, for the two younger girls played dressing-maids, and the two elder were absorbed in the all-important business of 'getting ready for the party'. Simple as the toilets were, there was a great deal of running up and down, laughing and talking, and at one time a strong smell of burnt hair pervaded the house. Meg wanted a few curls about her face, and Jo undertook to pinch the papered locks with a pair of hot tongs.

'Ought they to smoke like that?' asked Beth, from her perch on the bed.

'It's the dampness drying,' replied Jo.

'What a queer smell! it's like burnt feathers,' observed Amy, smoothing her own pretty curls with a superior air.

'There, now I'll take off the papers and you'll see a cloud of little ringlets,' said Jo, putting down the tongs.

She did take off the papers, but no cloud of ringlets appeared, for the hair came with the papers, and the horrified hairdresser laid a row of little scorched bundles on the bureau before her victim.

'Oh, oh, oh! what *have* you done? I'm spoilt! I can't go! My hair, oh, my hair!' wailed Meg, looking with despair at the uneven frizzle on her forehead.

'Just my luck! you shouldn't have asked me to do it: I always spoil everything. I'm so sorry, but the tongs were too hot, and so I've made a mess,' groaned poor Jo, regarding the black pancakes with tears of regret.

'It isn't spoilt; just frizzle it, and tie your ribbon so the ends come on your forehead a bit, and it will look like the last fashion. I've seen many girls do it so,' said Amy consolingly.

'Serves me right for trying to be fine. I wish I'd let my hair alone,' cried Meg petulantly.

'So do I, it was so smooth and pretty. But it will soon grow out again,' said Beth, coming to kiss and comfort the shorn sheep.

After various lesser mishaps, Meg was finished at last, and by the united exertions of the family, Jo's hair was got up, and her dress on. They looked very well in their simple suits – Meg in silvery drab, with a blue velvet snood, lace frills, and the pearl pin; Jo in maroon, with a stiff, gentlemanly linen collar, and a white chrysanthemum or two for her only ornament. Each put on one nice light glove, and carried one soiled one, and all pronounced the effect 'quite easy and fine'. Meg's high-heeled slippers were very tight, and hurt her, though she would not own it, and Jo's nineteen hairpins all seemed stuck straight into her head, which was not exactly comfortable; but, dear me, let us be elegant or die!

'Have a good time, dearies,' said Mrs. March, as the sisters went daintily down the walk. 'Don't eat much supper, and come away at eleven, when I send Hannah for you.' As the gate clashed behind them, a voice cried from the window, —

'Girls, girls! *have* you both got nice pocket-handkerchiefs?'

'Yes, yes, spandy nice, and Meg has cologne on hers,' cried Jo, adding, with a laugh, as they went on, 'I do believe Marmee would ask that if we were all running away from an earthquake.'

'It is one of her aristocratic tastes, and quite proper, for a real lady is always known by neat boots, gloves, and handkerchief,' replied Meg, who had a good many little 'aristocratic tastes' of her own.

'Now don't forget to keep the bad breadth out of sight, Jo. Is my sash right? and does my hair look *very* bad?' said Meg, as she turned from the glass in Mrs. Gardiner's dressing-room, after a prolonged prink.

'I know I shall forget. If you see me doing anything wrong, just remind me by a wink, will you?' returned Jo, giving her collar a twitch, and her head a hasty brush.

'No, winking isn't lady-like; I'll lift my eyebrows if anything is wrong, and nod if you are all right. Now hold your shoulders straight, and take short steps, and don't shake hands if you are introduced to any one, it isn't the thing.'

'How *do* you learn all the proper ways? I never can. Isn't that music gay?'

Down they went, feeling a trifle timid, for they seldom went to parties, and, informal as this little gathering was, it was an event to them. Mrs. Gardiner, a stately old lady, greeted them kindly, and handed them over to the eldest of her six daughters. Meg knew Sallie, and was at her ease very soon; but Jo, who didn't care much for girls or girlish gossip, stood about with her back carefully against the wall, and felt as much out of place as a colt in a flower-garden. Half-a-dozen jovial lads were talking about skates in another part of the room, and she longed to go and join them, for skating was one of the joys of her life. She telegraphed her wish to Meg, but the eyebrows went up so alarmingly that she dared not stir. No one came to talk to her, and one by one the group near her dwindled away, till she was left alone. She could not roam about and amuse herself, for the burnt breadth would show, so she stared at people rather forlornly till the dancing began. Meg was asked at once, and the tight slippers tripped about so briskly that none would have guessed the pain their wearer suffered smilingly. Jo saw a big, red-headed youth approaching her corner, and fearing he meant to engage her, she slipped into a curtain recess, intending to peep and enjoy herself in peace. Unfortunately, another bashful person had chosen the same refuge; for, as the curtain fell behind her, she found herself face to face with the 'Laurence boy'.

'Dear me, I didn't know any one was here!' stammered Jo, preparing to back out as speedily as she had bounced in.

But the boy laughed, and said pleasantly, though he looked a little startled, —

'Don't mind me; stay if you like.'

'Shan't I disturb you?'

'Not a bit; I only came here because I don't know many people, and felt rather strange at first, you know.'

'So did I. Don't go away, please, unless you'd rather.'

The boy sat down again and looked at his pumps, till Jo said, trying to be polite and easy, —

'I think I've had the pleasure of seeing you before; you live near us, don't you?'

'Next door;' and he looked up and laughed outright, for Jo's prim manner was rather funny when he remembered how they had chatted about cricket when he brought the cat home.

That put Jo at her ease; and she laughed too, as she said, in her heartiest way, —

'We did have such a good time over your nice Christmas present.'

'Grandpa sent it.'

'But you put it into his head, didn't you, now?'

'How is your cat, Miss March?' asked the boy, trying to look sober, while his black eyes shone with fun.

'Nicely, thank you, Mr. Laurence; but I am not Miss March, I'm only Jo,' returned the young lady.

'I'm not Mr. Laurence; I'm only Laurie.'

'Laurie Laurence – what an odd name.'

'My first name is Theodore, but I don't like it, for the fellows called me Dora, so I made them say Laurie instead.'

'I hate my name, too – so sentimental! I wish every one would say Jo, instead of Josephine. How did you make the boys stop calling you Dora?'

'I thrashed 'em.'

'I can't thrash Aunt March, so I suppose I shall have to bear it;' and Jo resigned herself with a sigh.

'Don't you like to dance, Miss Jo?' asked Laurie, looking as if he thought the name suited her.

'I like it well enough if there is plenty of room, and every one is lively. In a place like this, I'm sure to upset something, tread on people's toes, or do something dreadful, so I keep out of mischief, and let Meg sail about. Don't you dance?'

'Sometimes; you see I've been abroad a good many years, and haven't been into company enough yet to know how you do things here.'

'Abroad!' cried Jo. 'Oh, tell me about it! I love dearly to hear people describe their travels.'

Laurie didn't seem to know where to begin; but Jo's eager questions soon set him going, and he told her how he had been at school in

Vevay, where the boys never wore hats, and had a fleet of boats on the lake, and for holiday fun went on walking trips about Switzerland with their teachers.

'Don't I wish I'd been there!' cried Jo. 'Did you go to Paris?'

'We spent last winter there.'

'Can you talk French?'

'We were not allowed to speak anything else at Vevay.'

'Do say some. I can read it, but can't pronounce.'

'Quel nom a cette jeune demoiselle en les pantoufles jolies?' said Laurie good-naturedly.

'How nicely you do it! Let me see – you said, "Who is the young lady in the pretty slippers," didn't you?'

'Oui, mademoiselle.'

'It's my sister Margaret, and you knew it was! Do you think she is pretty?'

'Yes; she makes me think of the German girls, she looks so fresh and quiet, and dances like a lady.'

Joe quite glowed with pleasure at this boyish praise of her sister, and stored it up to repeat to Meg. Both peeped and criticised and chattered, till they felt like old acquaintances. Laurie's bashfulness soon wore off, for Jo's gentlemanly demeanour amused and set him at his ease, and Jo was her merry self again, because her dress was forgotten, and nobody lifted their eyebrows at her. She liked the 'Laurence boy' better than ever, and took several good looks at him, so that she might describe him to the girls; for they had no brothers, very few male cousins, and boys were almost unknown creatures to them.

'Curly black hair, brown skin, big black eyes, handsome nose, fine teeth, small hands and feet, taller than I am; very polite for a boy, and altogether jolly. Wonder how old he is?'

It was on the tip of Jo's tongue to ask; but she checked herself in time, and, with unusual tact, tried to find out in a roundabout way.

'I suppose you are going to college soon? I see you pegging away at your books – no, I mean studying hard;' and Jo blushed at the dreadful 'pegging' which had escaped her.

Laurie smiled, but didn't seem shocked, and answered with a shrug, —

'Not for a year or two; I won't go before seventeen, anyway.'

'Aren't you but fifteen?' asked Jo, looking at the tall lad whom she had imagined seventeen already.

'Sixteen next month.'

'How I wish I was going to college! You don't look as if you liked it.'

'I hate it! Nothing but grinding or skylarking. And I don't like the way fellows do either, in this country.'

'What do you like?'

'To live in Italy, and to enjoy myself in my own way.'

Jo wanted very much to ask what his own way was; but his black brows looked rather threatening as he knit them, so she changed the subject by saying, as her foot kept time, 'That's a splendid polka! Why don't you go and try it?'

'If you will come too,' he answered, with a gallant little bow.

'I can't; for I told Meg I wouldn't, because —' There Jo stopped, and looked undecided whether to tell or to laugh.

'Because what?' asked Laurie curiously.

'You won't tell?'

'Never!'

'Well, I have a bad trick of standing before the fire, and so I burn my frocks, and I scorched this one; and, though it's nicely mended, it shows, and Meg told me to keep still, so no one would see it. You may laugh if you want to; it is funny, I know.'

But Laurie didn't laugh; he only looked down a minute, and the expression of his face puzzled Jo, when he said very gently, —

'Never mind that; I'll tell you how we can manage; there's a long hall out there, and we can dance grandly, and no one will see us. Please come?'

Jo thanked him, and gladly went, wishing she had two neat gloves, when she saw the nice pearl-coloured ones her partner wore. The hall was empty, and they had a grand polka, for Laurie danced well, and taught her the German step, which delighted Jo, being full of swing and spring. When the music stopped they sat down on the stairs to get their breath, and Laurie was in the midst of an account of a students' festival at Heidelberg, when Meg appeared in search of her sister. She beckoned, and Jo reluctantly followed her into a side-room, where she found her on a sofa holding her foot, and looking pale.

'I've sprained my ankle. That stupid high heel turned, and gave me a sad wrench. It aches so, I can hardly stand, and I don't know how I'm ever going to get home,' she said, rocking to and fro in pain.

'I knew you'd hurt your feet with those silly shoes. I'm sorry. But I don't see what you can do, except get a carriage, or stay here all night,' answered Jo, softly rubbing the poor ankle as she spoke.

'I can't have a carriage without its costing ever so much; I dare say I can't get one at all, for most people come in their own, and it's a long way to the stable, and no one to send.'

'I'll go.'

'No, indeed! It's past nine, and dark as Egypt. I can't stop here, for the house is full. Sallie has some girls staying with her. I'll rest till Hannah comes, and then do the best I can.'

'I'll ask Laurie; he will go,' said Jo, looking relieved as the idea occurred to her.

'Mercy, no! Don't ask or tell any one. Get me my rubbers, and put these slippers with our things. I can't dance any more; but as soon as supper is over, watch for Hannah, and tell me the minute she comes.'

'They are going to supper now. I'll stay with you; I'd rather.'

'No, dear; run along, and bring me some coffee. I'm so tired, I can't stir.'

So Meg reclined, with rubbers well hidden, and Jo went blundering away to the dining-room, which she found after going into a china closet, and opening the door of a room where old Mr. Gardiner was taking a little private refreshment. Making a dart at the table, she secured the coffee, which she immediately spilt, thereby making the front of her dress as bad as the back.

'Oh, dear! what a blunderbuss I am!' exclaimed Jo, finishing Meg's glove by scrubbing her gown with it.

'Can I help you?' said a friendly voice; and there was Laurie, with a full cup in one hand and a plate of ice in the other.

'I was trying to get something for Meg, who is very tired, and some one shook me, and here I am; in a nice state,' answered Jo, glancing dismally from the stained skirt to the coffee-coloured glove.

'Too bad! I was looking for some one to give this to. May I take it to your sister?'

'Oh, thank you; I'll show you where she is. I don't offer to take it myself, for I should only get into another scrape if I did.'

Jo led the way; and, as if used to waiting on ladies, Laurie drew up a little table, brought a second instalment of coffee and ice for Jo, and was so obliging that even particular Meg pronounced him a 'nice boy'. They had a merry time over the bonbons and mottoes, and were in the midst of a quiet game of 'buzz' with two or three other young people who had strayed in, when Hannah appeared. Meg forgot her foot, and rose so quickly that she was forced to catch hold of Jo, with an exclamation of pain.

'Hush! don't say anything,' she whispered; adding aloud, 'It's nothing; I turned my foot a little – that's all,' and limped upstairs to put her things on.

Hannah scolded, Meg cried, and Jo was at her wits' end, till she decided to take things into her own hands. Slipping out, she ran down, and finding a servant, asked if he could get her a carriage. It happened to be a hired waiter, who knew nothing about the neighbourhood; and Jo was looking round for help when Laurie, who had heard what she said, came up and offered his grandfather's carriage, which had just come for him, he said.

'It's so early! You can't mean to go yet,' began Jo, looking relieved, but hesitating to accept the offer.

'I always go early – I do, truly. Please let me take you home? It's all on my way, you know, and it rains, they say.'

That settled it; and telling him of Meg's mishap, Jo gratefully accepted, and rushed up to bring down the rest of the party. Hannah hated rain as much as a cat does; so she made no trouble, and they rolled away in the luxurious close carriage, feeling very festive and elegant. Laurie went on the box, so Meg could keep her foot up, and the girls talked over their party in freedom.

'I had a capital time. Did you?' asked Jo, rumpling up her hair, and making herself comfortable.

'Yes, till I hurt myself. Sallie's friend, Annie Moffat, took a fancy to me, and asked me to come and spend a week with her when Sallie does. She is going in the spring, when the opera comes, and it will be perfectly spendid if mother only lets me go,' answered Meg, cheering up at the thought.

'I saw you dancing with the red-headed man I ran away from. Was he nice?'

'Oh, very! His hair is auburn, not red; and he was very polite, and I had a delicious redowa with him!'

'He looked like a grasshopper in a fit, when he did the new step. Laurie and I couldn't help laughing. Did you hear us?'

'No, but it was very rude. What *were* you about all that time, hidden away there?'

Jo told her adventures, and by the time she had finished, they were at home. With many thanks, they said 'Goodnight', and crept in, hoping to disturb no one; but the instant their door creaked, two little night-caps bobbed up, and two sleepy but eager voices cried out, —

'Tell about the party! tell about the party!'

With what Meg called 'a great want of manners', Jo had saved some bonbons for the little girls, and they soon subsided, after hearing the most thrilling events of the evening.

'I declare, it really seems like being a fine young lady, to come home from the party in a carriage, and sit in my dressing-gown with a maid to wait on me,' said Meg, as Jo bound up her foot with arnica, and brushed her hair.

'I don't believe fine young ladies enjoy themselves a bit more than we do, in spite of our burnt hair, old gowns, one glove apiece, and tight slippers that sprain our ankles when we are silly enough to wear them.' And I think Jo was quite right.

The Escape

J. MEADE FALKNER

John Trenchard, a fifteen-year-old boy, is involved with smugglers. In this extract from Moonfleet *(1898) he and his friend Elzevier are trying to escape from the soldiers who have ambushed them.*

The white chalk was a bulwark between us and the foe; and though one or two of them loosed off their matchlocks, trying to get at us sideways, they could not even see their quarry, and 'twas only shooting at a venture. We were safe. But for how short a time! Safe just for so long as it should please the soldiers not to come down to take us, safe with a discharged pistol in our grasp, and a shot man lying at our feet.

Elzevir was the first to speak: 'Can you stand, John? Is the bone broken?'

'I cannot stand,' I said; 'there is something gone in my leg, and I feel blood running down into my boot.'

He knelt, and rolled down the leg of my stocking; but though he only moved my foot ever so little, it caused me sharp pain, for feeling was coming back after the first numbness of the shot.

'They have broke the leg, though it bleeds little,' Elzevir said. 'We have no time to splice it here, but I will put a kerchief round, and while I wrap it, listen to how we lie, and then choose what we shall do.'

I nodded, biting my lips hard to conceal the pain he gave me, and he went on: 'We have a quarter of an hour before the Posse can get down to us. But come they will, and thou canst judge what chance we have to save liberty or life with that carrion lying by us' – and he jerked his thumb at Maskew – 'though I am glad 'twas not my hand that sent him to his reckoning, and therefore do not blame thee if thou didst make me waste a charge in air. So one thing we can do is wait here until they come, and I can account for a few of them before they shoot me down; but thou canst not fight with a broken leg, and they will take thee alive, and then there is a dance on air at Dorchester Gaol.'

I felt sick with pain and bitterly cast down to think that I was like to come so soon to such a vile end; so only gave a sigh, wishing heartily that Maskew were not dead, and that my leg were not broke, but that I was back again at the *Why Not?* or even hearing one of Dr. Sherlock's sermons in my aunt's parlour.

Elzevir looked down at me when I sighed, and seeing, I suppose, that I was sorrowful, tried to put a better face on a sad business. 'Forgive me, lad,' he said, 'if I have spoke too roughly. There is yet another way that we may try; and if thou hadst but two whole legs, I would have tried it, but now 'tis little short of madness. And yet, if thou fear'st not, I will still try it. Just at the end of this flat ledge, furthest from where the bridle-path leads down, but not a hundred yards from where we stand, there is a sheep-track leading up the cliff. It starts where the under-cliff dies back again into the chalk face, and climbs by slants and elbow-turns up to the top. The shepherds call it the Zigzag, and even sheep lose their footing on it; and of men I never heard but one had climbed it, and that was lander Jordan, when the Excise was on his heels, half a century back. But he that tries it stakes all on head and foot, and a wounded bird like thee may not dare that flight. Yet, if thou art content to hang thy life upon a hair, I will carry thee some way; and where there is no room to carry, thou must down on hands and knees and trail thy foot.'

It was a desperate chance enough, but came as welcome as a patch of blue through lowering skies. 'Yes,' I said, 'dear Master Elzevir, let us get to it quickly; and if we fall 'tis better far to die upon the rocks below than to wait here for them to hale us off to gaol.' And with that I tried to stand, thinking I might go dot-and-carry even with a broken leg. But 'twas no use, and down I sank with a groan. Then Elzevir caught me up, holding me in his arms, with my head looking over his back, and made off for the Zigzag. And as we slunk along, close to the cliff-side, I saw, between the brambles, Maskew lying with his face turned up to the morning sky. And there was the little red hole in the middle of his forehead, and a thread of blood that welled up from it and trickled off on to the sward.

It was a sight to stagger any man, and would have made me swoon perhaps, but that there was no time, for we were at the end of the under-cliff, and Elzevir set me down for a minute, before he buckled to his task. And 'twas a task that might cow the bravest, and when I looked upon the Zigzag, it seemed better to stay where we were and fall into the hands of the Posse than set foot on that awful way, and fall upon the rocks below. For the Zigzag started off as a fair enough chalk path, but in a few paces narrowed down till it was but a whiter thread against the grey-white cliff-face, and afterwards turned sharply back, crossing a hundred feet direct above our heads. And then I smelt an evil stench, and looking about, saw the blown-out carcass of a rotting sheep lie close at hand.

'Faugh,' said Elzevir, ''tis a poor beast has lost his foothold.'

It was an ill omen enough, and I said as much, beseeching him to make his own way up the Zigzag and leave me where I was, for that they might have mercy on a boy.

'Tush!' he cried; 'it is thy heart that fails thee, and 'tis too late now to change counsel. We have fifteen minutes yet to win or lose with, and if we gain the cliff-top in that time we shall have an hour's start, or more for they will take all that to search the undercliff. And Maskew, too, will keep them in check a little, while they try to bring the life back to so good a man. But if we fall, why, we shall fall together, and outwit their cunning. So shut thy eyes, and keep them tight shut until I bid thee open them.' With that he caught me up again, and I shut my eyes firm, rebuking myself for my faint-heartedness, and not telling him how much my foot hurt me.

In a minute I knew from Elzevir's steps that he had left the turf and was upon the chalk. Now I do not believe that there were half a dozen men beside in England who would have ventured up the path, even free and untrammelled, and not a man in all the world to do it with a full-grown lad in his arms. Yet Elzevir made no bones of it, nor spoke a word; only he went very slow, and I felt him scuffle with his foot as he set it forward, to make sure he was putting it down firm.

I said nothing, not wishing to distract him from his terrible task, and held my breath, when I could, so that I might lie quieter in his arms. Thus he went on for a time that seemed without end, and yet was really but a minute or two; and by degrees I felt the wind, that we could scarce perceive at all on the under-cliff, blow fresher and cold on the cliff-side. And then the path grew steeper and steeper, and Elzevir went slower and slower, till at last he spoke:

'John, I am going to stop; but open not thy eyes till I have set thee down and bid thee.'

I did as bidden, and he lowered me gently, setting me on all-fours upon the path; and speaking again:

'The path is too narrow here for me to carry thee, and thou must creep round this corner on thy hands and knees. But have a care to keep thy outer hand near to the inner, and the balance of thy body to the cliff, for there is no room to dance hornpipes here. And hold thy eyes fixed on the chalk-wall, looking neither down nor seaward.'

'Twas well he told me what to do, and well I did it; for when I opened my eyes, even without moving them from the cliff-side, I saw that the ledge was little more than a foot wide, and that ever so little a lean of the body would dash me on the rocks below. So I crept on, but spent much time that was so precious in travelling those ten yards to take me round the first elbow of the path; for my foot was heavy and gave me fierce pain to drag, though I tried to mask it from Elzevir. And he, forgetting what I suffered, cried out, 'Quicken thy pace, lad, if thou canst, the time is short.' Now so frail is man's temper, that though he was doing more than any ever did to save another's life, and was all I had to trust to in the world; yet because he forgot my pain and bade me quicken, my choler rose, I nearly gave him back an angry word, but thought better of it and kept it in.

Then he told me to stop, for that the way grew wider and he would pick me up again. But here was another difficulty, for the path was still so narrow and the cliff-wall so close that he could not take me up in his arms. So I lay flat on my face, and he stepped over me, setting his foot between my shoulders to do it; and then, while he knelt down upon the path, I climbed up from behind upon him, putting my arms round his neck; and so he bore me 'pickaback.' I shut my eyes firm again, and thus we moved along another spell, mounting still and feeling the wind still freshening.

At length he said that we were come to the last turn of the path, and he must set me down once more. So down upon his knees and hands he went, and I slid off behind, on to the ledge. Both were on all-fours now; Elzevir first and I following. But as I crept along, I relaxed care for a moment, and my eyes wandered from the cliff-side and looked down. And far below I saw the blue sea twinkling like a dazzling mirror, and the gulls wheeling about the sheer chalk wall, and then I thought of that bloated carcass of a sheep that had fallen from this very spot perhaps, and in an instant felt a sickening qualm and swimming of the brain, and knew that I was giddy and must fall.

Then I called out to Elzevir, and he, guessing what had come over me, cries to turn upon my side, and press my belly to the cliff. And how he did it in such a narrow strait I know not; but he turned round, and lying down himself, thrust his hand firmly in my back, pressing me closer to the cliff. Yet it was none too soon, for if he had not held me tight, I should have flung myself down in sheer despair to get quit of that dreadful sickness.

'Keep thine eyes shut, John,' he said, 'and count up numbers loud to me, that I may know thou art not turning faint.' So I gave out, 'One, two, three,' and while I went on counting, heard him repeating to himself, though his words seemed thin and far off: 'We must have taken ten minutes to get here, and in five more they will be on the under-cliff; and if we ever reach the top, who knows but they have left a guard! No, no, they will not leave a guard, for not a man knows of the Zigzag; and, if they knew, they would not guess that we should try it. We have but fifty yards to go to win, and now this cursed giddy fit has come upon the child, and he will fall and drag me with him; or they will see us from below, and pick us off like sitting guillemots against the cliff-face.'

So he talked to himself, and all the while I would have given a world to pluck up heart and creep on further; yet could not, for the deadly sweating fear that had hold of me. Thus I lay with my face to the cliff, and Elzevir pushing firmly in my back; and the thing that frightened me most was that there was nothing at all for the hand to take hold of, for had there been a piece of string, or even a thread of cotton, stretched along to give a semblance of support, I think I could have done it; but there was only the cliff-wall, sheer and white, against that narrowest way, with never a cranny to put a finger into. The wind was blowing in fresh puffs, and though I did not open my eyes, I knew that it was moving the little tufts of bent grass, and the chiding cries of the gulls seemed to invite me to be done with fear and pain and broken leg, and fling myself off on to the rocks below.

Then Elzevir spoke. 'John,' he said, 'there is no time to play the woman; another minute of this and we are lost. Pluck up thy courage, keep thy eyes to the cliff, and forward.'

Yet I could not, but answered: 'I cannot, I cannot; if I open my eyes, or move hand or foot, I shall fall on the rocks below.'

He waited a second, and then said: 'Nay, move thou must, and 'tis better to risk falling now, than fall for certain with another bullet in thee later on.' And with that he shifted his hand from my back and fixed it in my coat-collar, moving backwards himself, and settling to drag me after him.

Now, I was so besotted with fright that I would not budge an inch, fearing to fall over if I opened my eyes. And Elzevir, for all he was so strong, could not pull a helpless lump backwards up that path. So he gave it up, leaving go hold on me with a groan; and at that moment there rose from the under-cliff below a sound of voices and shouting.

'By God, they are down already!' cried Elzevir, and have found Maskew's body; it is all up; another minute and they will see us.'

But so strange is the force of mind on body, and the power of a greater to master a lesser fear, that when I heard those voices from below, all fright of falling left me in a moment, and I could open my eyes without a trace of giddiness. So I began to move forward again on hands and knees. And Elzevir, seeing me, thought for a moment I had gone mad, and was dragging myself over the cliff, but then saw how it was, and moved backwards himself before me, saying in a low voice, 'Brave lad! Once creep round this turn, and I will pick thee up again. There is but fifty yards to go, and we shall foil these devils yet!'

Then we heard the voices again, but further off, and not so loud; and knew that our pursuers had left the under-cliff and turned down on to the beach thinking that we were hiding by the sea.

Five minutes later Elzevir stepped on to the cliff-top, with me upon his back.

'We have made something of this throw,' he said, 'and are safe for another hour, though I thought thy giddy head had ruined us.'

Then he put me gently upon the springy turf, and lay down himself upon his back, stretching his arms out straight on either side, and breathing hard to recover from the task he had performed.

Rebecca of Sunnybrook Farm

KATE DOUGLAS WIGGIN

Rebecca Rowena Randall is one of seven fatherless children who live at Sunnybrook Farm in the state of Maine. She is sent by stage-coach to stay with her two crusty aunts. Rebecca of Sunnybrook Farm *first appeared in 1903.*

The old stage-coach was rumbling along the dusty road that runs from Maplewood to Riverboro. The day was as warm as midsummer, though it was only the middle of May, and Mr. Jeremiah Cobb was favouring the horses as much as possible, yet never losing sight of the fact that he carried the mail. The hills were many, and the reins lay loosely in his hands as he lolled back in his seat and extended one foot and leg luxuriously over the dashboard. His brimmed hat of worn felt was well pulled over this eyes, and he revolved a quid of tobacco in his left cheek.

There was one passenger in the coach, a small dark-haired person in a glossy buff calico dress. She was so slender and so stiffly starched that she slid from space to space on the leather cushions, though she braced herself against the middle seat with her feet, and extended her cotton-gloved hands on each side, in order to maintain some sort of balance. Whenever the wheels sank farther than usual into a rut, or jolted suddenly over a stone, she bounded involuntarily into the air, came down again, pushed back her funny little straw hat, and picked up or settled more firmly a small pink sunshade, which seemed to be her chief responsibility, unless we accept a bead purse, into which she looked whenever the condition of the roads would permit, finding great apparent satisfaction in that its precious contents neither disappeared nor grew less. Mr. Cobb guessed nothing of these harassing details of travel, his business being to carry people to their destinations, not, necessarily, to make them comfortable on the way.

Indeed, he had forgotten the very existence of this one unnoteworthy little passenger.

When he was about to leave the post-office in Maplewood that morning, a woman had alighted from a waggon, and coming up to him, inquired whether this were the Riverboro stage, and if he were Mr. Cobb. Being answered in the affirmative, she nodded to a child who was eagerly waiting for the answer, and who ran towards her as if she feared to be a moment too late. The child might have been ten or eleven years old, perhaps, but whatever the number of her summers, she had an air of being small for her age. Her mother helped her into the stage-coach, deposited a bundle and a bouquet of lilacs beside her, superintended the 'roping on' behind of an old hairtrunk, and finally paid the fare, counting out the silver with great care.

'I want you should take her to my sisters' in Riverboro,' she said. 'Do you know Mirandy and Jane Sawyer? They live in the brick house.'

Lord bless your soul, he knew 'em as well as if he'd made 'em!

'Well, she's going there, and they're expecting her. Will you keep an eye on her, please? If she can get out anywhere and get with folks, or get anybody in to keep her company, she'll do it. Good-bye, Rebecca; try not to get into any mischief, and sit quiet, so you'll look neat an' nice when you get there. Don't be any trouble to Mr. Cobb. You see, she's kind of excited. We came on the cars from Temperance yesterday, slept all night at my cousin's, and drove from her house – eight miles it is – this morning.'

'Good-bye, mother; don't worry. You know, it isn't as if I hadn't travelled before.'

The woman gave a short sardonic laugh and said in an explanatory way to Mr. Cobb: 'She's been to Wareham and stayed overnight; that isn't much to be journey-proud on!'

'It *was travelling*, mother,' said the child eagerly and wilfully. 'It was leaving the farm, and putting up lunch in a basket, and a little riding and a little steam-cars, and we carried our nightgowns.'

'Don't tell the whole village about it, if we did,' said the mother, interrupting the reminiscences of this experienced voyager. 'Haven't I told you before,' she whispered, in a last attempt at discipline, 'that you shouldn't talk about nightgowns and stockings and – things like that, in a loud tone of voice, and especially when there's menfolks round?'

'I know, mother, I know, and I won't. All I want to say is' – here Mr. Cobb gave a cluck, slapped the reins, and the horses started sedately on their daily task – 'all I want to say is that is a journey when' – the stage was really under way now, and Rebecca had to put her head out of the window over the door in order to finish her sentence – 'it *is* a journey when you carry a nightgown!'

The objectionable word, uttered in high treble, floated back to the offended ears of Mrs. Randall, who watched the stage out of sight, gathered up her packages from the bench at the store-door, and stepped into the waggon that had been standing at the hitching-post. As she turned the horse's head towards home she rose to her feet for a moment, and, shading her eyes with her hand, looked at a cloud of dust in the dim distance.

'Mirandy'll have her hands full, I guess,' she said to herself; 'but I shouldn't wonder if it would be the making of Rebecca.'

All this had been half an hour ago, and the sun, the heat, the dust, the contemplation of errands to be done in the great metropolis of Milltown, had lulled Mr. Cobb's never active mind into complete oblivion as to his promise of keeping an eye on Rebecca.

Suddenly he heard a small voice above the rattle and rumble of the wheels and the creaking of the harness. At first he thought it was a cricket, a tree toad, or a bird, but having determined the direction from which it came, he turned his head over his shoulder and saw a small shape hanging as far out of the window as safety would allow. A long black braid of hair swung with the motion of the coach; the child held her hat in one hand and with the other made ineffectual attempts to stab the driver with her microscopic sunshade.

'Please let me speak!' she called.

Mr. Cobb drew up the horses obediently.

'Does it cost any more to ride up there with you?' she asked. 'It's so slippery and shiny down here, and the stage is so much too big for me, that I rattle round in it till I'm most black and blue. And the windows are so small I can only see pieces of things, and I've most broken my neck stretching round to find out whether my trunk has fallen off the back. It's my mother's trunk, and she's very choice of it.'

Mr. Cobb waited until this flow of conversation, or more properly speaking this flood of criticism, had ceased, and then said jocularly:

'You can come up if you want to; there ain't no extry charge to sit side o' me.' Whereupon he helped her out, 'boosted' her up to the front seat, and resumed his own place.

Rebecca sat down carefully, smoothing her dress under her with painstaking precision, and putting her sunshade under its extended folds between the driver and herself. This done, she pushed back her hat, pulled up her darned white cotton gloves, and said delightedly:

'Oh, this is better! This is like travelling! I am a real passenger now, and down there I felt like our setting hen when we shut her up in a coop. I hope we have a long, long ways to go?'

'Oh, we've only just started on it,' Mr. Cobb responded genially; 'it's more'n two hours.'

'Only two hours!' she sighed. 'That will be half-past one; mother will be at Cousin Ann's, the children at home will have had their dinner, and Hannah cleared all away. I have some lunch, because mother said it would be a bad beginning to get to the brick house hungry, and have Aunt Mirandy have to get me something to eat the first thing. It's a good growing day, isn't it?'

'It is, certain; too hot, most. Why don't you put up your parasol?'

She extended her dress still farther over the article in question as she said: 'Oh dear no! I never put it up when the sun shines. Pink fades awfully, you know; and I only carry it to meetin' cloudy Sundays. Sometimes the sun comes out all of a sudden, and I have a dreadful time covering it up. It's the dearest thing in life to me; but it's an awful care.'

At this moment the thought gradually permeated Mr. Jeremiah

Cobb's slow-moving mind that the bird perched by his side was a bird of very different feather from those to which he was accustomed in his daily drives. He put the whip back in its socket, took his foot from the dashboard, pushed his hat back, blew his quid of tobacco into the road, and, having thus cleared his mental decks for action, he took his first good look at the passenger – a look which she met with a grave, childlike stare of friendly curiosity.

The buff calico was faded, but scrupulously clean, and starched within an inch of its life. From the little standing ruffle at the neck the child's slender throat rose very brown and thin, and the head looked small to bear the weight of dark hair that hung in a thick braid to her waist. She wore an odd little visored cap of white Leghorn, which may either have been the latest thing in children's hats, or some bit of ancient finery furbished up for the occasion. It was trimmed with a twist of buff ribbon and a cluster of black and orange porcupine quills, which hung or bristled stiffly over one ear, giving her the quaintest and most unusual appearance. Her face was without colour and sharp in outline. As to features, she must have had the usual number, though Mr. Cobb's attention never proceeded so far as nose, forehead, or chin, being caught on the way and held fast by the eyes. Rebecca's eyes were like faith – 'the substance of things hoped for, the evidence of things not seen.' Under her delicately etched brows they glowed like two stars, their dancing lights half hidden in lustrous darkness. Their glance was eager and full of interest, yet never satisfied; their steadfast gaze was brilliant and mysterious, and had the effect of looking directly through the obvious to something beyond – in the object, in the landscape, in you. They had never been accounted for, Rebecca's eyes. The school-teacher and the minister at Temperance had tried and failed; the young artist who came for the summer to sketch the red barn, the ruined mill, and the bridge, ended by giving up all these local beauties and devoting herself to the face of a child – a small, plain face, illuminated by a pair of eyes carrying such messages, such suggestions, such hints of sleeping power and insight, that one never tired of looking into their shining depths, nor of fancying that what one saw there was the reflection of one's own thought.

Mr. Cobb made none of these generalizations; his remark to his wife that night was simply to the effect that whenever the child looked at him she knocked him galley west.

'Miss Ross, a lady that paints, gave me the sunshade,' said Rebecca, when she had exchanged looks with Mr. Cobb and learned his face by heart. 'Did you notice the pinked double ruffle and the white tip and handle? They're ivory. The handle is scarred, you see. That's because Fanny sucked and chewed it in meeting when I wasn't looking. I've never felt the same to Fanny since.'

'Is Fanny your sister?'

'She's one of them.'

'How many are there of you?'

'Seven. There's verses written about seven children:

> Quick was the little maid's reply –
> "O master, we are seven!"

I learned it to speak in school, but the scholars were hateful and laughed. Hannah is the oldest; I come next, then John, then Jenny, then Mark, then Fanny, then Mira.'

'Well, that *is* a big family!'

'Far too big, everybody says,' replied Rebecca, with an unexpected and thoroughly grown-up candour that induced Mr. Cobb to murmur, 'I swan!' and insert more tobacco in his left cheek.

'They're dear, but such a bother, and cost so much to feed, you see,' she rippled on. 'Hannah and I haven't done anything but put babies to bed at night and take them up in the morning for years and years. But it's finished, that's one comfort; and we'll have a lovely time when we're all grown up and the mortgage is paid off.'

'All finished? Oh, you mean you've come away?'

'No; I mean they're all over and done with – our family's finished. Mother says so, and she always keeps her promises. There hasn't been any since Mira, and she's three. She was born the day father died. Aunt

Miranda wanted Hannah to come to Riverboro instead of me, but mother couldn't spare her; she takes hold of housework better than I do, Hannah does. I told mother last night if there was likely to be any more children while I was away I'd have to be sent for, for when there's a baby it always takes Hannah and me both, for mother has the cooking and the farm.'

'Oh, you live on a farm, do ye? Where is it? Near to where you got on?'

'Near? Why, it must be thousands of miles! We came from Temperance in the cars. Then we drove a long ways to Cousin Ann's and went to bed. Then we got up and drove ever so far to Maplewood, where the stage was. Our farm is away off from everywheres, but our school and meeting-house is at Temperance, and that's only two miles. Sitting up here with you is most as good as climbing the meeting-house steeple. I know a boy who's been up on our steeple. He said the people and cows looked like flies. We haven't met any people yet, but I'm *kind* of disappointed in the cows; they don't look so little as I hoped they would, still' – brightening – 'they don't look quite as big as if we were down side of them, do they? Boys always do the nice splendid things, and girls can only do the nasty dull ones that get left over. They can't climb so high, or go so far, or stay out so late, or run so fast, or anything?'

Mr. Cobb wiped his mouth on the back of his hand and gasped. He had a feeling that he was being hurried from peak to peak of a mountain range without time to take a good breath in between.

'I can't seem to locate your farm,' he said, 'though I've been to Temperance, and used to live up that way. What's your folk's name?'

'Randall. My mother's name is Aurelia Randall. Our names are Hannah Lucy Randall, Rebecca Rowena Randall, John Halifax Randall, Jenny Lind Randall, Marquis Randall, Fanny Ellsler Randall, and Miranda Randall. Mother named half of us and father the other half; but we didn't come out even, so they both thought it would be nice to name Mira after Aunt Miranda, in Riverboro. They hoped it might do some good; but it didn't, and now we call her Mira. We are all named after somebody in particular. Hannah is Hannah at the Window Binding Shoes, and I am taken out of 'Ivanhoe'; John Halifax was a gentleman in a book; Mark is after his uncle, Marquis de Lafayette, that died a twin. (Twins very often don't live to grow up, and triplets almost never. Did you know that, Mr. Cobb?) We don't call him Marquis, only Mark. Jenny is named for a singer and Fanny for a beautiful dancer; but mother says they're both misfits, for Jenny can't carry a tune, and Fanny's kind of stiff-legged. Mother would like to call them Jane and Frances and give up their middle names, but she says it wouldn't be fair to father. She says we must always stand up for father, because everything was against him, and he wouldn't have died if he hadn't had such bad luck. I think that's all there is to tell about us,' she finished seriously.

'Land o' liberty! I should think it was enough,' ejaculated Mr. Cobb. 'There wa'n't many names left when your mother got through choosin'. You've got a powerful good memory. I guess it ain't no trouble for you to learn your lessons, is it?'

'Not much; the trouble is to get the shoes to go and learn 'em. These are spandy new I've got on, and they have to last six months. Mother always says to save my shoes. There don't seem to be any way of saving shoes but taking 'em off and going barefoot; but I can't do that in Riverboro without shaming Aunt Mirandy. I'm going to shool right along now when I'm living with Aunt Mirandy, and in two years I'm going to the seminary at Wareham. Mother says it ought to be the making of me. I'm going to be a painter, like Miss Ross, when I get through school. At any rate, that's what *I* think I'm going to be. Mother thinks I'd better teach.'

'Your farm ain't the old Hobbs' place, is it?'

'No, it's just Randall's Farm – at least, that's what mother calls it. I call it Sunnybrook Farm.'

'I guess it don't make no difference what you call it so long as you know where it is,' remarked Mr. Cobb sententiously.

Rebecca turned the full light of her eyes upon him reproachfully, almost severely, as she answered:

'Oh, don't say that and be like all the rest! It does make a difference what you call things. When I say Randall's Farm, do you see how it looks?'

'No, I can't say I do,' responded Mr. Cobb uneasily.

'Now, when I say Sunnybrook Farm, what does it make you think of?'

Mr. Cobb felt like a fish removed from his native element and left panting on the sand. There was no evading the awful responsibility of a reply, for Rebecca's eyes were searchlights that pierced the fiction of his brain and perceived the bald spot on the back of his head.

'I s'pose there's a brook somewhere near it,' he said timorously.

Rebecca looked disappointed, but not quite disheartened. 'That's pretty good,' she said encouragingly. 'You're warm, but not hot. There's a brook, but not a common brook. It has young trees and baby bushes on each side of it, and it's a shallow, chattering little brook, with a white sandy bottom and lots of little shiny pebbles. Whenever there's a bit of sunshine the brook catches it, and it's always full of sparkles the livelong day. Don't your stomach feel hollow? Mine does. I was so 'fraid I'd miss the stage I couldn't eat any breakfast.'

'You'd better have your lunch, then. I don't eat nothin' till I get to Milltown, then I get a piece o' pie and cup o' coffee.'

'I wish I could see Milltown. I suppose it's bigger and grander even than Wareham – more like Paris? Miss Ross told me about Paris; she bought my pink sunshade there and my bead purse. You see how it opens with a snap. I've twenty cents in it, and it's got to last three months – for stamps and paper and ink. Mother says Aunt Mirandy won't want to buy things like those when she's feeding and clothing me and paying for my school-books.'

'Paris ain't no great,' said Mr. Cobb disparagingly. 'It's the dullest place in the State o' Maine. I've druv there many a time.'

Again Rebecca was obliged to reprove Mr. Cobb, tacitly and quietly, but none the less surely, though the reproof was dealt with one glance, quickly sent and as quickly withdrawn.

'Paris is the capital of France, and you have to go to it on a boat,' she said instructively. 'It's in my geography, and it says: "The French are a gay and polite people, fond of dancing and light wines." I asked the teacher what light wines were, and he thought it was something like new cider, or maybe, ginger-pop. I can see Paris as plain as day by just shutting my eyes. The beautiful ladies are always gaily dancing around, with pink sunshades and bead purses, and the grand gentlemen are politely dancing and drinking ginger-pop. But you can see Milltown most every day with your eyes wide open,' Rebecca said wistfully.

'Milltown ain't no great neither,' replied Mr. Cobb with the air of having visited all the cities of the earth, and found them as naught. 'Now, you watch me heave this newspaper right on to Miss Brown's doorstep.'

Piff! and the packet landed exactly as it was intended – on the corn-husk mat in front of the screen door.

'Oh, how splendid that was!' cried Rebecca with enthusiasm – 'just like the knife-thrower Mark saw at the circus. I wish there was a long, long row of houses, each with a corn-husk mat and a screen door in the middle, and a newspaper to throw on every one!'

'I might fail on some of 'em, you know,' said Mr. Cobb, beaming with modest pride. 'If your Aunt Mirandy'll let you, I'll take you down to Milltown some day this summer when the stage ain't full.'

A thrill of delicious excitement ran through Rebecca's frame, from her new shoes up, up to the Leghorn cap and down the black braid. She pressed Mr. Cobb's knee ardently, and said in a voice choking with tears of joy and astonishment: 'Oh, it can't be true – it can't! To think I should see Milltown! It's like having a fairy godmother, who asks you your wish and then gives it to you. Did you ever read "Cinderella," or "The Yellow Dwarf," or "The Enchanted Frog," or "The Fair One with Golden Locks"?'

'No,' said Mr. Cobb cautiously after a moment's reflection. 'I don't seem to think I ever did read jest those partic'lar ones. Where'd you get a chance at so much readin'?'

'Oh, I've read lots of books,' answered Rebecca casually – 'father's, and Miss Ross's, and all the dif'rent school-teachers', and all in the Sunday-school library. I've read "The Lamplighter," and "Scottish Chiefs," and "Ivanhoe," and "The Heir of Redclyffe," and "Cora, the Doctor's Wife," and "David Copperfield," and "The Gold of Chickaree," and Plutarch's "Lives," and "Thaddeus of Warsaw," and "Pilgrim's Progress," and lots more. What have you read?'

'I've never happened to read those partic'lar books; but land! I've read a sight in my time! Nowadays I'm so drove I get along with the Almanac, the *Weekly Argus*, and the *Maine State Agriculturist*. There's the river again; this is the last long hill, and when we get to the top of it we'll see the chimbleys of Riverboro in the distance. 'Tain't fur. I live 'bout half a mile beyond the brick house myself.'

Rebecca's hand stirred nervously in her lap and she moved in her seat. 'I didn't think I was going to be afraid,' she said almost under her breath; 'but I guess I am, just a little mite – when you say it's coming so near.'

'Would you go back?' asked Mr. Cobb curiously.

She flashed him an intrepid look and then said proudly, 'I'd never go back – I might be frightened, but I'd be ashamed to run. Going to Aunt Mirandy's is like going down cellar in the dark. There might be ogres and giants under the stairs, but, as I tell Hannah, there *might* be elves and fairies and enchanted frogs! Is there a main street to the village, like that in Wareham?'

'I s'pose you might call it main street, an' your Aunt Sawyer lives on it, but there ain't no stores nor mills, an' it's an awful one-horse village! You have to go 'cross the river an' get on to our side if you want to see anything goin' on.'

'I'm almost sorry,' she sighed, 'because it would be so grand to drive down a real main street sitting high up like this behind two splendid horses, with my pink sunshade up, and everybody in town wondering who the bunch of lilacs and the hair-trunk belongs to. It would be just like the beautiful lady in the parade. Last summer the circus came to Temperance, and they had a procession in the morning. Mother let us all walk in and wheel Mira in the baby-carriage, because we couldn't afford to go to the circus in the afternoon. And there were lovely horses and animals in cages, and clowns on horseback; and at the very end came a little red-and-gold chariot drawn by two ponies, and in it, sitting on a velvet cushion, was the snake-charmer, all dressed in satin and spangles. She was so beautiful beyond compare, Mr. Cobb, that you had to swallow lumps in your throat when you looked at her, and little cold feelings crept up and down your back. Don't you know what I mean? Didn't you ever see anybody that made you feel like that?'

Mr. Cobb was more distinctly uncomfortable at this moment than he had been at any one time during the eventful morning, but he evaded the point dexterously by saying: 'There ain't no harm, as I can see, in our makin' the grand entry in the biggest style we can. I'll take the whip out, set up straight, an' drive fast; you hold your bo'quet in your lap, an' open your little red parasol, an' we'll jest make the natives stare!'

The child's face was radiant for a moment, but the glow faded just as quickly as she said: 'I forgot – mother put me inside, and maybe she'd want me to be there when I got to Aunt Mirandy's. Maybe I'd be more genteel inside, and then I wouldn't have to be jumped down and my clothes fly up, but could open the door and step down like a lady passenger. Would you please stop a minute, Mr. Cobb, and let me change?'

The stage-driver good-naturedly pulled up his horses, lifted the excited little creature down, opened the door, and helped her in, putting the lilacs and pink sunshade beside her.

'We've had a great trip,' he said, 'and we've got real well acquainted, haven't we? You won't forget about Milltown?'

'Never!' she exclaimed fervently; 'and you're sure you won't either?'

'Never! Cross my heart!' vowed Mr. Cobb solemnly, as he re-mounted his perch; and as the stage rumbled down the village street between the green maples, those who looked from their windows saw a little brown elf in buff calico sitting primly on the back-seat holding a great bouquet tightly in one hand, and a pink parasol in the other. Had they been far-sighted enough they might have seen, when the stage turned into the side doorway of the old brick house, a calico yoke rising and falling tempestuously over the beating heart beneath, the red colour coming and going in two pale cheeks, and a mist of tears swimming in two brilliant dark eyes – Rebecca's journey had ended.